GRIM WOLVES MC SERIES

WILD CUB

JAMIE FRITZ

This one is for those who thought they couldn't do it but
did it anyway.

To my parents who always told me to reach for the stars.
(Also don't say I didn't warn you about what I write)

For my Mad Maxx, between you and the others keeping
my feet warm as I wrote.

Before you start reading, I want to give a warning that this
is intended for mature audience/readers. As I do in my
day job, I want to give transparency. Here are the trigger
warnings. Towards the end of this book, you will find
a list of helpful phone numbers and websites to further
help those who are seeking help.

Abusive relationship (past)
Death of a loved one (past)
Anxiety
Drugs
Gun violence
Grief and loss
Homelessness
Attempted murder and Murder
Organized crime
Trauma
Trafficking
Domestic violence

Cape Breton Lullaby

Driftwood is burning blue, wild walk the wall shadows
Night winds go riding by, riding by the lochie meadows
On to the break of day, close Mira stream singing:
Caidil gu la laddie, la laddie. Sleep the dark away

Close by Beinn Bhreagh's stream, wander the lost lambies
Here, there and everywhere,
Everywhere their troubled mammies
Find them and bring them home, sing them to sleep

singing:
Caidil gu la laddie, la laddie. Sleep the night away

Daddy is on the bay, he'll keep a pot brewin'
Save us from tumbling down
Tumbling down to rack and ruin
Pray Mary send him home, safe from the foam singing:
Caidil gu la laddie, la laddie. Sleep the stars away

Caidil gu la laddie, la laddie. Sleep the stars away

WILD CUB
JAMIE FRITZ

1:49
4:10

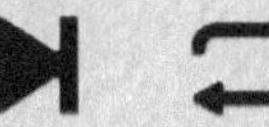

Chapter 1

Teresa

I don't know what's worse, waking up from a delicious, sex dream where the man is having his way with you or the fact that my needy dog is waking me up and not the man from my dreams.

"Seamus, five more minutes, bud. Please, let mommy sleep," I grumble under a pillow as my bed tries to lull me back to sleep.

His cold nose presses against my arm and the softest whines escapes his mouth.

I growl at him, and he huffs in response.

"Fine, I'm up, but not for you, you little fucker." I toss the pillow off my head, seeing a furry bubble butt in my face.

Seamus, my black and white Welsh Corgi, turns to lay his head on my chest. He's lucky he's so cute. I sigh. I have to get up for this party or else I'll be late. And Allie may have a fit if I don't show up.

Seriously, whoever thought a biker bar named The Devil's Whiskey was a fantastic place to host a kid's birthday party is insane, but little Allie wants her auntie to be there. I mean, how can you say no to a little girl with little dimples and a twinkle in her eyes?

Seeing Allie fills the hole in my heart of wanting one of my own. I'm okay being the godmother to my friends' kids while I wait for Prince Charming. Even if Prince Charming is lost and may have gotten burnt to a crisp by a dragon.

It's Saturday afternoon. After convincing myself to get up,I begin to get ready for what is bound to be an afternoon of sugar-high children.

This is the first Saturday afternoon I've had off, since the foundation decided to open a new building to house more families, provide more services, and have everyone's office under one roof. I have been putting in overtime in preparation for the transition and the hopes of a promotion.

The Lighthouse has been home to me for the past six years.I've been eager to make a difference in this community while working hard to bring resources to the homeless and vulnerable. But sometimes, a girl just needs a Saturday to herself.

Swinging my legs off the bed, I start to debate my life choices.

What do you wear to a kid's party at a biker bar?

Throwing caution to the wind, I choose my favorite ripped jeans, the ones that hug the curve of my thick thighs, and an old band t-shirt. I debate pulling out my old red leather jacket. I worry that it's a little too on the nose.

Seamus cocks his head from his bed. You can sense the judgmental thoughts that are going on in his head.

"I don't need your judgment, sir," I smirk at him before turning down the hall to my bathroom.

Looking at the time, I debate whether it's enough to make mego from sasquatch to princess. I put my contacts in, my mind spinning knowing what I need to get accomplished. As I rush to get dress, I let Seamus out once more. I check in the mirror, jerking back at the image before me, giving myself one last look. My eyes grazed over the final product.

Well, good thing I ain't going there to attract men.

I glance at the clock. I have to be out the door ASAP if I plan to be on the other side of Raleigh on time. Do I dry my hair or do my makeup? Decisions, decisions. I take a deep breath and decide on the makeup.

Anything to look more human, right?

Time doesn't seem to be on my side as my morning music surrounds my house. The minutes fly by too quickly. I topple, practically tripping over everything.

I'm going to be late.

It's a goal to be on time. Often that goal is never successful. Ask anyone, they'll tell you the same thing. I grab my backpack and keys, along with Allie's birthday gift.

Thank you, Amazon.

I bought her a little preschool art set. Michelle and Matthew might hate me for it, but I'll live. I tell Seamus bye, I go back to get my jacket and lock up the house. Red leather is always the way to go.

Am I looking forward to this party? Yes and no. I adore my Allie, I love my friends, but sometimes they don't always understand why I do what I do. One thing is for sure, I'm ready for food and maybe even a drink.

Today is Allie's fourth birthday and I promised Matthew and Michelle that I would make it. So yes, I'm excited to go. I know I have been elbow deep in work and being around them is important to me and them.

When I finished school in Richmond six years ago, Virginia didn't have much hold over me anymore. Dad retired from the police force, and he and mom are enjoying retirement in Williamsburg.

I really need to call Momma.

So, I moved to North Carolina, I didn't know anyone, unless you count my cousin Brittany. It took one night on the side of a road due to a flat tire, late at night and me to flag down someone to get help. Little did I know, a grizzly looking man on a motorcycle named Matthew came to my rescue. At first I was hesitant to trust this stranger, but his sense of humor matched mine. Before too long we were friends and then I met Michelle, and I quickly was adopted into their family.

Soon after I met Matthew and Michelle, Seth was introduced to me. Seth's a single dad, raising his teenage son and young daughter. He jokes that his daughter, Ella, loves me more than him. I truly believe it.

Matthew and Seth belong to a motorcycle club, so this biker bar isn't too farfetched. I joke with them about being part of the Sons of Anarchy, but all I get is an eyebrow raise. I feel like I poked a bear when joking with that.

I pull myself down from memory lane and finally find The Devil's Whiskey towards the outskirts of town. The parking lot is filled with bikes and decked out lifted trucks that scream country boys and compensation. From the outside, it looks like a typical restaurant, but I can hear the loud bass of heavy rock music. I smell whiskey, cigarette smoke, but above all I smell barbecue; a.k.a., heaven.

All eyes are on me as I walk through the double doors with Allie's gift under my arm.

Did I leave my zipper down or something?

I flip my Ray Bans on top of my head, I look around me,feeling more out of place than anything else. I walk to the nearest person, next to some empty bar stools, asking where the birthday party is. With a grunt, he points to the back, meaning the outside seating area where the smell of the barbecue is wafting in from.

I trail my hand on the empty worn down bar stools as I pass by making my way to the back of the bar. I wonder what stories this place could tell. The wall behind the bar is full of liquor, and I hear the whisper of a Jack and Coke calling my name. I pass tables with grown men and women who look like they could do some damage. Cigarette smoke fills the room, the sound of billiard balls cracking and the snap of pool sticks against them sounding in my ears. It might be mid-morning outside, but there's no sunshine in this place.

As you step through the doors, the newest kids' movie soundtrack is a stark contrast to the music inside. From a slight nervous energy to a calming, ray of happiness spreads through my mind. The sight of what feels like home eases the spine-chilling sensation I started to have back there.

The bright light hits everything, the bright colors swirl around like a princess's dream. Matthew is at the smoker while Michelle is fixing Allie's hair and a dozen kids are playing with bubbles, trampolines, and inflatable slides.

Catching Matthew's attention, I wave as he holds a beer while talking with Seth. Seth nods his head at him with a slight humorous grin on his face.

This was my family away from family.

I make my way over to Michelle only to get pulled into a tight hug from her. Something butts us in the middle, only to reveal the dimpled cheeked and bright-eyed little princess.

Allie pushes between us.

"Sasa, up please," she begs.

I release Michelle and swoop Allie up in a bear hug. Sasa is her way of saying Tessa, and I love it.

"Happy Birthday, Allie-cat! Have you been having fun?" I squeeze her tight, wishing she would stay small forever.

"Sasa, come jump," she says, bouncing in my arms.

"Oh Allie, I don't think Sasa wants to jump. She's too big for the trampoline," Michelle says softly.

Allie's face morphs into a puppy dog pout, the one I taught her.

"How about this, Allie-cat? What if I try and if I think I'm too big, I'll stop. What do I always tell you?" I say as I set her down before she could take off running to one of the trampolines.

She giggles, and with a little wiggle says, "Try before we say no." She takes it into a full sprint.

"You don't always have to say yes to her, Tessa. Also, you're late," Michelle starts as Matthew interrupts with a snort.

"Are you surprised? She'll be late to her own funeral. You could tell her the building is on fire, and she'll say *yeah, just give me a few minutes,*" Matthew finishes as he checks the smoker.

"Yeah, but you would die of a heart attack if I actually showed up on time," I say, punching Matthew's arm. Seth lets out a laugh. I pin a look to him, "You got something to add?"

He shakes his head no, miming that he's zipping his lips. Matthew rolls his eyes, and a wave of laughter breaks between Michelle and me.

As I quickly catch up with Seth and the latest on his kids, my eyes can't help but jump around and look at the outside.

The outside of the bar is adorable; it's definitely an interesting contrast to the rest of it. There's an outside bar, picnic tables, yard games, and a small fire pit. Add in the bubbles, toys, and trampolines, and it's heaven compared to the hell inside. The sun starts to shine brighter, illuminating everything around us, I flip my sunglasses back on.

My eyes catch Allie with her little hands on her hips giving me all the sass in the world. I look back at my friends, "I better go jump or little princess over there is going to drag me along."

As I walk to where Allie's is starting to jump and laugh, Inotice a pair of eyes looking at me out of the corner of my eye. I can't help but turn to see what's catching my eye.

But it's not so much of a what, but a *who*. A man holding my attention. There's something hypnotic about the grayish tint that gleams when the sun hits them, knocks the breath out of you. With a shiver, I shake my head.

Stop being a creeper Tessa.

"Sasa, come on. Jump!" Allie calls out to me, grabbing my attention, tearing me away from the tempting eyes.

I take off my boots and attempt to step onto the trampoline.

Okay, maybe I *am* too big for this. Having big boobsand thick thighs does not help, that's for sure.

Allie grabs my hand to help me jump, but I'm cautious not to send the kid into the parking lot. The more I jump, the more I realize I'm getting too old for this shit. Especially when there are more kids crowding and trying to get on. They're like a flock of seagulls, all wanting to go after the same thing or do the same thing.

"Allie, Sasa is going to get off," I finally say, giving up the notion that I could keep up with her.

"No, stay!" she says, sounding defeated but moving on to the next thing.

"How about I just stay and watch you jump?"

"Okay," she says, perking up and going back to jumping.

I put my boots back on before standing next to the trampoline to watch Allie jump.

After a few minutes, I notice another small child charging like a bull towards me. The wind gets knocked out of me as Ella practically tackles me into a hug.

"Tessa, you did come! Daddy said that there were no promises," Ella exclaims as her arms snake around my waist.

I glance over at Seth, who's looking my way.

"Seriously?" I yell in his direction.

He shakes his head and lifts his beer.

I peer back at Ella, the cheery look in her eyes makes you want to smile. "You know I wouldn't miss seeing my girls," I say, rubbing her cheek.

"Tessa, can you get me a lemonade?" Ella asks me sweetly.

"Sure, sweetie. I might as well get me a drink, too." I turn back to ask Allie if she wanted anything, she shakes her head as she continues to bounce around. I wave over to Michelle to switch places with me. Ella takes my hand in hers, gripping it tightly.

We head over to the bar, grabbing the bartender's attention.I lean across the bar. By the way, who keeps a bartender back here for a kid's party?

"Do y'all have lemonade back there?" I asked the bartender.

He looks at me then at the stock he has outside. "We did, let me check, sweetheart." After a moment he comes back and says, "I need to go get more inside, if you wanna follow me to the bar?" I nod and follow him inside.

When he rounds the bar, he nods to the bartender I noticed when I first arrived. He grabs a glass, filling it with Lemonade before handing it over to Ella.

Then his eyes meet mine, "You want a lemonade too or are you thinking something a bit harder."

I lean against the bar, immediately regretting it. It's sticky. I make a mental note to find hand sanitizer or wash my hands. The bar still seems loud compared to outside. The smoke is heavier. I frown at Ella.

I probably shouldn't have let her come in here with me. She starts to hum and swing my arm as she looks around. I'm shocked by how at ease she is in a biker bar of all places. Like the girl is comfortable.

Looking back to the bartender, I smile, "How about a Jack and Coke please."

I keep one eye on Ella who's in her own world and the other eye on the bartender making my drink that I suddenly get startled. I feel a smack on my ass. A man who could use a visit to a dentist sits down on my left, giving me his million-dollar smile.

It's not that the smack hurts, but the audacity to do it in the presence of a child. A bit of rage starts to boil, a flood of thoughts wanting to cuss him out start to form. Intrusive thoughts of what would happen if I did something and what the outcome would be floods my mind.

I roll my eyes and brush it off.

Not the time to start a fight, Teresa.

"You know, if you ever want to pop out a couple of those rugrats, feel free to give me a call," he laughs, sipping his beer, leaning against the sticky bar.

Breathe.

"Well, I appreciate that, but I certainly don't want that number. If you'll excuse me, I'm just grabbing our drinks and leaving," I rebut, Ella peering up at me with concern in her eyes.

I smile, showing her that everything's okay. Lead by example. Showing her that I won't be pushed into a corner. Neither should she.

Apparently, he didn't like my answer.

He sneers at me in response. "Well, I guess you don't know the rules around here about being a bitch. Bitches only have one place, and that's on their knees." He moves closer to me, gaining my full attention. My body tenses, the hairs on my neck standing on edge. This guy thinks he can talk to me that way in front of sweet Ella? It infuriates me that I can feel the heat rise, my heartbeat pulses.

"Bitch huh? Well, I've been called worse things by better men," I give him a withering look.

Fuck if I'm going to let him intimidate me.

"Randy, leave her alone and sit your ass back down by the pool table," the bartender attempts to come to my rescue. He gives me my drink, looking at me with empathy, knowing that I wanted to get away as soon as possible. As I go to turn, Randy snatches my left arm. I look from my arm back to him, with the drinks nearly spilling.

"I didn't say you could go."

This man is messing with the wrong woman. The ugly side of me is stirring, wanting to come out and play.

Chapter 2

Teresa

The man doesn't let loose, his hand still gripping my upper arm. I set my drink down, noticing that Ella still has hers with both hands.

I give Randy one of my fake smiles. "Ella, baby, take your drink outside. I'll be there in one second," She lets go of my hand and starts walking to the door.

Out of the corner of my eye, I see another barfly start to approach, but I turn my focus on Randy, reaching into my front pocket ever so quickly to flip out my pocketknife. I start to lean closer, aiming for his balls. I can feel another man behind me, but I keep my focus on the man in front of me.

I try to keep my voice stern and clear, "If you ever fucking touch me again and or use that language in front of a child, I will take these crown jewels, leaving you less of a man than you already are," I growl, not backing down from my stance.

I glance down and laugh harshly. "Doesn't look like there's much manhood to take anyway."

I'm prepared for there to be an issue, maybe even a bar fight, but no one moves. No one moves a muscle. Every eye is on me, waiting to see what'll happen. Randy looks at me intently, clearly debating his next move before he looks behind him.

Fucker, I'm the one holding a knife to your man parts.

Coming to a decision, Randy throws my arm down, backing away slowly. Barely looking away, waiting to see if I will do anything else. He sits his ass on the furthest bar stool, then realizing I'm not looking away. My eyes narrow, silently praying that he would try something else.

I flip the knife closed and shove it back into my front pocket. I turn to join Ella and run into what I think is a brick wall.

I haven't even started drinking yet...

"Everything okay here, darlin'?" a voice rings out.

I take a step back and look up into those blue-gray eyes I saw outside.

Damn!

This man could be a Viking. I say six foot three, maybe, blond hair swept back in a man bun, the sides of his head shaved as well, a well-maintained short beard. Those *eyes.* Something about them just draws you in. Judging by how hard I just smacked into him, he's got solid muscle beneath those clothes.

This isn't the time to eye-fuck a stranger.

"Yeah, I'm fine, Leif Erikson. Now, if you don't mind, I have a little girl waiting for me to go back outside." I back up taking my drink with me as I head out along with Ella.

As I brush past him, I get a whiff of fire and a wooded forest, one of my favorite scents. I take one last look at him over my shoulder, and I feel the butterflies explode in my stomach. He meets my gaze, so I quickly avert my eyes.

You better chill out down there, Teresa. We ain't got time for his "knight in shining armor" or southern gentleman type.

Ella's standing by the door, sipping her lemonade through a crazy straw. This girl is fearless, acting as if she's not phased at all.

"Tessa, I think that's your prince."

I give her a questioning look, but my answer lies where her stare goes.

The man that is behind, the handsome stranger built like a warrior. A small shiver courses through me, a small thought of him sends atingle. My body tries to shake it off. I take her hand, pushing through the door, feeling the sunshine and cool breeze on my face. "Jellybean, be your own prince, don't wait around for one."

I look down at her as she cocks her head trying to understand what I mean. "You have no idea what I'm talking about do you?"

She shrugs, shaking my hand away to grip her drink again with both hands. I start to chuckle, the pure innocence thinking of knights and princes is her world. We join her dad and brother, Jordan, at a picnic table.

"Daddy, Tessa was a knight!" she exclaims, excitedly. This five-year-old is not afraid to blurt anything out. It's her world, we're just living in it.

Wide eyed and apologetic, I try to shush her, to no avail. "I don't think Daddy needs to hear this, Ella."

Seth cocks an eyebrow at me. "Do I want to know?"

I shake my head. "No, you don't. I handled it in the most lady-like way." I hear a snort from the corner as Jordan gives me a side eye. "Got something to say, punk?" I inquire.

Jordan looks up from his phone. "Who me? Nope. Just didn't know you could act like a lady." For a teenager, he's smarter than most adults with twice the sarcasm.

Before he can react, I have him in a headlock, ruffling his hair as he struggles. Little punk has a mouth like his father.

"What did she see that she deems to be 'ladylike'?" Seth finally asks.

"Don't worry, she was by the door. Although, she watched me walk head-first into a brick wall of a human. She's calling him my prince now." I scoff, the mere thought that I always need saving, or that I need a man like that.

"Klutz, who the fuck did you run into?" Seth looks up at me in surprise.

I'm usually more aware of my surroundings.

"I don't know. I didn't get a name. I don't really care," I take a sip of my drink to avoid more questions.

I can feel Seth silently pressing me for more. Seth is too nosey for his own good.

Sighing, I give in, "Fine, he looked like a Viking. Blond hair, blue eyes. I think he was sitting near the outside bar when I first came in."

Seth goes quiet, his face turning white as a ghost. He remains quiet, averting his eyes to Matthew, who crept up behind me when I got to the table. Matthew stays quiet, I turn to look at him, his eyes are bugging out of his head.

"You gonna say something, or let it go?" I questioned. I turn back to Seth.

Seth looks down at the table, avoiding the question.

"Shouldn't you be saying that I need to avoid all men like that? Big, hulking men, I doubt that man had brains, as he didn't move out of my way." I start to laugh, usually this is where Matthew and Seth turn into big brothers and fending off guys that look my way.

Seth sucks in his lips, his eyes rapidly moving up and down. Without looking at me, he shakes his head.

I have an eerie feeling.

"Don't tell me Leif Erikson is standing right behind me." My Spidey senses are tingling.

"Yep," Seth mumbles as he takes a sip of his beer, looking down to avoid the chaos that might erupt.

"Does he have a puzzled look on his face? Like why did I brush past him or call him stupid?" I take a big gulp of my strong drink.

"I'd say so," Seth answers.

All I wanted to do was spend time with my friends and my munchkins; I don't have time for an alpha-male trying to "do a good deed."

I sigh, turning to face the giant. Might as well get this over with. It's not that hard to tower over me, but I'll be damned if I let some man make me feel small. His scent hits me before I see him. I can smell the fire and woods, it's intoxicating. I've always liked the smell of bonfires. It brings back memories of summer fun and roasting marshmallows, and days on grandfather's farm at night. Any other day, I'd be climbing him like a tree, a squirrel trying to get its nuts.

Lord, get your mind out of the gutter.

I take a deep inhale.

Woman, pull yourself together.

He speaks before I have the chance to form a coherent, non-sexual thought.

"I want to apologize for Randy, for his rudeness. Normally, we're very gentlemanly," the mysterious man says.

I can hear a faint hint of a southern accent. My mind lingers to the way he says things like it makes him more appealing.

"I can handle myself, this isn't my first rodeo."

And *probably not my last.*

He chuckles, "There's still no excuse for him to put his hands on you. Again, I apologize on his behalf."

I can see a smirk starting to form at the corner of his mouth which only irritates me further.

"Listen *sweetheart*," I sneer. "While I appreciate the sentiment and the gesture, you don't have to put on the knight in shining armor for me. I'm not the damsel in distress type. I've faced bigger giants than Randy before. That back there wasn't even a giant, more like a grumpy old troll under a bridge." I make Jordan scootch over so I can sit at the table.

Jordan snickers at the end of my joke.

Seth jerks my arm, hissing out, "Tessa shut up or keep digging your grave. I don't need to hand you the shovel."

All I want to do is enjoy the rest of the day without someone harassing me or coaxing me into doing something I might regret. He leans forward, standing behind me, inches away from my ear. I can feel the hotbreath, the pounding of his heartbeat against my back.

Do I smell peppermint? Did the man pop a mint before coming over?

"Seems like there's some bite in that bark. Just be careful of where you bite, some people bite harder. Folks around this place don't take kindly to mouthy women with your spitfire. I'm just trying to be respectful. Show some kindness. But if you think you can handle it, I'd be happy to test that theory." He says, low enough that I can only hear him. The bass of his voice vibrates in his chest against my back. In the coolest air, I feel a fire rising in me.

One day is all I asked for where I don't have to explain orbe condemned for my actions. I stand up to face him.

"Oh sweetie, you don't want to know what this mouth can do. Sorry to say, it might destroy that ego you've got going on, Leif Erikson." I smirk, throwing the nickname at him as I turn to go play with the bubbles, taking my damn drink with me.

"The name is Alexander Jackson Jones, but you can call me Jackson. But if you want to call me by a Viking, just know I'll fuck like one.Maybe one day I'll find out what the mouth can do, and you test the theory of the nickname."

I can just hear the smugness in his voice, probably topped off with a sexy smirk spreading across his face. His voice adds to the boldness of his words.

Somehow the world stops and, for once, everything is quiet. I know there's music playing, children laughing, the smell of barbeque in the air.

Please don't let this be one of my squirrel moments.

I stop dead in my tracks, glancing back over my shoulder. "Be careful what you wish for, A.J.," I shorten his name, hoping to get a rise out of him. I smirk at him for good measure. I turn back and sip on my drink, walking towards Allie, who is currently engaged in a bubble war.

I try to calm my raging emotions. Part of me feels the adrenaline flowing through my body. The other part feels it's rage at his audacity. Then there's this small part that is turned on by that asshole.

My phone dings, pulling my attention off the kids. I look to find messages from my group chat with Matthew, Michelle, and Seth.

Lord only knows what lies ahead in their messages, knowing them, pure chaos.

Matthew

> Girl, it was nice knowing you. You seriously don't know when to shut the fuck up.

> Don't know what you're talking about. Also, hurry up with the damn meat. I'm starving over here.

Matthew

> You do realize who that was right? Did you pay attention to the cut?

His cut? The thing that Seth and Matthew wear? Why would I need to pay attention?

> Translation?

Matthew

> Jesus, if you'd paid attention, you'd've seen the importance. He's probably going to bury you..

Maybe I want him to bury something in me. Tessa, get your mind out of the gutter. The messages keep flowing in before I can respond.

Michelle

Please be on your best behavior. Jackson ain't stopped watchin' you. Think you just threw down a challenge.

Must be missing something then.

Seth

Matthew, just tell her before we see her on 20/20.

Matthew

Nope, gonna let her learn her lesson the hard way. She threw down the gauntlet and challenged a bull. She'll get the horns. Nothing I can do. May God have mercy on your soul.

Seth

Wanna start a pool on how long she can last?

Matthew

twenty bucks says give her two weeks.

Seth

> Make it a month, she's stubborn as a mule.

>> Fuckers, all of you.

The messages are only making me more irritated, so I pocket my phone. I try to ignore the stares and glances that I'm getting from everyone around me, like they all know something I don't.

"Sasa, do you have a boyfriend now?" Allie pops by my side, taking my hand.

I crouch down to meet her eye to eye. "No, sweet girl, why would you think that?"

I'm hoping she doesn't ask me anything else.

"Mr. Jackie keeps staring at you. I think he likes you."

I look behind her. Damn it, she's right.

I pick her up, settling her on my hip, "Ah, don't worry. He couldn't handle Sasa." She squeals with excitement in my arms.

Chapter 3

Teresa

Work is never done in a world that is ever changing.

Papers and notebooks seem to be the common theme amongst Sunday afternoons. With hyperfixation on a high, I prepare for the week ahead. Sundays tend to be the prep day for what lies ahead. Although, in life we can't fully prepare for the world, one day at a time.

I chose the Lighthouse for the chaotic bliss it gives me.

The Lighthouse Foundation operates a domestic violence and homelessness hotline that helps out the community get connected with resources in the area. Within the foundation we have a shelter centered on helping those families get their second chance into a home of their own.

The Lighthouse is scattered into different offices and buildings which hurts the collaborative piece we need to operate. But all the moving parts are essential for progress and efficiency.

When I started, I was a standard hotline specialist then promoted to supervisor, eventually working my way into project management and director. Needless to say, I have worked to make a difference in a community that needs it.

Sure, all cities look pretty and shiny with their built up downtown, but it is the surrounding areas and the outskirts that no one wants to talk about and walk in, unless you are me. Needless to say, I will put others before myself and feel no shame with it.

Seamus lies on his back in his bed, warming his belly in the sunlight, while I take notes on the homeless shelters, budget meetings, and other responsibilities I have to look after this week. The comfort of Irish Tavern music atmosphere makes it the perfect afternoon.

It's calming with Seamus' little snores mixed with the quiet tavern music in the background. That is until a ding pulls me away from the quiet and my trailing thoughts.

The temptation to swipe it open and peek at who is texting might be too much. With my mind already down the rabbit hole, curiosity is the obvious winner, I open my messages. I'm welcomed by a new notification.

Unknown

> Did you know that Bjorn means Bear in several languages?

I shouldn't entertain the thought of replying nor flirting with a stranger over the phone, but I'm never one for rules.

> Well, Encyclopedia Brown, I did know that. Got any more interesting facts?

Unknown

Pretty bold to be talking to a stranger.

That's right. You could be a stalker or a killer. I better not give away my address.

Unknown

Little Cub, I'm not a stalker, but maybe your friendly neighborhood viking.

Something about the nickname little cub sends shivers down my spine. I don't know whether to blush or be insulted. No one has really called me little cub I mean unless they want to be creative, perhaps even meaningful; everyone seems to stay along the lines of my first name. Sasa, Tessie, Tess, Tessa, and the occasional "T".

Viking?

Shit, him again. How did he get my number? Matthew? Seth? When I see them next, I'm going to kick their asses. I have half a mind tattling on Matthew to Michelle, she'll kick his ass for me.

Is this your attempt at getting my attention again? Because if it is, it ain't workin'.

I add him to my phone as Leif Erikson, quickly naming the unknown number.

Leif Erikson

> Oh darlin'. There are a lot of ways I could get your attention. I'm still waiting for you to destroy the ego you think I have.

> How about I take you out?

This cocky bastard.

The words of my mother echo in my head. *"If the person truly wants to date you or be with you, make them show you. Don't go chasing."*

> Look. It'll be a cold day in hell before I let you take me out.

> Now, good day to you, sir.

Leif Erickson:

> Careful, little cub, I like a challenge.

> Promises, promises.

Leif Erickson

> I keep mine.

> Call me Jackson.

> I'll see you around Teresa.

I read the last message again, and my vagina starts to tingle with excitement and nerves.

You need to calm the fuck down. I'm not falling for that line.

Unfortunately, she doesn't listen to me.

I get fixated that I second guess this interaction. Do I want to poke the viking god a little more? He's reaching out for something or someone.

I can still feel the impact from his solidness against mine, I wonder how easily he could pick me up and pin me against a wall.

For a moment, I wonder what those lips would feel like brushing against my skin. Shaking my head out of the daydream, I notice another message.

Leif Erikson

> Try not to think too hard about me, darlin'. Too much filth will rot your brain.

Oh, two can play at this game.

> Someone's a little cocky, isn't he? Listen, when you are mentally tall enough to ride the ride, maybe we'll give it a chance.

Leif Erikson

> Playing fire with again. Don't make promises you don't intend to keep.

> I keep my promises.

I reply back, echoing what he just said.

Jesus, instant regret. I know I meant it, but that was my vagina talking, not my mind.

Another squirrel moment again leads me to think about the kind of package he's working with.

Jesus, it's been almost seven years since my last relationship which is also the last time I've had sex. That's what this is. My body reacting to a man flirting with me after so long. It has nothing to do with Leif Erickson himself.

I can't do another relationship, not when my last one ended so poorly. I won't let this affect me, I've come too far in life to get starry eyed with need. I'm not about to let a motorcycle, Viking God of a man, break down my walls. I let a man break down my walls only to have to rebuild. It got me nowhere but more heartache and a sense of mistrust in myself. No, I just need to find a different distraction.

Chapter 4.

Alexander

I know I should stay away.

How can I when this woman walked through my doors with ablazing passion and fight. I'm having to restrain myself, to keep myself from automatically claiming her, taking her as mine.

She's a fighter. A beautiful puzzle of a woman that I want to solve. Something makes me want to know everything about her, which isn't hard knowing the right people.

I want to see the fight in her as her darkest desires a reset free.

The nagging feeling that I shouldn't take an innocent woman like her into a world that she's not ready for.

But the next steps are not from the heart but a command that I can't ignore. No matter how breathtaking this woman is, I don't want to have to drag her through a hell that's not her's. This life isn't for her.

I still want to be selfish. Her energy, her heart is everything I want. I may not be deserving of her.

Watching her from a distance, the temptation of taking her and keeping her is strong. For now, I'll follow through with my task. As much as I need to stay away, I'm not.

But first coffee.

Chapter 5

Teresa

Morning comes quickly and the endless list of things I want to do rolls through my mind.

I drive through the town roads before getting on the highway to get to the main office that's tucked away downtown. I head towards my exit onto the avenue where my favorite coffee shop is located. I've been coming here since I moved to Raleigh.

The Angry Dog, the coffee house, calls my name, the place I visit the most. As long as I get my latte with my extra shots and my muffin, we're in business. On my way in, I spot Mr. Jeremiah sitting at the corner of the street.

"Ms. Tessa, Ms. Tessa. I ain't seen you in a long while. Foundation's been hiding you, miss. We miss seeing your bright face at the center." I can hear his sweet southern charm peek through.

His smile may not be the brightest, but it lights my heart.

"Mr. Jeremiah, you know I try to come by as often as I can. Are you staying out of trouble?" I ask him, seeing his backpack next to him.

He's holding some flyers, and I glance at them, recognizing the emblem of the Center.

"I promise, Ms. Tessa. That I've been nothing but a gentleman. The center got me helping them pass flyers. They have enough resources there now they want my help."

It warms my heart that they're trying to help others. If anyone could rally others and point them in the right direction, it would be Jeremiah. I'm blessed that he has been there from the start when a very young social worker took to the streets of downtown in her first week on the job.

"You don't look like you belong here, sugar. Best get off the streets before anyone gets the wrong idea," Jeremiah says to me.

He's dressed in brown pants and a black sweater with a vest, plus a brown news cap. His kind eyes, and warm brown skin and handsome face brings a certain welcomeness. But I think this man must be confused. I'm no sex worker. I look down at my outfit; okay, the V-neck shirt isn't helping my argument right now.

"No sir, I'm not a worker. I'm an intake specialist at the Foundation. I'm just trying to find the Center over here and I think I'm lost," I clarify, looking at my phone for directions.

This is not Richmond.

Realization dawns on his face. "Oh, you work for Ms.J ean! Okay. Can I give you a piece of friendly advice, sugar? Wear a sweater. Some folks around here would jump at a chance with you with just one wrong look. You look like a nice girl. Where you from?" I'm not feeling any ill will from him, only sweet vibes.

"Richmond, Virginia. Still fairly new, so Jean thought I could do some visits before getting on the phones and

start intake. My first stop is Ms. Aggie," I slump my shoulders. I definitely don't feel like I belong here.

Jeremiah wraps his arm around me, guiding in the opposite direction from where I was going. "Listen, sugar, I'll help ya get to Ms.Aggie. I'll be honest with ya, though, you gonna need to be a little more vigilant around these parts. These are tough times for folks like us. You come to ol' Jeremiah and I'll help you learn the community. If you don't believe me, talk to Ms. Aggie, she'll tell ya."

As we walk to the center, I recognize the area immediately. I swear I must have passed it three or four times.

Jeremiah has overcome homelessness back in the 90's. He opened up a mechanic shop that he partners with community centers to help out those needing employment or training. He's a long-standing advocate for the community and volunteers his time with the Center. He's a good man, overcoming the challenges with strength.

"Ms. Tessa, I have news on the streets." Jeremiah's voicesnaps me out of my memory. He leans forward, grabbing my attention. "The streets have been really quiet lately. I hear whispers of someone asking for help with jobs. You know people around here do anything for money, but quiet ain't good."

I stare at him intently, not having the faintest idea what he's talking about.

"I'm watchin' out for peoples, but you know, good things never come when it's quiet. Some people are saying that people have gone missing. Never to see again, not even at the Center," he continues.

I wince. "Jeremiah, I'm sure the Center and other agencies have their ears on the ground. Please, just make sure you take care of yourself, and let the police know if anything dangerous happens. Don't be a superhero. You're too important to the community and me," I say as I rest my hand on his shoulder, half-heartedly joking with him about the hero part.

"Ms. Tessa, I know you care. I leave the cape to you. I hope to see ya soon." Jeremiah picks up his backpack and turns to leave. I watch him walk down the busy street, vanishing into the crowd.

Sighing, I turn to walk through the busy traffic towards the coffee shop. The shop bell rings as I open the door, and the baristas look up with smiles.

"Tessa! Right on time. Caramel latte with three shots of espresso." Danisha, one of the baristas, slides my latte towards me.

"Thanks, D. Can I get one of the wild berry muffins, please and thank you?" I walk towards the register, looking down to reach for my wallet.

"Put it on my tab, D," a voice from the corner rumbles.

It's a deep growl that sends a shiver down my spine. I know that voice. Maybe Michelle was right; did I throw down a challenge and now someone wants to stake a claim?

Would that be such a bad thing? He could stake something.

The phantom feeling of someone watching you, creeping up behind you, makes me freeze. My feet stick to the floor, fighting off every urge to turn around and peek at this phantom. I can feel his body heat searing onto my skin, the intoxicating lust of temptation. The same heat that brings back the spine tingling

Teresa Saoirse, get your fucking act together; you are not falling for this brute.

I can smell that campfire smell, caressing my senses. Mymind begs me to step closer, to melt into it. I'm scared to turn around, to allow myself a glance at those eyes I could get lost in forever.

Danisha places the muffin down next to my coffee order. I take my items as I turn around, but he's already gone, sitting at a near by table. Anger builds inside of me, tension building in my muscles, a slight shake of my body occurs.

Tessa, count backwards before you do something you'll regret.

The asshole smirks and sips his coffee. There's a twinge in his smile, like he thinks he's won the game.

I drag in a breath for courage and walk over to his table.

"You know, the polite thing to do would have been to thank the person who paid for your muffin and perhaps sit," the Leif Erikson wannabe taunts as he takes a sip of his drink.

He surveys me slowly, so as to take a mental picture of every curve and inch of my body. The feeling of his eyes gives me a rush of need. The audacity of this man that after two days his actions have turn into stalking. The way his eyes lay on me makes me feel like he's circling for prey.

I give a condescending smile. "Oh honey, I never said I was polite. Especially not to men who have a tendency to stalk me, so, good day."

I turn to walk away, and I hear the screeching of a chair scraping the floor.

I don't give him a chance to speak before I'm out the door.I take a bite of the warm muffin, fresh from the oven. A tiny little moan escapes me. I can't help it.

"Now that's a sound I'd like to hear more often." Wide eyed,he does not give up. He wants a rise out of me. I turn around with a mouthful of muffin, trying my best to retaliate, as he stands before me, "Oh, darlin'. Sounds like you got your mouth full. Maybe you'll let someone talk first,"Jackson leans against a nearby wall and smirks at me.

Before, I thought this man was a brick wall, casting a shadow over me, and now that I keep looking at him, he had broad shoulders filling out the top of his jacket, jeans hugging his bottom half, outlining histoned, muscular legs. He's even wearing boots. He's wearing a dark blue V-neck,exposing a little curly chest hair. I cock my head to the side and wonder what this man would look like without clothes.

Tessa, stop gawking at the stalker.

I finally swallow a bit of muffin. "Keep begging, A.J. This is as much interaction as you'll get from me. What do you want?" I don't have either the time or the patience for his boldness today.

"Trying to be a gentleman and check in on you, maybe I wanted to grab your attention, run an idea by you. Matthew spilled some information about you, and I think you might be interested in what I have to offer," he said, walking a little closer to me.

I'm going to kill Matthew later.

Jesus, now I smell peppermint. Did he have peppermints in his pocket?

I snort. "Not interested in being a sweet butt, no matter how much my friends told you about my sexual history." A hint of heat flushes my cheeks, divulging too much information.

He snickers at my assumption, "I was talking about your day job as project manager, but nice to know where your mind is at."

Well, that blew back on me. I'm going to end horny before I even get through my day.

I continue to ignore him.

I hear his footsteps following me.

"I wouldn't be too quick to turn down something before you know it. We need your expertise on a common matter," his smooth voice starts to pique my interest.

I shake my head and ignore him as I continue to get to my car.

"Not interested," I say, unlocking my car.

He steps forward with no personal space, forcing me to lookup at this tree of a man. He starts to gently caress my cheek, brushing the back of his index finger up and down. He brushes his fingers across my bottom lip. Leaning down, he brings his mouth to my ear.

Jesus take the wheel please.

"Quick to say no before you try. Isn't that what you told Allie to do?" He glances down at me one more time, presses a smooth soft kiss on my cheek before opening my car door for me.

I got in feeling like a doe in headlights, feeling flustered and heated all the way down to my pussy. I watch him vanish in the morning street crowd. I can still feel the heat swirling through my veins. Something inside wanted more but the other half wanted to know what he would want with me being a project manager. A biker and a social worker together, not seeing the possible connection. Now, I'm pissed. Fuck and it's only Monday.

I get to work without further incident, attempting to calm myself down by blaring music on my way. I've not been that flustered or infuriated in a long time. The only time this happens is when I am fighting for causes dear to me, like advocacy programs or more community resources.

I stomp into my office, which isn't much since I'm hardly there. Most of the room is taken up by an L-shaped desk with an opening underneath where I store emergency items for when I'm in between locations. I've lost count at how many times my emergency deodorant has saved me. I glance at my desk and notice a new water bottle, filled and chilled.

Reva.

"Reva!" I scream from my office as I set down mybackpack.

A petite blonde woman with square framed glasses pokes her head through my office door.

"Yes ma'am, you hollered?" she says, full of smugness.

"What is this doing on my desk?" I ask, pointing to the bottle of water.

She just chuckles, "My friendly reminder to stay hydrated,or else I'm going to stick you on an IV."

She trots into my office and plops into one of the chairs.

"Water is overrated," I retort. "Plus, we already have a busy day ahead and I don't need any more distractions."

"Distractions? I thought you seemed heated. The slight attitude and energy you're giving off says a lot," she looks at me skeptically.

"I'm not heated, just distracted, which I can't afford right now," I deflect, sitting down in my chair to check my email and travel schedule.

"I think maybe it has to do with a guy," she smirks.

I practically choke at her cheekiness.

"Reva, does it seem like there's man. I don't want to be a housewife and pop out two point five heathens. At least not right now," I remind her, packing my bag to get ready for a meeting downtown.

"I'm just saying, some days I wish you would get laid and relax." Reva leans across the desk to lay her hand on mine. "By the way, if you give me more attitude, I'll kick you into the parking lot."

That's my friend and co-worker.

As peaceful as we think our Canadian friends are, she is *not* afraid to choose violence in the morning. She keeps me in line and has a lot to offer the Foundation. Some days, I can't live without her.

Speaking of friends. I pull out my phone to send a message, throwing a shot in the dark. I start with Matthew, only to work my way down.

I see where your loyalties lie.

Matthew

sips tea

I glare at the screen as I grab the things I'm going to need for our meeting. Then I follow Reva as she heads to the elevator. Reva and I head back downtown for our meeting, in a rushed manner.

As we get into the elevator, I see Sheldon, looking back in our direction, "Well, if it isn't my two superstars coming to save the day." Sheldon, the Foundation's CFO says.

He tends to step in to pick up the slack when the other executives are away on business so we see him a lot.

I give a small wave as we get closer. We don't say much as we make our way to the elevators, which we take to the sixth floor board room.

The only reason why I'm here is because our board of directors wanted to go over the budget for next quarter and get an update on the systems. Sometimes these go on for a drag, but the passion in me burns. When I get on a subject, I feel like the only relief is when someone physically shuts me up. It's the fixation aspect. That's where Reva comes in; shutting me up when I've gone too far.

I shake myself out of my thoughts.

"Tessa, are there any updates on the shelter building?" one of the board members, Richard asks me.

"I should have more of an update in the next two weeks. The foundation is good and the construction of the shell is almost done. Reva and I are going to be visiting it in the coming days," I report.

Nothing like blank stares from a board of men. If only I could get them to experience the field, even if only for an hour. Maybe then they'd understand.

"Tessa and Reva have been very diligent with this project. They're meeting with service committees in the neighboring cities and will report back. We all know resources are limited and even with the expansion of the shelter, it may not be enough. We're working on the donor aspect," Sheldon explains.

Sometimes, Sheldon annoys the hell out of me, but in this moment, I let my feelings slide because he saves my ass with the board, *again*.

In a sense, that's what Reva and I are trying to explain. Of course, from a male voice, they accept it. I feel my blood boiling already.

Reva sees my cheeks getting red and my eyebrows furrowing and gives me a look. The more I think about it, the more my anger boils. Reva senses the anger and touches my thigh to help ground me.

Driftwood is burning blue, wild the wall shadows
Night winds go riding by, riding by the lochie meadows,
On to the break of day, close Mira stream singing
Caidil gu la laddie, la laddie, sleep the night away

Momma and Granddaddy used to sing to me when I was little, as I got older, it's been the one thing that can ground me, allowing my mind to focus. I take a silent deep breath.

"I'll be able to give a more detailed report in the coming weeks. As far as we know, we're on track to open in the fall of this year." I'm being cautious of a set date, between the weather and the workforce, the date keeps being pushed around.

"We understand that leadership has changed, but don't bite off more than you can chew, Tessa. A lot is riding on this," another board member, Dale, points out.

I nod. In all honesty that is all I can do to fight back the internal words I want to say.

As the meeting ends, Reva pokes me in the side, "You want to text Sam and ask her about lunch?"

I nod and pull out my phone to text Sam to join us at the outdoor barbecue place a block away.

Sam has been another blessing in my career. Sam's been in charge of the hotline for a couple years now. She's the heavy hand and the advocate all in one. She can be shy at first, but once she's fired up about something she is a whirlwind.

"Did Tessa tell you how she was flustered this morning? I was about to smack the attitude right out of her," Reva says bluntly.

I couldn't respond, as she perfectly timed it to when my mouth is full of the best barbeque outside of Memphis. Jesus, I have to take smaller bites.

"Oh, who ruffled *your* feathers this morning?" Sam says, wiggling her eyebrows.

I finally chew through the meat and swallow. "Do y'all have anything better to talk about that's not my sex life?"

They both look at me and smirk, and shake their heads no. I sigh, "I ain't saying nothing. If I don't think about him, my mind will forget about him."

"So, there was someone!" Sam's giggling now. "By the look on your face, I'd say this man left you speechless." The smirk on her face intensifies my reaction, although I'm still speechless.

Reva smirks. "You sure you don't need a good dusting down there? Seeing as the cobwebs have built up and all." I wanted to smack her. Damn, I chose violence today. "Sweetie, we're just concerned that you need some release from all the stress. I could set you up with my neighbor, Adam."

"Last time you set me up, he was the most vanilla man I've ever met. Seriously, I make too many damn decisions in a day. I just need someone else to take the lead," I finally exclaim.

"Would you even give a man the chance to take the lead?" Sam asks. She's got a point.

"Possibly. I'd just make him work for it," I shrug, trying to finish my lunch before I go back to work.

"So, what I'm hearing is that you're choosing to keep downstairs closed for business," Reva grills me.

"Trust me, the man this morning was infuriating. Stupid Viking country looking motorcycle god," I mumble under my breath.

"So, there *is* a man and he's getting to you. Can we help him? Does he need a road map?" Reva scooches over to me, bumping my shoulders.

"No, and I don't want to talk about him," I grumble as I get up to throw my trash away. Something or someone in the corner of my eyes catches my attention, but I brush it off as stress-induced paranoia.

All I wanted to do was leave and bury my nose in work. As we walk, a shiver trails down my spine. My dad used to tell me that whenever that happens, it was a bad thought trying to exit the body. The feeling as if someone is watching me, following my every move.

I am so screwed.

Chapter 6

Teresa

Between virtual meetings and overseeing the hotline, I'm ready for home. Just me and a bottle of whiskey in my hands, with Seamus snuggled in my lap.

Something pulls my attention as I pull into my makeshift driveway and see the lights on in the living room. Seamus paws with excitement at the bay window. Something in the pit of my stomach, though, is screaming at me.

Something's not right. The glimpse of someone from this afternoon, the shiver down my spine, this eerie feeling; something bad is about to happen. This is when I regret not having an alarm system. My anxiety starts to ride high.

I grab my softball bat from the back of my car and creep slowly to the back to unlock the door. Fuck, it's already unlocked.

Someone's in my house and I only have a bat as my weapon of choice.

I slowly let the door swing open, hearing the blasting of music coming from the kitchen. I relax my shoulders in relief. Only one person would dare change my music in my home.

"If you don't turn down that fucking music, I'm going to beat you into tomorrow morning," I scream over the music, watching my cousin make herself at home, opening a merlot.

Last time I checked, I don't own merlots. She turns to grab a glass, only to jump when she sees me.

"Jesus, Lord in heaven. You can't sneak up on people like that!" her southern twang rings out. "Tessie, put the bat down, you'll scare the neighbors."

"Doesn't help when the neighbor is your cousin. I gave you the key for emergencies and to let Seamus out during the day. You have your own home, right next door!" I toss the bat on the couch and plop down. I scratched Seamus' ears as Britt turned down the music.

"Figured you might want this," Britt hands me a glass of red. I'm not a fan of dry reds, but after the weird day I've had I'm desperate. Seamus plops on my lap nuzzling his nose between my legs, already starting to fall asleep.

"Sam or Reva already called you. Y'all are big yentas, I swear," I say as I take a sip of wine.

"Cous, we're southern. We ain't Jewish. Change your references. But also yes, they told me. Viking country God or something like that." she says, waving her hands about.

I throw my head against the back of the couch with a groan. "Shut up. If we don't mention him, he won't show up."

"Tell me everything," she cozies up to me on the couch, her own glass full of merlot. Her whole presence is full of giddiness.

"Nope. Suffer. If I don't talk about him," I begin.

"He ain't in your mind. You sound like a damn broken record. I swear, sometimes I feel you've been touched too many times by God almighty," she groans, practically downing her glass already. Before I can retort, she makes her way to my kitchen.

"Hey, while you're in there, make me a quesadilla," I call. I know exactly what reaction I'm going to get, but I thrive off the chaos.

She's screeching now, banging around my kitchen, "Last time I checked, God gave you two legs and a capable body, you can make your damn food." I laugh at her, knowing that she'll cook anyways.

Brittany is my only family here. She escaped from Alabama a few years before I came to North Carolina and was instrumental in helping me find this house. Thank God, because I don't know what I would have done without her.

"You wanna tell me why you brought in the baseball bat?" she asks from the kitchen. She rummages through my kitchen to make dinner.

I sigh, with her there's no getting around this conversation she's like a dog with a bone, "I just felt paranoid. Just a weird morning, an awful board meeting, and I got the shivers in the afternoon. Today's felt like someone took my voodoo doll and poked me with all their needles."

"So, it has nothing to do with someone making you flustered?" I can hear the sizzling of the skillet with what smells like butter. My stomach is growling at me, the hunger pains setting in now.

"Me? Flustered? Never." I start to brush off her interrogation.

"You wanna drop the act? Seth already told me what you did at Allie's birthday party," she says pointedly, setting out our plates for dinner.

"Jesus, do you all have anything better to talk about than my life?" I mutter.

"Look, I ain't going to press you on it. But knowing you, it's going to eat at you, I think you'll never know until you try," She walks and hands me a plate.

I give up arguing with her and tuck the plate close. It was food and I wouldn't dare bite the hand that gave it to me.

Britt ends up staying the rest of the night, and together, we finish the bottle of wine. Once she leaves, zig zaging through the yard to her house, sleep beckons me.

Sleep finds me easily when I hit the pillow. I pray for a dreamless sleep, but it doesn't appear to be in the cards tonight. All my anxieties rush into my head, creating nightmares from another planet. I swear I can feel the flames on my skin. I see a looming shadow, nothing but the shape. I scream, reaching for help, but no one hears me. My screams are quiet, but loud in my ears.

I feel a wetness, stirring me from sleep. I blink, opening my eyes to Seamus' wet tongue. I laugh, giving him a pat on the head as a thank you for saving me. Seamus snuggles his nose against my hand, grounding me as I attempt to find sleep.

Nowadays, nightmares feel more like a reality. That's the most frightening truth of it all.

The week flashes through fairly quickly and somewhat productive. My training sessions with my intake specialists are complete. I've run reports to apply for state funding, gotten heckled by the girls, had virtual meetings for city committees, and even helped out the hotline when it got busy.

I glance at the time on my computer screen as it reads three in the afternoon. I try to open my screen to my calendar, praying that I can end the day early.

"Reva, do we have anything else on the schedule?" I ask. I squint my eyes at the screen.

"No, I think that's all on the agenda. Why? You trying to cut out early today?" Reva shouts from her desk.

While my office is attached to the hotline area, there are two doors that separate my office. This building used to be an old shipping place, so I have a bathroom and shower near my office. I get privacy when I'm in meetings but sometimes, I feel secluded. Reva's desk is near the first door, so I only see her when it's intentional. It works in our favor when we have interactions like this.

She walks down the hallway towards my office. "Let me guess. You want to run by the center?" I swirl around in my chair.

"You got it! You want to come along? I've wanted to check in with Ms. Aggie and see how everyone's doing," I say as I pack up my backpack to head out for the day.

"Yeah, I guess I'll go with you," Reva shrugs, walking back to her desk.

"Got a hot date or something?"

She looks too coy for it to be anything else. "Maybe, maybe not."

I can't help but rib her about it. "Uh huh, another online dating match?"

Silence falls between us.

I'm right "Called it. Do I need to be on standby?"

"Maybe. We'll see, Tessa." she says with a hint of a smirk on her face.

While we don't have enough shelters in the area, we at least have a couple day centers that provide different services. The one near the city is highly utilized, with countless people in need of help.

Reva and I call it a day in the office and head towards downtown. I like to volunteer my time outside of the office to check in and talk with Ms. Aggie, the sweet, vibrant soul that she is.

Ms. Aggie is an incredible soul, a powerful woman that has one goal in mind, to help those in need. She's a patron saint in this community. She runs the Center like clockwork and nothing gets past her.

When I first came to Raleigh, Jeremiah and Ms. Aggie were the people who helped me acclimate. They've truly opened my eyes to the needs of these people. Just shows that even in this community, it's a smaller picture that shows the bigger problem.

Reva and I park as close as we can before walking to the Center. "You think Ms. Aggie is gonna be there today?" Reva asks.

"I'll wait to answer that," I answer, reaching for the front door.

"TERESA SAOIRSE BJORN, as I live and breathe. She's graced us with her presence. Child! Get yourself in here," a booming voice flies through the doors, a deep old southern accent bellows out.

"There's your answer." I laugh as Reva shakes her head.

I open the door to be greeted by a vision in plum. The dark skinned beauty wraps me in a warm, strong hug before I can get anything more out.

"Ms. Aggie, do we have to use my government name?" I squeeze her back with just as much love.

"Well, when you don't come visit as often, you'll find that you are missed." She says, patting my shoulders, giving me a look over.

"And you brought Reva. Tessa have to drag you or something?" Aggie snickers.

Reva and Ms. Aggie are like oil and vinegar sometimes. I laugh, "No, she came all on her own."

"You ever going to give me credit for coming?" Reva reaches for a hug, Aggie playful denies her but brings her back in for a full hug. To Aggie, everyone is family, as long as you don't piss off mama.

"Y'all come to help out and check in?" Ms. Aggie walks us through the hallways to the main room. It's supper time, so everyone's in line for food. I inwardly sigh. Something's been eating at me all week, and only one person may know what to do. I've been trained by the best, the memories of the first time she saw me and never wanted to let go.

"Ms. Aggie, I have Ms. Jean's new girl. She got lost, but I found her." Jeremiah walks me into the center to meet Ms. Aggie.

"Jeremiah has a knack for picking up lost pups. I'm Ms. Aggie. Jeremiah's harmless, just a pain in my behind sometimes." Ms. Aggie extends a hand for me to shake.

"He said you're a good judge of character," I shake her hand.

"He's one of the good ones. Listen child, I've been doing this for years and Jeremiah here is godsend. Be a good one to keep in your back pocket."

"That's what I told her, Ms. Aggie. Might take her under my wing." Jeremiah smiles at me.

"Actually, that's not a bad idea. Nothing gets past him here. Between him and me, we know everything. You'll get used to it, honey child." Ms. Aggie leads me around the center. It's not much, but it looks like it does wonders for the community. Maybe they're right; if I get out of my shell and immerse myself, maybe I can make an impact.

She sat me down, putting a hand on my shoulder, "You'll get eaten alive out here, taken advantage of, and you seem like a good girl. Stick with me, hunny, and I'll educate you on this community. Maybe one day, you'll go places and be like me," Ms. Aggie says to me. "Don't give up. Be a voice to those who don't have one."

"Aggie, Jeremiah had told me something and it's been nagging me. He was saying that people are disappearing, being offered jobs but not returning anywhere. Is there a job corporation that somehow appeared overnight? Numbers at the hotline haven't dropped. Have you seen or heard about people disappearing? Any families or individuals gone missing? I don't know if I'm overthinking it, but something about it all is just unsettling." I look at her hopeful as Aggie puts a hand up to stop me.

The rambling probably didn't help. My mouth went faster than my mind could keep up.

"Girl, you're fixating because it's something you can't control. You know if I saw something, I'd tell you. Honey child, take a deep breath. I think the Foundation got you overworked." She rests her hands on mine and I feel like someone has knocked me back down to earth and reality. "Why don't you see if there's anything in the kitchen to help out? I bet the chef will give you a cookie," she smiles, patting my hand.

Maybe she's right, maybe there's more going on in my own head causing me to flip between fact and fiction. When I get fixated on things, I tend to overreact. I shrug off my thoughts and give a hand in the kitchen to take my mind off things.

Chapter 7

Teresa

My phone screams at me as a message pops up. Placing the cookie down to the table, I read the messages.

Seth

Ella wants to see you. She asked if Tessa can come over pleeeeease! Her words, not mine.

I wouldn't mind seeing Ella, just the thought of her makes me smile. Seeing Seth and the kids beats what I had in mind for the rest of the night, namely a late night boxing session and a pint of ice cream on the couch. I'd much rather see the kids and watch a Hurricanes game.

I'm leaving the center now, should be there in about 20 minutes.

Seth

Cool, mac and cheese on the stove and garage is open if you want to get a beer or something.

Free beer.

The decision was practically made for me. Hurricanes game, mac and cheese, Jordan and Ella, and beer. Count me in. At least the drive won't take forever, the traffic has eased up since it's post-rush hour. I've made the trip to Seth's house countless times, so much so that I know the route like the back of my hand.

I make my way down the winding road through the neighborhood to Seth's house. The garage is open, with a spot for me to park my car near his driveway. I park, wiping the exhaustion from my eyes.

I trigger the light in the garage and notice something shiny, almost blinding my eyes. I knew Seth had a bike, but this may be a new one. I don't think much of it; I've learned my lesson this week about thinking too much and being fixated. I go to the beer fridge and pull out a cider.

I twist off the cap, opening the door that leads from the garage to the kitchen. "Seth, hello, hello!" I spot the casserole dish of mac and cheese and practically run to take a plate from the cabinet.

I hear the game blaring in the living room and Seth yelling at the screen. After finding a fork, I take a sip of my drink and turn around to head towards the living room, heavenly mac and cheese in hand.

All the air in my lungs suddenly disappears. As if I was underwater and reaching for the surface. I spit my drink out. I toss the plate aside, attempting to save it from shattering from my nerves. Shock isn't the word to fully describe what I see. The hairs stand up on my arm, a cascading effect down my legs.

Sitting on the couch with a beer in hand and Ella sitting on his lap talking his ear off is Jackson. Coincidence? I think not. What game is he playing at? All eyes are on me. Ella squeals, jumping off his lap and running straight to me. For a tiny little thing, she has some speed on her. Her arms are outstretched, indicating that she wants me to pick her up.

"Tessie, look, look! He's here. The knight is here. Jackson was asking about you," Ella wiggles in my arms. The little devil in disguise.

"Yes, I see that, Ella bella," I sigh as I give her a kiss on the cheek before setting her back down.

God, you're really testing me.

I was beginning to forget about him. I see the smirk on his face. I debate on whether to suffer the tension in the air, or retreat to the kitchen and suffer from afar. I chose the former. I attempt not to look at the giant, gorgeous man sitting on the couch, looking as if he belongs there, easing back with his arms stretched out.

"Hello, Teresa." The Viking waves at me.

I don't move an inch. The way he says my name, a rush of heat went to my cheeks. Why is this man suddenly appearing everywhere? I didn't ask for this to happen. I can feel my eyes twitch.

"Tessa, hun, you know you can eat in here," Seth gestures to the living room, asking me to unfreeze from my spot. I search around for an excuse, any excuse to stay in the kitchen.

I notice a box of crayons and a coloring book sitting in a mess of papers, probably from Ellie before I got here.

"You know what? I thought I would color here with Ella. You know *she* was the one who wanted me to come over," I start to say, hoping to God that Ella picks up on the hint and starts coloring.

My smart little Ella picks up what I'm putting down. "Daddy, can I color in the kitchen with Tessa? Pleeeeeease."

"Sure, just let Tessa eat, please. Judging by what she did first, she didn't get anything to eat today," Seth states. He may have a point. When you're on the go, you tend to forget about necessities, that and the ADHD. I chug my drink down, hoping the quicker I drink, the faster the buzz.

"Sometimes, I forget to eat during a long day of work, okay? You know me, I can't stay still long enough," I say as I devour my food, Ella hums as she colors at the same time. She hands me a crayon to color in the chicken from the princess movie.

"Sounds like you have a lot of responsibilities. You've been able to handle it?" Jackson asks smugly.

"Sweetie, there isn't anything I can't handle," is my automatic response. Before I can take it back, my mind's giving me a slap in the back of the head. I stuff my mouth with more mac and cheese. Maybe this'll prevent me from giving Jackson anymore ammo.

"Darlin', I'm sure you can handle... a lot," he snickers, sipping his beer. Seth looks at me with a question on his face. Seth is innocent, but completely obvious to what is going on.

After another serving of mac and cheese, the Hurricanes game goes into a second intermission when I hear, "Alright, Ella Bella, it's time for bed. Let's get teeth brushed before story time."

I freeze again, letting my anxiety get to me. What is it with me and not wanting to be alone with Jackson? I'm typically an extrovert, but Jackson is different. He radiates strength and heartache. Even the thought of being alone with him, I might implode.

He keeps glancing over at me, trying to steal moments of time. My heart races faster with the thought of him near me. I barely know him, but half of me wants to feed my curiosity and the other half wants to run in the opposite direction.

"Tell Tessa good night," Seth calls from the living room as he stretches from sitting on the couch so long. Ella puts down her crayons and gives me a hug goodnight and a kiss on the cheek.

After me, Ella turns to Jackson. "Goodnight, Mr. Jackson," she sings as she hugs his leg.

He laughs and smiles so big, it might melt my heart. The hearty laugh silences all that is around us.

Seth and Ella head upstairs for their bedtime routine, leaving me alone with Jackson. I finish my food and decide to clean up the kitchen. I hear footsteps sounding heavy against the old wood floor with every creak. I know Jackson is on the move.

"It seems others take care of you, I could help with that, too" Jackson pulls one of the bar stools out to sit as I continue to wash the dishes, ignoring him.

He's not there, he's not there.

I glance over my shoulder. Damn it, he's still there. "Oh, now you won't speak. Is someone actually speechless?" That's it.

I slam the dishes down in frustration, sending bubbles and water everywhere. "Momma said never to talk to strangers. I barely know you. So please, just walk away."

"It's merely an observation. I'm just offering to help with anything you need. Be your knight."

I snort. "What's your fascination with that reference? Ella rubbing off on you or something?"

"She may have given me ideas, especially when it comes to a strong-willed, beautiful woman," his smirk makes me even angrier.

I wink. "Strong-willed and stubborn as a bull."

"Maybe if you put the horns away, we could stop being strangers."

Words fail me, as my mouth hangs open. I turn back to the dishes, grumbling to myself. This man is assuming that I'm not capable of taking care of myself. That I need a knight?

"You think that I'm not able to take care of myself? Do I look like someone who is incapable of self-care?" I turn around, my hands on my hips, the sponge soaking into my shirt.

He rests a finger on his chin inquisitively. He stares at me, scanning me from head to toe. I won't let him play me like that; I stare right back, right into his eyes.

Well, that backfired. Just staring at him makes me tingle all over. Damn this man is like a walking wet dream. I feel my body heat intensify. If he doesn't speak soon, I'm going to melt right here.

"Darlin', I'm just wondering if you would allow someone in and give you what you need. Can't help but wonder what if..." he starts to say.

I break eye contact and turn back to the sink, trying to finish the dishes before Seth comes back.

"What if what?" Maybe I shouldn't ask questions I'm not ready to know the answer to. I need another drink. Something stiffer.

Bet he's got something stiffer.

Jesus, get your mind out of there. I'm not following that yellow brick road.

I don't hear him move around the counter. There's a silence that fills the air, and my mind starts to wonder if he's even still there. Should I turn around and look?

Suddenly, the smell of peppermint and cedar takes over my senses. I get goosebumps from my legs up my spine. He's behind me. I know it.

"What if I kiss this spot on your neck? Would you shiver?" He brushes my long hair over my shoulder. I feel his lips taking the place of his fingers between my ear and my shoulder. It's the perfect stop. I stay still, sinking into comfort.

He places two more kisses down my shoulder before his mouth grazes my ear. I haven't been touched like this in a long time. Not since Aiden.

"I wonder. If I were to brush my hand across your stomach to your thighs, would you sink further back to me? Fit your body closer to mine?" I feel his hand heavy on my thigh as his other hand travels across my stomach. I can feel the pressure, taunting me, between fabric and skin.

My breath quickens. I can feel my shirt lift, feel a rush of cooler air on my skin. His hand makes its way under my shirt; I can feel the rough pads of his fingertips brushing across my stomach towards my chest. His hand almost skims the bottom of my breast.

His other hand is circling and rubbing against my thigh. A rush of sensation. I want this man to devour and touch every inch of me.

I lift my head to see our reflections in the window. I make eye contact with a pair of icy blue ones.

He's watching me.

Why does this turn me on, to be watched? I'm putty in his hands. His eyes never leave me, watching my chest heave as he touches me. He knows exactly what he's doing to me. His eyes and his hands seem hungry, begging to feast on their prey.

I let a moan slip out, letting my body take over. Jackson nips at my ear at the sound, and I sink into him, my hands wrapping around him from behind, using him as leverage. I feel unbalanced, unsteady.

"I wonder, if I reach down, will you be wet with the thought of me? Letting your body give in," his hand travels down but I stop him. I've been here before, letting my desire call the shots, and it led to nothing but pain.

I twirl in his arms to stare directly into his eyes. "Keep on wondering, sweetheart."

He wraps his arms around my middle, securing me against the counter. He smiles wickedly and bends down to whisper in my ear. "Little Cub, I plan to make it happen. Why not take a chance."

He looks down at me then, those eyes sparkling with curiosity. I start to wonder who's the hunter and who's the prey. I feel my cheeks rush with heat. He's getting closer and closer to my mouth with each second of silence.

Lord knows the cobwebs need to be swept. I would love to feel those lips on mine, on my neck, my breasts, all of me. We're so close. He's centimeters away from undoing me when a stair creaks and we shoot apart.

I feel flushed, anxious, silently praying that Seth didn't see anything. I quickly finish the dishes, trying to calm myself.

I can hear Jackson snickering as he sits back on the stool, Seth joining him. "What'd I miss?"

Jackson answers first. "Nothing. I was just asking Tessa if she would let me take her out some time. She turned me down cold."

Seth laughs, but the bullshit story has me panicking, rambling like an idiot.

"Wait, what? No, no. That is not what happened," I scream, before I remember that Ella probably just fell asleep.

"Then what happened?" Seth presses me for an answer.

I need to act quickly, but I'm slowly realizing that I'm not going to win this battle. I lower my head. "Fine, he asked, and I turned him down. Strangers turn me off."

Seth snorts. "Yeah, okay Tess. Throwing down another challenge." He's really digging his own grave here.

"Oh yeah, she's heartbroken. But don't worry, she'll say yes and I tend to get what I want." Jackson stands from his stool and heads towards the garage. "I'm getting another beer real quick and making a phone call. Y'all want anything?" Jackson asks with a light laugh.

"I'll take another one or two of these," I say, holding up my empty bottle.

"As the lady wishes," Jackson responds as he leaves the room. The moment that Jackson leaves, I land a smack across the back of Seth's head.

"WHY DIDN'T YOU SAY THAT HE WAS HERE, YOU ASSHOLE!" I whisper-shout. "Seriously, a heads up would have been great."

"I didn't think it was a big deal! I mean, you only met him once and sometimes he comes over for the club business when I need to be involved. Did I miss something?" He throws his hands up in surrender.

Breathe Bjorn.

"Seth," I begin, really thinking about the words about to come out of my mouth. "That man gives me a vibe."

Seth furrows his eyebrows. "A vibe? Care to elaborate?"

I sigh. "A vibe. You know, like I need to stay away from him. Red Flag. Danger. Do not pass go, do not collect $200."

"You feel a vibe?" Jesus asks fewer questions than Seth.

I hang my head. "Yes, a vibe. Listen, the day after the birthday party, he messaged me."

"Did he threaten you? Did he harass you?" Seth doesn't look surprised. Apparently, I missed the memo. He tries to fish out answers.

Obviously, I'm losing this argument. "No, I didn't feel threatened. I just.. I'm not used to the attention. I'm an awkward goldfish."

"An awkward goldfish?" Seth tilts his head.

I start to get frustrated. "Are you going to question me about everything? Look, something's just off and it may just be me. I just need to know something, Seth. Should I be worried? Should I be watching my back?" I have to ask. Seth may be the only person who will give me an answer.

Seth runs his hands through his hair with a sigh. "Look, I won't sugar coat it. I'm not as involved with club business 'cause I have my kids, but even I know that Jackson is a serious man. I know he can be ruthless, protective. He's determined, with a stubborn streak a mile long, but he doesn't hurt people who don't deserve it. So, to answer your question, as long as you don't do stupid shit, you won't be on his radar." He sighs again.

I know he's being honest with me and it's all I can ask for right now.

He's not done, "What's the harm in going on a date? I mean, I think he would treat you right. It might be time to get back out there," Seth says, rubbing my back in comfort.

I know he means well, but I still feel like I need to watch my back.

Before I can respond, the door swings open and I shut my mouth.

"Oh, don't stop talking about me on my account." Jackson hands me my drink and I quickly twist the cap off, downing half of it before I march myself back to the couch

"Since Tessa is not going anywhere, y'all want to watch the Vegas game after?" Seth asks from the kitchen. Fucking hell. I will murder him in his sleep. I must've looked like a deer in the headlights because Seth tacked on a "no pressure,"

"Maybe. I still need to get home to Seamus," I blurt out. I turn my focus to the game, then realize I picked the wrong spot. I tuck myself in the corner on the L-shaped couch.

"What kind of name is Seamus?" Jackson asks.

"He's her corgi, but I'm assuming Brittany's watching him, so he's fine," Seth says, sitting back on the couch.

Yep, he's going to die by my hands, and I'll make it look like Winnie the Pooh did it.

Jackson sinks down into the couch, nothing but solid muscle positioning itself directly next to me. He swings his arm across the back of the couch and I feel my heart rate climb. I don't let it phase me; I continue to drink and watch the game.

Slowly, so slowly I didn't realize it at first, he starts to squeeze the back of my neck, spreading his fingers gently through my hair. I turn back into putty. He twists the little baby hairs underneath, just playing with them. He drops them to trace his finger across my shoulder blades. If he keeps doing this, I'll fall asleep on this couch.

Suddenly, he stops. I let out a whisper of a whimper. Thank God for the volume of the game. Otherwise, I'm sure Seth would've heard. Jackson peeks me out of the corner of his eye and smiles into his beer. The sweet caress is intoxication, my body asking for more. Perhaps a few minutes longer and I would give in, might even say yes. But with that I decide against it and stand up and head towards the door, in the most "awkward goldfish" way possible.

"Thanks for the food and the drinks and the game, Seth, but I'm tired. Long day. I'll text you when I get home." I gather my keys and quickly shuffle out to my car, before anyone else could protest. I need to get home soon as possible. Thankfully, I don't live too far.

As soon as I reach home, I lock my front door, then turn and slide down to my backside. What did I start to get myself into?

I get in the shower to scrub this day away, the feeling of Jackson against my skin. Do I regret him touching me?

No, I don't.

I wanted it; I could have turned away at any time and I didn't.

I've built so many walls, and his touch is starting to melt away a part of myself that I didn't know I could take down. Maybe I'm just shocked someone wanted to touch me.

My last relationship had made me feel like I was nothing, that I wasn't worthy of love. He's the reason why I built so many walls; I can't let someone destroy all the work I've done. I get out and change into my pajamas as my phone goes off on my bedside table.

Leif Erickson

Sweet dreams, little cub.

I'm stunned. Seth's right. He *is* determined.
Fine.
I gather the courage to message back.

Be like the wind and change directions.

Leif Erickson

As long as that direction is towards you.

You can't catch the wind.

Leif Erickson

But I can catch you. Go to sleep.

I turn off my phone for the night and drift off to sleep, Seamus at the foot of the bed snoring. I pray for a dreamless sleep. That's until the morning comes quickly.

Saturday mornings also mean boxing at this little hole in the wall gym Sam found. I started going when the dreams got worse, and I needed an outlet.

Romero, the owner, allows me private time before opening as long as I say good things about him to Miss Aggie. That's not something I'm about to meddle in.

"Seamus, you wanna go to the gym?" I scratch his ear, knowing his answer. I quickly get ready for the gym and put Seamus' harness on him. Seamus is harmless when we go to the gym. He just prances around and stares out the window at the passing cars.

Seamus stares out the passenger window of my car and starts to wiggle his butt. He knows where we're going. "You gonna help Momma out?" I ask him.

He glances back over his shoulder, his tongue hanging out. We park in the back and I help Seamus down. He huffs and puffs trying to hurry me up to open the gym door. I find the key and carefully let us inside.

"Hello, old friend. I've missed you," I announce when I flick some of the lights on. Seamus does his normal laps, and I see his head poke back around the corner of the boxing ring. I lay out my gloves and my wraps. I'm not a professional by any means, but Romero and his crew taught me enough over the past few years. I can handle more than people would guess.

I plug my phone into the stereo and start up my playlist. *Raging on a Sunday* by Bohnes echoes around us. Seamus is already in a corner, making himself comfortable.

I head towards the mat for a stretch and warm up with the jump ropes, attempting to work on footwork and endurance.

I start to wrap my hands while heading towards the speed bag, praying to God I don't hit myself in the face. I'm not the most graceful person. Music continues to blare through the speakers, loud enough for me but not enough to wake the neighbors. My workout makes me sweat worse than a sinner in church, making my legs feel like jelly and my arms burning.

Something shiny catches my eyes. Down a long empty hallway that I think once held champion photos is a target board.

Now *that* piques my curiosity.

Seamus notices my irregular movement and pops up. I look down the hallway and see the board is above a storage box. A Cheshire cat grin spreads across my face as I open the box. Seamus pokes his head through and looks at me.

"Oh yeah buddy, I'm trying it." Seamus scatters; smart choice. I've thrown axes for fun at one of those entertainment spots, and I have been around knives my entire life. How different could this be?

I take out three knives that look doable. I plant my feet, winding my arm back and releasing one of the knives. It hits the target board lower than I wanted. Brushing it off, I adjust my feet a little bit. I wind my arm back behind me, releasing another one. I hear a *thunk* as the knife lands in the outer ring of the target.

I'm starting to get frustrated.

Come on Bjorn, get it together.

One more time, I ground my feet, already feeling the sweat running across my face. I wind my arm back behind me.

Aim for the bullseye.

I am about to throw it when, "If you release it sooner, you'll hit it," a voice calls out and I quickly react, not realizing that the blade has slipped through my fingers.

"Good morning, little cub." he says with a smirk on his handsome face.

Chapter 8

Teresa

Alexander Jackson Jones is a fucking parasite.

Just when you think you got rid of him, he comes back with a vengeance. Sitting there in a hoodie and black gym shorts, arms crossed in judgment and awe. I realize now that the knife I threw is lodged in one of the wood panels on the wall behind him.

Damn, that got some distance.

Squirrel moment.

I start to wonder why Seamus didn't signal that someone was here.

Wait a second.

"How the hell did you get in? I locked the door," I shouted.

I step closer to him, closing the space between us. Jackson sits there at the edge of the boxing ring, possibly plotting his next step, taking inventory of what he sees. Even sitting down, he has height on me.

"Funny thing doors, they tend to open when you have a key." He holds up a key. "Did you really think you're the only one Romero lets in early?"

"Funny, never seen you here before," I spit sarcastically.

Jackson grabs the waistband of my leggings and pulls me closer, meanwhile I get a full breath of his cedar scent.

"Are you always this sarcastic this early in the morning or am I that special now?" He traces my mouth with his index finger.

"Don't flatter yourself, A.J," I deadpan, attempting to bite his finger.

Maybe I can distract him so I can leave. But something whispers to me, to stay and ride this out. Fight back, show him that he didn't get under my skin.

He crosses his legs around me, effectively trapping me between his legs, "Call me Jackson," he rumbles out.

I hear Seamus growl, and Jackson growls back at him with a deep rumble.

I roll my eyes so hard it hurts. "Are you seriously having a possession fight with my dog? Jesus, maybe I dodged a bullet."

He looks back at me. "Oh darlin', it's no fight. More of a claim or protectiveness"

"You think I need protection," I shove his chest, trying my best to push myself free. Also ignoring the word claim.

He just chuckles, "We all need help once in a while, especially a beautiful woman who wants to save the world."

Flattery can only get him so far, but not to me. I still don't know him. But maybe Seth was right. I shake the thought.

I go to shove one more time into his chest, but Jackson is faster. He captures my wrists in each hand and places them to my side. I'm pinned, unable to move. His brute strength takes over, and unfortunately, I don't know how to get out of it.

But do you really want to?

I'm caught by surprise when he yanks me forward and slams his mouth onto mine.

The kiss immediately starts to melt away my rough exterior. I sink into the kiss. It's a hungry, brutal kiss, a game of give and take, almost a power fight. I can feel the heat of our bodies against each other. It's been a long time since I've felt this. His kiss is intoxicating, sending butterflies in my stomach, like a siren calling to the sea.

He pries my mouth open, slipping his demanding tongue in for a taste. I hear nothing but our breathing and the sounds of our lips connecting. He releases my wrists, and my hands fly into his hair, wrapping around the strands of blonde hair and tugging.

I try to control the kiss, give myself something to anchor me, but Jackson nips at my bottom lip. It's not hard enough to draw blood, but it's enough to send a shot of pain down my core. I let out a small whimper of defeat.

He lets go of my lip with a pop and gives me a small look up and down as he releases a low grumble. He licks his lips, "I have wanted to do that for a few days now."

He goes to kiss me one more time, but I shove him back as I lean to the side, hoping to escape from him. With enough force, I scramble out from his legs and into the ring.

Jackson bends the ropes to let himself in. He stalks around the ring, trying to intimidate me into bending. "Tell me, Teresa, what brought you here this morning?"

I snort. "Not that you care, but everyone has their outlet to escape the world every once in a while. I'm sure a man like yourself hits the booze or finds a woman to satiate his needs," I keep my space, not wanting to give into temptation.

"Whatever happened to never judging a book by its cover? Maybe if you give me a chance, you'd be surprised." He moves in the opposite direction.

I'm not getting out of this, I know it. "You know what A.J, I'll make a bet with you. If you pin me, I'll agree to the date. If you can't and tap out, I win, and you leave me alone." Okay, I know it doesn't seem fair, but I can take him. Plus, part of me wants to bruise his ego, knock him down from his almighty throne.

"Any rules?"

I nod, "Don't kill me. I have people counting on me."

He grins, "I wouldn't dream of it."

I turn my back from him and fix my ponytail, but before I know it, I feel a yank on my hair. I grab his wrist, steading myself as I sweep my leg with his. We land backwards, the initial shock allowing me to swing my legs over his lap and straddle him, landing a couple of punches to his abdomen. I attempt to pin his arms, to no avail.

Instead, he fixes them behind his head. "Darlin', I know winning is the goal, but I must say, the view ain't half bad. I could get used to you being on top," he laughs like it's nothing, and here I am panting as if I sprinted a mile.

Something primal leaves his lips, and for a split second I think I need to run. I watch him wide-eyed; I know I won, but he hasn't tapped out. He goes to buck me off him and I try to maneuver into an arm lock but it fails me.

Jackson flips me to my stomach, so that he's straddling my backside. I go to buck him off, trying to use my arms to push off, but to no avail. He quickly grabs my wrists and locks them behind me with one hand. There's strength there; there's no way I'm getting out of this hold.

Sweat drips off of me in sheets, but there's a strange, heated sensation fluttering across my skin.

No ma'am, now is not the time to be horny.

I grunt in an attempt to get him off, like a donkey he's pissed off. He trails his other hand down my spine in response.

I feel him lean down, bending towards my ear. I feel the warm whisper of his breath against the side of my face. "Just give in. It's easier than fighting me," he nips at my ear, I try to kick out again.

I don't know why I try, because he grabs my ankles with his other hand. I'm truly trapped, all my energy exerted. Maybe this is a sign: things happen for a reason.

I sigh and tap my back to let him know I'm out. He eases up, removing his weight from my spine. As he does so, he tenderly kisses my cheek.

"Don't paint me as a villain in your story yet, beautiful," he murmurs as he eases up on my backside.

I think I'm out of the woods until I feel a sharp pain across my ass as Jackson smacks it hard. I gasp, expecting irritation and instead feeling particularly turned on.

"That was for the attitude and stubbornness, Little Cub."

Heat rises to my cheeks. This is the first time a man has said that and here I am, turned on by a man more than I've ever known what to do with. We sit up and face each other, as if he knows what he just did.

I cross my arms. "So, you won. You never said *when* you wanted to take me out."

He just shrugs. "I'll let you know the date and time."

I'm flabbergasted. "What? No grand ideas? You're gonna leave me hangin' and guessing your next move?"

"What better way to keep you on your toes?" He grins, his smile splitting wickedly. He moves suddenly, crouching down to get closer. He cups my chin, tilting it up. I blink, still flush from our previous interaction.

"Teresa, maybe give me a chance and we'll have both our ways. You deserve someone who wants you the way you are." He leans to plant a soft kiss on my lips.

This kiss is different from the others. It's sweet and light, but still makes me yearn for more. I pull back and watch Jackson walk away, disappearing to the back into Romero's office.

And you think you're that person, Jackson?

We went from strangers at a children's birthday party to hungry for another kiss in a matter of days. This is not like me.

Maybe he's right. Maybe I should give him a chance. His words strike a chord in me, and I almost feel like breaking down in the middle of the ring. I hear Seamus whimper and a small tear rolls down my cheek.

"Are you ready to go buddy?" A small bark tickles my ears. I pack up my stuff and we head home, almost feeling like I need to go back to sleep and shut out the world.

Mid-week stretches on forever, the hotline seems to be in a crazy busy spell, enough for Sam to ask me for help. I try to help out as much as possible, but I can't help floating back to the memory of Jackson. It's been hard to forget about our interaction, every heated sensation, every what if. What if I had given in earlier?

I'm shaken out of my daydream by the ringing of the phone. *Definitely not the time, horny Bjorn.*

"Thank you for calling the housing hotline, how can I help you today?" My customer service voice comes out like a southern princess.

The caller is irritated by our lack of resources, needing housing, saying someone was offering the homeless population work. If only we had more funding, the ability to reach further.

I log the call and continue to help the numbers go down to a manageable level but something about the last call haunts my thoughts.

Something that keeps nagging at me.

It rattles me, my mind is circling back to Jeremiah and Ms. Aggie. I call Sam into my office; maybe she can put me out of my misery.

"Sam!" I yell across the hall. She scurries in with a pissed off look.

"A normal person would send a message or email, not yell across the office," she grunts.

"Yeah, but I'm not normal," I grin. "Have you been getting calls from anyone saying that there's someone offering people work?"

Sam's eyebrows furrow. "Hm, I haven't. You want me to ask the team?"

I nod. "Probably something worth mentioning. I don't know, maybe it's just a vibe. At the end of the day it may not be anything."

Sam gives the look of confusion wondering where my mind is heading towards.

I have to laugh at the quirk in her eyebrow. She knows me too well. Maybe it's just my paranoia again.

Sam sits in one of my chairs to continue our conversation; at least she'll tell me if I'm spiraling or obsessing. My phone starts to ring, and, still leaning on my desk, I press the speaker button.

"This is Tessa Bjorn. How can I help you?"

"Saturday, 7 am, I'll meet you at Devil's Whiskey. Make sure you wear a jacket." I know that voice.

Jackson booms through the speakers. I turn to Sam and the look on her face is full of curiosity and delight.

I grimace. "Ah, yes. Our date. You know, it was unfair."

He chuckles softly. "I remember tapping out when I pinned you underneath me, although I had liked the view of you on top." Heat rushes to my cheeks. Sam's mouth drops open in shock and holds back her laughter, and I know I'll have to explain this later.

Fuck.

"I can admit defeat. You won your prize." I cross my arms against my chest.

He audibly tsks. "No, Teresa, our date isn't my prize."

"Then what is?" I say, leaning towards the phone.

"Your heart." He says it with confidence, like it's a given. Sam goes into an "awe" explosion, squealing in my ear.

Two can play this game of his. "My, my, does Mr. Jackson have a soft spot? Color me surprised." Sam giggles in the background.

"Darlin', there is nothing soft about me." He lets out a deep laugh. I'm not usually bashful but at this moment, I am.

"You do realize he is talking about his dick, right?" Sam intervenes.

My eyes go wide with her words. "Samantha! I'm hanging up now before I regret anything else." I punch the button with more force than I intended.

Sam sits with her hands intertwined, her index fingers touching her lips. I groan, leaning my head back on my chair. "Shut up, your mind is too loud."

"Wait until I tell Brittany and Reva. This is him, the one you were talking about last week? I need more details. Are we talking 'touch her and you'll die'? Climb him like a tree? What?" Sam continues to ramble, but I don't listen. I shake the intrusive thoughts that stir in my head.

Suddenly, Sam's waving her hand in front of my face. "You ain't even listening to me!"

I scoff. "Yeah, yeah climb that tree like I'm searching for nuts, I heard you."

"Yes ma'am. Also, don't you have a meeting with Sheldon?" I look at the clock, my heart flying into my throat when I realize I'm ten minutes late. I'm like the wind and gone. I hope Reva's there, covering my ass.

A quick sprint down the hall and I'm walking into our small conference room. Sheldon looks pissed, which is not a good sign for me.

"Thank you, Tessa, for taking time out of your *busy* schedule to meet with us." Sheldon taps his watch. "Good thing we don't have a multi-million dollar building we have to get reports on."

I notice a red-haired woman clad in a tight navy blue dress also joining us. I would know that red hair anywhere.

"Carla, finally coming out of the shadows? How's Mr. Connors?" I ask, taking my seat next to Reva. Carla Jenkins is a snake of a woman if I've ever met one. She flaunts herself around the office like she owns the place, when she's just a highly-paid assistant for the CEO, Mr. Connors.

"Mr. Connors is taking some much needed rest. That's why I'm here. You know, to ensure his program is going well," she says as she stares at her freshly manicured hands.

I must be making a face because Reva pinches my thigh. "I'm glad to hear that. I apologize for my tardiness. Sam needed some relief with the hotline."

"Let's get to it then." Sheldon waves his hands in an attempt to move the meeting along. *Breathe Tessa. Some battles aren't worth it.*

"Reva and I visited last week and everything seems to be in motion. The site leader said we're on track, with a soft opening potentially in September," I report, eyeing Reva nodding in agreement.

"But it could be pushed back, from what I am hearing," Sheldon announces.

"I was told our timeline is still good. Nothing has changed," I rebut.

Carla pouts. "Mr. Connors wants to see this through and I'm sure we wouldn't want to disappoint him. He's worked so hard for this. I want to be able to give him good news."

It ain't your fucking job on the line, bitch. Move along.

I plaster on the fakest smile I can muster. "No, we wouldn't want to disappoint him. Which reminds me, I wanted to ask about the annual Masquerade silent auction. Were we trying to host the event at the new location or still at the Main Hotel?"

The Foundation holds an annual masquerade silent auction in the hopes to raise money for our services and programs. It's a fun event where we cozy up to donors and ask for more money. Every year, we get so close to our goal and this year, I have an ace up my sleeve.

Lucie Lynn.

Lucie Lynn is a volunteer but two years ago, she went through our shelter program. Her story touched my heart and I saw passion and hope in her as she worked to turn her life around. I want her to tell her story at the event, in the hopes the donors will see success. "We're still having it at the Main," Carla interrupts, although she knows my question is for Sheldon.

Sheldon nods his head in agreement. "We just need to keep to the plan. No changes. I know you have ideas, Tessa, but right now is not the time when we have so much going on. I need you to take a look at next quarter's budget and make sure there isn't anything I'm missing." Sheldon doesn't look up from his phone.

"Oh Tessa, I'm sure you can handle that, right?" Carla snickers.

Reva is pinching my thigh again, warning me not to choose violence. Anger begins to bubble and all I want to do to wrap my hands around Carla.

"Of course. I'll take a look and have them on your desk in the next couple of weeks," I give him the slightest of smiles. I've done these tasks every time and he acts like I don't know what I'm doing. Whenever Carla's in the room, he turns into an asshole.

You've come this far, Tessa. Don't ruin it now. One day at a time.

"Tessa, we need to get back to the hotline. Sam said there's been an increase in calls." Reva pulls on my arm to escape this hell hole of a meeting.

As we walk, I start to hum to calm myself down. This day needs to end. I'm even looking forward to my date.

Chapter 9

Teresa

The alarm goes off reminding me that I have a date with Jackson. I don't know whether it's nerves or fear that strikes me. I shake my head, wondering why I agreed to this.

Cause your ass hasn't had a date in years and you could stand to get laid.

Seamus looks at me with curiosity. "Just ignore me, bud," I tell me as he huffs at me in agreement and continues to bury himself in the blankets.

As I hurry getting ready, I lift the jeans over my ass, and find a shirt that doesn't attract too much attention to my "God-gifted" boobs. I scramble to find my red-leather jacket that Jackson told me that I needed to wear, which I'm arguing with him about. I take one look in the mirror, natural yet not dead looking. A splash of perfume and I'm ready.

Seamus looks at me with his ears perked up. "Alright, sweet boy. What do you think? Too much? Too little? Am I going crazy?" I bend down to give him scratches. He barks at me but leans into my hands. I lean my face in for our nose boops, then text Brittany to let him out in the afternoon if I am not back by noon.

Brittany

Don't worry, I have your location if you get murdered by the viking.

I head out, giving myself enough time to warm up my car and head towards the Devil's Whiskey. Meeting him at a bar seems awkward; are they even open at 7am? I mean is that normal? Would it surprise me that a biker group has a bar open this early?

I pull into the parking lot, filled with bikes. Peering at the clock on my radio, it's 7:10 am. I feel bad, but tardiness is my style, a reputation to maintain.

Gonna be late to your own funeral.

I smell the familiar smoke mixed with the morning scent. I take a deep breath and attempt to open the bar door. To my surprise, it flies open and I'm greeted with the dark scene of the bar.

A few men sitting at the bar look my way, another few at the pool table racking up balls. Heavy rock or country plays lightly in the background.

I walk through the bar, nodding my head in an attempt to look friendly. Last thing I want is a scene because I look out of place. Thankfully, I spotted a familiar safe face near the back.

"Well, look what the cat dragged. The tiny but mighty mouse. Come for round two, sweetheart?" The bartender from my first time here smiles at me.

"Oh, you know, once you get a taste of the wild side, apparently you can't go back," I joke as I take a seat at the bar. I know I'm late.

"Sweetheart, are you here to see someone or are you looking for trouble? Because I'll warn you, this isn't the place for it," he offers, cleaning glasses and pitchers. He hands me a cup of coffee, as if he read my mind. "Especially if someone has not gotten their coffee."

Before I could explain, a booming voice echoes to the left down the hallway. "Now Johnny, we wouldn't want to scare off a pretty young lady."

A giant of a man with salt and peppered hair and a matching stumble pops into view. His eyes are gray eyes, like when the early morning fog hits the dark forest. His skin is sun kissed, a bit rough skinned, his frame holding rippling muscles. What was with this bar filling a woman's wet dream? Is it a requirement that you should be handsome and rugged?

"Sorry boss, I didn't intend any harm. She's a spitfire, though," Johnny throws his hands up in defense.

I finally take a sip of my coffee, wishing I had a splash of Baileys or creamer. Silver fox turns to me again, "I'm sorry, I don't mean to be rude. Name's Rawlings, and pretty much the boss around these parts. I'm assuming you're here for Jacky-boy? He's doing me a favor right now, seeing as you kept him waiting," Rawlings extends his hand to greet me.

I grip his hand, shaking it powerfully in return. Curiously I say, "What favor is that?"

A small chuckle escapes Rawlings, "A mess that needed cleaning up."

"I'm sorry I'm known for being a little late." I give a faint smile, turning my attention back to my coffee.

"Prez... Boss, this is Matthew and Seth's friend," Johnny announces.

"Ah, you're the one who started shit in my bar," Rawlings leans on the bar near me, grasping his hands together.

I feel myself going slightly red with embarrassment. "Wouldn't have had to if your man had any respect for women. He had enough respect once he met my knife, though." I take another sip of coffee.

"Ah, so that's what's in your pocket," he says with a wicked grin, giving me a wink.

There's something cocky in his grin. Unfortunately for him, though, he isn't my type.

I feel a brush of lips tingle my cheek. I turn around and spot Jackson in a leather jacket with a Grim Wolves patch, dressed casually in jeans and a t-shirt.

Now that's more like it. I let out a small moan, I guess he's growing on me a little bit.

"Now, Prez, I told you to be nice to the woman. I had high hopes of trying to keep this one," he drapes his arm around my shoulders. The way he says "keep" sends a small warmth through me. The thought of letting down my barriers would make my therapist very happy.

"Be careful what you claim brother. Some feral cats aren't worth it in the end," Rawlings says as a warning in my direction.

I stand up to say something, but I feel a gentle tug pulling me back against him pulling me out of the trouble I was about to make. A swirl of peppermint surrounds my ear. "Careful, Little Cub. I may know how to control my temper, but that is one lion you don't want to poke." Jackson may have a point.

I turn and throw my arms around his neck, "Alright Jackson, I'm here and it's early and you promised me a date at a god forsaken hour..." He dives straight to my lips, distracting me from the people behind me. He fights to control the kiss and I let him. He's the first to break it.

He rests his forehead against mine. "For someone who hates mornings, you talk a lot. Also, you kept me waiting."

"Yeah, and?" I say while my finger travels down this arm.

"I don't like to be kept waiting. You'll learn that in time," he smirks. Without hesitation, he picks me up and tosses me over his shoulder.

I slap against his back. "Put me down, you brute. I'm capable of walking. You afraid I'll bruise your ego and leave?"

Smack.

That was no love tap either. His palm landed hard across my ass cheek. The sting and the heat come all at one. I whack at his back and wiggle to get loose. He holds my legs tighter as we head to the parking lot. I can see the smirks and hear the snickers of the men in the bar. "Jackson, put me down!"

"Anyone tell you that you talk a lot, darlin'? Let me handle things," Jackson declares as he lands another one across my ass. This is a strange sensation.

Dear god, do I *like* this? I feel wetness flooding my panties. *Jesus.*

We finally reach outside and he sets me down next to a bike. Jackson starts it up and reaches to hand me a helmet.

He straddles the bike and looks at me. "You coming, little cub?" I walk around the bike to the left side. "What are you doing, Teresa?"

"I'm making sure my pegs are down. Last thing I need is the muffler burning my ankle. Again." I strap on the helmet.

My father had a bike when I was growing up and I used to love riding alongside him. I used to joke with him that I'd get my license and take his bike. My first ride with him, the peg was not down on the right side. I went to swing my leg over and my exposed ankle met the hot muffler.

I get on the back of the bike and search for his belt loops to hold on. Jackson swats at my hands and pulls my arms to wrap around his waist, forcing me to scooch closer. My heart's thudding wildly, my breathing starting to hitch. The rumble of the bike pulses against my thighs. The smell of exhaust mixed with gasoline unlocks memories from the past. I can't help but smile. I'm happy I chose the leather jacket, as the wind whips against me. I don't know where we're going, but I know he has something up his sleeve.

It takes us half an hour to arrive at the Sal's Branch Trail. Two cars sit in the parking lot and it's still pretty early. I'm about to swing my leg over when I feel two strong hands pull behind my knees and cross them over his lap.

"You're in a rush," he chastises me. "Slow down. Take a breath."

I take my helmet off and hand it to him. I look around, seeing the trail up ahead and the sun peeking through the trees, cascading through the woods. I hear birds singing up high in the trees. Before I know it, Jackson swings around to face me, my legs still wrapped around him.

Okay, his love language is physical touch. This is new.

I search his eyes for what to say. Nature continues to hum its morning tune. I start to get nervous.

I haven't had a man look at me like this in years, like I'm a beautiful, unknown creature. I can feel the heat coming from my cheeks and look down at our hands that are somehow intertwined.

"I'm sorry this just feels strange," I say shyly.

Jackson slides a finger under my chin and tilts it up to look at him.

"You don't have to apologize, Darlin'. Tell me to stop and I'll stop," Hell must have frozen over because that's a new take.

He caresses my face and I lean into his hand, wanting to stay here at this moment. I know it's a fantasy, but I'm here. I get lost in the moment, time is frozen. "You want to stay like this, or do you want to go on a walk?" Jackson says to break the moment. I nod my head and unwrap my legs. He picks me up and swings me off the bike before straightening to his full, towering height.

"Lead the way," Jackson says, gesturing towards the entrance.

If I'd known we were hiking, I would have chosen more appropriate footwear. The trees are in the beginning stages of showing their full color. I don't know where I'm going but the little kid in me doesn't care. The little kid in me sees adventures.

A few moments go by, lost in my head, afraid I would talk Jackson's ear off and have my squirrel moments. I'm jarred out of my revelry by his deep voice. "Penny for your thoughts?" He strides up closer to me.

I shrug, "Nothing too exciting. I guess I'm imagining what the little kid in me would do. Most likely, wander off into the woods like I'm Robin Hood or something," I shove my hands in my pocket.

"I imagine you have an active imagination," he playfully bumps into me.

"Oh, I do. When I was younger focusing was hard," I try not to say too much.

"What changed?"

I shrug again. "I learned I had a superpower."

And medication was introduced.

"You could fly," he laughs teasingly.

I joked with him, "That would make my life easier, but alas, no."

He ticks up an eyebrow. "So, what's your superpower then?"

"Mr. Jackson, why would I give away my secrets so early?" I chuckle again.

"Does that mean I'll have more chances to find out?" He questions.

The conversation keeps flowing for another twenty minutes. He probably thinks I'm crazy with my rambling by now. I jump from the topic of my work to my family to my not so proud drunk moments.

I decided to change the topic. "Okay, you know way too much about me. Tell me about you. Unless you want to tell me you are secretly a viking prince waiting for the ship to take you back to the fjord?"

Jackson grabs my hand, twining our fingers together, as we walk over a small wooden bridge. "My story is simple. I grew up in North Carolina, towards Gastonia. Didn't stay there too long; mom passed away when I was three from breast cancer. Pops went back to the Raleigh area where Uncle Thomas took us in. Pops patched into the club a year later. Uncle was president of our club then. When I was ten, Dad was shot by a rival club and Uncle was my last living family member."

I could see a little sorrow in his eyes.

"Was? Wait, for real you're in a motorcycle club?" I ask, even though I already knew the answer.

He looks a bit grim, "Club members aren't known to have a long life span. By the time I was 21 and patched in, he lost his life protecting the clubhouse. Everyone wanted me as president, to keep it in the family, but I couldn't take on that role. Rawlings, the man you met at the bar, stepped up and told me that he'd take the role as long as I was vice president." All his family is gone; my heart aches for him. I itch to comfort him, but I'm sure he doesn't need my help. All I do is rub my thumb across the top of his hand.

Maybe that's why they were switching between Prez and Boss, trying not to reveal too much.

"I'm sorry you went through all that. Losing family is never easy."

He brushes it off. "I didn't mean to put out the sob story. Look, I've devoted most of my life to the club, but every now and then it's good to escape it like cooking when I can, fixing cars and bikes, getting my hands dirty." The thought of his hands sends shivers down my spine.

Fuck.

He continues. "I like walking trails with an intriguing woman. We're not villains, but we are not overly good people, either."

We must have walked half the trail by now because it looks like the halfway mark is looming closer.

"Jackson, are you saying you're not good for me?" I grin, taking it as a joke, but I don't think he does.

He stops in his tracks and pulls me closer, so I can feel bulge in his pants. "Teresa, I'm not a good person, I've taken the lives of others, some of them haunt me. I've had to make decisions that might result in blood. We've hurt people. I guess we never thought that someone would be okay in the world we live in." He starts to say.

I want to reach for his hand, and grasp it in mine.

He goes on, "But you came in that bar, like a bright ball of sunshine and I don't know it's hard to explain." He stops.

I look at him, searching in his eyes for something to grab onto, "You can try. I'm not going anywhere."

He huffs out a deep sigh, finding the words to say, "Maybe I'm trying to see if you would paint me as the villain in everyone's story or will you allow me to show you the other side. I want to be in your dreams every night. I want every touch to haunt your skin. I want."

He lets go of my hand and walks to stand behind me, sweeping my hair back to plant a kiss on my favorite spot.

Is this supposed to happen? Where instantly you can be swept into your dreams, where someone shares an inkling of a desire yet untold.

"I would want you to make memories with me, to bring a smile to your face. Because when you smile, it knocks out all the damage and horror in my mind." He says

I pull back a little bit. "I'm not anyone's savior or redemption."

He steps back around, "And I'm not asking for you too." He cups my cheeks in his hands. I simply melt in his touch. The slight possibility of an adventure or making memories with him. "But I want you to feel like you can be who you want to be and do whatever your heart desires around me, and trust me."

My anxiety peaks a little at the contact, so I try to turn the conversation. "Do you want to make a new memory now?" My mouth goes dry, searching for the answer in his eyes.

"Perhaps a game of sorts," a grin spreads across his face.

"What did you have in mind?" I say as his eyes darken, igniting with my words. "A game of hide and seek?"

My eyes widened, "A wager?"

"Run, run, run, little girl, away from the big bad wolf,." He growls low.

Fucking hell.

The growl makes the lower half of my body tingle, like sparks igniting across my body. "I'll give you a 20 second head start." There's a huge lump in my throat.

He's awakening sensations that I haven't felt in years. Even has me curious.

"Aren't we a bit old for a game of hide and seek?" I nervously laugh.

"Afraid that this wolf could find you?" Jackson inquires.

 I go speechless.

"What's the wager?" my voice sheepishly lets out.

His eyes darken for a moment, a curl of smile lifts his mouth, "If I find you, you let me unleash a hidden desire. You let go, for a moment."

"And if I win," I propose.

He kisses my cheek, "Whatever your little heart wants."

I want a lot of things.

"I don't see you running, little cub. One," Jackson starts to count. I try to take off like a flash of light.

Legs don't fail me now.

Half of me wants him to find me and enact whatever fantasy is playing in our head; the other half wants to challenge him. I count in my head, hoping to find a thick area or tree to hide behind. I see a huge oak and slip to the side, calming my breathing.

Chapter 10

Alexander

Run little one, let me unleash your desires.

I can smell the hidden arousal, the thoughts that spin in her head are loud.

I shouldn't want this, even knowing what I need to do.

But she is my wild one, my heart calls out to her even if she doesn't recognize it.

Her take off is exhilarating, and unlocks something primal, possessive.

But, I always find what I want, and I go after it.

Chapter 11

Teresa

It feels like forever. The anticipation has me in a death grip. I'm thankful there isn't anyone else around.

A few more quiet moments pass when I start to hear the crunching and rustling of leaves.

"Oh, Little Cub, you can't hide forever. I see something I want, and I won't stop until it's mine." The moment he says mine, I'm done. Heat rushing through me,

I have to cover my mouth with my hand to keep quiet. I move around the tree, out of his line of sight. He's watching every corner and crevice. Praying silently that he continues past me so I can run, and an idea pops in my head.

I pat the ground to find a decent sized rock, something with weight to it. I wind my arm back and toss it as far as I can.

My chance to run the opposite direction, hopefully towards the bridge, rests on that rock. Jackson cocks his head towards the rock and starts to pick up speed.

Maybe I have a chance.

As soon as he's out of sigh, I sprint off again, hoping that I'm not making too much noise. I run as fast as my body allows, realizing that I'm nowhere near the bridge or people.

Fuck!

I hide again, near a tree and bush, hoping the leaves will camouflage me.

I hear the rustling of leaves and snapping branches again. "You're lasting longer than I anticipated." The sound inches closer and closer. "But in the end, we both know who's going to win." He snickers, and I practically lose my mind.

I've never been so scared and turned on at the same time. I crouch down, readying myself to slide around the tree when he gets closer. His footsteps are getting closer and closer, his voice still carrying on, "I can smell you. Lemon and the sea. Intoxicating." I peek around the tree, and then: *snap.*

Shit, please don't turn around.

Nothing.

Absolute silence.

I peek again, wondering if I have time to run. He's gone. Like mist in the morning. I straighten up and look around.

I've watched enough scary movies in my life; I refuse to be the first one killed. I ready myself to open my knife.

Like a lightning flash, two huge hands grab my upper arms and pin me against the tree. Jackson tsks, his chest heaving and his eyes dark with hunger.

The predator has found his prey. And he's ready to devour.

"Well, Little Cub. It seems like I've won." He takes my wrists and pins them above my head as he licks the bottom of his upper teeth. His hunger and need are showing. I shake my head, lust already clouding my vision.

"Time to unleash those hidden desires, Teresa. This is your chance to stop me." A warning, he's giving me a way out.

In the heat of lust and want, I answer him. "And what if I don't want to stop you?"

He plants a hard kiss on my lips in response, and I gasp, allowing him to deepen it. Our bodies grind against each other, moving in sync, like we've been doing this forever.

He growls when I tear my hands from his grip to reach for his jacket. The feral look in his eyes warns me off; he needs control. His kisses travel down my neck as his hands work their way beneath my shirt, pushing it up, practically ripping it off in his haste to have me naked. I feel my bra fall to the ground, and his fingers tease my nipples into hard peaks. I'm practically on the edge already, and he's barely touched me.

"God, please," I burst out, not caring if someone hears me. There's a low chuckle against my skin.

"Patience. I'll give you what you need." He travels down to my waist and grazes his finger along the top of my jeans. "What will I find Teresa? Will I find you wet and hungry for my touch?"

I practically buck against him. "Alexander, please. If you don't, I will," I moan.

He pinches my nipple. Pain radiates across my breast.

My mind goes blank, his name coming out as a plea, but only Alexander.

This side, asking for Alexander, another side.

"I'll stop if you don't control that mouth of yours, and right now, I don't want to stop," Alexander warns.

He's not Jackson anymore, at least in my head. He's a man taking what he wants. I battle to keep calling him Jackson, but my heart and mind make their decision.

Alexander.

My mouth clamps shut. I whither, needing him to touch me, but his words almost make me come on the spot. I can feel my orgasm building, and it terrifies me.

He unbuttoned my jeans, easily sliding his hands down to my core. He kisses me again and his fingers travel across my wet heat. I need release soon or I'm going to spontaneously combust. I buck against his hand.

He chuckles against my lips. "Oh, so soaked for me. Was it the words, the game, or your need for my touch?"

He's teasing me now, rubbing back and forth lightly, never finding the spot I truly need him to touch. My clit swollen with need aches, and before I know it, he finds it, and my knees start to buckle.

"If you answer me, I'll give you what you want."

"Please," I whimper.

He pulls his hands away, leaving me a puddle of built-up heat. He stalks around behind me, wrapping his arms around me as he pushes my jeans all the way down my legs. I press against him, feeling his cock thick and hard in his pants.

"Mm, don't worry, darlin'. I have plans for us, including burying myself right here." He punctuates his words with a smack to my pussy before cupping it. One hand is circling my thigh, the other rubbing my clit in small, torturous circles.

I'm barely hanging on by a thread at this point. "Alexander, *please.*"

"Then answer my question," his rhythm picks up, his other hand slowly making its way to my entrance.

Before I can register his movements, he plunges a finger inside, and I feel like I'm dying. "So tight, Little Cub. I wonder how well you'll stretch around my cock," he murmurs into my hair. I grab his shoulder behind me, steadying myself. My head falls back onto his chest as I ride his hand.

"Answer. Me," he whispers against my neck, moving his finger in time with his words.

"Everything! It's everything. Please, let me come." My words come out like a tidal wave, giving in to his demands.

He adds another finger, curling as he thrusts, while his other hand rubs my swollen clit. I'm almost there, and the build is agonizing. "Let go, Teresa. Let everyone know whose fingers you're coming on like the good girl you are."

"Yes," I breathe. "So close."

He doesn't lessen his strokes, the intensity building. "Come for me."

His words break the wall of my orgasm. The rush of it frees me, the ecstasy clouding my eyes, my body trembling with the aftershocks. My breathing hitches as he slowly extracts his fingers. His hands leave me in a pool of my own desire, and I slowly come down from my incredible high.

I scramble to fix my clothes, lest anyone see me naked in public, and look up to see Alexander tasting his fingers. My eyes widened with shock.

He licks his lips, as if not wanting to lose a drop. "Oh, I'm going to enjoy our adventures. And you might be my favorite flavor." He leans down and wraps his arms around me to kiss the top of my head.

"Come on, let's finish the trail and I'll take you to lunch early." He grabs my hand, leading me back to the bike before I can answer.

Welp, there goes that brick wall. A desire unlocked.

I'm in way over my head with him, I should retreat. Go back to my comfort and normal side. I can't help but think this is a dream that I haven't woken up from.

Alexander takes me to a small mom and pop diner. I don't know if I have much of an appetite, not after what we just did. Still, I order some fresh fruit and a broccoli and cheddar soup, knowing I'll need the calories later. I sit there, lost in thought, revisiting our rendezvous, wondering if this is crazy.

"I can see the wheels turning, Teresa. Talk to me." He reaches across the table to take my hand. I purposefully avert my gaze from his face; if I take one look at him, I'm done, I know it.

"Don't want to scare you off, Jackson. Look, back there..." I struggle to find the right words. "That was a first for me, unusual, strange. But I found it exhilarating. It's been a long time since I felt like that."

He strokes my hands in comfort. "I liked when you called me Alexander, no one calls me that anymore." He's gentle but yet the same man from the woods. "You don't have to explain yourself. If you need time, I understand. I let things get a bit rushed."

Silence falls between us again, and it prompts me to admit something I may regret. "There were two people in this decision," I start to say, avoiding his gaze, "But I want more."

I look up to see him smirking now, obviously proud of himself.

Great, I stroked his ego.

"I can do that. What do you want?" He asks a million dollar question.

"Not even the second date yet and you're asking about future intentions." I'm nothing if not great at turning awkwardness into sarcasm.

He smirks. "So there's a second date."

I threw a grape at him. "Maybe." I sigh, how do you explain what you want to burly biker gang man with the looks of a god.

Was he ready for a potential family or seriously dating? I continued, "Look. I want fun, but I want someone to come home to at the end of the day. I want the laughter, the memories, and hopefully, one day, a family. I can't afford the games that lead to heartache. And if that is not for you, then we can just get the bill and leave."

"I can't promise perfection." he starts to say.

Well there goes the idea of a future, my mouth twists until he says, "All I wanted was a chance. You gave it to me. So, there's no one else I'd rather have." He looks serious about that, too. I find that hard to believe, but maybe that's just the toxic thoughts surfacing.

"You mean *right now*," I correct him, and he shakes his head.

"No. Not just *right now*," he implies.

"I'm not expecting perfection. So I guess we just see where we go from there?" I say, turning back to my food.

"Can we get back to the fact that you enjoyed yourself." Jackson says as he takes a sip of his water.

"Don't let that get to your head there, Jackson," I cock an eyebrow at him.

"I liked when you said Alexander." He says in a rumble, almost at a whisper like it's a secret.

"I was in the heat of the moment." I mutter. We become silent again, letting the air settle, fighting the urge to call him Alexander.

"Jackson, if you break me, I'll kill you," I say half-heartedly. We both know I wouldn't.

"Darlin', I'll hand you the knife." Just like that I'm on the road to hell with the hound from hell. Into the flames of what is to come.

Chapter 12

Teresa

When did I become the romantic type? The one who fawns over the little things and sidetracks herself more than she already does. Jackson may look like he can snap someone's neck and he probably has, but damn, I didn't expect romance.

We've been out a few more times, but even I was surprised by the flowers on my desk, a card reading "to the many adventures to come".

It's been a few days and I haven't heard from him. My anxiety tells me I should check in, hoping I didn't scare him off. Maybe I let down my guard too soon, said too much. I'm pulled away from my thoughts when Sam walks through the door. "Hey boss lady. Got a minute?" I swivel my chair around to meet her gaze.

"What's up? Is this a good minute or a bad minute?" I inquire.

"Depends on how you take it," she says. Sam looks down at the floor, knowing I might not take the news well. "Carla was looking for you."

I snort and groan at the same time. "What does she want now? Did she forget her broom?"

"Apparently, you forgot to look over the budgets? She went tattling to Sheldon."

Motherfucker. I knew I was forgetting something.

But I should have expected that this would happen, the first moment I forget or she finds an opening, she takes it. I bolt to Sheldon's office. I'm careful, I've always been careful. There Carla sits, talking with Sheldon. What a snake of a woman. I want to reach across and yank her by her fake red hair. The smug look on her face tells me I'm screwed, like she has Sheldon wrapped around her bony pinky.

"Sheldon, I'm so sorry..." I begin but am stopped by Sheldon's hand, forcing my mouth to snap shut. I can feel my body start to tremble.

"Carla has already taken care of it. Look, I understand if you're overwhelmed, but all I asked was for you to look over the budgets. Thankfully, Carla was able to step in." Carla grins like the bitch she is, acting like she already won.

My blood is boiling. All I see is red. I'm not surprised this happened, she wants the spotlight and tends to throw everyone under the bus.

"Sheldon, I'm truly sorry. I overlooked my to-do list. This wasn't intentional," I try to ease the situation.

Sheldon isn't backing down. "Tessa, you're a hard worker, but sometimes I worry this is going to be too much responsibility." No one on the face of this earth wants to hear those words, the fear of being let go. I can feel the tears collecting behind my eyes. "Look, just try and do better. If not, maybe this is too big of a job for you."

"I believe she can do it. She's worked this hard," pouts Carla, patting Sheldon's hand. But the look in her eyes is devious, conniving.

I want to yell, scream, and smash the condescending bitch in the face. But Sheldon's words become an echo in my head, telling me I'm not fit for this or anything else. The self doubt sets in. My body paralyzed with the thought that I'm not enough.

Instead, I just nod. "I understand, Sheldon. Now, if you'll excuse me, I have shelter check ins and supervision notes to complete." I practically run out the door, putting on my brave face, not allowing anyone to see my emotions, when all I want is to shut out the world behind me.

"Tessa," I hear Reva and Sam call out.

I slam the door shut before they can get to me. I find the closest, non-breakable item, a Rubik's cube, and chuck it across the office. Still seeing red, I swipe all my papers off my desk. I feel like a volcano erupting, rage spewing out of my pores.

I find a pillow on one of my chairs and press my face hard against it, letting out screams of frustration. The release stings my throat. I sink down the wall, still holding the pillow to my face as I cry.

I hear the creak of the door open. "Boss lady?" The quiet call stills me. I need to gather myself. I can't afford for anyone to see me like this. The door swings wider, and Reva and Sam softly plop down next to me. I look over at them, wiping the tears away, taking deep breaths.

"I'm okay," I just want to get back to work.

"This is not fine. What happened?" Reva asks me. I stand up and walk around my desk to sit in my chair. I look around, seeing the papers on the floor, dents in the wall, not recalling if I threw anything else. Sam starts picking up the mess.

"Sam, leave it. Look everything's fine. Just give me a few minutes and I'll be back to normal," I snap. The blank stares are all I need to know that I screwed up.

Sam and Reva know I'm lying, but I won't admit it. "Whatever you say, ladybug," Reva says as they leave my office. I hang my head in disappointment. I let the anger explode. Before the door closes, Reva speaks again. "By the way, Jeremiah is on line 1." The door closes behind her with a click.

Emotions are running high, and I feel like I can't see straight. I just want to call it a day, go home, and leave it all behind me. The light on my phone keeps blinking; I almost forgot Jeremiah's waiting for me.

"This is Tessa."

"Ms. Tessa, Ms. Tessa. You definitely know how to keep a man on his toes," a small chuckle echoes through the receiver.

"Jeremiah, I don't mean to be rude, but I am a tad busy. Is there a purpose to this call?" The attitude hangs thick in the air. But a sniffle is released.

Jeremiah ignores my rude remark. "I told you I'd keep an ear out in the streets. I've noticed more and more people missing. Like one day they're here and then the next, gone."

"I know the housing list opened up. Do you think they're just getting help?"

I can practically hear his head shaking. "No ma'am. Jeremiah knows all. I swear, Ms. Tessa. Someone's out here taking people and luring them to a trap. I thought I saw some vans earlier this weekend. Maybe the old eyes are playing tricks on me."

I sigh. "Jeremiah, look. I know it seems strange. Do you have proof?"

"Yeah, yeah, just ask Ms. Aggie. She'll tell you the truth."

Feeling defeated, I scribble down on my to-do list to speak with Aggie. "Alright Jeremiah I'll look into, please don't do anything or look into this anymore." I'd already put my suspicions in the back of my head, but I guess it's time to revisit them.

Throughout the month, I've pushed aside the thoughts of someone hurting our homeless community. I can't do anything without concrete proof. I have other items on my list to get through. March is ending and I have six months to oversee the shelter project and not screw up. I pack up my bag and decide to work from home.

I head out the door and tell Reva I'm finishing work at home and to call if she needs me. She gives me a small nod. I get in my car and the earlier emotions come back up. I can't stand losing control like this.

I know I'll have to talk to my friends about it, but now is not the time. The drive home is uneventful. I go to unlock my door and find it already open. *Brittany. I do not have the time nor the energy to be around her, not today.* I swing open the door and there she is, sitting on my couch, a fresh pizza and a glass of whiskey in hand.

"Reva messaged me code red. I'm here whether you want to talk or not." She pats the couch and hands me the glass. *Hello old friend.*

"I'm sorry Britt," is all I say before I'm a puddle of tears, staining her shirt. She hums the familiar tune that only calms me down.

Driftwood is burning blue, wild walk the wall shadows
Night winds go riding by, riding by the lochie meadows
On to the break of day, close Mira stream singing:
Caidil gu la laddie, la laddie. Sleep the dark away.

Most of my life, I rely on the songs to soothe and ground me. When I slipped into my dark depressed days, the songs of the past brought me back.

We stay like this for what seems like hours, until I finally notice when darkness casts a bright moon glow into the living room. I get up to finally change out of my work clothes and into my yoga shorts and an old college hoodie.

I'm starting to feel that half bottle of whiskey I've emptied with Britt. As low-country music fills the void of silence, drowning out the emotions that escaped the day with his deep soulful voice.

Suddenly, there's a knock at my door, startling all of us. Seamus barks and aims straight for the door. I think I stood up too fast, because my legs wobble. I debated opening the door, but I can't imagine who it could be. I get to the door and look through the peephole on my toes.

My heart starts to race. The gruff sound of his breathing answers the quiet.

"Darlin', I know you're there. Open up," Jackson sounds, but I can't see his face. After days of silence, I shouldn't answer him, but I do.

I swing it wide, and the first thing I notice are small beads of red on his face. I step closer, not speaking a word. He's sporting a fresh black eye and a couple open wounds on his head. This man is bleeding, and in my house, or more like my porch..

"Jackson, what.. who.. why..." I caress his cheek. I need to get him some medical attention.

"Don't ask questions you don't want answers to," there's a hint of laughter in his voice. "Are you gonna let me in or are we gonna stand here all night? Because I'd much rather do something else with you." His voice is deep, lower than normal, he chuckles softly.

"Who the fuck is at the door?" Brittany gets to her feet and comes face to face with the man who has a chokehold over my thoughts. She takes a long, wandering look over Jackson. "Fucking hell, you look like shit," she starts to say, then looking at the fuller picture, a hot-ass man leaning against the open way, hunching over. "Hot damn, she's been hiding you. Guess those cobwebs are cleaned out," she says, back at me as she winks.

Heat and shock cover my face almost instantaneously. "Britt, I think it's time for you to go," I say as I shove her out the door.

Jackson steps into the house as I push Britt out of it and shut the door behind me. This is the first time he's seen my house, and the sudden need to clean is strong. Seamus trails behind him as he walks, huffing and sneezing to get his attention.

Jackson bends down and scratches his ears. A strange tingle washes through me as Seamus isn't too keen on men, but Jackson appears to have won him over. "Go to the kitchen. I'll get my first aid kit and some ice."

Thank goodness that I'm extra prepared, I think I have enough supplies to get me through the end of the world. I've taken enough first aid classes to do fine and at one point, I was a medical social worker intern, where I learned a thing or two, especially in the emergency department. The stories that I could tell people.

"You've been drinking, Little Cub." His voice booms through the hallway with a hint of judgment. The wash of guilt rushes through me.

"I'm fine; I have a higher tolerance than many people believe," I rush down the hallway with my supplies, "Plus, it's either me or the hospital."

He's sitting at the island, waiting for me. Something about him waiting for me and the thought of being his nurse.

Alright, I'm cut off.

"No hospitals," he gruffly answers.

"Then you're stuck with me," I open the kit and grab my supplies.

"Good, I like this choice better," Jackson says with a glint in his eye.

"One second, let me get a stool. Even sitting down, you're a giant. I need to see these cuts better." I go to turn but I'm picked up and set on my kitchen countertop before I can draw my next breath.

Jackson steps between my legs with a stool pulled behind him. "This works better," he says with a sly smile, sending electricity coursing through my body. *Focus.*

"Fine, but no funny business," I chastise him. "You ain't in the hottest state right now."

"Awe, Little Cub. You think I'm hot," I apply pressure to his wound and he flinches.

"Sweetie, there aren't enough words to describe you," I say as I try to clean up the wound. The cuts aren't too deep, so maybe a butterfly bandage will work.

Jackson lightly brushes his fingers against my thighs. The feeling, combined with the alcohol still coursing through my system, may be enough to put me to sleep. "Sir, if you don't stop, I won't be able to finish taking care of your wounds."

"Can't stop thinking about it," his eyes heavy from probably exhaustion, as they almost droop shut.

I roll my eyes. "About what," asking as I continue to work on his head wound, pondering what the hell happened.

"Your soft skin under my touch," he says as his fingers start sliding up my legs sending prickles under this touch.

"Maybe you took more to the head than I thought, Don't get cocky with me."

He smirks, "You ain't seen cocky yet." I smack his hands away, but he moves to put them back. I bandage him up with the butterflies, then tilt his chin up to check for any more cuts or bruises. About to clean any more, then he continues.

"I appreciate the help," he softly lets out, the silence surrounds us again.

I'm the first to break it. "Do I wanna know how this happened?"

He grunts. "Something I needed to take care of. Someone disagreed with me." I wet a washcloth to clean off the remaining dried blood. It must have been a heated argument.

"What's this *thing* you needed to take care of?" I rinse off the cloth to clean his face again.

"You." He turns my face towards him, a finger under my chin. I look him dead in the eye, wondering when I became the damsel in distress.

I scrunch my eyes. "As much as that doesn't make sense, I don't need to be taken care of; you don't need to worry about me. But how did this have to do with me?"

"But what if I want to, Teresa?" I throw the washcloth into the sink, as he said that. I attempt to make my way off the counter, but I'm trapped against him.

"You didn't answer my question." I stare at him.

"Nothing you need to worry about." He inches closer to me. His hand trailing alongside my thigh.

"You don't have to tell me everything, just if it relates to me, what kind of trouble happened?" I incur. If he wants me to trust him, he needs to start here.

He rests his head on my lap, avoiding my glare, "Someone had certain thoughts about you and we disagreed. We fought, end of story."

I didn't like his answer, truthfully. We've known each other for a little bit and the feeling that he's hiding something is making my skin crawl.

He pulls me out of my thoughts, I pat his hand. "You're all clean. You don't need me anymore. If you please, I would like to continue my date with a man named Jack." He stands up, pushing the stool out

"Trying to get rid of me? Or are you taking your anger out on something else?" He brushes his nose against mine. I see red, my temper about to go full sail.

"Fine. You show up here like you haven't been ignoring me for days. I had a shitty ass day where my boss made me feel like I was drowning, then second guessed my ability to take on a job I have worked my ass off for for years. So no, I don't need someone to take care of me when I am doing just fine at handling shitty days," my anger keeps bubbling, I should stop, but maybe the combination of alcohol allows for the truth to be free.

I continued, watching him take every dagger of words I throw, "Last I remember, you said you aren't a good man. Why would you want to take care of anyone other than yourself?" I try to wiggle out of his reach, avoiding his contact. I've taken care of him and in response he becomes cryptic. I don't have time for mind games or second guesses or even second choices.

Jackson's face changes as I speak. He goes from flirtatious to stern, his eyebrows knitting together. He grabs my face, pulling me to look him in the eyes, but I refuse to back down.

"When I called your office, your assistant said you were going home. I asked what happened and she didn't want to tell me. But, I can be *very* persuasive. She sang like a bird after a moment, about how you screamed and wrecked your office. She said she hasn't seen you like this in ages. I got concerned, I told Rawlings I was going to check in on you after I got done with *work*, he gave me some choice words, and another disagreement with a brother, and now I'm here," his anger matches mine, but never aimed at me.

His icy blues are staring back at, "Yes, I know you can take care of yourself, but maybe it is okay to let someone who cares about you be there too."

His words hit me hard. Why am I worth it to him? I haven't done anything worth anything. "You called my office? Why?"

Jackson scoffs. "Why? Just because it's been a few days doesn't mean I forgot about you. I wanted to see you, but apparently, you found another man to be with tonight," his anger broke off. He lightly kisses my forehead, tucking a strand of hair behind my ears, "I'm sorry if you thought I was ignoring you, but business comes first. At least right now."

Right now? Why wouldn't it be later?

"Mmm, Jack D. Never disappoints," I release a soft laugh, my buzz quickly fading. Damn high tolerance.

"I won't disappoint. Right now, I'm having to make certain choices." He kisses my cheek. "You can be the most hard-headed, stubborn ass woman with a smart mouth, and I'll still be here."

I turn beet red. "Most men would be turned off by my mouth."

He grabs my hand and places it on the crotch of his pants. He's turned on. He's hard for me. No, *because* of me. A rush of emotions fights to come up my throat. "I wanted to see you. Let's go." He walks to the couch and grabs the blankets under one arm and Seamus, who is growling at him, under the other.

Okay, now I'm confused. "Where are you taking my dog?"

"You're following me to the backyard and I'm going to kiss you under the stars. I want the wonders from above to look down in awe."

I practically whimper. He's saying all the right things. He wants to release a part of me that's still caged in like a wild animal refusing to be tamed. The rest of the night, he fulfills his promise of kissing under the stars. For a moment, my body eases into the bliss of the night, wondering what the stars will tell me, what whispers will come my way.

Chapter 13

Teresa

Between getting lost in thoughts and time moving, April quickly approaches.

Jackson's a constant now, ever since that night in the kitchen, patching up his wounds, I tend to see more of him throughout the week, but the man is biding his time.

This week's flowing better than last week; I felt myself spiral, becoming the person I've tried so hard to not become. Anxiety is a bitch.

I've apologized to Sam and Reva for allowing my monster out. They didn't deserve how I spoke to them, and I don't deserve them as friends. I've been lying low at work, sticking to my to-do list. When I got to the office the day after the disaster, my office was put back together like nothing happened. Thank you, Sam and Reva.

A knock sounds at my office door. "Boss, Ms. Aggie just called." My head jerks up. It's rare that Aggie calls the Foundation, nevertheless me. Shivers again. I have a bad feeling about this. The concerned look on Reva's face doesn't help either.

"Did she say what she needed? Is something wrong?" I feel the need to forget my to-do list. My mind races with the endless what ifs. Reva shrugs, giving me motivation for my next steps. What if she's calling because something is wrong with the center? What if someone in the community died? My stomach is in knots. I dial Aggie's number.

One ring.

Two rings.
Three rings.
Voicemail.
Fuck.

I grab my keys and dash out of the office, telling Reva that if anyone asks, I'm out doing outreach and talking with partners. The anxiety keeps building as I drive through the city, dodging traffic as much as I can. My phone beeps with a text message. My mind's telling me to answer it in the hopes that Aggie messaged me. For a brief moment, I stop at red light and open my phone.

Leif Erickson

Tell me I can see you tonight.

Tonight? I don't know. Can I call you later? I'm dealing with something at the moment.

He doesn't respond right away. I don't imagine him waiting by the phone for my reply. After our night in the kitchen and the stars, he calmed my mind, my mind wanders back to it.

"Look Teresa, I guess I should've warned you that between the club, the bar, and the shop, I may get carried away with...work. It's never intentional," he says, laying on his back on the blanket. Seamus cuddles into the crevice of his underarm.

My head lays on his chest, listening to his heartbeat, counting the vibrations against my cheek.

I sigh. "I know, but my head was saying other things. It's hard to silence those thoughts sometimes."

"So that's not your superpower, quieting your mind."

I smack him on the chest lightly as he laughs. "Look, I thought I said or did something wrong."

Jackson rubs my side, soothing me into sinking closer to him.

"You've done nothing wrong; I guess I'll have to remind you between your legs and ease your mind?"

I practically choke at his insinuation. "Alexander, my cousin is currently peeking through her blinds with buttered popcorn."

The sound of his first name stirs something in him. He looks down at me with a wicked grin. "Maybe we should give her a show." He flips off his back and starts to wiggle my shorts down. Brittany would approve and probably with popcorn.

My heart's still beating out of my chest. I know there are things that I can't control, something I've covered extensively with my therapist, but this has me rattled. I park the car near the Center and sprint to the entrance. It's mid-afternoon, which means Aggie's probably in the big room. I pop open the doors with a "Where's Aggie?" at the receptionist, already anticipating the answer.

"And you are?" Either she's giving me attitude or she's new.

"Tessa Bjorn from Lighthouse Foundations! Aggie called my office. I need to see her. Now!" I slam my hands on the receptionist's desk. The slam echoes down the halls, slightly scaring me with the intensity.

"Don't get your panties in a twist, I'll call security." The side twang and her attitude are heating me up and my patience is running thin. For a month, a side of me has been uneasy. Something within the community is changing and it isn't good.

I bypass her and sprint to the larger community room in search of Aggie. I can feel the sting of incoming tears building under my eyes. I keep going down the hallway, looking into each room and office. I make my way to the very back of the building, silently praying to God that she's in the donation room. Sweat drips across my forehead as I pump my arms.

I push through the swinging doors, huffing out my breaths. "Aggie! Please for the love of God and all things holy, please be back here."

I look across the space, peering down the aisles. The room starts spinning, colors starting to mesh together. Tears run down my face, my mind a mess with anxiety. My chest heaves up and down, my body going numb.

A hand on my shoulder wakes me up and whips me around. I stare into the chocolate eyes of Aggie.

"Tessa, child."

I immediately wrap my arms around her neck, continuing to sob. "Child, what's wrong?" The question is so simple, yet so loaded.

I incoherently sob into her shoulders, my body failing me, going weak and numb. Her arms wrap around me and her hand cradles my head. "Shh, hey, I'm here, I'm here."

My emotions have betrayed me.

How do I explain this to her? I let fear take over and rule my actions. I let myself and my thoughts cause an outburst. Although it feels like a lifetime has passed, I know it's only been a few minutes. Aggie takes me to her office and hands me a box of tissues. The amount of black coming from wiping my eyes tells me I don't have mascara left.

"Now, would you like to tell me why Keisha said there was a mad woman looking for me?" she says, easing back into her chair. I know she's waiting for me to explain myself.

"You called my office, which you rarely do." I put the ball back into her court.

She nods. "I called because I did need to talk to you. Obviously, I may have needed to give Reva the message if I'd known you would react this way."

"I tried to call you back, Aggie, but you didn't answer." I tap dance around the real reason I acted the way I did, with no apology.

She scoffs. "Do I ever answer my phone?"

She may have a point. There's a beat between us. I overreacted. I breathe in and out a few more times, gathering myself back to composure.

"Well, I'm here now. What did you need to talk about?" I start to get back to myself.

She doesn't let me off the hook. "What I'm about to say is strictly an observation. I figure you and I are more involved with our city, enough that I thought you would want to know."

She rummages through the stack of paperwork on her desk.

"You know we have our daily check-ins, and we add them into the information system. I was running reports for the grants and committees for next week. I noticed a slight decrease in the amount of people we had over the month of March. Compared to last year, it doesn't seem like that much." She pulls out charts and the reports, similar to what I pull for the hotline.

"Aggie, how much is it?"

"30."

Okay, not bad. "Okay, but that's compared to last year. What about February? I would understand if there was a decrease there. You and I both know that over 6,000 people are reporting home-lessness. Perhaps half of them visit the center."

She huffs, getting even more annoyed at me. "I know that! Jesus, keep talking and something intelligent might come out."

"Aggie, I don't see the need to worry over something mean-ingless." I start to stand up, but I'm stopped by Aggie raising her hand.

"Listen, I saw the report from March and February. There was a decrease by 70. March reported 253 regular individuals checking in, February was 323. I know Social Services aren't that quick with housing 70 people. So, Tessa, where did they go?"

"Regular meaning?" I ask, making sure we were both on the same page.

She leans over, "Regular as in, uses the center daily."

The numbers and the coincidences are telling me one thing.

I pause, thinking about my next words. "Jeremiah told me on more than one occasion that he noticed people missing. But, people come and go every month here. I'm not sure what to believe."

Aggie sighs, clearly not willing to fight with me, "Look I'm just telling you that I think something fishy is going on and maybe it's time we become fishermen."

Was Jeremiah right? The thought of people disappearing without a trace, no else looking for them hurts me. The idea that no one is thinking about them forms sorrow in my soul.

My head gets fuzzy at the thought of what we may have stumbled across. Let alone the thought that the foundation is intertwined with this somehow, we should have noticed something by now if this was true.

"I can't promise anything, but I'll keep an ear out. I'll run my reports to show proof." I offer, trying to suppress the guilt that starts to bury inside me. Aggie nods at me, and she stands to give me another hug.

"Tessa, Something's got you spooked. Don't let it get to you. You're stronger than you give yourself credit for." Her words echo in my head. Are her words echoing my feelings forming towards Jackson or is this bombshell that there's more to these whispers of vanishings. Her embrace is enough for me to gather back that strength or at least on the right path.

"We'll figure it out," I say, leaving her office.

The time to listen to instinct rather than numbers or suspicions, starts now. My instincts tell me that I need more answers, more than I can find on my own. An idea pops in my head, dangerous but perhaps necessary.

I dial the number, taking a deep breath. Nerves rattle me as I sit in my car, my fingers tapping on the steering wheel. A couple rings go by, then the click. *He* still makes me nervous

"Did you handle your situation? Or do you just miss me?" his rough, but sweet voice rings out. I swear I could feel the vibration of his voice through the receiving end.

I chuckle. "And what if I just missed you?"

"Then you must have fallen for me." The cockiness in his answer washes away some of my anxiety.

My chuckle turns into a full-blown laugh, "More like tripped on the sidewalk and busted my face."

"I'll kiss your wounds better, Little Cub," he growls and a smirk paints my face.

Deep breaths, rip the bandage.

"You still wanna see me?" I nervously ask, even though his admiration and slight obsession makes for an obvious answer.

"I think you know the answer. I can come see you, unless you have other ideas. I have some ideas of my own. Including your bed."

As much as I desperately crave his touch, his affection, there's other things that beg my attention. "Mm, someone's in a mood."

I can hear the rumble in his chest from here. "Always for you, darlin'. Now, what do you have in mind?"

I blurt it out before I lose my nerve. "You want to visit the new shelter with me? Tonight?"

My proposition is met with a laugh. "Is Teresa Bjorn asking me out on a date?"

"Don't let it go to your head. To both your heads. But yes; I talked a bit about what I do, but now I want to show you."

He agrees faster than I expect. "Okay, I'll pick you up at seven?"

I shake my head, "I'll meet you there. The day has been... unpredictable, but I'm hoping to be out later this evening."

I withhold the truth until the timing is perfect. My hope is that maybe through his connections or the club's, he could find out more answers than I can. There's a deep gut feeling that there's illegal or criminal behind the disappearances. Jackson I hope could be a solution to my problem. I beg that this is a misunderstanding and people are getting a second chance in their own homes.

As the rest of the day passes by, one look at the clock tells me that the day needs to wrap up. I message Jackson that I'm leaving the office in a bit and sent him the new address. Even in a rush, one look in the mirror and the rat nest that I call hair is everywhere and dark circles cascading on my face, I'm a picture of beauty.

I dial Britt to ask if she'll take care of Seamus, and the tone of her voice tells me all I need to know. With a gentle reminder from her to "wrap it before I tap it".

Time escapes once again, I'm running late, Jackson surely is going to be waiting on me. Again. Jackson might have my ass, literally. I yell good night to my late shift people and practically run out of the office and out the door in a breeze.

The new shelter is outside the city. Where the city is more hustle and bustle, we needed a place to immerse within the community even more. Allow the families and women to feel a connection to the neighborhood rather than a city where life seems to pass us by.

The plan starts formulating in my head, what I want to say and what to avoid. I didn't want to be fully immersed in Jackson's world, but with him staying closely by me, it's inevitable that my world and his will collide.

The sun's setting and the golden hour's here. I already called Hammitt, the project leader, letting him know I would be at the work site. I enter the dirt parking lot and notice Jackson's bike with him leaning against it, and a smirk across his face. I look at the clock; I'm only ten minutes late, which is my personal best.

I park the car.

Breathe Bjorn, don't make yourself anxious.

Yet, my palms are sweaty and my heart rate increases.

"What did I tell you about being late?" A hint of tease comes from his lips.

A sly grin comes across my face, "I believe that you said I'd be rewarded with a kiss." Even in my wedges, the brute is tall.. I press my lips against his, sinking into it with a soft laugh. What is this man doing to me?

Opening your eyes to how you should be treated.

Jackson presses harder, going from playful to passionate without warning. His hands travel down my back, sending goosebumps all the way down. Jackson cups my ass in both of his strong hands, and a fire grows in my belly. A smack lands where his hands used to be and a gasp escapes my mouth. He leans over to my ear, knowing Hammitt is in the trailer, waiting on me.

"I would take you over this bike if I didn't know we have an audience. You know I don't like to be kept waiting." His breath is hot on my ear.

"And yet, Leif Erickson, you're still here and touching my ass. We have a date to get to." I grab his hand off my ass to lead him towards the trailer. With a nod from Hammitt, we don our hard hats and enter the building. Not an ideal "date", but one to remember.

It feels like the building is a blank canvas, waiting for the color to explode within. The shelter portion is on one side, with three floors, including a cafeteria and tutor rooms. The other half of the building will be administrative departments, case managers, and volunteers. We build, rather than lease, so that we can give more hope to others in our community.

The work lights are still on, shining through the open spaces. The echo of our footsteps fills the hallway.

"So, am I going to actually get a tour, or will I have to be creative and imagine it?" Jackson says from behind me.

I chuckle. "I like to start off my tours by asking what would they like to know first?" It's not a total lie, but something stirring inside of me is making me feel like a ball of nerves.

Jackson plays along. "Okay, what's the purpose of the shelter and why such a large one?"

"Currently, we're operating a shelter within an older home. We saw a need for a bigger space for individuals escaping a domestic violence situation and families experiencing homelessness. There's more to homelessness than just not having a home. Think of an onion: as we peel back someone's story, we can start to understand what led to their current situation," I start to explain, which leads my mind into many directions of conversations.

I can talk about this subject for ages and still be able to further have discussions.

"That's commendable, trying to get people off the streets. What happens after they enter the shelter?" I lead him through the empty rooms towards the staircase to the second floor.

"Our hope is to find them permanent housing, which can be difficult. Honestly, there's a lot we can and can't do." The second floor is just as bare as the one below, but it fills me with hope that the shelter will be filled.

"I don't know how you can do this every day and not feel attached," he says, looking through the empty spaces intended to be family rooms. Seeing the curiosity in the caring giant I've gotten to know melts my heart.

"Who says I don't get attached? That's why people in my field usually see a therapist."

"You still see a therapist?" He turns to look at me through the open space, a fire simmering on low in his eyes.

"Some demons are hard to get rid of," I admit softly, not giving him a chance to peer through the looking glass.

"Are you still fighting your demons?" He steps closer.

That's one way to scare someone off.

Wait until he sees the ugly side of your mind.

"Mm, nope. Not the time or place." I look down, kicking the dust. Suddenly, his boots line up with mine.

"When you're ready, I'll be here waiting." He tilts my chin up to his face and plants a soft kiss on my lips. For a moment, my eyes close, like this is all a lucid dream. His hands caressing my sides.

I pull back to give him a faint smile. "Can I admit something?"

That cat-like smile is back across his face. "Of course, Teresa." Dammit, why did he have to say that with so much sex? My mouth starts to go dry.

"There's more of a reason why I needed you here tonight." I take his hand in mine, dancing around the hidden truth.

I see the twinkle in his eye. "Hm, a repeat of the woods. A taste? A chase?"

Okay, not saying that thought didn't cross my mind. I shake my head. "No! You sex demon. You really think I'd look like this if I wanted sex? Let alone bring you here?"

"Mm.. what would you look like?" He starts to trail a finger across my chin and down my neck and my eyes start to flutter. I smack his hand.

I take a deep breath. "Okay buddy, focus. I didn't want to involve you in this, but I was hoping for some help. There's been a development brought to my attention and I don't know how much more power I can exert."

"So, you want me to do *what* exactly?" he says, tucking a strand of hair behind my ear.

"I don't truly know what your club does, but my hope is that you can ask your connections about a problem. Maybe have the club look into a problem that is becoming a great concern for my community." There, I said it.

He thinks about it for a moment. "Well, if I were to get information, I would need to know the problem."

I huff at him. "I was getting to that, but you're distracting."

"You have no idea..." he says, kissing along my neck. I give him a shove.

"Seriously, Alexander, I need you to focus," his name escapes me with such ease.

He snickers. "I like my name on your lips. It sounds.. welcoming. Needy."

"Alexander," I growled in warning.

"Yes, Teresa," he smiles, his eyes soften, finally giving me what I need. "Okay, darlin', what's the problem causing you to tense up?"

"A person I trust, Jeremiah, approached me a few weeks back saying he was noticing odd things, like people disappearing, rumors about people getting jobs and then no one hears from them. I didn't think anything of it nor saw anything myself."

Jackson's face turns serious. "These people, are there any records of them? Or direct evidence. Missing person reports?"

"Well, like I said, I didn't think anything of it. Jeremiah tends to linger and ramble sometimes. Then, I had Aggie tell me she ran a report and noticed some discrepancies. My mind's telling me that it's not true, but some things aren't adding up..."

He looks at me skeptically. "So, you brought me here to butter me with the hope that I'd help find something?" Well, he catches on pretty quick.

"Confirm or deny the issue. More or less," I walk further down the hallway. I just need him to say yes. Maybe I can ease my mind into facts.

"What do I get out of it? What's in it for me?" His question hangs heavy in the air. I can't tell if he's serious or not.

"The feeling that you helped a community and made me happy," how does he want me to answer? Would it make me happy? Yes, especially knowing if someone is on my side or he's just entertaining the idea.

"Mm, sounds tempting"

"Are you needing more convincing?" The words come out faster than I anticipated, the smallest taste of anger forms.

"And if I do?" He pushes my buttons. I thought it would be an easy thing, get the hulking man who is in awe of you to say yes.

But, if I have to convince him in other ways, one part of me wouldn't object. What I wouldn't do to this man. I want to wrap my legs around him, pinning me to the wall. I want his lips all over me, covering every inch and corner of my body. I want to get lost in him and never come up for air.

"Darlin', if you keep looking at me like you want to devour me, I will happily oblige. Just say yes," he says, licking his lips.

The temptation is maddening. The deflect in the true conversation becomes more obvious. I want to say yes, but the practical half of me is saying no, to wait, don't be too eager. "And what if I want to wait?"

I can feel the heat of his body behind me. He brushes the back of his knuckles down my arm. "Then we'll wait. But know the longer you wait..." he starts to say.

Suddenly, a sound echoes across the empty hall sounding like clanking metal falling. The endless sounds startling me. My heart races and I worry someone's here. Call it paranoia or gut instinct, but the thought of not being alone scares me more. Before I can focus enough to call 9-1-1, Jackson pulls out a gun that was tucked away in his holster.

"Teresa, get behind me. Now!" The urgency in his voice is not a warning.

We creep down the hallway, Jackson readies his gun for an attack, his protective instinct kicking in. I stayed close behind him, wishing I'd brought my knife. I look around the first floor again, noticing that the place doesn't seem disturbed. Jackson freezes and my anxiety ratchets. The area doesn't appear out of sorts or phased.

Maybe it's my mind spiraling down an early rabbit hole.

Jackson keeps me behind him at all times. For a brief moment, I feel secure. "I think we're in the clear," he says as he holsters the gun.

As my mind settles that it was nothing, something catches my eyes. I push past him and immediately freeze in my tracks. In front of me is a busted work lamp, filament shattered everywhere. A few scuffs of fresh mud, still wet.

Somebody was here and I don't think it was Hammitt.

"Alexander, come here." I holler, as he quickly comes to my side. As he looks at the scene, I turn to see a stern look, I can't read it as anger or concern. I hide my face from him, my own guilt of bringing him into a mess I don't even know how to clean or anything else.

"How big is this thing you need me to look into?" he asks, but I'm asking myself the same thing. What the hell did I even myself into. I didn't even choose to chase this, more like a snowflake turned into a rolling snowball before my eyes.

"I don't know myself. Does this give you motivation now?" I look at him over my shoulder.

"Darlin', I didn't need another reason. This isn't any coincidence. But I need you to promise me something, and I'm not fucking around." He grabs my shoulders and spins me around. It doesn't hurt, but the intensity is there. "You call me, day or night. I don't fucking care. If there's something going on, you find me. Do you understand?" I nod my head.

"I'mma need those words from ya," the hint of his twang coming out.

I gulp. "Yes, sir."

He tosses me over his shoulder like a rag doll, a habit he is picking up but I don't mind. "Come on, I'll ride behind you to make sure you get home."

I smirk at that last statement. "You'll ride behind, huh?"

Smack, landing on my ass. "Yeah, I deserved that." I mutter.

I saw the fear in his eyes. Eyes don't tell a lie when it comes to something that's hidden. I know what I'm afraid of, what he's afraid of.

Chapter 14

Teresa

What did I get myself into? I'm immersed in something that may be more than I can chew, and I'm enlisting the help of a man I just started to trust. He stays close and doesn't seem to take his eyes off of me. My only hope is that it's just someone trying to scare me, and there's no true danger.

But I would have been told by Jackson if I'm truly in danger... right?

My faith and trust in a man that I barely know, forcing himself to break down the walls that I spent so much time building.

Looking at my computer my emails start to pile up, but then I get distracted. My phone buzzes, pulling from my endless thoughts, fully expecting it to be Jackson checking in on me. At this point, I need to make a guard post for him. I peek at my phone.

Michelle

I was told that your ass needed to come over for a family bonfire.

Told by whom?

Michelle

One guess, sweet cheeks.

Jackson? Why would Jackson make Michelle tell me to come to bonfire night? I dial his number.

"I was wondering when you were going to connect the dots." He sounds amused.

"Wanna tell me why?" I inquire.

"Figure you'd have some fun with friends and be safe while I make some runs."

I'm confused, "Wait, you're not going to be there?"

"Not tonight, some business came up," he explains.

"What do you mean keep me safe?" I'm a little insulted, "I can take care of myself. I don't need folks looking after me."

He laughs, "Yes, but trouble follows you and we can't be too cautious."

What is he hiding then? "Unless I'm in danger, I don't like being told where to go and what to do. So, I'm not going," that's half a lie as I want to see a special little girl.

For a moment there's dead silence, I thought the call had ended, but a growl told me otherwise. "Teresa, I don't fuck around with protecting folks, especially with my girl. There'll be a prospect with you tonight."

Those words haunt me. I haven't been anyone's 'girl' since my ex. My body freezes as if I'm stuck with the words circling around me.

No, this is not the time to break down or freeze. Time to get back to the Tessa everyone knows.

I growl in response. "Jackson, I have neither the patience nor the brain power to explain this to you that I'm fine taking care of myself. You don't need to have someone watch me. Don't need a babysitter."

As soon as it leaves my mouth, I regret it. No going back now.

"Careful Little Cub, that mouth can still get you in trouble even if I'm not there. Hate to leave you with a red ass and wet pussy as punishment."

"You're not gonna spank me," I test him, pushing his buttons, attempting to win this fight.

"Be careful what you wish for," he warns me.

"Awe, Alexander, promises, promises." I giggle, just to annoy the fuck out of him.

The silence is deafening. "I'm going to say this nicely once: Go to Michelle and Matthew's tonight until I get done and do not leave their property. Have a little fun, I just need to know you're safe. But disobey and I'll lock you up in a safe house and not look back. Straight there after work; no pit stops. Do. You. Understand?"

I swallow thickly, more turned on than I should be. "Yes, sir. Geez. Temper. I still don't like it."

"Darlin', you haven't seen a *temper* yet. Now, be a good girl and do as you're told. Have fun with your friends. You're in safe hands tonight. I'll see you soon."

He never answered about me being in danger, he danced around that fact. I'm confused, I want to make him happy, but still demand independence.

Either I have a death threat on my life or someone is overprotective since I have brought him into the fold. I hung up the phone before I could say anything else. I immediately dial the one person who would love to help me make him rethink who he's talking to.

"You wanna come to a bonfire at Michelle and Matthew's?"

"Can I bring the rum?" Britt asks, her excitement palpable.

I laugh. "Would I say no to you?"

After work, saving all emails until Monday, I see the prospect tailing me. Jackson isn't lying about the prospect. I don't know his name, and I don't ask.

Fuck it. He wanted someone to babysit me? Fine. But I wasn't going to make it easy. He thought I couldn't get into trouble if I'm with Michelle and Matthew, Alexander Jackson Jones doesn't know me then. It's starting to be a mistake early on that I involved him.

How did disappearances lead into making me stay where people can see me? What about those people who can't see them, no one protecting them?

The prospect, a term I never thought I would use in my life, seems young, like fresh out of college or something. He's a cute kid, with curly ginger hair and freckles dotting his cheeks. He looks lean underneath the plaid shirt and faded jeans. Medium build, poor kid. I hope they don't break him.

"Hey Sparky, we're stopping by my place so I can change and pick up my cousin." I start to get in my car.

Sparky boy looks bewildered. "Ma'am, he wanted you to go straight to Matt's place."

I look back at him. "You gonna tattle on me to A.J.?" I know he hates that nickname, but he ain't here.

His face twists in discomfort. "I'm just following orders, ma'am."

"Sparky, you have two choices. I can be your friend, or I can make your life a living hell. Let me say this again. I am going home to change and take care of my dog and then my cousin and I will be going to the bonfire. Do I make myself clear?"

My dad used to say that I can stare into someone's soul and scare them straight to the grave. Most of the time, it works. This is one of those times.

Sparky gives me a nod and I head home to change into some shorts that may or may not rise a bit in the ass area, plus a sweatshirt. Brittany's already there, bottles of rum in hand.

"Who's the young buck in your driveway? And why do I have a feeling that he could do some damage at the same time?" She peers through my office window.

"Oh, that's Sparky. Jackson has him acting as my personal watchdog so I don't go looking for trouble. He just never said anything about finding trouble within common ground." I yell from my bedroom.

"And that's why you're bringing me along, hoping to awaken the soul even more?"

I smile. "And to piss him off."

Brittany laughs, knowing full well I mean it. This has been a long time coming. She grabs my arm before we head out, that chaotic look in her eyes, "Matthew, you still have the four wheelers?"

"Yeah, why? Where is your mind going?" She's cooking something and I'm all for it. She concocts an idea, something may have Jackson rethink about trying to handle me like a doll. If his focus is on me, it's already time to get him to refocus.

We're welcomed by the ash and burning fire smells that seeps into my soul. The night is young and I have a point to be made. My compass is pointing in a different direction. I look back at my personal shadow for the night, "You coming Sparky, or are you just going to stand out here all night?"

He grunts and moves behind Brittany and me as we enter the backyard. I finally hear the bumping of music. I anticipated that Michelle would just have the family over, but there are a few extra people I've never met or at least seen before. Something attacks my legs, and when I look down, I see Allie hooked onto my leg.

"Sasa, you're here!" Her cute smile distracts my racing mind. What is it about her smile that makes it so easy to love her?

I crouch down to meet her eye to eye. "You miss me or something, kid?"

"Paint? You wanna paint?" I pause for a moment to think about what she's talking about. Then I remember the art set I got her; maybe she's talking about that.

"Maybe later, sweetie." I start to leave, but something illuminates in my mind, something to add to this plan. "Hey, you wanna ride around tonight?"

"Do we ask daddy?" Her eyes go wide.

"Maybe if we ask real nicely, he'll say yes. Where is he?" I ask, grabbing her hand as she leads me to Matthew, sitting in a lawn chair with a beer in hand.

"Oh god, who let the trouble in?" he exclaims, getting out of his chair to embrace me, before someone clears their throat. I see Sparky sitting, shaking his head, which I promptly ignore.

"Ease up, Sparky. Matthew's like my brother. And happily married to that fine woman over there." I point over to Michelle, who blushes under the embers of the night.

Matthew laughs and turns to introduce me to the others around the fire. "Tessa, this is Keola. He's the treasurer of the club. "Sparky" over there is Greer, a prospect." I look at Keola, a stern look on his face, a sour expression from a person I hardly know.

I extend my hand to shake Keola's. He grips mine so hard I'm nearly on my knees, attempting to make a point about something. I remove my hand, shaking it out, looking towards Matt, "Keep Brittany away from him. Last thing I need is for her to break this one."

"Which one, grump face right here or Sparky behind me?" Matthew chuckles.

"Someone say my name? Oh, hey boys." Brittany pops out of thin air with a red solo cup, handing me another one. Matt and I look at each other before turning back to Britt, saying together, "Both."

"Daddy, can I go with Sasa on the four wheelers?" I nearly forgot that Allie's still standing behind me, being very patient. Matt reads the room, jerking his eyes from behind me to beside him, rubbing the back of his neck.

"Don't think that is a good idea, baby. Maybe another time. We don't want Sasa in trouble." Matt takes Allie's hand, plopping her down on his lap as he takes his seat again.

"She's the reason why Jackson raised the flags about? I see nothing special." Keola peers at me, examining me before taking his seat again, adjusting the leather vest he wears.

I rear back a bit at his directness. "You act like I asked for it? Unless you know something that I don't." Keola shuts his mouth before saying something. That's more of an answer than I asked for.

"Well, ain't this just fun. I think we need more alcohol," Michelle yells from where she's laughing with Brittany. I down my entire cup, mustering up the courage for what's next. Michelle comes up behind me refilling the empty cup.

Fine, two can play at this game. I reach for my phone to call him. I hope he picks up; time to cause a little trouble. One ring, two rings, three rings, *click*.

"This better be about you behaving yourself." I hear him grumble under his breath.

Chapter 15

Alexander

Lies. Lies keep building up. Unseen danger rearing its ugly head.

She doesn't know what she's stumbled into and now is a part of the chessboard. Jesus, this wasn't supposed to happen.

I have to tell her.

Memphis stirs next to me as we look out at the train tracks, waiting to see what these whispers are about. I just hope she's understanding that I don't mean to be as controlling as she thinks, but I need her safe. She'll fight me every step, but for what to happen with the club business and her, our worlds will collide.

Her sweet sass and submissive will be the death of me. She'll learn either the easy way or hard way. She'll learn some truth soon. Right now, she's testing her limits with me. Greer messaged me earlier saying that she's still not completely happy, even taking a detour before Matt's place.

"Brother, your phone's buzzing," Memphis elbows my side.

My phone?

Teresa.

"This better be about you behaving yourself," I answered the phone.

"Jackson, you have some scared henchmen, like one wrong move and they're plotting an early funeral. Your man Keola is an interesting man..." she says sternly.

"They're just protective and following orders. You on the other hand, might not be. Are you drinking, Little Cub? I told you to have fun there." I say as Memphis holds back a laugh.

My girl hums a yes, "Just started, babe. Listen, speaking of fun, Allie and I are gonna go ride on the four wheeler. You don't mind, do you? I mean, nobody is trying to kill me. Except Keola, the way he looks at me, does he think I'm stupid or naive or I have you under my spell," she says, toying with me, coaxing me to overreact. Her ranting is adorable.

"Don't think that's wise. Stay on the property, like I told you. Greer should be watching you and Keola is harmless, he means well," I remind her, keeping my cool. My own nerves and thoughts tell me fuck the run and wrangle her ass.

"If you don't trust your men, then why use them? But, I'm not hearing a no.. so I'll take that as a yes." She challenges me. The effect of a chase, waiting for me to see what I'll do. This is a retaliation for telling her what to do.

"Don't think you heard me. Stay on the property and out of trouble; someone's always watching you." I growl out, "We'll discuss later. I promise. Just not right now." My blood starts to boil. The more she pushes the more she's proving some point. The point that you can't tame a woman like her.

"When is a good time?" her anger roars out, "Look, unless you can tell me a better reasoning, I'm going to have my *fun*. Okay, bye."

"Teresa!" I yell as she hangs up the phone.

Oh little cub, bad mistake.

Chapter 16

Teresa

"Come on Allie, let's go for a ride." I take a final sip of my drink and put it aside. The gawking stares around me are all the motivation I need. With a giggling Allie in tow, we head into the garage, where I find the key in the ignition and helmets ready to go. Allie puts on her little pink helmet and hops in the front, waiting on me. I put on the helmet and straddle the wheeler quickly.

"Allie, you wanna take a picture for Mr. Jackson?" She nods her head and I click my phone on, ignoring the missed text messages. I snap a picture with me kissing her cheeks and her with the biggest smile, tempted to set it as my wallpaper, and send it to Jackson.

Allie taps me on my arm. "Sasa, daddy's coming."

News travels fast. I turn on the beast and let the engine rumble, revving it up. Matthew screams at me over the motor.

"Tessa, please. If you're trying to get back at Jackson, this isn't the way to do it." His eyes glint with worry and anger.

"I'm sorry, what did you say? Can't hear you," I yell back, knowing good and well I did. Something has broken within me, and my body and mind are starting to feel a tiny bit of freedom.

I rev it up more and hit the gas out of the garage, making a move towards the fire, towards everyone else. Brittany and Michelle raise their cups in salutation. A couple of people are missing, but I don't focus on that. The rumble of the machine underneath me brings memories of riding on Jackson's motorcycle.

You can't keep a woman who doesn't want to be kept.

"You ready, Allie-cat?" She does a small bounce in the seat. I can't help but smile. I hear something in the background' it's Sparky and Keola starting up the other four wheelers. I can see the panic and distress in their movements. Party's going to be over sooner than I expected.

We head towards the trails in the back. I know them pretty well, as we've ridden them before. I know every twist and turn and little bump. The adrenaline pumps through my veins with the rush of temptation and danger.

I know I'm walking a fine line with Jackson's patience by disobeying, but that's part of the fun. I'm doing this not just to piss him off, but to bring myself back to life. The sense of danger may awaken that feeling.

I slow down a bit to glance behind me, to see if they're following. Sure enough, the headlights lightly peer through the backwoods. I'm not going to make this easy on them. They want to see wild Tessa? They'll see wild Tessa. I speed up and head toward a section of the path less marked and easier for Allie and me to hide.

Something in me wishes Jackson was here to play this little game. He wanted to play more games and find adventures. We get far enough away that I drift us and reverse back even farther into the woods before quickly shutting the engine and lights off. I give myself a brief moment to look at the sky full of stars, watching the twinkle of them overhead.

I remember one more thing, turning my ringer off my phone. I've watched enough horror films to turn it off. I glance at my phone and see some angry text messages.

Leif Erickson

I swear to Jesus, if you don't get your ass back to the bonfire, it'll be more than your ass being punished.

Teresa. I will fucking duct tape you to a chair.

Hehe, keep going babe. Don't make it easy on them.

Family is sometimes the worst influence.

Teresa Saoirse, you wanted my temper? Might want to keep your doors locked. Because when I get a hold of you, you might wish you'd listened.

Just let me know you're okay.

I send her back an emoji.

I hear the motors and the lights of the other bikes getting closer and closer. I push a finger to my lips to tell Allie to stay quiet. She does it back to me.

Good job sweet girl. You'll give your daddy a run for his money one day.

The sounds are within yards of us, and if I calculated it right, they'll breeze right past us with their speed. A few moments go by, and the sounds disappear further into the woods. I give it a few extra moments before I get Allie and I back on the wheeler.

Suckers.

I start the engine back up. "Alright Allie-cat, I think we had enough for now. Let's get back and we can make smores." I kiss her little cheek and we ride at a slower pace than our original speed, giving us the chance to enjoy more of the ride or what's left of it. Allie kicks her legs against the wheeler, as if riding a horse, to "giddy up." God bless the man she marries.

The edge of the trail is getting closer, and I can see the illumination of the bonfire. I see everyone standing, and I can't help but smile.

Checkmate, Jackson.

I park the wheeler in the open space around the fire and turn it off. I set Allie down as she runs into Michelle's arms, recounting the story of how we hid from the boys. I glide into an empty seat next to Brittany as she hands me my drink.

"Was it worth it?" she asks.

"Abso-fucking-lutely." I take a big swig of my drink, pulling out my phone to send Jackson a message back.

I'm safe. Not a scratch on me, you big oaf.

Matthew glares at me through the fire, shaking his head. "At least you kept her safe. I can't say the same for you, though. I'd tell you to run, but apparently, you'd like that too much."

Heat rushes to my cheeks. Did Jackson tell everyone about what we did in the woods that day?

"What fun is the chase if you make it easy?" I say.

Matthew laughs, and I'm glad I have at least one person on my side. The music continues to blare through the speakers until the rumble of Sparky and Keola arrives through the trees. A small snicker escapes me. They park the wheelers, and I can see the death in both their glares. Keola marches over to stand in front of me.

"Can I help you there, buddy?" I sip my drink again.

"You stupid woman, you have a death wish. If you don't die by the people after you, you will by Jackson"

I scoff. "If you haven't guessed by now, I'm not afraid of him. You may be, but I'm not. Look, if you live long enough, you'd realize that I'm not one to listen without reason. Now, sit your ass down and enjoy the rest of the night." I stand to face him. Just like Jackson, Keola has height on me and I refuse to back down. It's a stare down.

"It's not him you have to worry about," he mumbles.

"Well, I don't see anyone else," I spread my arms out showcasing the emptiness and no one else around.

"I'll take care of Keola," Brittany exclaims from her seat.

"No, no, it's fine. He won't do anything to me, afraid his pretty face might get rearranged," I warn him, not knowing the power of that threat.

Keola rolls his eyes. "You're lucky he's planning on claiming you. In the meantime, might wanna listen closer next time."

My eyes grow wide, Keola's words settling in the pit of my stomach. His claim? I've only known Jackson a few weeks. Yet, the thought is both unsettling and calming. My phone buzzes again.

Leif Erickson

I will see you soon, Teresa.

No Little Cub, no darlin'.

A slight spark of regret might be settling in. I brush it off. I'm surrounded by people who love me, and I have rum. If I drink too much, I'll just make Sparky or Matthew take us home. There's too much tension, and, while I don't think Keola is a bad person, he doesn't think too highly of me. I'd rather keep my distance.

The night continues on with blaring music, fireworks, more rum and some whiskey, and dancing. The night is ending, and I somehow gave my keys away.

I make it home, but the night ends in black and a dead sleep captures me. My body spins trying to decide what direction it wants to feel.

The morning brings a bright as fuck sun. I don't know what time it is, but the pounding of my head throbs full of regrets and bad decisions. Some more than others.

I can hear the soft snoring of Seamus in the corner of the bed. I reach around to scratch his head, and when I do, I suddenly feel the brushing of my sheets against my breasts.

My bare breasts.

Panic floods over me.

I'm naked as the day I was born.

Where are my clothes and why did I decide to sleep naked? Oh god, please tell me I didn't strip for someone.

Crap, what if Sparky saw? I sit up slowly, clutching the blankets to me, draping them to give me some decency. I look away from the window as the sun punishes my eyes, and my next sight isn't any better.

Fuck. My. Life.

"Good morning, little cub."

Chapter 17

Teresa

Jackson sits in the well-loved bedroom chair as if it's his throne, dominance exerts from him. The smell of roasted coffee swirls around my room. With one look at me, he rests his coffee cup on his thigh as if to wait for sudden movement.

It's some god forsaken hour and this man looks freshly showered, casually dressed in a black tee and faded jeans, watching me like I'm prey. Either I'm about to meet my maker or I'll be seeing stars *very* soon, again. Is it possible to be horny and hungover at the same time?

I look at Seamus; he hasn't moved. It should concern me that Seamus trusts him.

So, my dog trusts him, but I can't?

The irony rings through my head. I look around for any scrap of clothing, possibly ones from last night. I don't have to look too far as I see them folded in a neat pile behind him. My eyes dart back and forth between him and my clothes.

"Are you going to keep my clothes hostage?" I say roughly in my morning voice. A running list of what I need to do within the next hour begins to rapid fire through my mind.

One thing is to shower and brush my teeth.

"You're free to get them. Your choice." He sips his coffee.

I smell a trap, "If you want to see me naked, all you have to do is ask nicely."

I scooch towards the end of the bed, still draped in blankets. His eyes grow darker. If this is punishment, then Lord save me.

"Darlin', I got enough of a view last night," he places his coffee on the floor and folds his hands. In that instant, I drop the blankets and sashay over to my clothes.

There's no sense in hiding, if he's already seen everything. I reach over to grab my clothes to high tail it to the bathroom, but before I can, I'm snatched by the waist, hands forced behind my back with one of his massive ones, legs straddling his lap.

My stomach tries to hang in there, but the swift movement makes it churn. My mouth is left gaping, trying to form the words I wish I knew to say.

"Do you have anything you would like to say?" He peers into my eyes.

Speak Bjorn. You've come this far just to piss him off, play his little game.

"Mm.. you smell nice?" That's not a lie. Aside from the coffee, he smells like mint and the woods, like fresh pine with a hint of smoke. He shakes his head at my answer.

"Try. Again." He wraps his free hand around my neck lightly. I'm trying really hard not to be turned on, but my nipples don't receive that message.

"Um, I'm sorry I wasn't nice to your men? Poor Sparky, I think I scared him," I answer.

Again, Jackson shakes his head. His hand travels down further, lightly brushing against my hard nipples. I try my hardest to steady my breathing.

"One more time. Try. Again."

I know he wants me to apologize for my "disobedience," but I won't. Not because of this torturous morning, but because I don't apologize for doing nothing wrong.

"I'm sorry that you have a stick up your ass." Whatever is coming my way is like a storm brewing, that I definitely deserve.

A spark of rage in his eyes sends a warning that I might need to shut up before my mouth gives me more trouble. His hand travels down around my stomach and curves to my ass, his mouth rising in a smirk. Goosebumps fall across my ass as his circles it.

Smack.

His hand makes contact with my flesh and the sound echoes through the room, making Seamus pop his head up.

"Seamus, out! Now!" Jackson growls at him. Seamus, the little traitor, does what he's told with only a small bark.

"Up. On the bed, ass in the air. Now," he commands.

Oh shit. Maybe I've overestimated him. I slide off and make my way towards the bed. I assume the position, exposing me to his gaze. I feel a slight breeze as he stalks up behind me. The bed dips as he joins me, and I swear my blood thrums faster in my veins. His hand grazes down my back, the brush of his fingertips smoothing down my spine.

"How many, little cub?" He circles my ass, caressing every inch of my behind. He's waiting for an answer. This man is actually going to spank my ass. Question is, how many is he expecting? I say the first number that pops into my head.

"Three." Lord, let it be right.

"Six," he says quickly.

"Six? You just doubled my answer," I gasp. Honestly, I was being a brat last night, but it was necessary. I'd felt locked up in my own body for too long.

"Six. I'll be generous and explain. You'll learn that I care too much about you to see you hurt, but actions have consequences. Three are for the text messages you didn't answer while you pulled that little stunt. Another for making my men chase after you, especially knowing that game is ours. Another one is for hiding from them, a naughty girl. Don't think I don't know you did, because I do. The last one is for putting me in a state of constant worry and making me lose my temper while I was on a job." His fingers trail along my back, making me agonize in anticipation.

"Do you understand?" he says as he readies himself. Six, I can handle.

"Yes, Alexander," I whimper out, preparing myself for what comes next. Jackson's name escapes me.

"If you're a good girl and learned your lesson, I'll reward you after," he whispers in my ear, automatically making me wetter than I thought possible. Sweet Jesus.

"Count, Teresa," is all he says before I feel the first pop of his hand. A gasp leaves my mouth, my skin tingling under his palm.

"One," I counted. Another lands on my cheek before I can steel myself, moving me forward from the force of his hand. "Two."

I can feel the sting even more with this one, the heat of my flesh intensifying. This is a heady sensation, pleasure mixed with pain; part of me wonders if I want more.

He takes a small pause, palming my ass and inhaling a deep breath that turns into the low hum of a growl. He's enjoying this, the way he takes his time, the anticipation makes me tremble.

My head is turned away, but I want to peek around to see him. I turn my head in his direction to see his hardness pressed against his zipper. I can feel the fiery desire to unzip his pants and take care of him, feel his hardness in my hands, knowing it's because of me. I want to brush and stroke him, watch his face twist in need and lust.

He lands another and pain vibrates through my body. My mind begs to tap out but my pussy wants more. I'm soaked; I ache for him to touch me and let me come. "Three."

"Little cub, this may be punishment, but the look of this pussy glistening with need makes me want to do terrible things to you." His low laughter sends even more heat rippling to my pussy. I try to slip my hand underneath me, hoping to slide it to my clit, but he yanks my hands back out and over my head.

He clicks his tongue at me. "That's not being a good girl." He swats another one on my ass, harder than the last. Now I'm getting mad. He's taking his sweet time, the fucker.

"Mm, your ass blushes so well for me, little cub."

"Four."

He chuckles at me. "Good girl. Hang on for me."

Smack. "Five." A tear creeps out of my eye. The pain is about to be too much. I bit off more than I could probably handle.

It's like he knows I'm reaching my limit. "One more and then I'll take care of you, darlin'. Doing so well, little cub."

For his last one, he uses both hands; they land on both cheeks simultaneously, releasing a mix of a whimper and yip from my lips.

"Six," I breathe out, almost out of oxygen.

He circles again, massaging my tender and sore ass as he goes. "Do you remember why I did this, Teresa?"

I nod my head. I don't necessarily agree with it, but he's not used to losing control. He's not used to emotions, whether they be positive or negative.

"Say it. So I know that you do."

I obey, if only to hurry him along. "I disobeyed and acted out, which worried you, possibly put you in danger." I feel his weight leave the bed.

I hear him directly behind me now. "Not me, possibly put you in danger. I protect what's mine. Can't do that if what's mine is acting like a brat. If you want to be a brat, darlin', you better run, because I will find you. You won't like your punishment, I promise you." The echo of the word *mine* resonates. We have only been with each other for almost two months.

Before I could say anything in rebuttal, his tongue found my clit.

Thank you, God. A long moan escapes my mouth as his tongue presses into me and my release starts to build. The mix of pain and heat from my ass and his gifted tongue lapping at my pussy only lifts me higher. Alexander feasts like a man starved. He sucks my clit into his mouth, and I feel like I'm about to explode. When I feel him thrust a finger inside, curling in time with his tongue, I lose my mind.

"Please, Alexander." I'm agonizingly close. I need this release.

"You taste like the sweetest of fruits. So needy. You wanna come in my mouth?" he speaks against me.

"I'd much rather come around your cock," I say breathlessly.

"Mm, soon, darlin' but not today." He pumps into me with two fingers now. I feel myself stretch around him, but it's a tight squeeze. I can't imagine how I'm going to take his cock.

"You're not ready, still so tight. Your pussy is fighting my fingers." I'm almost there; just another moment and I'll be seeing stars.

"Stop playing around and make me come. Please." I'm begging now, more than I ever thought I would for a man.

The vibrations of his answering laugh ripple against my clit. "Only because you asked so nicely. Come for me, Little Cub. Let me feel it around my fingers." He hooks an arm around my waist, keeping me in place as he feverishly works his tongue against my clit. My legs start to quiver.

I'm right there, his fingers curling inside me threatening to launch me into a full orgasm. A mixture of so many different sensations sends me flying, my pussy pulsing around his fingers, my release like a bottle rocket. Stars explode behind my eyelids. He releases my waist as I come down and withdraws his fingers, making me shudder at the loss.

I slump down as all the energy leaves my body, and he flips me onto my back as he walks to the side of the bed. The glistening of my release is still on his fingers, and an idea sparks. I find the energy to grab his hand and bring his fingers to my mouth. Two can play at this game.

I suck on his fingers, tasting myself. His eyes grow wider and darker. I release his fingers with a smile. He bends down and plants a kiss on my head. The sweet tender affection puts a cherry on top.

"Go shower, I'll cook you some breakfast. We have things we need to discuss." He leaves the room, and a frown spreads across my face.

Why won't he let me touch him? I push aside the seed of doubt. It feels like the brokenness in me is back. I just want to make him as happy as he makes me, well when he's not commanding me. Maybe this is just a moment of weakness, a slight happiness, a short term thing.

The shower feels like heaven, hot water spraying across my skin, the Advil I took helping my headache.. I know I need to get my life straight. Easier said than done. After the shower, I quickly change into fresh clothes. I glance at the time on my phone: 9:00 am.

Jesus, I could have gone back to bed.

Sizzling and popping comes from the kitchen. I round the corner, finding Seamus wagging his tail at Alexander's cooking. He's barefoot in my kitchen, as if it's his home too.

"There better be coffee, or else I'm kicking you out of my house," I grumble as I sit at my island.

"As if I'd ever disappoint you." He slides a cup of hot coffee over to me, accompanied by a plate of bacon and eggs. Damn, how long was I in the shower for?

"Hmm, the love of my life, finally." I bite into the bacon as Jackson whips back around with a startled look.

"Chill out Erickson, I was talking to the bacon. You said we need to talk, so talk. You didn't come over just to smack my ass." Food and coffee are the answer to my hangover, and damn, are these some good ones.

He quirks an eyebrow in my direction. "And if I did? Last I checked, you were dripping."

I don't dignify that with an answer. "Stop deflecting. Talk!"

He sighs, running a hand through his hair. "Teresa, I wasn't joking around last night. I took a look at the information you were talking about, and I don't think the noise and the mess at the site was a coincidence. Someone is looking into you and you stumbled into something bigger than anticipated."

I freeze. Am I actually involved in something? People missing, I knew that, but I didn't mean to involve myself in anything dangerous. I shake my head. "Keep talking, Jackson".

He lifts his eyebrow again at his name, he's not Alexander right now.

"Someone's been watching you and my guys are looking into it. My question is, what did you get into, darlin'?"

A small tear rolls down my cheek. All I wanted was to be a social worker and make a change. Jackson reaches to touch my cheek, but I jerk away before he can. I can't do this. I'm a mess. My emotions are all over the place. I trust too easily and then pull back. Everything seems like it's crumbling down around me. My heart races, and I stand to pace around the kitchen. I look through the window, the outline of the mountains in the background. Jackson doesn't move. He doesn't chase me.

Driftwood is burning blue, wild walk the wall shadows
Night winds go riding by, riding by the lochie meadows
On to the break of day, close Mira stream singing:
Caidil gu la laddie, la laddie. Sleep the dark away

"What's that?" Jackson walks a little closer. Was I singing? I must have zoned out.

"Cape Breton. It's a lullaby my grammy and momma used to sing to me."

"You should sing more." He inches closer to me.

"Stop deflecting." I huff out. Maybe I need to go back into my shell.

"I needed you safe last night; with a lot of unknown factors I wasn't going to take a chance. From what we found, it doesn't look good." He stands behind me, wrapping his arms around my waist, pulling me closer to him. I stay still, lost in thought, fixating on the blindness of everything around me. Unknown threats or dangers, I couldn't protect myself.

He whispers, "Where did you go, Teresa? Don't hide from me. Don't lose yourself."

"Jackson," I try to find the words, "I need you to include me, none of this cryptic crap. I can't be left in the dark, having to pick out what's fact versus fiction. You can't suffocate me and smack my ass into submission..." I try to say.

"Unless it's in the bedroom?" he finishes.

"Deflection," I grit out. "How can I protect myself without knowing what's out there?"

"That's life," he tried to answer bluntly.

He turns me around to face him. If he keeps doing this, my stomach may make an appearance. "I wasn't fucking around, Teresa. Until the threat of someone stalking you, hurting you, putting a hit out on you, is neutralized, I need you to think before you act. Once everything is over, then you can be the wild person you want to be. As long as it's with me." The soft kiss on my forehead seems to seal the deal.

With him? He's easily inserted himself in my life, and didn't wait like I needed. My mind isn't used to someone like him. Assertive, protective, possessive, and one step ahead of me.

I need air, I need space.

But I need to not let myself go too far.

"I should let Seamus out," is all I say in return. I really wish I had a bottle of whiskey and a pair of sunglasses right now.

Seamus trots around the yard without a care in the world, as if my internal struggle doesn't exist. I'm surprised Jackson didn't follow me, but I'd much rather have this silence. I'll keep my distance, knowing there could be something worse coming my way. If I ignore it, maybe the problem will resolve itself or disappear completely. The last month has been a roller coaster, and I need time to think, time to come to terms with where I'm at.

I walk back inside and find my house empty. I see a cleaned up kitchen and spot a note next to my coffee cup.

One breath at a time. I'm here when you need me, little cub. Don't hide from me.- A

What did I get myself into? How did I, a simple social worker, get into this? Time to get some work done. Maybe hiding is the best way to protect myself.

Chapter 18

Alexander

I'm way over my head, she seeps into my thoughts, my desires, the little fantasies. I needed her safe, but the deeper she's in this mess, the more someone's going to get hurt. Leaving her is hard.

I pray that it's me. I hope it will be me that gets hurt. I don't know if I can bear to think of the pain that she may feel if anything comes to her.

She's not fully ready for my world, but I'm so ready to have her in mine and permanently. Only thing that keeps me going is knowing that the light in her eyes silently begs me to keep her. Keep her close, rather in my arms.

Until then, when she's ready to accept it, I'm here. I'll keep a distance if that's what she needs, but she can't hide from me.

There's a part of me prays that for her safety and others, and the truth that she stays hidden away from me.

My mind is in a tailspin. She causes my mind to spin like a childhood ride at a carnival. She's just as addictive and tempting to me. A light in a dark time.

She hides maybe because it's too much and she should feel like that.

I pushed too far.

And yet I can't stay away from her.

In the end I have one thought as I watch from afar, watching her mind spin in not knowing what she wants to do, whether to call out to me or move on and forget about it all.

Come back to me, little cub.

Chapter 19

Teresa

I can still feel the faint sting of my ass, even though it has been a week.

But it's been quiet,

I guess I got half of my wish. I haven't been able to see him, and part of me is worried that he's keeping his distance, and now I'm too far away.

On the other hand, I've attempted to reach out, but my fingers always hovered over the call button. Perhaps my notion of hiding and keeping quiet put him off. Another part of me is saying *let it go* and to remember the last time we put someone else's happiness before our own.

"Hey Tess, you ready? We have the luncheon with those donors, remember?" Reva pops in, tugging a sweater on over her dress.

I shake my head yes, when the real answer was that I forgot. But then, I remember we're bringing Lucie Lynn so she can tell her story to the donors. I'm not supposed to have favorites, but she is a survivor, an image of strength and proof that the work the Foundation does pays off for those that come through it.

We pick Lucie up at the corner of her apartment building parking lot. She's wearing a bright blue sundress, highlighting her light caramel skin that shines in the sun. Her bouncy curls are pulled into a half updo. She reminds me of a little fairy who just wants to make you smile.

"Miss Tessa," she shrieks from the back seat, wrapping her arms around me from behind. "Thank you for picking me up while my car's in the shop."

"The shop where your boyfriend works, from what I hear." I peer behind me, winking at her. She just giggles and turns red in response. She deserves a good man in her life to treat her like the queen she is.

"You ready to tell your story, love?" I always check with her, knowing that some days are harder than others. I know what that feels like. The shame, the anxiety, the memories.

You're lucky you have me, no one else wants you. You embarrass me. I shake those words away. This is not the time.

"I got this, Miss Tessa." She nods her head.

As much as I know this is part of the job, luncheons and meetings break my heart. I wish I could do more on-the-ground responsibilities.

Still, if I have to pimp myself out for the Foundation I'll do it. A few of the most prominent families, the ones from old money, are in attendance. It'll be worth it in the end. Lucie Lynn is a charmer, and her story is powerful.

"Boss, I think we have a tail," Reva whispers so Lucie can't hear. I look in the passenger mirror, spotting a white Ford pickup truck. Alexander drives a blue Dodge when he's not on the bike. I dialed him for the first time in a long while.

Pick up.

A few rings go by unanswered.

"What do you want, Teresa?" His tone is rough, like I'm a nuisance. The slight crack in my heart deepens.

"Gotcha, no term of endearment. Fine, I'll keep this brief." That stings a bit. I guess I deserve that. "White Ford pickup, I think either 250 or 350. Is that you or one of your men?"

"That's Joaquin." Nothing else. No smart remarks, no tender warning. Back to the coldness, like the beginning. A brief silence falls between us. It's as if my heart breaks in the cold silence. No warmth to undo the ache that I'm feeling.

"Got it." I hang up before I let myself talk more.

Fifteen minutes later, we arrive at the restaurant and head towards the private dining room. Wine is already being served, and I can sense Reva looking at me like it's a bad idea. I give her a look like I'll be fine.

"Mr. and Mrs. Carter, it's nice to see you again! How're the grandkids?" I screw on my fakest smile, selling enthusiasm. On any given day, this wouldn't be so hard.

Today, however, the ADHD and anxiety are in high gear. "Thank you all for coming today. We are only a few months away from the silent auction, which I know most of you plan to attend. I wanted you to meet Lucie Lynn. You may have seen her around the agency as a volunteer. What you don't know is that she is a graduate of our shelter program. Lucie, take it away."

I take a sip of my wine, enjoying the strawberry and cherry notes. Allowing the notes to flood my mind with the ease of comfort of the pain in my chest. My eyes close if only for a moment.

My phone buzzes with a message, but I ignore it. My eyes and ears are on Lucie.

After she finishes her awe-inspiring story including her journey with the foundation and the triumphs of leaving an abusive situation, one that we fought hard to get her out of. She has been through so much, but she is the image of strength in my eyes and perseverance. I follow with a toast. "To Lucie, and to the future of the Foundation and the many individuals we will continue to help regain their lives."

As we take a collective sip, my phone buzzes again. I take another sip.

Leif Erickson

Don't drink too much wine.

I look around to see the intrusive notion that he's watching. I don't know where, but my eyes keep searching among the restaurant patrons.

Leif Erickson

And yes, I see you.

Asshole. A lot of nerve to dictate what I should be doing, as if he has any say in my actions.

This hot and cold treatment is giving me a migraine. Reva raises an eyebrow at me.

I respond back with a middle finger emoji, hoping he'll leave me alone so I can enjoy the rest of this meal and get back to work. I turn off my phone for the rest of the meal.

"Do I want to know what that look was about?" Reva leans in my direction.

I smirk. "Just putting an asshole back in his place."

Reva isn't buying it. "Are you going to be okay? You've got a couple more meetings today."

"Yeah. I'll be fine, Revs. This is Lucie's time to shine." I nod towards her, and Lucie gives me a grin as she sparks a conversation with Mrs. Carter. Lucie may have convinced more people to our silent auction than I ever could on my own.

After lunch, I throw myself back into my work at the Foundation, flipping between my own research and running reports and meetings. I'm starting to feel like bringing Jackson in was a waste.

Again, I'm having to take things into my own hands, like a broken record. Close to the end of the day, a knock sounds at the door.

"Hey, boss lady. Got a minute?" Sam walks through the door and closes it.

"For you, Sammie, all the time in the world. What can I do for you?" The look on her face is a mixture of confusion and worry. Something uneasy boils in my stomach.

She wrings her hands, like something's happened. "What do you need from me? I've been combing my brain trying to find a way to help. "

"You help me out tremendously with the hotline. I got caught in a spider web and I'm going to get myself out of it. Don't worry about me."

"I know, but I do anyway. Just give me something, please."

I let out a breath. Maybe a second pair of eyes on reports would help. "Okay, look at the past few months' reports and the call volume compared to last year as well. Maybe look at the call times and notes and see if there's a trend or something out of the ordinary. Who knows, maybe we're missing something."

"I can do that. I'll be like Nancy Drew or the Scooby gang." She perks up and walks out.

I shoot a message to Brittany asking if she wants to come over with the bottle of Jack. Like lightning, she responds.

Brittany

> I don't have the old faithful, but what about Jameson?

> Irish women with Irish whiskey, what can go wrong?

You know damn well what could go wrong. Drunk texting and hangover the next day.

I'll be fine, brushing off the possible consequences. Brittany will know when to cut me off. I still need to get through my week.

Silence.

That's all I'm given. Last week, over whiskey, I burst into tears from the stress and the fact that Alexander hasn't spoken to me. I'm surprised that we made it through mid-April and I'm still on Sheldon's good side, as long as Carla stays away. There is some cause for celebration.

I spent the rest of last week combing through every report and call record of the past few months. I spoke with Jeremiah for community updates. Aggie's still looking into the decreasing numbers. Sammie's still burning the midnight oil. I find myself bringing Seamus to the office when I work longer hours. I thought about a caffeine IV drip. Sleep fails me most nights.

On the plus side, I've gotten to know my tails and their names. I've seen Sparky a couple times and he always gives me a gentle nod. I met Coda, he's got a slight accent and looks like he belongs in the mafia more than a motorcycle crew. I caught him one day listening to some instrumental music. He tried to tell me he couldn't talk to me because of Jackson, but I ignored him and carried on conversations about music. For a few minutes, we spoke about composers and music. It was nice to have a decent conversation.

Finally, there's the former soldier, Darius Richard, or D.R. I joked that I'm going to call him Doc, which did not go over well. Jackson was never among them. Why would he be? Silence and coldness, that's all I get.

I need to move on, he's not chasing, and all the horrible thoughts in my head come out true. Maybe for a brief moment, I allowed myself to open up to the possibility of a new relationship and found myself trampling over my own wants to fulfill his.

Later in the week, routines come out normal. I have an hour beforehand and typically, I slack off and walk around. With meetings planned back to back, I distract myself, fixating on something from Sam's research, hunches turn into plausible facts.

My phone rings, and I pick it up without looking.

"This is Tessa," I chirp while I gather files I need for my meetings.

"I need to see you." Almost two weeks of radio silence, that's his choice of words.

Don't give in, Tessa. Be the person you want to be.

Wild, untamable, resilient, humble, a fighter.

"Make an appointment," I retaliate.

"I'll just do a walk-in. I'm ten minutes out." He's persistent. The nerve of this man. I shake my head, fighting the small urge to say yes.

"Sorry, I don't do walk-ins, especially from ghosts. Make an appointment with Reva." I hang up before he has a chance to respond. Of course, he doesn't take that lightly. He calls two more times and two more times, I ignore him.

I've had time to think. If he wants me that bad as he desires, he has had plenty of time to tell me. Why would I grovel for a man's attention? I know that he can see in my mind the fear, knowing that time has been a barrier to wanting someone in my life.

I push the thought of him, putting myself in my work. Distracting myself from the faint memory of his touch, his caresses.

Knowing my meetings are starting soon, a second cup of coffee sounds like heaven. My phone rings; Reva's calling.

"Yes, Revs, I know I have my first meeting in like twenty minutes."

"Yeah yeah, you're getting your coffee. Mr. J.J called at the reception desk asking for a walk in. I think he's a donor."

I brush it off. "Fine. Hopefully it's a big check. Just put him in my office." I click off. I know we have a Mr. Jacob Jones who's a donor, but I haven't heard from him in a while. I make it back upstairs and Reva rushes to meet me. The sorrow, grim look on her face, scares me.

"So... my mistake." the nervousness in her voice.

"Oh, it wasn't for me?" I sip my coffee.

"No, it's for you, but.. he won't leave." I brush past her and behold, the dead has risen.

"Reva, call Ghostbusters back, they forgot one."

Jackson, or Mr. J.J, sits at my conference table. His hair is pulled back into a bun, the edges shaved clean. Sharp suit and tie, dark navy blue to compliment his skin tone and eyes.

"Thanks Reva, I'll handle this."

"You want me to backhand him?" she whispers.

"No. I'll call if I need back up." I close the door and look back at him, giving him a scowl.

"You have some nerve, Jackson, showing up unannounced!" I walk around to my desk. "And what's with the suit? Last time I checked, bikers don't need a suit," I say, checking my email, pretending to do work, not giving him the attention he's craving.

"When I said I needed to see you, it wasn't a request." He eases back into his chair, hands folded on his lap. I glance around my computer, noticing the tattoos peeking under his jacket, across the nape of his neck. My mind jumps from wondering if the placement hurt to why there and why those designs.

Don't pay him any attention. He wants a chase? I'll give him a chase.

"Oh hell no. You don't get to command anything. I gave you a chance, and you went silent on me, perhaps moved on. So, thank you, but your services are not needed nor wanted." I turn back to my computer.

"No." One word. One word can spark anger so infuriating, it lights a house on fire.

"Excuse me?" I say, challenging him.

"You're excused," he says, a smug look on his face.

Be the bigger person.

"What the hell do you want? Or you are here to just annoy the fuck out of me?" I peer back at him with a bite in my voice.

"Business and pleasure." The sensuality in his voice turns up the heat.

I swear, this hot and cold treatment is going to give me whiplash. "You can forget about the pleasure. Skip to the business."

"I told you not to hide," he says, completely off topic but not looking at me as he says it.

"Yeah, but apparently you didn't heed the warning label. I don't listen very well. You know where I am and where to find me. Exhibit A," I snarl out. "The silence explained it all."

"Silence... you think I was ignoring you." He leans forward.

"Think? I know buddy. Trust me, the bottle of Jameson has been a better lover than you were." I think this is the part where everyone would agree that my mouth might get me into trouble.

Jackson stands up and walks towards the front of my desk. The intimidation might work on others, but the look in his eyes tells me something different. At this moment, I don't know if I need to run, tase his ass, or smack him. I put my walls back up; I am not backing down from a fight.

"Has been? Last time I checked, that's past tense. I don't believe we're a past." He places his hands on my desk, leaning closer to me.

"You know, I found you attractive, until you opened your mouth."

Brave. Stupid, but brave.

"Last time, you had no issue with my mouth. Need a reminder?" The possessiveness in his voice sends little reminders of last time down my spine.

"No, I'm quite fine. Now, leave," I growl out.

"No." There's that word again. Maddening, enraging.

"Jackson, I'm not asking. I am *telling* you to leave. Do you need more brain cells to figure it out?" I turn my chair to stand up but am trapped by his arms, forcing me back in my chair.

"It seems we have some issues to work out. Let me make one thing clear: when I said I protect what's mine, that meant you." His words whirl around my head, my eyes growing wide. "You are mine. I told you not to hide, and you did. I intended to let you breathe and figure things out. The phone works both ways."

When did he think the answer for me was silence? Then I reconsider, perhaps I'm the problem, like I have always been in some capacity.

"And the last time I called, I received the cold treatment. You decide to hide as well. You relied on your men to keep tabs on me. News flash, I've enjoyed their company more than yours recently. With you, fucking Antarctica. Could freeze to death with your demeanor," I say to him. "Jackson, please leave. I gave you a chance. You blew it."

More like we both blew it. More emphasis on my end.

"That, darlin', is not my name. You needed time, time to accept it, but maybe someone should have trusted that I wouldn't leave you. Letting you come to me when you were ready. But someone didn't lean into that trust. Why is that?" He inches closer to my face, and I know that time is ticking away before real work requires my attention.

"Jackson, I'm not perfect. But this is not the place nor the time to have this conversation. " Those are the only words I have in me.

"That is *not* my name. Let me refresh your memory." He whips my chair back around and lowers himself to my ear. "Just say yes."

"I don't have time for this." My meeting alerts dings to turn my camera on for my meeting. "I have a meeting and you're an example of an unpleasant distraction."

"You might reconsider in a moment. Turn on the camera, little cub, and don't let them know." He slides over to the other side, a pillow in hand. He adjusts my chair then slinks underneath my desk, adjusting himself.

"Let them know what, exactly?" The video is starting and then the realization hits me. Jackson pries open my legs.

Fuck yes.

I mute my video. Thankfully, I'm wearing a dress. He pushes the material up, exposing my legs to the coolness of the air.

"Jackson, not the time or place for this." My mind wonders how comfortable he is down there. I want to peek, but my chair is pushed in thankfully, the camera is only from the chest up.

"Lift your ass and say yes." He wants a game of uncle? Game on. I lift up a little and he yanks off my underwear, to the point where I think he ripped them. My breath quickens. "Yes."

But he doesn't start right away. Like a predator, he plays with his prey, waiting for them to cry for mercy. "Good morning or afternoon everyone..." the chairperson begins to take the role. Jackson's peppering kisses along my inner thighs. They're slow and agonizing. I hear my name called, realizing the committee was calling my name.

"Yes. I'm here, sorry, spotty connection, here."

I can feel the small laughter from Jackson below and I kick him, but he nips at me. "Behave or I'll stop." I turn my head away from the camera, covering my mouth.

"You do and you'll lose the battle, my friend." I sit back up as the meeting continues.

Jackson continues his quest, his lips hovering over me. He kisses right above my clit, but when I adjust to get him closer, he pushes me back. Without warning, he drags a long lick up my slit, causing me to straighten up. He's like a grown man with ice cream, eating his favorite flavor.

"Jackson," I growl. I swear, this man will be the death of me.

"Tessa, do you have any objections?" asks one of the members.

Crap, I'm supposed to be paying attention. As soon as I try to answer, Jackson inserts a finger, and I yip, "Nope no objections." I've never hit the mute button so fast.

There's something intoxicating about a man opening you up like his favorite play toy. I can see the wild part of me enjoying this way too much. Jackson's fingers pump in and out while he sucks on my clit, pulling every ounce of pleasure out of me.

I have to quickly turn off the camera. "Jackson, if you don't hurry up down there, I'm going to lose it."

He adjusts my chair again. I still hear the muttering of the voices in the meeting. "Jackson?" He says, "Try again, this time with your knees in the chair and lift up." Lift up? Jackson wickedly grins and situates his head on the chair, looking up. "Sit. Camera on."

"Sit where?" I fumble over my words.

He jerks me onto his face. This man said sit and in doing so, wraps his arms around my thighs. Jackson's tongue goes to work, lapping at every inch of my wetness. A gentle smack on my pussy makes me yelp. "Camera on."

Crap, nope. I'm about to tap out.

I turn the camera back on, trying to keep my composure. My orgasm starts to build quicker than anticipated. I keep the mic muted to let out a few moans. Then, in a swift movement, Jackson rubs his calloused thumb over my clit. My eyes grow wider and I lean over and cover my mouth. "Jackson, please, you've made your point. Just let me come."

He doesn't stop. The combination of his hands and his mouth takes me over the edge.

I'm close, ready to release. Then, he stops.

"Wait, wait. No. I'm so close," I cry out.

He picks me up a bit to speak. "Tell me what I want to hear."

My mind can't remember if the camera is turned off or not. I look up and it's not, so I turn it off. "What do you want me to say? Beg?"

A slow drag of his tongue makes my brain short circuit. "You'll figure it out. Better pay attention to your meeting, darlin'." Jackson returns to his position, torturing me with his tongue. Dragging me back to the edge again, he chuckles as more moans escape me.

My body is aching for more than this. I start to move at my own pace, getting in sync with him, riding his face like a toy for my own pleasure. Everything fades away, no voices, just him and me.

"Please." He's relentless again, keeping a steady pace. The build of my orgasm reaches the top; just a few more moments and I'll be soaring. His name, he wanted me to say his name.

"Alexander, please." With that, he gently pinches my clit and I'm done.

I'm a mess, soaring high in clouds of euphoria. My body feels like I just ran a marathon. He lifts me off of his face, sliding from underneath the desk.

I will never look at my desk the same again; I'm going to get Reva or Sam to spray holy water in here. I feel my body easing off the high. Realizing that the meeting is still happening, I sent a message that there was an emergency that needed my attention. Which there is: the cleaning up after myself. I quickly exit out of the meeting.

Alexander is leaning against my desk next to my chair. He adjusts his suit and tie and I can't help but admire him.

"Excuse me, I need my underwear and to clean up. Then, you have some explaining to do." I look around for where he tossed them earlier. My eyes bulge when I see he's holding them in his hand.

"Mm, I'm taking these for safe keeping," he says as he pockets them. He leaves my mouth wide open in disbelief. He's leaving me bare. I start to feel heated again.

No ma'am, no round two for you. You better get a fucking grip.

I march to the bathroom attached to my office. I spend the next few moments composing myself, convincing myself to not let his man think he can have his way.

I open the bathroom door and see Reva pop her head out from around her desk, looking down the hallway. The smirk on her face makes me blush even harder. She tosses something my way: a small perfume bottle. "Sweetie, you reek of sex. Just a little something to get through the day."

Fucking hell. I quickly spray myself and toss it back.

I open my door and leave it open; no more chances for him. He sits at the table, leaning back in the chair. I take my seat. "Speak, Alexander." But he pulls me into his lap.

"I will but that means you have to shut up for two minutes," he says, leaning forward. Tight lipped, I gestured for him to continue.

"I need you to know, I didn't leave you. I've seen many women come and go from the club and when women tend to hide, men never leave them alone to figure their shit out. Never worked out in the end, so I figured you needed the space. I can see that I was wrong. But Teresa, you hid. You shut down after everything." He doesn't finish. Instead, he takes my hands and for a moment, his eyes are sincere.

"I think we can both agree that whatever you got mixed up in, coupled with my demands, gave you a lethal dose of reality that maybe you weren't ready for. But I never left you. I couldn't," his soft, stern voice tells me.

"You're right, I needed time, but you left me with my thoughts, I needed you near," I interrupted.

He just nods. "I'm sorry that I didn't know. Lesson learned."

"My god, the world is ending, you apologized. How did those words taste coming out?" I have to laugh and revel in the moment.

"Just as sweet as your...." he teases his hand traveling around my ass. I smack his hand in response.

My eyes go wide. "Jesus, you're going to give me a heart attack if you keep it up."

"Teresa. Please. You have to talk to me. You have to trust me," A simple demand.

"I'll try," is all I say.

"You will try..." he starts, waiting for me to finish.

I roll my eyes. "I will try, Alexander. Happy?"

"Very. Now, I gave you pleasure. Here's business. I've had my men keeping tabs on the streets. I think your person is right. People are missing. We put tabs on one, call it an experiment. She was pitching a tent near the tracks on the outskirts. She'd been doing that for a couple days, then gone. They asked around, but it was like she didn't exist. No one's seen her. We have a picture if you want to pass it around." He reaches into his jacket pocket and pulls out a photo.

Unfortunately, I don't recognize her.

"Jeremiah and Aggie aren't wrong, then. Which means I need to face reality." I put the photo on my desk. "Thank you. Now, out of my office." I start to push him off the chair and towards the door.

"Kiss me first and I'll get out of your hair" I place both my hands on his face and bring him down to my level, kissing him gently and tenderly. He pulls away and swipes his tongue across his lip. "Much better. I'll text you later." I lean on the door frame and watch him walk away.

"Um.. I'm going to plan the funeral," Sam yells from across the room.

"I'll get the gravestone," Reva remarks.

"Excuse me?" I gape.

"He's going to be the death of you," Reva says nonchalantly.

"I call dibs on him next!" Sam yells, raising her hand.

I said I wasn't going to give in, but I won't completely forgive and forget. I will not be made a fool in the end. Still, maybe I need to let go of the mistakes. I realize now that I started to free fall too fast and suffered the consequences. This time, I'll try to relinquish this chokehold I have on my fear of the unknown.

Chapter 20

Teresa

The man learned his lesson apparently because not even a day and the man checks in periodically. I promised myself I wouldn't give second chances, but something about him begs for it and my gut is telling me to allow it. My thoughts stop as a sudden knock at my door startles me. I got lost in thoughts during a phone call, call it lust haze.

Carla peeks through. One sight of that red hair through my door instantly is ruining my day. I jokingly send Reva and Sam a message to have bail money ready. I gesture to her to hang on as I finish with my phone call. It also gives me a moment to gather my strength for whatever bullshit is about to spew out of her mouth.

"Carla. To what do I owe this pleasure of a visit?" It hurts to say the words.

"I just came to check up on you and see how you're faring. You know, I was talking with Mr. Connors, giving him updates, and he's just so excited to have the new building soon."

I swear, I could kill her in seven different ways and make it look like Winnie the Pooh was the mastermind. If she's here to chit chat, I don't have time.

"I am doing just fine. The new building is being drywalled and wired. Reva and I plan to visit with some donors next week. The hotline is still buzzing and from what I hear, we have lease signings in the services department, although I know Lillian can tell you more. The shelter is running smoothly; Angela and Mason have it covered." I stand up and stretch my legs, hoping she takes the hint.

"I know you can handle things, but I don't want you to get burned out. We women have to stick together." I swear her southern accent is about as fake as her boobs.

"Yes, we women have to stick together. Anything else I can do for you?" I grit my teeth, faking a smile, warding her off.

She apparently didn't get the hint. "Well, I wanted to talk with you about something for the auction. I was wondering if you would like to be one of the hosts? Before you say anything, I think you would be great."

No, absolutely not. "Carla, I already have my marching orders. Development runs the auction; talk to them."

She waves her hand, dismissing my argument. "I've already checked with them and they love the idea. Oh, please do it for me. Better yet, do it for Mr. Connors," she pleads, pouting her lip as if her charm will work on me. Before I can say a word, my intercom interrupts me.

"Tessa, you have mail here that needs your signature," our receptionist says.

"Alright, one second. Carla, excuse me." I walk past her. The nerve of this woman.

I get to the lobby and see a delivery person patiently waiting for me. I know I'm not expecting anything, and it looks like priority mail. Something in me stirs. You would think after so many crime shows and Alexander telling me my life is in danger that I would be worried or cautious. Instead, there's a sense of calmness.

I sign for it and give a small nod to the delivery person. I dial Alexander, and after the first ring, he picks up.

"Little Cub." Shivers run down my spine at his voice. The way his voice can just melt me away into a Tessa puddle is crazy.

I regained my strength from pushing the horny thoughts that circle my head, "I got a random priority mail. Looks like no return address. I would say it's harmless, but I'm guessing not." You could hear a pin drop. The rolling death of silence is deafening.

"Stay where you are." He clicks off. Within seconds, he appears at the agency's front door. Anger and frustration looms over him, or rather concern. The receptionist is startled when he taps on the door.

"Go ahead, he's with me," I tell the receptionist.

He rushes over, pulling me to the side away from prying eyes and ears. "Alexander." I give him a slight smile, looking up at him.

"Teresa."

"Got here awfully quick, were you in the parking lot already?" I try to break his seriousness, but it wasn't effective, he reached out his hand. "Hand it over and I'll have Joaquin look into it."

I shrug my shoulders. "It's probably nothing, but I won't stop you."

"You're a quick learner, darlin'." I hand him the envelope but don't release it. The puzzled look on his face tells me I threw him off guard.

"No secrets, Alexander. I mean it."

He just nods. "I'll let you know if I get any news." I rise to my toes and kiss him softly. "You better."

I turn to leave back up the stairs, but before I can react, he yanks me back to him, pressing our bodies closer. Grabbing the back of my head, he bends to steal another kiss. This one sets me on fire, sending sparks everywhere. The slip of his tongue leaves me in a breathless heap. I could stay here all day, if there were no eyes watching us. He pulls away, releasing a deep breath. He leans down to my ear, whispering, "Could give them a real show darlin'."

"Nah, I want you all to myself." I plant a chaste kiss on his cheek. Once he's gone, I march myself back to the office with the fluttering thoughts of what I would do to that man if given the chance.

Now who sounds possessive?

"Think you forgot about the pest control problem in your office," Reva warns. Fuck. I forgot about Carla.

I make it back to my office and shut the door. "Carla, I apologize. Think someone is pranking me with fake mail. Sorry, you were saying?" I take my seat again.

"Hosting, you know, being in front of the crowd? Say yes. I think you would be perfect. Just say yes." She is practically begging and just to shut her up, I concede.

"Fine, yes, I'll host." As much as I don't want to, I'll try to put on a smile if it gets her the fuck out of my office.

"Oh, goodie! Wait until I tell Sheldon." She prances out of my office. I lean back in my chair, twisting my claddagh ring before getting back to work. The one that sits on my right hand with the heart pointing out, he hasn't turned it the other way, but time will tell.

I finish the day on time and give myself a breather from falling down the rabbit hole again. Fresh eyes, fresh mind. I grab my things and let myself out of the office. The light from the sunset is fading, as street lamps start to turn on.

"Miss Tessa, Miss Tessa! I'm glad I caught you." I'd know that voice anywhere. I mutter to myself, cursing that I didn't leave earlier.

I turn and face him, holding my keys in my hand, hopefully showing him that I was getting ready to leave for the day.

"Jeremiah, buddy. I'm seeing you more times in the last two months than I did all last year. What can I do for you?" I grit through my teeth.

He doesn't beat around the bush. "Listen, I was doing my rounds, like you know I do, and I told you I'd keep an eye out for anything sketchy between there and my shop. Anyway, I told Ms. Aggie. Did she talk with you? I know she did, she told me." He starts to ramble.

"Jeremiah, a point needs to be made," I interrupt him. After a long day, I can't think anymore.

"Alright missy. Look, I seen them take them."

"Them who?" I put emphasis on who. Knowing Jeremiah, it's like a dog chasing their tail.

"The people I warned you about. I especially seen them by the tracks, you know, people be camping near there and everything. They convince people they have jobs and housing, and you know, some people are desperate. You and I both know how long those waiting lists are, Ms. Tessa. You have to do something about it. We gotta put a stop to them," his last words echo in my ears, stunning me.

"What would you have me do? Jeremiah, I know this is a problem, but we need evidence, you know that, before we can take this anywhere. I have people looking into it. " I release my answer, and it feels like a bubble has finally burst.

"Who's looking into it, Miss Tessa? They people you trust?" A simple question and a loaded answer.

"Sam, Aggie, Reva, and my friend Jackson. He's got his men surveying, I think." Thinking that it might be wrong to call him friend, but Jeremiah doesn't need to know the extent of my relationship with him.

"What men?" Jeremiah's eyes grow wider. He's hiding something and the silence speaks louder than words.

"Jackson has his crew looking into it," I ramble off, feeling like it's beside the point.

"What crew, Miss Tessa?"

I avert my eyes, knowing how Jeremiah will take it. "Wolves. At least that is what the patch on his jacket is."

Jeremiah stumbles back, shocked, worried, angry, all wrapped up into one expression. "Child, that is not a club you want to mess with. Why? Why?" He's yelling now, more worked up than I've ever seen him. "Miss Tessa, they are bad people, not ones to trust. Don't trust them, even if your own life depends on it. They a shady bunch."

I'm exasperated now. "I don't have the power, Jeremiah! People rely on me to do the impossible and the moment I get sucked in, I'm powerless. What would you have me do?"

Silence falls between us, the truth out in the open now.

"That's where you're wrong, Miss Tessa. You have power, you just haven't seen it yet." He sinks down, as if I wounded him. "I'll get you the evidence. Then people will see."

He turns to walk away. "Jeremiah, please don't. I don't need you to get hurt or get yourself into trouble."

"That's the thing, Miss Tessa. People are already getting hurt." He walks away before I can respond to him.

Everything seems to be spiraling. I'm not a detective or police, but things aren't adding up. Someone is taking people like a plague. A million questions spiral through my head. Where are these people going? Who's taking them and why? Is this trafficking? Why is it that people expect me to be the one to solve this? I'm one person with normal limitations.

I shake it off and continue to do what I do best: do the best I can and be content with that. I've worked enough to know what I can control and what I can't. I drive home and turn off my phone for the rest of the night. My system feels overwhelmed. I have not heard from Alexander, not knowing if he found something useful or not. Sleep finds me into a dreamless sleep.

The morning comes, and I feel like a train hit me head on and left me in the dust. I turn my phone on and wait for the antics to start. Seamus sits at the end of the bed, staring at me with his head tilted, and I know damn well I'm being judged. "Let the games begin, boy."

My phone starts to light up like the Fourth of July. I have missed three phone calls: one from Britt, one from momma, and one from Alexander. Fifteen emails, most likely junk. Ten text messages, five of which are Alexander concerned about my lack of response.

I may have to come to terms with the fact that he's overprotective, and that I unfortunately put him in a situation that requires his participation. Jeremiah's words resonate again in my head. I guess we'll be having a difficult conversation. "Seamus, mommy might just run away with you to an island and call it a life at this rate." I have a feeling that tonight will be a long night.

I head into the office, where another day can go by and I can focus on getting myself back together. The hotline is holding steady, and I say good morning to my team before heading into my office. I walk through and notice a man sitting at my desk.

"Good morning. Can I help you?" Translation: what the fuck are you doing in my seat. He's typing away, wires popping out of places I'm sure they shouldn't be.

"Oh. I'm sorry ma'am. They just told me to come in here. Sorry. They said I can work here." He fumbles around his words and his movements.

"Who said?" Daggers shoot out of my eyes.

"Carla. Sheldon? I think." He's sweating profusely.

I beeline for Sheldon's office. Carla stands behind Sheldon, looking at his computer. "Sheldon, a heads up would have been nice." Is she always with him?

"Oh, Carla said she sent you an email." Sheldon appears baffled. I may not be a fisherman but something's fishy.

Carla, cool as a cucumber, slinks her way across the room. Scrambling for her phone to check her email and looks back at me, "I'm so sorry. I thought my email was sent."

"Okay. Why do I have a random man sitting at my computer?"

"We got an alert that your system has been tampered with, and someone may have gotten ahold of your files and client system. We called technical support to make sure there isn't a bug in the system. We're still analyzing, but your computer is in quarantine. We'll figure it out. I think you need to be more careful with your computer. Let's hope that it wasn't a hacker and the confidentiality of the system and folks are safe." I can see the factitious smirk on her face.

"Okay. I appreciate the heads up." I turn to leave, and I can hear whispers. The fear starts to ruin me.

They're blaming me, as if I had something to do with this. I'm just as worried as they are, even more probably. My body starts to shake with the racing thoughts of *what if.*

Returning to the hotline, I sit in a random chair and slump down. I'm tired of giving myself damn pep talks in my head. I take one step forward to get knocked five steps back. I lean over, placing my face in my palms. Someone clears their throat. I look up to see Sammie handing me a cup of coffee.

"You look like your life's motto should be the middle finger." I know that should make me laugh, but I just zone out, staring into nowhere. I see Sam's mouth moving, but words fail to translate. Information overload. Sam jolts my body.

"Tess, Jesus, the zone out moment was real." Her hands are on her hip, a headset dangling from her neck.

"Sammie, at this moment, I need a mental slap of words." Not a direct request. At this moment, my past brokenness and old habits are seeping to the surface.

"Like what? How's being alone in your little pity party?"

"Sam, did I put on this persona of knowing everything, that I can fix everything? My brain has enough squirrels looking around for nuts. Apparently, I can't do anything right. Am I seriously that blind or have I just been ignoring reality, waiting for someone else to take care of it?" I spew out the words in a rage.

"Wow, your ass must be jealous of all the bullshit you just spoke," Sam retaliates at me.

"Care to elaborate before I reconsider firing you?" I raise an eyebrow.

"Is shit getting complicated and out of your control? Yes. Would you rather things go your way? Yes. Is it? Nope. Did you ever realize that being you is why people come to you? I don't think they're asking you to change anything. Just keep fighting and being you. Tess, you got lost. Go be found. Don't give up now when you're so close to finding the solution. This is when we need you the most, not the person you are trying to become." She lays her hand on my shoulder, looking me dead in the eyes too.

"Tessa, get your fucking head out of your ass and get to work. You have made it this far, keep going." She pats my cheek playfully.

This is the kick in the guts that I needed to get myself out of this self-induced pity party. I didn't make myself into this person. I've worked too hard to become the person I am today, this strong, balls-to-the-wall, independent, "you hurt someone I love and I will injure you" person. My life is not a hot mess; it's a spicy disaster that keeps on giving.

Still, Sammie's right. Why change the person I am if there's nothing to change?

Techie's still working on my computer, and lord knows what he's going to find. I dial Alexander; I'm probably going to get my ass chewed out for turning my phone off and not responding to him, which I still have yet to do. A couple of rings go by, and a voice picks up the other end, a few octaves higher.

"Jackson's phone." The little voice rings out. I've dealt with callers enough to know when a "teeny-bopper" comes on the phone.

"Excuse me, I'm looking for the owner of this phone." I hide my true tone before I do something incredibly stupid.

"Oh Jackson. He's currently occupied, I guess taking care of something. You know, taking care of *business*." The high-pitched southern drawl stings my ears, and the giggles just piss me off.

"May I ask who this is?" I'm annoyed, for lack of a better word currently.

"Oh, this is Topaz." Please tell me that's her birth name and not some sugar baby bullshit.

I internally groan. "Topaz, dear. Why do you have his phone?"

"He left it with me, told me to keep an ear out. You know, he can be sweet, takes care of us and all." I'm ready to toss a coffee cup across the room.

"Us."

Don't ask questions you don't want the answers to.

"Us, waitresses at the bar, people of the club, the businesses. Wait, is this Tessa? Aw, he talks about you. It's nice to talk to you finally." On any given day, I would want to befriend someone so sweet. But I'm ready to rip the hair off this Topaz, something feral and maybe even jealous. Two can play the possessive game, Alexander. I hang up the phone, raging like a bull seeing red.

"Reva, I need you to come with me somewhere, in case I need an alibi or an accomplice to bury a body."

"Whose car are we taking, and will I need bail money?" Reva grabs her purse.

"Mine, and we'll see." I storm out. I race down the stairs and out the back door.

"Where're we going?" she asks as we open my car doors.

"We're going day drinking." I pull out of the parking lot, spotting my tail. Darius Richard, you better warn your boss that his wild woman is on the warpath.

Chapter 21

Alexander

"Come on Jacky boy, you're telling me you have nothing new? Coda hasn't picked up on anything?" Rawlings blew smoke in my face as he takes a drag of his cigarette.

I wouldn't say I don't have anything new, but not enough answers or ways of explaining what I do know and keep her at arms length from everything.

"So you're telling me this girl ain't got nothing, but yet something was found in that letter," Rawlings isn't having my bullshit today. I don't know how much longer I can hold him off.

I don't know how much longer I can hold him off, I need to come up with a plan.

Or I need to tell her the truth.

What is it about the truth that makes us as humans scare to share it? Fear of rejection? Fear of acceptance?

"We're working on things, Prez," I admit, avoiding his eye contact.

"That's not good enough," Rawlings raises his voice. He snuffs out his cigarette before plopping down his office chair at Whiskey.

It's true that the turf war has been worse the past few weeks. We've had more members get hurt, making D.R work extra hard on patching people up. The Falcons are getting crafter. Unfortunately it has taken us for a loop, thrown into an unknown that has no answers.

"I'm having second thoughts of pulling that girl into this mess. She's got trouble in her name and sooner or later it's going to come our way." he says, tipping his head back against the chair. "Never fully trust a pussy, even if it's so damn tempting."

Before I can answer, my phone *dings*. My face turns red. "No, but she's got something coming her way."

I turn on my heel and burst through the door from the office. She's going to have a hand painting her ass red.

Chapter 22

Teresa

Arriving at the Devil's Whiskey, I adjust myself. The parking lot is semi-full, keeping up the appearance of a normal bar and "restaurant." My striped button up shirt, french tucked into my jeans with the top two buttons undone, showing a bit of skin, is just enough to tease. Loosening the bun on my head, I let down my natural waves.

"What's the plan, boss? Storm the castle? Grab a bitch by the hair?" Reva searches in her purse for a knife, bigger than my pocket one.

"Well, if the big man behind us was smart, he would warn Alexander. But we're gonna go in, order a couple of drinks, and wait for the explosion." I tuck my pocket knife into my pocket and keep my sunglasses on.

We walk through the inside seating area and push through the back doors. I don't care about the stares and whispers that fly our way. A wicked grin comes across my face. I hear a friendly, familiar voice behind the bar out here.

"The wind brought back the spitfire and a beautiful friend. Aren't you two supposed to be working?" Johnny says, already pouring me a whiskey and coke.

"Oh, I am. It's a bit of a business and pleasure thing. You know, early afternoon brunch with drinks." I grab my drink. Reva isn't far behind me. Rendering him speechless, I brush past other patrons as I plop into a chair, crossing my legs, basking in the sunshine. "Lover's quarrel? Jealous rage? Boss man won't like it." Johnny hands me my drink and a drink for Reva.

"Well, he shouldn't have been a dumbass and pissed me off." I sip on my drink.

"Hell hath no fury, you're here to do what? Shake the shingles off the roof?" Johnny continues to grill me. I hear the hinges on the door creak. Peering through my sunglasses, I see Keola and Darius bolt through the door. Both sporting a look of confusion and possible frustration.

"Boys, glad you can join us. I believe you have probably seen and stalked my friend and project assistant, Reva. Reva, the one on the left with the vein popping out on his forehead is Keola. I told you about him. Calm, cool, and collected and grumpy, but will snap you in half. The man on the right is Darius Richard or Doc, as I call him. Surprised it took this long, boys." I take a long sip. "What did you do, take a power nap?"

"I'm starting to think you're back to your old self, boss." Reva raises her glass to clink mine.

"Hey, would y'all mind getting a waitress? I'm starving. You know, make yourself useful instead of brooding in the doorway."

Keola mutters something under his breath and Darius walks over to the bar, shaking his head. "T, you're walking a fine line between understandable and questionable."

"Doc, look. For some reason, y'all think that if I do what I'm told and keep my head down, I'll survive. But I climbed my ladder by pressing questions, getting answers, and bending the rules. Sorry to disappoint." I wave my glass for Johnny to pour another.

A bouncy, medium height woman, with caramel skin pops through the door. Short blue jeans ride up her ass and a shirt two sizes too small perks up her boobs. Her braided blue hair cascading around her face as she walks over to the chairs. "Hi y'all, I'm Topaz. I'll be your waitress. First time here?"

She seems so sweet and sunshiny. Part of me doesn't want to hate her, but I'm currently here to make a point to an audience.

"No dear, been here before. I'm Tessa and this is my friend Reva. We just want an order of fries for now." I don't know why I said fries.

She starts bouncing, giddy and everything. "Oh my god, you're Tessa. You're even more beautiful than I imagined. Oh, Jackson is a lucky guy." Reva looks at me and sinks a little in her seat.

"Yes, yes he is." I start off slow and easy, keeping my voice low.

"You are simply beautiful. No wonder he is so enraptured by you." Topaz beams. Crap, now I feel like a possessive bitch, shrinking down in my seat. I'm a bit taken back. I anticipated a bit more of a fight or a sign that she wanted to sink her claws into Alexander. I think I made a mistake.

"Um, thank you." I shutter, "I wanted to see the woman who answered his phone..." I pause in the middle of my statement. Her face drops almost into a roaring laughter.

"Oh sugar, you thought I was one of the biker bunnies? Oh you don't have to worry about me." She gives me a wink. "Alexander, not my type. By a football field. But your friend on the other hand," She leans on the table, her bright blue braids cascading down her arms. She is striking.

"And here I thought I was going to give a word of warning." I hunker down the liquor quickly taking effect.

"A word of warning? I can promise you, you aren't going to scare me off." Her angelic smile spreads across her face.

Reva looks at me and shrugs, telling me to entertain the thought. "Um. Well. I was going to say 'if I see a single strand of blue on him, you won't have to worry about keeping it blue. It will be bloody red once I'm done. Are we clear?' And now I feel like a storming possessive bitch for thinking that. I'm sorry." I said.

"Oh trust me, I think you could hold your own against all the bitches some of these men bring in. I'll get your order in and be back in a jiffy." She laughs it off and bounces back to the kitchen.

The fear had washed over me when she had picked up the phone. I heard Matthew and Seth talking about girls the club keeps around for company, and I don't play by those rules. Alexander wants to be possessive with me? I'll do the same, but after I make a fool out of myself on the wrong woman.

I walk over to the bar, grabbing my next drink. I attempt to make myself presentable. Keola and Darius are holding back laughter as they had just watched the train wreck.

Darius laughs at me. "Oh girl, you almost crossed the line. But hey, you gotta do what you gotta do. Topaz is harmless, I mean not completely, but."

I slap a hand on his back. "Doc, I think you and I are going to be best friends."

Walking back to the table with my drink in hand, everything seems to stop. I turn around to see him, chest heaving, blue eyes staring at me. I turn back and sway to my chair, plopping back down with my legs crossed. A vicious but shy smile spreads across my face. Silently hoping that the two in the back don't blow my cover.

"Ah, I was wondering when I would see your face. Reva, I should have bet money." Sipping lightly on my drink, I cock my head at him. "Damn, it would have been good money too."

Reva sips on her drink, choosing the accomplice side of things. "Jackson, it's very nice to see you. Now that I know that you're alive and decidedly not under another alias."

He marches over to the table, beelining to me. Casting a shadow down on me, he's seething. "Darlin', care to explain yourself?" Alexander demands.

I tsk. "Oh, no. I don't have to explain myself to you. But you do." I take one final sip of my drink before standing up to face him. He's the one playing with fire.

"Apparently, you also need reminding that if you're going to be stupid, you better have the bravery to back it up." I play with his gray shirt, fingers twisting the material. I lick my bottom lip, tempted to strip him bare here. "The next time a woman answers your phone and I hear how *sweet* you are on them or how you *take care* of them, she better run, and you better have the balls to face me, Alexander." I walk behind Reva's chair to watch him squirm a little in confusion.

"D.R., did I fucking miss something?" Something tells me that no one told him about Topaz. Darius throws his hands in surrender, not knowing what to say.

Reva raises her hand.

Oh, this oughta be good.

"Yes Reva, would you like to help out our dear confused Alexander here?"

"Yes, boss. Your girl tried to call you on what seems to be a crappy morning for her. She felt bad she didn't respond to your messages last night. To her surprise, a girl answered your phone and said, and I quote, *He left it with me, told me to keep an ear out. You know, he can be sweet, takes care of us and all,*" Reva says beautifully, better than I could.

We're chaos in the making. She fists bumps me, as he stands there puzzled, confused.

"Sounds like someone has fucked up, boss," Darius chirps in the background. Alexander doesn't say a word. Topaz comes through the doors and hurries with the fries and ranch, a way to my heart. She flashes a devilish smile.

"Thank you," I say as she plops down next to Reva, taking out a cigarette and starts to light it.

Suddenly, the light bulb comes on across his face. A small snicker releases from his lips. "You mean to tell me, you heard a woman's voice on the phone and got jealous. And lucky enough it was Blue over here?"

"I don't take too kindly that, when I call you, a woman says you were "taking care of business," if I know what she means." I stuff a French fry in my mouth, leaning on Reva's chair.

"Oh darlin', green isn't your color." He walks over to the bar where Darius still sits.

I signal Reva to take the basket of fries with us as I count out some cash to pay for the food and drinks and hand it over to Topaz, giving her a nice tip as well part of my guilt.

"Alexander, I'm going to say this once and only once. I'm not a forgiving woman. If I hear another woman *speak* your name in a tone I don't like, be prepared. I don't share." I warn him, "And I will allow Topaz to help me." I walk up to the bar and pat Alexander's cheek, handing Johnny a tip as well.

"She's a keeper, and I won't hold her back from scratching a woman's eyes out." Topaz chuckles out.

"Darius, I'm going back to the office, if you are still on tailing duty. Don't worry, Reva is driving. Alexander, I'll be home tonight. But if you come over, behave, I'm having company over." I exit the bar with Reva in tow. The alcohol is still taking over a bit of my control. I'm hoping the point was made. But a part of me jumped to conclusions and almost made another mess that would need to be cleaned up. Bright side, I made a new friend and she is feisty. I must admit, it was invigorating, empowering, not according to plan. This is exactly the feeling I wanted years ago.

⟫⟫⟫➤ ⟪⟪⟪⟪

Sam, Reva, Britt, and I meet at my house, and I clear my office area, giving us room to Nancy Drew this shit. I need to look at the whole timeline and evidence. I honestly haven't heard anything from Jackson and the feeling inside that he's withholding information isn't sitting well with me.

I sip my wine. Alexander's been silent but I'm sure a watchful eye is never far. I feel like I need to check in, but I push the thought away. Was I dramatic, a bit. But two can play his little possessive game.

We sit in the office, going through reports and notes Sammie and I made. We're racking our brains with what we have, feeling like there's a puzzle but no indication of a photo. Pens and sticky notes lay all over the floor. A couple of hours pass by, and we look like we've been at it for weeks. My wall is looking like a conspiracy theory in motion.

"Okay. Staring at the papers ain't helping. Let's walk the timeline from the beginning. By the way, llamas?" Brittany holds up my llama sticky notes from Ella.

"Leave me alone. I love them and they're all I have."

"Okay, so let's get at it. When did it start again?" Sam asks, stuffing another slice of pizza in her mouth.

"It was after Allie's party. I believe it was the Monday after, because that was before I ran into Jackson." I scribble the early March time frame on a sticky note, handing it to Britt.

"And what were his words?" Sam asks. Reva sits in the chair at my desk, feet propped up, notepad on her lap. Sam lays on her stomach on the floor, papers surrounding her with a pen sticking out of her messy bun. Seamus lays silently between Sam's legs, pancaked on the floor. I'm laying down with a pillow over my head, blocking out the light and possible distractions.

"Said that he had *heard* there were people missing, something about jobs and housing," I say, rubbing my forehead.

"To which you said…" Reva continued.

"Please be careful, if he sees anything to call the police," I say.

"Alright, so the start of March, then what? Where did the white rabbit lead you?" Brittany asks, putting one of the notes on the wall.

"I had asked Aggie if she heard anything as people were entering the center. She said if she heard anything then she would have told me by now. She didn't say anything was going on."

"Uh huh, so where did the white rabbit take you next?" Brittany asks again.

"Didn't you have that call? That's what prompted you to tell me to look into reports and any strange calls," Sam pipes in.

"Oh yeah, okay. So basic call, looking for housing. I believe he said his buddy was telling him about it and asked if the hotline had the phone number. I explained that we didn't have that resource. I think my mind started to spiral because I remember shivers went down my spine and too many connections to make it a coincidence. Which is where you came in Sam." I point to Sam, giving her the chance to explain her information.

"Within the month of March, we didn't have any decrease in calls. I went through calls and looked into everyone's call notes. There were five additional calls about a group having jobs and housing, promising that if they worked, they would be housed outside of the city," Sam reads off her reports and information she printed out.

"Was there any information regarding names or even a location?" Reva chimes in, scribbling some notes and thoughts.

"Nope. One call mentioned vehicles coming to pick them up, but no mention of a location," Sam answers. Part of me feels this is an endless circle, and there isn't any clear proof. I'm hoping, with this information, I can take it to the committees and local police to make a plan. As much as I would like to find the people associated and end it, this is as much as I might be able to do.

"Alright, so that's March. Let's look into April; what do we have? Please tell me y'all have something," Brittany continues.

"Okay, so again, April reports so far are not bad. Still within the average range," Sam reads on.

"Wait. Did we look into separating the calls from their categories? Like those reporting homeless versus just needing resources or assistance?" Reva chimes in, making a valid point.

I pop up, knocking the pillow to the floor. Sam jerks up to look at me. "No, I didn't. But I will this week when we get back into the office. Maybe there's a distinction there." She scribbles a note to herself to look into the reports.

"But also, Tessa had that call from Aggie. Aggie was looking for you early on," Reva says, bringing back the memory of my panic attack.

"Yeah, a day that I'd rather forget. She said that in February, there were a total of 323 people who visited the Center. Then in March, there were 253. Maybe I need to get the lists from Aggie and compare. Find the names, possibly," I say, rubbing my forehead.

"Could we use the list to track the call history? Worth a shot?" Sam contributes.

"We could run into confidentiality issues. If the committees get a whiff of us going through people, we would be under siege." Reva makes a point. Hotline is about confidentiality. We only intervene if there's a problem with coordination.

"But you could ask Jeremiah. See if he recognizes the names," Brittany adds in.

"I'm guessing your reports didn't have anything either," Sam says. "Unfortunately, Reva wasn't able to get the reports. Something about not being able to open them or something. I don't understand." I lay back down. It seems like we have a point, but we're going back down a slippery slope.

"Okay, so let's look at it now. What's been going down this past week that seems sketchy?" Brittany asks.

"The random piece of mail that Jackson took and said he'd look into. I have a feeling that maybe there's something there but he's keeping it to himself. Then there's Jeremiah's warning." I finish out what I know.

"So, he just showed up last night and said beware?" Reva asks.

"Not exactly. He said he has seen more on the streets, seen people in a van. There one day and gone the next. Especially near the tracks. Then he warned me about Jackson and his club. "Not good people," I believe he said.

"Do you trust him? I'm not talking about within a relationship, but personally, with your life, this work, and what's going on within the community?" Brittany asks me the million dollar question.

"That's the thing: half of me does. He's shown enough to care about my well-being. Shit, he has a watchdog sitting in a car right now watching over us. The man has claimed me or whatever that shit is. My gut tells me I can trust him. I wouldn't have asked him to help if I didn't." I sit back up and give out all the evidence I have.

"And the other half?" Sammie asks in a soft voice.

"The other half is telling me there's something more I need to be looking at but it doesn't know what. It's like the vibe I'm getting. There is so much more, and I don't know what to expect."

"Well, isn't it time to get some questions answered?" Brittany chimes in.

"No time like the present, I guess."

"We still have nothing but an inkling and some reporting factors. Right? Cool. I don't think even the Scooby gang can solve this one." Reva throws her hands in the air.

We might need the whole gang at this point. One thing for sure is that work needs to be done.

Chapter 23

Teresa

Well, work has provided any clearer answers, and I feel there is still more head way.

Alexander is silent again and the anxiety creeps in again, flooding my mind with the worst thoughts, and I need them to quiet down. Call it insecure or past trauma with relationships. Sam, Reva, and I have been busy all week looking into the information. Sam has been pulling the reports, separating it out between different calls.

After I got my computer back, unfortunately, Sheldon says that half of my personal files were compromised and deleted, so I've been frantic, trying to restore the majority of my files from an external hard drive. Sam and I have been working into the night. Answers needed to come or more trouble could be brewing.

"Boss, I'm out for the night. Please text us when you leave and get home safe," Sam calls out from the office hallway. Out of everyone, she is more scared of what is to come than myself and tends to worry about me. While I sit back and worry about everyone.

Still burying my nose in the computer, my glasses at the bridge of my nose, I swear, the more I look at reports and notes, the faster my head spirals and I feel like I'm slipping.

Quietness can drive a person mad, alone with their thoughts, using it as a weapon for destruction. I can't handle the silence at night. With the aid of music to calm my mind, it allows my thoughts to formulate and comprehend all this information. I'm feeling like I've been caught in the middle, with no understanding of where it all started. *You may never know.*

Night falls with the sun disappearing from view. Darkness invites loneliness and for now, I welcome it. I accept it. No distractions other than the sounds of the background. My best work tends to come at night, maybe because I seclude myself from others.

I put my head in my hands and let out a frustrated yell.

"Sounds like someone needs a distraction."

I take a deep breath or two and peek through my hands, finding the one man I thought knew better than to sneak up on me. Alexander leans up against the doorway, peering into my office, taking in the scene, probably second guessing his involvement with me. Leaning back into my chair, I push my glasses to the top of my head.

"Do I want to know how you got in?" I get up and walk around to the front of my desk, leaning against it. I fold my arms across my chest, hiding the possible excitement of seeing him. Something about him sends pleasure and exhilaration zipping through me. The sight of him is unbelievable.

"Little birdie let me in. I can be very persuasive." He smirks. *Sammie.*

"Little birdie may not have a job and I'm fully aware of your tactics." I look away, because if I look at him any longer, I might regret my next move.

"I'm surprised, darlin," he says, inching closer.

"Surprised about what?" I cock my head at him.

"I'm not getting a tongue lashing from you or something not being thrown at my head." He laughs.

"I would have thrown something at you or kicked your ass if I deemed it necessary. Plus, there's a better use of my tongue," I say brazenly. A spark of curiosity rages in his eyes.

"Oh, do tell." He walks closer, inches away from sitting between my legs.

"I like to show, not tell." I turn to walk away when he grabs me from behind and pulls me back to his chest. He inhales me, before letting it out in a fast rush.

"I've missed you."

"It's only been a few days. Also, did you just smell me?"

He shakes his head, his lips rubbing against my neck. "Yes, I did. Lemons and sandalwood, that's you. I'll always find you." He engulfs me in his arms, embracing every inch of my body. This moment. I wish I could freeze time and live in this moment. For a brief second, a sense of trust and protection settles over me. Maybe this is my chance to trust him.

"Mmm, wait until I tell Doc you've turned into a sap," I snicker.

"Oh, him and the others are aware. That's not a secret," he tells me. "You're working later than usual. What has you burning the midnight oil?" He lets me go and slinks into one of the chairs.

"I'll show you mine if you show me yours." I sit in my chair, twisting back and forth. "Look, Jackson..." I continue but I'm interrupted. I let it slip again.

"Nope. Try again," he lets out. I know what he wants.

"Look *Alexander,* I have some questions. I think now's time for some answers." I lean forward, catching his attention.

"I can try. But first, I need to make sure you eat something that's not cereal." He stands up, offering his hand.

"How do you..." He's not wrong. He gives me a look, like I should know the answer. "Never mind. You see all." I pack up my backpack and laptop. I shoot Britt a message that she's on Seamus duty for the night and let her know my location is on. "Alright you brute, let's go. Feed your woman." That is the first time I've actually admitted that I'm his.

He grins from ear to ear. "I like the sound of that." He takes my hand as I lock up the building and walks towards the parking lot.

Alexander scans the parking lot. I assume he took over for the previous watchdog. I walk in front of him, trying to grab my keys from my bag when I hear tires screeching in the darkness. The sound echoes, as if the world is only making that sound. I turn to look around but it's too dark to have any indication of what's coming. I whip my head around, trying to find Alexander.

I hear the bang of shots ricocheting off the building, and then a slight inflection of pain, then my body is shoved to the ground. I try to brace my head for impact, but pain radiates across my skull and adrenaline starts to surge through my veins. Alexander barricades himself around me, firing off his gun. My ears are ringing, muffling the sounds around me. I can't see anything. His weight is still on me and everything goes still.

Moments go by, I try to balance myself and understand what happened. I turn my head as Alexander gets up, on the phone. He's angry, yelling, but I can't make out what he's saying. I groan in pain; he's no soft blanket and pillow. I must have said his name, because he looks at me with concern. Shock, confusion, and pain are not the combination I want to see. He rushes back to me, and the ringing softens. I can start to hear a few of his words, but not all of them.

He examines me, every inch of my body. His eyes dart to my right arm, and I follow his gaze. Blood drips down my arm, coating it. With the adrenaline, I must not have felt it at first. He rips part of my shirt off to bandage it up. My eyes don't leave my arm. Then all I see is darkness, like a gentle sleep.

I must be dreaming. Granddaddy's here. We're sitting on the back porch of his old farm, swinging on the porch swing. He died when I was young, but this isn't a memory. I'm my normal self, but granddaddy is still the vibrant man he was when I was nine. The sunkissed wrinkles from the days on the farm and the freckles on his nose are too real. I can feel the tears starting to form; I've missed him so much. "Granddaddy?" I say it like a whisper in a dream. He looks at me with his kind eyes and rests his hand on my cheek. I lean into it, his calloused hands warm against my cheek.

"My brave angel. Hang on."

I clutch his hand to my face. "Granddaddy, I miss you."

"I know, a stóirín." My little treasure.

"Why are you here? Why am I here?" I question him. I'm so happy to see him, whether or not this is heaven. Or my mind playing games with my memories.

"Rest. You're here to rest." His eyes, like honey, stare into my soul. "Oh, a stóirín. You've been through so much. I'm so proud of you." His hands intertwine with mine. "Give yourself to love. Know that I will always be here." I hear him hum Cape Breton as he kisses my forehead, as a bright light breaks it all.

My eyes flutter open, waking from the hazy dream. I'm lying on an unfamiliar couch, my arm bandaged, the blood cleaned up. My head's pounding and an ache runs through my body with every slight movement. I groan. This is worse than a hangover. I slowly adjust my balance and sit up.

"Alexander?" I call out.

This place looks like it belongs in a magazine: industrial, painted in dark earth tones. It's masculine but soft at the same time. It's obviously been converted to serve as both a living space and a garage, and I'm not surprised. A motorcycle sits at the edge of one of the garage doors.

"Alexander?" I call out one more time before I get to my feet. I regret it instantly; my balance sucks, and I'm holding onto anything I can as I make my way into the nearby kitchen.

No one's here, but I spy one perfect companion: whiskey. I'm not sure if this is Alexander's place, fuck it. I was just shot: I deserve this. I gather enough strength to sit on the counter and take a big swig, allowing the warmth of the alcohol to wash through me. I have no idea what happened nor how long I have been out. Something tells me that I have been out of the loop on a few areas.

I lay my head back against the cabinets and gently close my eyes. Pain is still radiating through me. I hear the flushing of a toilet and my eyes pop back open. I rest the bottle on my thigh, waiting for the person I'm assuming will be Alexander.

I'm not wrong. He emerges in basic jeans and a shirt, molded to every cut and edge of his body. Rubbing the back of his neck. *I want and I want now.*

He glances over at the couch, realizing the dead have risen like Easter morning. He scans the room, panicking, before finally finding me on the counter.

"Hiya." I wave at him.

"You're awake." He leans against the kitchen island as I take a sip from the bottle.

When he sees what I'm drinking, he walks over to me, nestling between my legs, and moves to grab the bottle from my hands.

"If you touch this again you'll lose a hand." I snatch the bottle away from his grasp.

"I just don't think that this is smart with possible head injuries. D.R says you should be okay, he suspects that you passed out due to stress and fear." He places his hands on my thighs. I swear to Jesus, this man is infuriating and tempting at the same time.

I scoff. "I was promised answers and until I do, I'm going to drink myself into a stupor because that's how I'm coping with this crap right now. Start talking cowboy." I drink again.

"I don't think you *are* ready, darlin'." Fucking hell, what's with him? I push him off, or at least attempt to but his strong hands grip me.

"Fucking spare me the rod. I've been patient, I've played by your rules. *Go hifreann leat!*" Apparently, when I'm extra angry, my childhood Gaelic lessons come in handy and becomes prominent.

"You speak Gaelic?" He raises an eyebrow. I just raise one back at the poor attempt at deflection.

He sighs, and that's how I know I've won. "You're right. You deserve answers. Ask away." He grabs a chair and sits, still settled between my thighs.

"A few nights ago, Jeremiah warned about what was going down in the community, then proceeded to give me a few words of warning about you. What do you do, Alexander? What do you really do? What is the club into? I'm sucked into this world now, so I deserve to hear the truth." The alcohol is kicking in now.

He looks me square in the eyes, steeling himself for my reaction. "The club handles the transportation of goods and storage of certain exports. Different businesses need a provider to overlook shipments. We don't ask questions, and we get a cut of the profits. The only thing we don't handle is drugs; too much shit happens with drug contracts. We own a few businesses to keep out of trouble."

"Like the Devil's Whiskey." I connect the dots.

"And the Angry Dog," he adds. My mouth drops.

"No fucking way. A biker gang owning a downtown coffee shop?" I laugh lightly, but he squeezes my thighs in warning.

"We dip our hands in a lot of things, keeping things legit, but shipping and transportation is our biggest one."

I take another swig as he continues. "I'm not a good person, Teresa. I have done things that tarnished the halo and added the horns, if you will. I've taken down people that jeopardized our operations or put our people in danger. Jeremiah has a right to be worried. But there's something about you, the way you care and see the world in a different light, that draws me in, makes me want to be a better man..." He kisses one of my hands, and the butterflies start to flutter. And the alcohol, but I'm choosing to ignore that for now.

"Will you tell me? About what you've done? Give me more insight on those darker parts?" I ask, knowing I'm pressing my luck.

He shakes his head no. "Perhaps one day, but I think you might have more pressing questions."

I let that one go for something else that's bothering me. "I want to know about the mail I gave you." I go to take another swig, but he stops me.

"Joaquin didn't find anything. No trace of it being laced or tampered with. It's being kept somewhere safe though, just in case."

I can feel the warmth of the whiskey circling around in my head. I'm not drunk, but I'm tipsy enough to ask my most loaded question. "Why?"

"Why what, little cub?" His eyebrows furrow.

"Why am I a target? I'm just a project manager for a non-profit for fuck sakes. I don't run into circles like you."

Alexander moves to take the whiskey bottle from my hands, slowly setting it down out of my reach. "We can talk about that more when you're sober."

This time, I didn't fight him. Instead, I twirl the hair falling into his face around my fingers. He'd tied it up into a bun, but I reached around to untie it, letting his hair float around his face. My fingers intertwine with the white blond strands, and I move to kiss him gently. It's a soft kiss, one that makes you swoon for more.

Alexander guides me into another kiss, this one passionate and starving. He pulls me down off the counter until I'm straddling his lap, and I feel his hands roaming my ass. Before I know it, I'm moaning into his mouth, slowly grinding against him, feeling how hard he is against me. My hands caress his chest, down to the top of his pants. This is my chance, if he'll let me. My hand slips across the rim of his briefs. Alexander tenses up, possibly a bit shocked.

"Let me take care of you," I whisper against his lips, practically begging for a taste. "Please."

"Since you asked so nicely." He presses one more kiss to my lips, fumbling to take his shirt off. I slide off his lap, standing back to admire the planes of his stomach, itching to touch him. . He pushes the chair out of the way, leaning against the island as I slowly make my way to my knees. I trail kisses down every inch of his body, feeling his heart beat faster with anticipation. As I venture further, my hands pop open his jeans, pulling him out to my hungry eyes, spreading a bead of pre-cum across his head as I go.

I grip him lightly, feeling every muscle and vein. It's bigger than I imagined, thicker, and it thrills me. Alexander hasn't taken his eyes off me, watching every movement. I pull back a moment to get a better look, and he cups my chin.

"What do you want, little cub?" he asks, gripping his dick.

I lick my lips. I want a taste. But one word escapes me, "You."

He just smiles down at me, his eyes soft. "You have me, Teresa. Until our roads end."

His words echo his promises. I see the man that wants to take care of me, wants to continue to see the good in me. He has put up with the chaos in my heart and in my mind. He fights back and puts me in my place, he's not afraid to be with me. He's not expecting perfection, but is admiring the brokenness. He does not know the whole story of my past, but at this moment, I know that wouldn't scare him away. My heart is opening to this man.

I lick him along the length of him, taking my time, giving him a show. I run a circle around his tip, flicking under the sensitive flesh. He lets out a groan, his head tipping back as he sets his hand on my head. My hand grips him at the root, pumping as I suck on his tip. I finally take him all the way down, letting myself become accustomed to his size. I bob my head up and down, my hand following suit, setting on a rhythm of long and slow drags.

"Fuck," he hisses. I can feel myself growing wetter with each of his groans. He tenses up as I take him deeper, his head hitting the back of my throat. My thighs rub together, desperately trying to get pressure to where I'm throbbing. I moan around him, letting the vibrations surround him.

"Sucking my dick gets you wet, Teresa?" he mumbles between breaths. In response, I fondle his balls as he hits the back of my throat. He bucks off the counter, hands tightening in my hair, desperate for control.

"Teresa, if you don't stop, I'm going to come before I can bury myself in that weeping pussy." I ignored him; I wanted to push him, and I'm not stopping now. I can sense he's close; as I feel him start to thicken, I bob down, pausing as he goes as far as I can take him. As he grunts, I peer up at him with round eyes.

He taps the side of my cheek. "You have five seconds to get your ass on the bed."

I release him with a loud pop before I sway over to the bed in the back of the garage, leaving him slack jawed behind me. Within seconds, I'm lifted up and tossed onto the bed. Clearly, I wasn't walking fast enough.

"Clothes off. Now," he growls. I sit up at the command, slowly peeling off my tank top and bra. My breasts pop free, and he grabs them before I have the chance to get my pants off. Before I can comprehend what's happening, my nipple is in his mouth, hot and wet, and my back arches off the bed as he gives it a teasing nip.

"So sensitive, are we?" he coos.

"Fucker," I gasp out.

"Mm, dirty girl."

I rush to get everything else off, wanting this man to devour me. He pushes me back onto the bed, his hands trailing a soft path to my pussy. I whimper as he ghosts over my folds with his fingers, bringing them to his mouth for a taste.

"Wet and sweet. Just how I like it." Before I could retort, he slams two fingers inside of me, knocking the breath out of me.

"Please," I choke out.

"Please what? What do you want?" He pumps his fingers at a slow pace, enough for me to come to my senses.

"Fuck me. Take me," I demand.

"With my fingers or.." he trails off, adding his thumb to stroke my clit.

"I swear to all things Jesus, Mary, and Joseph, Alexander, if you don't bury yourself in me with your cock soon..." I begin but don't need to finish as he thrusts into me. I gasp at the sensation of my pussy deliciously stretching to accommodate him.

"Mm, look how nicely your pussy takes me, like it's starving for more." He says, slowing kissing my neck, teasing me.

I feel *so full*. If he doesn't start moving soon, I might actually lose it. He doesn't take the hint, though, and bends down to kiss me, slipping his tongue between my lips to take control.

As much as I love kissing him, I buck against him, needing more friction.

"I got you, little cub." He slides in and out slowly, waiting until I squirm to pick up speed. He's angling his hips just right, so that he's teasing my clit with each thrust. I let out a moan that's quickly silenced by his mouth. I can feel myself tighten around him, spasming the closer I get to the edge.

He looks down and groans at the sight. "So tight. You feel like a dream. Look at you, taking me so nicely."

Without warning, he lifts my legs together, flipping them to one side. Suddenly, he feels deeper, bigger, *more*. The sensation of him floods my veins. I feel myself clenching, almost painfully, ready to explode. I feel the smacking of his balls with every movement, and he drives into me faster, like he's devouring me, like I'm his.

"You gonna come for me, darlin'?" He slams harder, tears running down my cheek. If his unrelenting pace is punishment for my sins, I'll just sin more.

"Please," I let out on my way to seeing stars.

"Please what?" He grins wickedly.

"Make me come, please Alexander," I scream out. I'm a mess with every movement he makes.

Suddenly, he flips me onto my knees, my ass in the air. I know I won't last long like this, and I have a feeling he knows that. He slows down his rhythm, drawing out the moment, seizing control.

I groan as I clutch my hair in frustration. "Wait, no. I was so close." I'm practically sobbing at this point, whimpering at the closeness of release.

He runs his hand across my backside, his featherlight touches stirring back the excitement. "I know you were, darlin'. I've dreamt about this, your sweet cunt taking me, driving you wild for my cock." I press back into him, begging for more, and am rewarded with a stinging smack to my ass.

"Greedy, aren't you? I want to hear you say something, and then I'll let you come." He picks up the pace, adding his hand to my clit, rubbing in slow, torturous circles.

Breathless I say, "What? Please."

He hums. "So polite when you want something, but I want something. You were already mine in the woods, but I need to hear you say it."

I shake my head, which earns me another smack.

"Stubborn woman." *Smack.* His hand rubs my clit in daunting circles and matches the rhythm of his dick driving into me, the heat blooming on my ass only adding to the pleasure.

"Say it." The build is coming again, and my soul is feeling the fire.

"Alexander," I whimper out, beginning to feel every fiber waiting to explode in bliss.

He wants me. At this moment, he chooses me. He wants me to let go, to be his. I have to put my faith in love.

"I'm yours, Alexander. *Please.*" I'm basically crying from frustration at this point. I'm his. It took me time to see that but I am.

"With pleasure." He smacks my ass and grips my hair as leverage, adding a bit of pain to the pleasure.

He thrusts a few more times before I'm seeing stars and riding out my orgasm. Alexander continues to slam into me until his dick twitches in release, filling me with his cum. I'm a puddle of sweat and euphoria. He slumps over me, placing small kisses on my shoulder. After a moment, he pulls out, his cum leaking out of my pussy. I twitch as he cleans me with a warm cloth. I've never experienced such tenderness and care. I can feel my walls coming down. It's been a long time since I've let myself feel these things. I can't help but smile. Slowly, this man is changing my thoughts of happily ever after.

Alexander slithers back to bed, pulling me into his chest from behind, kissing the back of my neck. I let out a sigh and mumbled something incoherent.

"I never noticed this." He trails his finger between the bottom of my neck and the top of my back.

"What's that?" I nestled back to him.

"Your tattoo. The only one you have." He kisses my tattoo, a bear paw with a mountain scene in the paw.

"It's for my granddaddy. Our last name means bear in a bunch of languages. He died of cancer when I was young. He was one of the most important people in my life." I'm word-vomiting now, letting it all hang out. He holds me tighter, his body saying everything he doesn't have to say.

I nuzzle into his chest, feeling his heartbeat in his chest. "I'm serious, you know. Until our roads end. You are mine."

"I could get used to hearing that." He kisses the top of my hair and sleep finds me easily, with Alexander wrapping me in his arms. For once, my mind is quiet and the world around me has given in. Slowly, the bricks start to come down.

Chapter 24

Alexander

Everything has gone too far, the lines have been crossed. Last night, she became a part of the problem more than ever. When she said she was mine, it was the moment that I knew the truth needs to be said, and I'm not ready to let her go from my arms.

Rawlings told me last night to bring her in, and unfortunately our paths will be one.

She lays in my bed, her hair tousled across the pillows, her naked body beaconing to be worshiped, touched, loved.

"Teresa. Teresa, darlin', wake up." I say as her eyes gently nudge open. The sun barely peeks through the windows as she refuses to move. I place a kiss on her forehead, "Darlin', we have to be somewhere. Get dressed. We'll stop by the agency and get your car."

When she finally wakes up she scrambles to her feet when she sees me fully dressed with my gun holstered to my side. She searches for her clothes and belongings, shooting me a look of frustration, "Mind telling me where you're taking me? There'd better be coffee." she grunts as she reaches for her boots.

I shake my head, "I wish I could. Just trust me, okay?"

My races through what I wish I could tell her now, her eyes full of concern, silently begging me not to break her heart.

Once we picked up her car, it wasn't long before I brought her to the compound, the center of our command.

When she steps out of her car, I rush to her, gathering her in my hands, "Listen. Please, listen to me. Do not look at anyone. Stay behind me. If you know what's good for you, keep your mouth shut until someone talks to you."

She studies the scenario, finding her ground before she steps forward with me. She searches my own face for any indication of hope or sense. I want to console her, tell her that everything will be okay.

We continue down a long hallway and stop at a door, I give a knock. "Yeah." One word vibrates from behind the door and through us.

I open it, leading her to where she sees Prez. His burning brown eyes sear into her skin. A feeling of uneasiness and shakiness immediately takes hold. Dark lighting barely gives details of his face, the only lighting is a large desk light.

"Have a seat. Please." He gestures to the leather seats in front of us. She makes small steps, surveying her surroundings. She's a cautious little thing.

I stay behind her, avoiding the anxious, sadden eyes, "Jackson has filled me in on the excitement from yesterday. I see that you are alive and well. I know you know the current...issues in the city. We have collected some information, but before I divulge, I have a proposition for you." He searches for a cigarette and lighter, lighting up as he gives her time to consider. She plays into Rawlings' hand, playing the little theatrical game.

"How can I be of any help? I'm not a biker or a criminal. I doubt I can be of any help," she leans back in my chair, folding her hands against her chest. I finally sat next to her, sitting straight up, silent, not even glancing in her direction. Guilt washes over me.

"You bring more to the table than you give yourself credit for." Rawlings leans back in his chair, propping his feet up on his desk.

"Nope, I'm good. I somehow got myself into this mess and I'm not interested in a deeper dive. Now, if you'll excuse me, I have to go." she moved out of my seat.

Rawlings glares at her and pops up out of his seat. "Sit your fucking ass down. Jesus, compliments don't work with you, do they? I don't know how he did it, but it worked," Rawlings growls out.

Her eyes widened, possibly thinking, wait, who did what? She lowers herself back down to the chair.

"Your choices are simple, dear one. You're either with us," Prez starts before pausing to let the silence settle in. "Or against us," Rawlings growls as he finishes his threat. She scoffs; he's asking her to choose between two true evils.

She's worked her whole life not being intimidated by those in power, those who want nothing more to stop her.

She glances to the back of the worn-out office. Two other members with Grim Wolves leather jackets stood guard near the door. She turns back around, eyes trained on the ground, shaking her head.

The smell of the cigarette smoke, whiskey, and wrong decisions hangs around us like a noose. She doesn't know what to say and when she finally looks back up, she catches my glances, the ones that helped lead her down many rabbit holes, given her lies.

She's now questioning everything, how her normal life got turned upside down.

Rawlings is not a patient man, he waits for his answer, and I can't make the choice for her now. But not all the truth has come out, and it's an explosion waiting to happen.

"If I had known a kid's birthday party was going to land me here, I'd have stayed home with Seamus," she mumbles. She raises her voice to respond to Rawlings. "You know at this point in a movie, the villain reveals his plan, and the hero realizes she fucked up. Do I at least get that?" I can see the itch to reach for a knife, the one in her front pocket.

Rawlings sighs. "I guess I won't beat around the bush, then. We have a common enemy, Ms. Bjorn. I asked Jackson to keep tabs on you, make sure you wouldn't be a problem or nuisance. When you met Jackson and enlisted his help, it just made his job easier. I'm not interested in why you were involved, but I gave him a task: extract information and push people in the right direction."

And there's the explosion, the truth of what it was in the beginning, but not now. But she won't hear or believe that part. Her mind is now overwhelmed with the worst thoughts of being used or lied to, something I wish never happened.

She rubs her temples, "Aggie didn't know what to look for in her reports, so I thought Jackson could help. But you pushed Aggie into pulling them."

"Ah, Ms. Aggie, an angel woman, but in need of a nudge." Rawlings puffs out a ring of smoke.

"What other tasks did you send him on?" she asks. Rawlings looks at her through the smoke. Exactly the answer she needed: her.

"May I remind you that *you* enlisted his help. He's a good VP, very convincing and charming. He got you here after you opened that door and made it easier to get what we want. In more ways than one." He lets out a rumble and a snickering laugh.

"I told him to keep tabs on you, even try to convince you to join us. Accessing your computer was a nice touch. He wiggled his way into that for us. All in all, seems like he did a bang up job getting you to say yes to him. You've seen the evidence so far and I'm guessing there's more to uncover." Rawlings finishes his cigarette.

Fuck.

I forgot about the computer. Another little detail. Once we got the information, Joaquin couldn't stop the security protocols in time and resulted in her being corrected at work. *I'm not a good person.* My own words echo in my head.

She turns her focus to me, begging me that it isn't true. "That was you? You hacked my computer? I thought it was Carla because she was slinking around my office. That day when I had my meetings and you wanted to talk about what you found?" She lunges at him but is stopped by Coda.

"You just gonna sit there like a bastard and not own up to what you did?" she spits out, I can't find my words. "No, I didn't think so. Manipulation from day one."

She turns my attention to Rawlings. "What exactly are you asking me to do? *Sir.*" she starts to ask.

Rawlings snickers, finding some of this funny. "You're right, Jack. Quite the mouth on her." He leans forward, his elbows on the desk. "Simple, gather intel, do some more digging, report back to us. We're trying to get a plan together and need your help." The instructions sound so simple but teaming up with the Grim Wolves feels like the road to hell for her.

A road that I wish she didn't have to travel on.

Rawlings can sense her hesitation, hell I can too. The tightness of her jaw, her solid expression is enough to back away from her.

It's like waiting for the volcano to erupt after the pressure has been building.

Rawlings continues, "Listen, we want this to end just as much as you do. People disappearing, toxic people are leading the city, not good for business. You do good work, and you seem to actually care. We know that your boss, Sheldon, is mixed up with some wrong people. He's working with someone, not completely sure who and how, and by some association, so are you. You want to make people safe again? Help us. It's up to you, but I'd choose wisely."

Her eyes widened at the mention of Sheldon. She didn't know.

Fuck she still doesn't know a lot of things.

She's holding everything in her, like her breath is gone. She's seeing red, blinded by the pure rage that is building in her. Everything in me is wanting to reach out to her and calm her.

I know she won't. She's holding back from releasing all her anger.

Rawlings leans back, continuing to catch her up. "You're a smart lady. Mouthy. Got an attitude. You're a fighter. I wish it didn't have to come to this, but people trust you. You just needed a little push, someone to pull you in without a fight. Don't look too hurt, my dear."

It's hard not to look hurt when hurt is not even the right word.

I hurt her. I backed her into a corner that has no way out. Her eyes are welling up in tears.

"Fine," she bites out, forcing herself to stay and not run. "I'll help, but only because these are my people. I only have one condition."

"I'll entertain it," Rawlings smirks.

"I want in on the planning. These are my people, my community to protect, to help. I can't afford to be left in the dark. I walk if that does not happen. You need my knowledge, my ties, my access," she stands firm in her position.

"Honey, is that a threat?" Rawlings cocks his head at me.

"Don't ask questions you don't want the answer to, Rawlings," I warn him.

"No sir, that's a promise. And I..." she narrows her eyes at me, "keep my promises."

Another blow to my own heart. A point of fact that I didn't keep my promise.

"Deal. But Bjorn -- you get one chance. We call the shots." He extends a hand for her to shake. She reaches out and grips it, signing my life away.

"Your rodeo, your bulls. I'm just the clown. In more ways than one." her eyes burn a hole in me. She lets go of Rawlings' hand and beelines out the door.

I stand up to go after her, not before Rawlings tells me, "Brother, it was good for the club. They'll be another like her. Let it go."

I growl, "There's no one like her. Just because you screw around with anything on two legs and have closed off any chance of love doesn't mean I have to."

I continue to take off after her. I know this is not what she's expecting and for another thing, I had fucked her, claimed her as mine last night.

My hands grab her once I have her in sight. Her body spins bringing her close to my chest. My hands grip her sides, enough to be bruising, leaving marks that will fade over time. She shoves me with enough force that I stagger back, having to find my footing.

I watch her as she reels back and goes to throw a left hook at me. I catch her hand, having to let go of her to do so. The fight in her continues as she tries to front kick me away. I move out of the way as she turns back around to take off. I'm not ready for her to leave without letting me make it right.

I know she's pissed, she has every right. I'm letting her go, I'm not staying away.

She's mine and I'll beg on my knees to prove it.

I lunge to wrap my arms around to try to bring her back to my chest. She lands a strong stomp on my foot. The slight pain in my foot makes me let her go as she takes off again through the main room.

I scream her name. She stops, turning back around slowly. I walk up to her, closing the distance between us. All eyes are now on us, waiting to see who will be the winner.

Her chest heaves from anger and exertion.

"You dirty ass motherfucker. I was starting to trust you. I started to let my guard down. I *felt something*. You fucking used me! I started to think that you wouldn't be that person. Congratulations, you fooled me." she punctuates each statement with a punch to anywhere she could reach.

I take every hit, I fucking deserved for being less of a man and being honest with her. I let club life dictate my every move. I let it take me down the same road as everyone else, choosing between the club and a decent life.

She continues as tears stream down her face. "Do you even understand how many people you put in danger, keeping this from me? I could have helped sooner, I would have understood. But you didn't allow me the fucking chance. And don't get me started on my computer! That's private information, someone's life story. I could have lost my job, Jackson. You manipulated me, and you could have destroyed *lives*."

She shoves me more with each statement. The pain in her voice trembles. She's fighting every ounce from crumbling on the floor. I didn't move, I'll give her the space to express everything.

I lower my voice, staying calm, "The goal wasn't to manipulate you, Teresa. Maybe it started out as a job, but it wasn't like that in the end. You're not an assignment to me."

I just stare at her. She looks like she's ready to tear my eyes out of my head. I keep going now that I have her attention, "I got a taste of you and wanted more. You make me forget about the job, you give me a peek of what a life with you can be, I want that. I saw something different than expected and I made a few mistakes in the end, but I kept pushing the truth from you for my own selfish needs." I inch closer to her.

Her face starts to get redder, ready to explode. "You asshole. You coward. You selfish asshole, thinking only of yourself. You want a life with me, the idea of it, something built on trust. Then boom, the same situation I put myself in last time. Look where my trust got me again: used and abused and fooled."

Everyone starts to tense up around us, not knowing if they need to intervene or not yet.

She hisses out again, "Perhaps you can make good on one promise. Hand me that knife, and I'll put us out of our misery."

I go still, like her words were bullets to my chest.

Gone is her Alexander that started to love. She sees the monster, the one who broke her. She sees me as a parasite sucking the life from her.

I reach out to touch her again, which she smacks away.

"Don't fucking touch me. If I need to talk with someone from now on, I'll talk to Rawlings. I fucking learned my lesson." she shoves me, because that's all she can do to release any kind of emotion. "The choice is clear here. You chose to hurt me, taking orders like a little bitch," she roars.

That last part made people move closer. Standing guard in case blood were to spill.

Her fight made me fall for her even harder. I want to piece everything, every emotion, every scar I made back together. I want to heal her pain.

"Sweet words that turn into tragic lies," she whispers. She starts to walk away from me, searching for my keys.

"Teresa, you know I wouldn't choose to hurt you." My own anger begins to show, but eases back down. "None of this was supposed to happen this way," I let out with a sigh, the truth is too late.

"Well, it did. I know now I'm not making the same mistake three times. I was the fool who didn't see the signs, the quiet, the distractions, the overprotectiveness," she walks further away, pushing through the doors to her car. The gravel crunches under each step.

She's walking away from us. She's not choosing to fight. "You're just going to walk away instead of talking it out?"

She practically chortles. "You had so many chances to talk. I was in an abusive relationship, a relationship that broke me."

And I broke her again.

Everything's coming together. All her anxiety, her questions, her walls. Someone else did this to her.

I raise my voice, "How was I supposed to know? You never told me."

"Don't turn this around on me!"

"I want you. I fucked up yes. But give me the chance to fix this. Stop being fucking stubborn, you feel played, I played you. That didn't stop me from still wanting you, choosing you."

"Choosing me means you hide from me, hide secrets that landed us here," she keeps her voice low, but soft.

I force out, "If you think you can walk away now, you've got another thing coming. You're mine, you belong with me."

She shakes her head, revealing words that she forces out, lies that are bitter, "I was never yours, you asshole! *You* ruined us. You did that all on your own."

I step closer to her, she steps back accordingly. "I'm not going to be a fucking pawn in your games any more. I agreed to help gather information because I care about people, care for a community that is no longer safe. But you? I don't owe you a damn thing. You're just another demon in my way," her words like venom.

She unlocks her car, the sounds of the doors clicking open. I try one more time. My hands reach to her.

"Teresa Saoirse." I raise my voice. She smacks me hard across the face. The sting of her hand radiates across my cheek. But that's not what hurts.

"You don't get to say my name. You lost that right." her voice trembles.

A rush of people come through the doors, watching what had just happened. Everyone's staring now, waiting to see what Jackson will do. "Tell Rawlings I'll be in touch." After that she runs to her car. Fighting her own self to get into the car.

She's not running me, I refuse to let her go.

 "I'm not giving up."

I know she hears me. She knows I'm not going to let her go.

She's mine. I'll give her time. I'll remind her.

For now I'll give her space. I won't be too far from her.

I watch her leave, high tailing it out of the compound. I turn back to the audience, my brothers and their ol ladies. Keola hangs his head. Memphis comes closer, placing a hand on my shoulder.

"I'm sorry, brother," he says. His words feel empty.

"Give her time, man," D.R echoes from behind.

Rawlings shows his traitorous face, stern, hard. "It was time."

Everything in me rages, I charge him, only to be blocked by my brothers. He doesn't move from his place. "You couldn't give me a chance. She didn't fucking deserve this!"

"The club, your family comes first." he warns me, reminding me where my place is.

"I wanted to make her family, introduce her to this life. You fuck it up. Your ancient ass believes it should be done one way. You keep being set in your ways and you'll die alone."

"We have our ways for a reason," Rawlings argues with me.

"Ways can be changed, Rawlings. But you won't allow it." I spit out.

This club is going to suffer from blind loyalty. The club can use some change, only if the Prez allows it.

My brothers shove me back. Memphis stares at me, silently telling me to cool down. I bump into Greer.

"She doesn't leave your sight." I command.

Greer nods, leaving to follow her.

I'm not going anywhere, little cub.

Chapter 25

Teresa

Tears sting my eyes. My heart feels like it's empty, non-existent within my chest. There's a pain in my throat from choking down the tears. He's not worth my tears, but I sure in hell wasn't going to let him see them.

The roads blur as I rush home. Everything around me blanks out. The heat rises in me as I get home, slamming the car door.

My legs start to give out on me, buckling underneath me. I crumble to the ground, the gravel imprints on my skin, indents causing physical pain. That's not the pain that hurts the most.

My tears spill out in a hot stream. A scream that turns into a groan releases.

He'll never get it. The look on his face, I hope he feels the same pain, knowing that he caused this.

I'm the way I am because I finally started to love myself.

I finally let myself feel again.

To know it was all a lie, that I opened up for nothing, is painful, agony.

He only proved my point: when they see me, they see a pawn.

For once, I wish there's no strings attached when they see me. That they would choose me.

I want to crash hard and forget everything. I want to scrub every inch of my body to erase his touch. I get home feeling like an empty shell of myself.

My movements are slow as I make my way through my house, the padding of Seamus' feet following me. I hear a small whine, like he senses my pain. I gather enough energy to get into bed and barricade myself in my covers.

I can hear the ding of my phone as it continues to go off, but I ignore it. I curl myself in a ball, as a darkness cradles me. I try to lull myself to sleep, praying for no dreams.

Days go by in a blink.

I take off from work. I pulled myself together enough to notify work. Sam and Reva attempt to check in with me. I ignore them, needing time to pull myself up again.

The days go by since Jackson's betrayal. The pain still creeps deeper and deeper into my chest with every creeping thought.

I've gone completely off the grid.

Keeping myself alone. Just me and Seamus.

I don't have the energy.

The number of text messages, missed calls, and emails pile up.

It becomes overwhelming.

The only message that haunts me is the one from Jackson: "Don't hide from me, little cub. I won't accept you walking away from me."

He's still holding out hope, and that scares me.

The doorbell rings, breaking me out of my thoughts.

Seamus perks up and walks down the ramp by my bed, spinning at the door, waiting for me to open it.

The longer I hesitate, the more the bell rings and a fist pounds on the door. I run through who it could be in my head.

Sam and Reva would've used the key under the St. Francis statue.

Britt would have busted down my door with no hesitation, and any of the club members would just appear like smoke.

Peeking through the peephole, seeing familiar faces that bring joy to my heart. Before me is Ellie, Seth, and Jordan, patiently waiting for me to unlock the door.

A sigh of relief washes over me. The slightest of happiness spreads knowing it isn't *him*.

Opening the door, I wrap Ellie in a big hug, which Seth just makes bigger. I mess with Jordan's hair as he walks by with a pizza in hand. I smile as we part, a flood of butterflies roll through my stomach.

Everyone heads into the living room, making themselves at home. I lean on the arch way, gawking at the scene of pleasance. Seth looks at me skeptically, surely noting the messy hair and darkened eyes. I plop on my the couch, grabbing a slice of pizza from the box.

"You wanna talk about it?" he asks.

I shrug. "What's there to talk about? I let my guard down, started to trust someone I thought could help and come to find out he was sent to manipulate me. What else can I say?" I ramble out. "And yet, I have a small feeling of empathy for him. He was sent to do a job and he accomplished it. Just didn't care who got hurt"

I get up from the couch and head into the kitchen; they need plates and I need Jack.

Seth isn't buying it. "I heard you let something slip. You neglected to tell him about Aiden and then proceeded to tell him at the wrong moment?"

Aiden. The name I hadn't heard in ages, I left him in the past. The same past where I got broken the first time.

I shake his name away, not giving him the power anymore.

"You're taking his side?"

I look back at him, he shakes his head, "I'm both sides of the devil's advocate. You really think he'd come this far to hurt you. Like it was his plan all along?"

My gut kicks me, Seth may have a point, though it doesn't mean I'm forgiving that quick. He has a point but not enough for me to go running back into Jackson's arms.

I've tried not to replay my words in my head, but I can't help it.

Abused and used may have caused some concern, I won't lie. "It was my story to tell."

I come back to sit back on the couch, stuffing my face and my feelings, while sipping on the jack.

At that moment, Ellie asks me to do her hair, almost like she could sense I needed the distraction. I grab a brush and methodically sweep it through her strands as Seth pipes up.

"Just like you have your story, Tess, he has one too." Seth looks me directly in the eyes as I loop Ellie's hair into braids. "Maybe you need to let him tell you, tell his story, listen to him. I know your heart is broken, but you may not know the whole truth."

I sigh.

Maybe he's right, but my mind shakes it away. Jackson had his chance. He let time move on, dictating what he was going to say or not.

Tears threaten to spill, but I can't cry in front of Ellie and Jordan. I finish with Ellie's hair. I lean into Jordan, squishing him as he plays on his Switch. "Bud, heartbreak sucks."

"I bet it does. It's not a good look on you," he says. I practically snort.

"Then what am I going to do?" He can at least give me some advice if he's going to be an ass.

"What did you do before him?" I give him a puzzled stare.

"Well, you were Tessa before him and you're going to be Tessa after him." I look at him, shell-shocked.

I quickly shoot Britt a text with an idea.

> Time to go short.

Brittany

> I'll get the scissors.

I smile; maybe a little change will spark the fire. I was Tessa before Jackson came into my life, and I'll be Tessa after. The sweet motivation lights a fire under my ass. I'm beginning to be at the next stage of this grieving.

The "fuck 'em" attitude.

Another ding sounds from an unknown number, and I click open the message. A video pops up, and I grow wide with concern. I click play, seeing a video showing Seth and the kids at my door, which opens as I let them in.

Someone's watching me.

It's one thing to be followed by the club, it's another level of stalking.

Unknown

> Wouldn't want anything to happen to little ones. Walk away.

This isn't the club. This isn't some ploy for me to come back from a heartbreak like that.

Someone is following me, watching my every move. My heart races, my breathing quickens. I can't breathe.

I drop my phone, my hands shaking with fear.

"Seth" I whisper out. "Seth!" At this point, the whisper's more like a yell. He strides into the living room, rushing to my side. My hands quake with anxiety

"What is it?" he asks, staring at my hands as he picks up my phone. He searches through the messages and finds the video. He stares at me as I stare back, fear and shock reflected back at me. Words don't do this justice.

"I'm calling it in," Seth says as he walks away with his phone to his ear.

My heart beats in my ears, deafening all sound around me. All the dangers that I was warned about, now here.

I keep wondering why these people think I'm a threat. Does this mean I'm close? I look back over my shoulder as Seth returns

"I take it he knows."

Seth just nods. "Yes."

"Anything else I should know?" I ask, telling myself that I wanted to be in the know.

"You'll have a detail again. Wouldn't be surprised if there's more than one. Rawlings will be in touch."

I grimace. Another guard? Great. "And Jackson? He asked about me, didn't he?"

The only response is a nod. "He's giving you space."

He may say he's giving me space, that won't stop him from actually keeping tabs on me, knowing my every movement. Then again, he told me not to hide. He doesn't sway my thoughts anymore.

My pain is still there, but anger is emerging, ready to fight.

The day comes where I have to return to work. In the midst of all the chaos, Britt made good on her promise.

I walk into work, just like the month May, I have a spring in my step. A new found lightness, that and my hair was gone and I lost around two hundred pounds of dead weight.

Walking into the office after my personal days will be a task. Reva and Sam have been quiet but not distant. I flounce into the building, knowing what lies ahead of me.

There's something to be said when internally you know there are problems, but the fear stops you from telling anyone else.

With all the thoughts of who continually to involve, surprisingly, I feel lighter, poised. Perhaps the lighter feeling is due to my shorter hair brushing against my shoulders, wavy and bouncy.

Reva gawks at me, then her jaw drops suddenly. "Okay, anger and heartbreak looks good on you, boss." I grin back at her. "Before you go in, you have a visitor."

I stop dead in my tracks. Maybe I'm not ready.

My heart drops. Who do I have to deal with now? Or has he come for me? "Will I like this visitor?"

"Well, she flew on her broomstick," Reva whispers.

Oh great. Carla. The witch herself landing in my office. My body fights the urge to cringe and walk the other direction. I don't know how much longer I would be able to keep her away.

Let alone just punch the office bitch.

I straighten my black blazer, holding my head high. Marching into my office, I find Carla sitting in a chair near my desk, legs crossed. She peers at her phone obviously not caring about her surroundings.

I don't have any inkling why she's in here.

Deep breaths.

"Carla. To what do I owe this pleasure?" I let out with a hiss, sitting in my desk chair, adjusting myself.

"I heard through the grapevine, that you'd taken some personal days last week and I wanted to check in and see if you needed anything," she lets out, allowing her accent to pop out.

Is that a hint of sincerity? Or a fake attitude? She's never this nice, let alone offer to help in any capacity but for herself.

"That's considerate of you." the pure shock of the words that fly out of my mouth are unfathomable and foreign. "The stress of it all has come and gone." I continue, though clicking away to get into my schedule for the day and week.

"Well, whatever happened, you look amazing," she gawks and awes in a high pitch, "The hair suits you. Well, I know when I'm not needed. If you need anything, we women have to stick together," she says, pushing herself out my door. Jesus, hell's frozen over.

Talk about a quick hello and goodbye. The whirlwind leaves my sight.

My mind wanders towards thoughts of what to do and who to speak with. With the added information from the past week or so, there's one person I need to speak to.

Jeremiah.

It's been a while. I still sense the need to apologize. Nothing about our last conversation sits right with me. I feel as if I disregarded him, playing him a fool, like he didn't know what he was talking about.

As I dive more into my thoughts, my fingers trail over a stack of papers. When my thumb hits the edge of the stack, my fingers spread through the pages. I start to pull from the spiral of thoughts of Jeremiah and look into the reports.

It looks like Sam and Reva made some notes on them while I was gone. If anything, it looks like an academia paper,

Going through these reports and notes, I feel numb.

I see numbers starting to decline, the faintest data points tell the biggest stories. I can see where the decline started. The numbers showed that the number of calls have decreased in the span of a quarter. Typically, that is the hope, that people are being helped and taken out of a tough situation where they have to choose between a roof over their heads or food in their stomachs.

The question is, when did it become noticeable?

"Boss, you got a call on line one," Reva yells to me, breaking from my focus. The line blinks at me, and I press it, readying myself.

"This is Tessa Bjorn," I answer, leaning back in my chair.

"Bjorn," the devilish gravel voice on the other line rasps.

Not the voice I was expecting, but nevertheless a surprise.

Chills run through my body. "Rawlings. Coming to check in on the clown?"

He laughs lowly, "My dear, you're no clown. Still haven't forgiven the poor boy have you?"

"Is this a social call or do you have something for me?" I snark, refraining from rolling my eyes at his comment.

"Straight to the point or still pissed." his cheekiness echoes through the phone.

"You tell me," I hiss, growing even more irritated than when I answered.

"You'll forgive him, he's determined."

"Rawlings, this is my last warning. You're not calling to get me to take him back. What. Do. You. Want," with one last warning, he relinquishes a heavy sigh.

I see Reva slinking in to hear the conversation, her eagerness to bear witness to this exchange is also entertaining.

"Mm, I can see why he's so captivated by you. The challenge and the threats. No wonder he took you to the woods." Heat rises to my cheeks. Reva mouths "the woods" and I hold up a hand to her.

I refuse to explain *that* one.

"Past tense, my friend, no longer," I grit out. "Okay, I'm bored and I'm hanging up."

"Next Friday." Two words is all he says.

"What about next Friday, Rawlings?" I ask.

"You're going on a field trip. Someone told me that you needed evidence for that drive of yours. We have a lead on who may be behind everything, but perhaps you may be able to give us your perspective." he says.

Rawlings can be convincing, of course when he wants something. He's a man of his word though.

Maybe there *is* some loyalty to people outside of the club.

I don't jump on his offer. "I work until 5 on Fridays. I'll be free after."

There's a snicker at the end of the line, it's almost like a growl.

"Cute you think you have a choice. You're going regardless," he says.

"One condition." I say before he has the chance to hang up on me.

I can practically hear the eye roll on the other end of the line. "I'll entertain it, Bjorn."

I don't let him get to me. "No Jackson. I told him my dealings are with you and you only."

"No guarantees." The pure ignorance of this man. If I wasn't afraid of the consequences of it, I'd smack him across his cocky smiling face.

I just laugh. "I'll walk. You can forget about my expertise, and I'll do this on my own. And if I do it on my own, if I get hurt, your precious vice president will kill you on the spot for not listening." I grin.

They need me just as much as I need them. He grumbles at the end of the phone.

Checkmate, Rawlings.

"Stubborn ass woman."

"Damn right." I hang up the phone before he has the chance to say anything else. I'm not going to ignore that Jackson is probably still getting reports of my comings and goings, but walking back into my life will take copious amounts of groveling and begging.

If you're even willing to give him a chance.

"Your thoughts are speaking very loudly, boss." Reva glances at me, knowing that if I don't answer, Sam will pry too.

"Just a lot of what ifs," I say as I sit again.

Reva doesn't let me get away with my pitiful explanation. "Let's rephrase that. They're not scenarios because that means you're entertaining the possibility. Your what ifs are just the spiraling part of you itching to come out." She shrugs, as if this is normal information for her.

"You been in my therapist's notes or something?" I kid with her, knowing that would be something my therapist would say.

"I don't want to talk about your therapist. I want to know about the woods." Reva wiggles her eyebrows at me.

I shake my head. "Not exactly something I want to relive right now. Are we ready for the shelter visit? I know if we don't leave now, I'm going to be late." Reva pops up, getting ready to leave.

I watch her gather her things as I wander, do I want to forgive him?

The agony of waiting for this dreadful field trip is going upon us. I just need to get through the last couple of days. Although Jackson's attempts to reach out to me have me wondering if I should block him, his words echo in my mind.

I see something I want, and I won't stop until it's mine.

I'm not giving up on us.

His touches still linger, no matter how hard I scrub at my skin.

The ghost touches of the last night we spent with each other.

The ache on my arm where he wrapped my gunshot wound. I miss the person he was in the beginning. He was sweet, caring, attentive, and mostly felt like a piece of me was complete.

That was before he fucked it up with hatred and hurt.

I have to get my mind off of Jackson. I need to get through the day focus on what I know and what I see in front of me.

Sam had separated the call records yesterday and found another can of worms. Sam, with her nose of a bloodhound, found that the tiny decreases have gone back an entire year.

What's more intriguing and concerning is that, when separated out by gender, women have decreased at a higher rate. My questions keep growing and the answers aren't there. I start to think of seeing Aggie tomorrow at the center, just to run everything by her again. Surely she knows more about what's going on since the last time we saw each other.

I make my final notes for the night and realize the sun has well set, and darkness has spread across the sky. We have the proof of the trend, but the physical evidence is lacking. Maybe I can't completely Nancy Drew this, but I'm close.

My cell phone starts to ring unexpectedly. "Aggie, I was just thinking about you," I smile.

"Child, you need to get to Memorial," she says with haste, having no time to give detail.

"Wait, Aggie, are you okay? What happened? Who's hurt?" Fear washes over me, leaving no breathing room.

"It's Jeremiah. I'll explain when you get here. Second floor, east wing." She hangs up and like lightning, I'm gone in a flash.

I race to the parking lot, spotting a black truck under the streetlamp. I rush over, knocking on the window frantically. I must have startled someone because I can hear the curses. The window rolls down: Keola's on duty tonight.

"Jesus, you know how to sneak up on someone." He shakes his head. Apparently, this man's oblivious. Not a great trait for a tail.

"Keola, I don't have time for the quick snarks. You're following me to Memorial Hospital. Something happened to Jeremiah," I yell as I sprint to my car.

At this point, all notions of a normal reason for being in the hospital fly out of my head. Did Jeremiah not heed my warning? I hope this is just a false alarm, that he's completely fine. Damn speed limits and traffic.

Arriving at the hospital is a blur. I don't remember where I parked, and frankly, I don't care. Keola's in tow as I make my way down the hospital halls, quickly on my heels. I frantically press the elevator button, but nothing's coming. I bolt towards the stairs to the second floor. The stomping of footsteps behind me gives off a pounding echo.

"Fucking hell. If I'd known we were doing cardio, I'd have prepared myself," Keola lets out, breathless.

"Oh grumpy, always be prepared to run." One of my golden social work rules.

I slam open the door to the second floor, scaring every doctor and nurse in my path. As I get closer to the east wing, my intrusive thoughts start peaking. I pause for a brief moment, realizing what the east wing is.

Bold letters scream at me: *Intensive Care Unit.* The threat of tears sting my eyes.

I reach the nurses station, sucking in gulping breaths, asking for his room.

"Ma'am, you have to be on the approved list," the nurse tells me.

I don't bother with formalities or kindness. "I was called by Aggie Williams. She should be the emergency contact."

The nurse gives me a sad but firm look. "I cannot confirm that, ma'am. I cannot divulge any information at this time."

I almost crumpled to the floor, my fists closing tightly enough where fingernail imprints bare into my skin, and I feel a pair of arms catch me, pinning one of my arms to keep me steady. "Mm, dead man walking," I hiss.

"Ma'am I'm officer Johnson, Ms. Bjorn had received a call from Ms. Williams regarding their friend." Keola's tone changes, changing from grouchy troll to respectable authoritative.

I peak over my shoulder, throwing him a cocked eyebrow, trying to say, "Officer?"

The nurse throws her hands on her hips, tossing them to the side, "Were you a part of the scene?"

There was a scene? My heart races.

"I was not, but my squad let me know. I was already with Ms. Bjorn at the time. Look sweetheart, she is just here for her friend, Jeremiah. If it makes you feel better, I'll be in the room with her." he works the room.

I'll give it to Keola, he knows what to say.

I shake out of his grip, plastering a fake smile to the nurse as she thinks of Keola's proposal. Without her looking, I retaliate by reaching behind my back to smack him, which he catches.

He leans down to my ear to where I can only hear him, "Either you control yourself, or I'm going to handcuff you, toss you back in the truck, and hand you off to Jackson."

I lower my head, keeping my voice low. "You wouldn't dare," I growl.

I turn to see him quirks an eyebrow. "Try me."

He lets go of me and I rub my wrist. The nurse whips her head back in our direction. Her intense eyes are frightening.

"Fine, but under supervision," she wags a finger at me like a toddler.

Before I can make my way in the direction they're sending us, a hand meets my shoulder and turns me around. Aggie, with irritated red eyes and wet cheeks, pulls me into a fierce hug. I can hear Aggie speaking with the nurse, but I don't register the conversation. Probably giving me more credit for being here.

All I know is that I'm being pulled further down the hall, the sound of the bustle of the hospital sends chills down my spine. Welcoming a fear that didn't get an invitation. I turn back to see Keola wasn't following me but on the phone. Aggie ushers me into Jeremiah's room..

The beeps are high pitched, screeching in my ears. All the air seems to have been sucked out of the room. Jeremiah lies on the bed still, no movement. Wires poke out everywhere, the beeping of the heart monitor telling me he's still with me.

My heart beats slowly, to the point of questioning whether I'll be seeing heaven soon. There are tubes in his throat, his face almost unrecognizable, eyes black and blue against his aged dark skin, possibly swollen shut. How I wish I could see those dark caring eyes staring down at me again. His left leg is lifted above him for elevation, pins peeking out from the blankets.

I grab his hand, holding it close to my chest. Tears spill down my cheek. Everything's hazy, my vision gone, my body numb. I sink down to my knees, holding his hand. Guilt, disappointment, it all rushes at me at once, and I sob lightly. "I'm sorry, my friend. Please, come back to me. Please." I repeat the apology over and over. He doesn't deserve this. A hand meets my shoulder, stirring me back into the present.

"This is my fault. I didn't listen. I wasn't there." My voice cracks with every word.

"Child, you know there isn't anything that man could be talked out of, not if he really wanted to do it," Aggie says, rubbing my shoulders. Tears continue to roll down my face; I can't stop thinking about what could have happened to him.

"What happened, Aggie?" I ask again with grit in my voice. Anger rolls through my veins.

Aggie sighs and sits in one of the chairs across his bed.

I can sense the heaviness in her heart.

"Jeremiah called and said he was following the white van. Said that he wasn't wasting time again, waiting on people who didn't care. I told him to wait for me, but he didn't. I know he left the garage after he called me. Child, he must have found something, because he left a voicemail. I didn't listen to it; I figured you'd want to listen as well."

I choose to wait on that for a more important question. "Aggie, how did you find him?"

The long pause doesn't bring me comfort. "I was walking out of the center and he... he was laying there. Motionless, blood everywhere. His face was contorted and starting to swell. Tessa, he was dumped, like no one cared. I called the ambulance. Thankfully, I'm an emergency contact, and they allowed me in. That's when I called you."

Pain and guilt radiate through my body. "I'm not leaving until I know he's safe."

A light bulb flits on in my mind and I reach for my phone. Instant regret hits my blood. I'm certainly asking for a one way ticket to hell.

"Little cub." My heart sinks, the wounds bursting back open at the breathless way he calls to me.

"Jackson."

He doesn't wait for me to say anything more, "I know. Someone's coming up there to watch out for him. Johnny will be there soon. Figured you'd want someone you know. Perhaps even trust."

He's always two steps ahead of me, has me figured out. Yet, he couldn't see or figure anything else out. I don't know what to say anymore. Silence takes over again.

"Teresa. I know I hurt.." he breaks, "I'm sorry."

I don't let him finish any more thoughts. "Thank you, Jackson." I hang up the phone, choking back tears.

Aggie soothes me, placing her hand on my shoulder once again. In her hand is Jeremiah's phone. I know and she knows that it should be in the hands of the authority. In this moment where I'd want to follow rules, for once I'm happy the rule book is out the window.

"You want to listen, honey?" Aggie's voice sounds to me from the other side of Jeremiah's bed. I nod my head, closing the distance between us.

"Keola, get your ass in here," I yell out to the hallway.

Keola walks in with eyebrows furled, mumbling something. "You hollered?"

"Listen to this with us and give it to Rawlings. I don't care much to check in with him, but I'm a trusted member." He nods and eases up. Maybe I *am* melting away the hard exterior. "Go ahead, Aggie."

Aggie presses play and I almost tear up at Jeremiah's voice on the recording.

*Aggie I told you. I was right. Listen, get people here to the southside of the tracks. They're poaching like these people are animals. I can't see much, but I see birds on their jackets. Jesus, they are rough. I think I can get a closer look. I told Ms. Tessa I'd get proof. Then she can get away from them wolves. Wait, there's the camera, one second. *click* See, got it. They roundin' folks up into that white van. Wait, hold on. *inaudible noises* Shit, they must've seen a flash, they comin' at me. Aggie, get her and tell her. Hey, hold up, what you doin'? *crackle and mumbles.**

"Bastard was doing cover work for you?" Keola peers down at me.

I punch his shoulder in anger.

I shake my head vigorously. "Watch your mouth about him! No! I just told him to keep his ears down, to let me know if he heard anything. I told him to let the police know."

"Child, you know he's determined," Aggie says, patting my hand.

"And stubborn," I mumble under my breath. "Aggie, I pushed him off as if it was another rumor. I told him he could trust me. Look where that got him."

"Stop trying to blame yourself. We don't know what's other there. We have enough battles in our lives that we can be blind to other dangers. There's a threat here, and I don't know what we need to do." Aggie slumps over, looking defeated. I crouch down to her, taking her hand in mine.

I look at Keola, a questioning look on my face that I know he'll understand. "Might as well start somewhere. At this point, we need all the help we can get."

I take a deep breath before peering up at Aggie. "Aggie, I need to explain some things to you, and it's a good thing you're sitting down."

I tell Aggie everything, from the moment Jackson entered my life, to the computer virus, to the reports Sam and Reva ran, to the moment I made a deal with Rawlings himself. Aggie deserves to know the truth.

"I understand. What do you need from me?" she says. No expression of anger, confusion, or even shock.

I'm shocked, fully expecting a bit more shock or horror on her face, but Aggie cares for Jeremiah. Perhaps not in the way he'd like, but she tends to put herself last compared to others.

"Right now, continue on like you don't know anything but keep your eyes and ears open," I say simply. I don't need another person in a hospital bed or the morgue.

Aggie nods. "There's one thing I can't get over, child. In his message, he said birds." Aggie ponders the thought. "It's a weird detail."

Keola avoids eye contact.

Fucker knows something.

I see red, but I force myself to take deep breaths to calm down a bit. "Keola. I swear, if you're withholding information, I will beat your ass so badly, you'll be the next person laying in a hospital bed." I get up and yank his cut, gripping with fire in my hands.

He sighs. "You'll understand more tomorrow." He grabs my wrist and pries my hands off.

I just roll my eyes. "Your boss is turning into a thorn in my side, buddy."

"You gave him the rose," he shrugs.

"The fuck does that mean?" I shake my head. I'm not in the mood for cryptic messages right now.

"I don't fucking know, not all of us are as good at comebacks as you," he mumbles and returns to the hallway. I just shake my head. It's a weird way of commenting.

I look at Jeremiah laying in the bed. I have a million questions, and a million unanswered prayers. I walk over and place my forehead on his.

"Siochan leat." *Peace be with you.*

Chapter 26

Teresa

The following day rolls in and I'm no closer to calming my nerves.

Aggie reassured me that everything is fine at the hospital. There's been no change in Jeremiah. She mentioned that Johnny's still there, watching over him, which sets me a little at ease. Johnny is a good man from the few times I've spoken with him. He's also the only one from the club not silently judging me for exploding on Jackson or begging me to take him back. He doesn't look at me like I'm weak, like I'd go crawling back to Jackson if given the chance.

I stand outside the agency, not so patiently I might add.

I can hold my temper, I can hold my tongue when the time calls for it.

I keep glancing at my phone checking between the time and any missed messages. Before I can make the decision to leave and forget it, I hear the purr of a large black truck pulling up to the curve.

I can't see through the tint, not until the passenger window rolls down, and I thank the heavens it's Sparky.

His ginger locks catch the light from the interior. A sense of relief waves through me.

"It's about damn time," I bellow, tossing my hips to side, "Thank fuck, it's you. Guess your boss finally listened," I say as I lift myself up to the passenger side and buckle myself in. It's not long before we are zooming through the highways, particularly dodging through cars.

Sparky speeds through the street to the highway, like a man on a mission.

"Remember when you said that you thought that he listened," Sparky comments as he drives, keeping his focus on the road.

"What do you mean?" I raise an eyebrow at him. I've been good. Other than the call at the hospital, I haven't thought about Jackson as much. I'm starting to accept fate and move on, but maybe I've spoken too soon -- something stirs in the back of the truck.

"He means, he's going to pull over and I'm driving," a haunting voice says. One that somehow still held power over me.

A chill rushes through my body, a spine tingling one. I keep staring straight out the window, not wanting to look into Jackson's eyes. The truck starts to veer over onto the side of the road. This is my moment to start to plot my escape route.

I could walk on the highway, maybe hitch a ride. And possibly get murdered along the way. Which wouldn't be a far consequence if I stayed.

We park on the shoulder while Greer and Jackson swap seats. I quickly unbuckle my seatbelt and grab the door handle. I can't open it. I continuously pull on it.

Fuck.

Plan B, initiate. I go to move into the driver seat but I'm met with arctic blue eyes of the man destined to break me into pieces again.

"Going somewhere, little cub?"

Words, you idiot. Say something. Anything.

I'm speechless, shaking my head like a loose bobblehead.

"Then I suggest you crawl back into that seat like a good girl and buckle up," he commands, growling as he does.

My pussy throbs at his praise. It hasn't been that long, but it feels like a lifetime.

Fuck. Down, girl.

Jackson sits down, slamming the door, pulling back into traffic. His tense features unfortunately make him intoxicating.

I comply with his demands, staying put like a good girl, not arguing with him. His face just makes me infuriated, his sense of command is demeaning, yet it calls to me.

He eases into driving, making confused on the path we are taking. I keep looking at the window watching the city lights fade and country mountain roads are welcome. I stay quiet, but not for long. Jackson snakes his hand onto my thigh, caressing it creating goosebumps under his fingertips. I shiver with a slight ache.

Bad Tessa.

I slap it away. "Do you mind?" I let out.

"I do when you're sitting next to me, aching for a chance at my touch," he responds, the cat-like grin on his face. He tries to get back onto my thigh.

"I've made myself perfectly clear, I don't want you touching me," I bite back. I remind myself I have a singular mission, to avenge Jeremiah and protect my community.

"I've made myself perfectly clear, too. I'm not giving up. You are mine," There's seriousness in this voice. My mind wanders back to that day, when I thought I heard him say that exact sentiment. I thought it was my mind playing tricks, hoping that the villain was really a hero.

"Jackson, just let me go, easier to let go of something that wasn't real. I have," The lies taste like vinegar. I don't know why I think they were lies. I keep telling myself it's over, when obviously the truth overpowers everything.

"Darlin', you can keep lying to yourself, but I won't." He places his hand back on my thigh and I tense up.

This is nothing; this means nothing to me.

"Too late for that," I mumble under my breath, resulting in a squeeze of my thigh. A snicker comes from the back.

Little traitor.

"You know, you're on my shit list, Sparky." I glance behind me, glaring at Greer, as he pushes his long spring red hair out of his eyes.

He spots mid track. "Do you mind telling me where we're going? I need to know if I should text Britt about planning my funeral."

He just shrugs. "You'll see when we get there."

Great.

"Where we're going, do I need to update my will or something? Or will death just allow me to get away from you," I sneer out.

"Darlin', not even death would stop me. I'd follow you and bring you back."

I roll my eyes at Jackson's intrusion. "Funny, heaven doesn't allow demons."

"Even Lucifer was an angel once." He smirks at me.

Smug bastard.

It's a long car ride, but I see signs for Wilmington.

I haven't been there in a long time other than to visit and do some shopping with the girls. There's something that Wilmington also houses, something or somewhere I would never think to think about.

Darkness is broken by lights as we enter through a massive gate, crowned with barbed wires and a blockade of postings, signs reading *danger, hazard.* All that's missing is "I'd turn back if I was you."

Jackson parks the truck once we're next to the fence. He takes a moment to just stare at me as I get my seatbelt off. His gaze is something you can't resist. He captures you, tells you everything without uttering a word. Those eyes that could make you feel like everything was right in the word. He gives a nod to get out the truck, not before he turns to Sparky in the back saying, "Greer, stay here. If anything happens you know what you need to do."

Greer nods and pats his hip, which I imagine is holstering his weapon. He switches places with Jackson, before Jackson can make it beside me. His striking warmth is alarming.

Jackson turns to me. "Darlin', follow behind me, and if you run," he starts, licking his lips. "Well, you know I don't mind the chase."

I shove past him. "Never again."

He chuckles darkly. "Never say never, always up for a challenge."

"Whatever gets you off at night." I walk towards the fence, watching as Jackson pops the lock and gestures to me to move along.

We're greeted by shipping containers of various colors, stacked higher than some buildings. The rows and rows of them swallow us like we're ants. A maze of steel and metal weaves around every corner. Nothing but the glowing lights from the work lights that surround the area. They attempt to illuminate the darkest corners. It's not until I feel a brush of his hand guiding me that pulls me from my thoughts, his hands playing with the tips of my hair.

"Mm, you cut your hair?"

"Wow, you're observant," I scoff.

"I mean, there's still something to grab onto." He teases, twirling a piece around his finger. A rush of warm spreads to my cheeks.

Damnit, Jackson. Stop making me blush.

I make a quick comeback, shutting down any possibility of flirtation, "Damn. I should have shaved it," I retort. I'm glad the darkness of the sky has taken over and only the work lights are on or else he would have seen the true color of my cheeks, hot red.

My feet seem to take me without hesitation, even not knowing where I'm heading, but I guess I'll find out when I get there.

Suddenly, I'm yanked backwards and spun to meet his eyes. He tilts my chin, meeting his expressions, "We're here for a purpose, but don't think that just because you're pissed at me, your ass isn't mine. The urge to bend you over a container and spanking your ass redder than a Christmas light is very strong. That mouth of yours is going to get you in more trouble than you'd like."

He bends closer to my face. "I seem to remember someone loving that *particular* form of punishment."

"Can't have someone if they were never yours," I say, testing his patience.

I blush redder than a sinner in church. I look into his eyes, searching for a glimmer of a joke, but I find none. He still believes I'll come crawling back to him. While my body betrays me under his touch, my mind is screaming to get away.

Jackson's intensity grows, his chest heaving with anger. His face is sharp with intent, a light stubble covering his chin. I want to touch it, feel it scratch my hand.

I'm taken by surprise when his lips slam hard against mine. It's needy, animalistic, it's heavenly fire. I could easily get lost in it, though the withering pain of the past few weeks overpowers me.

No. I'm stronger than this.

Anger bubbles as I bite his lip tasting the sticky coppery tang of his blood. To my surprise he doesn't jump at the shock, but rather accepts. He pulls back, scanning my face.

"Mm, my little cub turned into a wild cub," he says, grabbing his lip. "Not many people can make me bleed."

"Consider that your warning. Stop playing around like I'm some toy. Just take me to where we need to go," I sneer back.

"Yes ma'am," he continues, leading the way into a nearby building. I don't know what it's called, but it looks like an empty hanger bay, like the ones my uncle used to work in during his Navy days. We move closer, but before we step inside, Jackson pulls me aside.

The man is extra grabby tonight. Like he's finding every excuse to be able to touch me.

"You need to stay absolutely quiet. Do not, under any circumstances, try to stop what you're about to see. I would rather you live than be covered in bullet holes."

I jerk back at his harsh words. "And what is it that I'm about to see?" I question, crossing my arms.

He doesn't hesitate to answer this time. "Proof that we're not your enemies and who we believe is behind all of your problems. The people behind harming Jeremiah and many others. It's the proof you need."

He doesn't wait for my gaping mouth to snap shut, or for an answer. Instead, he leads the way into the building. The closer we get, the more voices I hear, and I pick up on the voices, sounding familiar from Jeremiah's video. I can't fully prove it or be able to pull someone from a line up. But the bass in their voice, the aggressiveness leads me to the truth.

The further we go, the closer the voices become. Jackson presses up against a shipping container, and I notice he's packing some heat.

Maybe I should learn how to shoot.

I shake my head damn squirrel thought.

Focus, Bjorn.

I focus on the voices, and peer around the corner. Three men huddle around each other, all wearing the same cut. I notice the emblem, a falcon clutching a human skull. Are these the club's rivals? What do they have to do with the disappearances?

I look back at Jackson.

"Keep looking, Teresa," he murmurs in my ear.

I turn back and try to focus on their conversation, regretting that I don't have a solid grip on the language. I hear car engines start, headlights shining into the building. The revving of the engines signal the men to stop.

White vans. The shock of the truth is soul shattering.

Jeremiah. I'm so sorry for not believing in you sooner.

The tiniest details are starting to make sense, to become real. It's not a game anymore.

The vans halt and I want to look closer, but Jackson grips me not to move.

A man steps out, his head shaved, a black bandana wrapped around it. He's dressed in the same cut and dirty jeans as the rest of the men. Tattoos pepper his forehead and the corner of his eye. Something about him feels familiar, but my mind draws a blank. The slamming of doors makes me wince. My heart's racing out of my chest.

Bandana man lights a cigarette, taking a small drag as he approaches the group. I can make out a word or two of their conversation, something about money, people, and maybe bitches, but it's been a while.

"Any more demands, boss?" one of the men asks Bandana.

"Nah, same old same old from the bitch herself." Bandana takes another drag of his cigarette. The feeling of uneasiness creeps up my chest.

He snaps his fingers, grabbing the attention of his other people, "Ready to move these people? That idiot from that night cannot happen again," Bandana announces.

I jerk away from Jackson. These assholes were the ones who hurt Jeremiah, harming a man that would give you his shirt off his back. The thought of charging at them, giving justice to Jeremiah and the many people before him that they have done God knows what to them, is silently shaken off when Jackson pulls me back.

"You can't. Not right now, there's nothing we can do right this moment. You'll get another chance, little cub, I promise," Jackson whispers in my ear.

The little distraction almost makes me miss their next move. The vans reverse further into the hanger bay. The men crowd around the back, swinging the doors open to reveal dozens of people, all knocked out cold.

"Dose'em again, and we'll start shipping them out. Remember what happened last time." Bandana shoves a guy on the shoulder.

"Yeah, but she was a scrapper. She was fun, unlike your ex, Benedict," the man laughs. *Benedict.* Bells ring in my head.

Benedict, Benny, the fucker who abused Lucie for years.

Fuck, the Falcons.

"You gotta be shitting me," I whisper.

I can feel Jackson's movements, turning to see him nod. He knows that I know.

Seriously, how the hell did I get trapped into this? Everything knocks together to finally make sense.

The Falcons. I knew all too well what they did to women like Lucie. The Falcons deal heavily in human trafficking and drugs. But why keep it a secret that the Falcons are apart of this? Why go to lengthy measures? Did they think I wouldn't believe them and their accusation if they knew that I have historical hatred for them.

These are the people that Rawlings was talking about that Sheldon has gotten mixed up with. My heart sinks in my chest. A well of tears threaten to shed, how much of this goes back to the foundation? How long have I been a puppet with invisible strings?

The ache and heaviness of my heart wearies me.

All I can think about is how I have to save the people in the vans. I notice a few vials of what I assume are drugs to knock out their victims before transport. I calculate plans in my head, running through every scenario I can think of. I may be impulsive, but I have my reasons. I don't need permission. I just need a good cover.

"Jackson, do you trust me?" I peer into his eyes. His eyes grow wide with concern, unable to answer. He's not stupid, he knows what I'm about to do.

"Go outside and shoot off some rounds into the air." I give him the simplest of instructions. "Then run, and I'll meet you there."

Jackson starts to protest but I loosen myself out of his grip and scoot closer to the edge of our hiding spot, still in the shadows, waiting for him to comply with my orders.

I keep my eyes on vans; I'm not going down without a fight. The voices get louder as I get closer, waiting for my chance. Jackson must have given in, because the next thing I know, gunfire rings outside the bay and the Falcons scatter like ants showered with water. They race outside toward the sounds, and I quickly snatch up the vials before sprinting for the exit.

But not before I open the van doors, looking at the scared individuals, their eyes pleading for help. A few men and women fighting for their lives. "Go," I quickly say, "hide, get to safety please."

I start to take off with prayer for their safety and freedom and the vials in my hand.

If they don't have the vials, they can't give the innocents, and if they don't have people, they can't harm anyone any more than they already have.

Although I would have wished the Falcons were a little bit dumber, they might have caught very quickly. My feet pick up speed as voices come hunt me down as their prey is on the way.

Angry voices, practically spitting out insults and threats at this point, reach my ears. My heart's beating in my throat; I'm only a few feet from the maze of shipping containers.

Thank goodness for my memory and sense of direction, because I hear gunfire ricocheting off the containers as I slip into the maze. The sparks sizzling as they miss me, zipping through the air.

I'm dodging and weaving at every turn to get back to the truck. I don't know where Jackson is, but he's done his job and he's not my problem anymore.

Quit lying to yourself, Bjorn. You are not a job to him anymore and you ain't over him yet.

I see the truck and fencing, the roar of gunfire still trailing behind me, but the truck lights blind me. I raise my hand to block the blistering light, and see two figures at the doors of the truck, firing back.

Jackson must have made it back before me. I get closer and closer to the truck, heart still racing, pounding in my chest, when I feel something ping me in the shoulder. The harsh sting and the pounding of aching flesh tell me one thing, I've been shot. *Again.* I keep going, I refuse to come this far to be stopped by a bullet.

I gather enough adrenaline to move past the fence and jump into the back seat of the truck. "Jackson, motherfucker drive!" I yell out, letting them know I've made it out.

The pain in my shoulder radiates through me. They fire off a few last rounds before Jackson quickly puts the truck in reverse and guns it out through the gate. We make it quickly onto the highway, and I swear, my heart isn't going to make it.

The truck rumbles under me as we speed away from the chaos. Thirty minutes on the road and I can't take it anymore. How I have made this far before a rush of screams is behind me.

I lay down on my back with my head resting on the bottom of the window. Pain shoots up my arm and down my back with every bump and hole we hit. I lay down in the backseat, trying my hardest not to pass out again.

I don't know if they realize I was shot, but I can't take anymore bumps or jolts to the shoulder. It's like Jackson purposefully hits them.

"Jesus Christ, can you avoid the potholes? Some of us may be injured back here," I yell from the back. That got his attention.

Chapter 27

Alexander

"Jesus Christ, can you avoid the potholes? Some of us may be injured back here," she yells from the back. The moment those words leave her lips, I slam on the brakes. I attempt to get the truck pulled over to the shoulder. As soon as the truck comes to a stop, I park the truck, leaving it to run. The amount of horns echoing as cars pass us.

We don't have a tail. They didn't follow us, but it won't take them long before they pull everything together.

My mind sees red, we have been on this road for a long while and now she says something. She infuriates me, the pure stubbornness.

Though I can't help but feel a sense of guilt. Putting her in this situation and now she's harmed again.

I fling the back door open in a flash, her head hanging along the opening of the door. A spill of her now cropped hair fans out. Her face twists, the pain radiating along her face.

"Can I help you, ya big oaf?" she bends her head back to look at me, "I would get up, but I'm coming down from an adrenaline high and I'm pretty sure I'm going to need some pain meds."

I take her head and lift it to make her sit up even more, her back still facing me. She winces at the movement as it jostles her left shoulder. I pull down her shirt, revealing a nasty wound. Her shoulder bleeds, enough to cover my hand. In the pale highway light, I can see the dark red spreading across my palm.

Her breathing becomes heavier, "I'd make a joke right now, but I don't think it's a great time," she softly laughs.

"Why didn't you say anything?" I growl out, reaching for something to press on her wound. She'll hate me for the pressure, the ache and pain sprawling across her back side.

She shrugs her usable shoulder, wincing when that, too, smacks pain down her side. "I'm sorry, I didn't think it was a good time, as we were all attempting to *survive*. I figured you saw and was making me live with the consequence of my actions," she retorts.

As if I could punish her. More like I punish my own self for allowing her to think I would hurt her anymore than I may have already done.

"Greer, get us back to the fucking compound, D.R. is going to hate this, again." I bark out orders. In a flash the man is already, pulling at high speed into highway traffic. The darkness chases us.

I hold her, it isn't my dick that suffers, it's my heart. Her pain is my pain.

"Just hang in there, darlin'. You think you can listen to me for once?"

She groans in response, her back sinking into me, like one whole person.

I adjust her shirt, as the temptation still eludes me. My forehead rests on the top of her head. She deeply sighs, as I join her. Her ragged breath chips away at my already broken heart. All I want to do is cradle her, take every ounce of her physical and emotional pain and ease it away. Maybe this was my true punishment, the true consequences of my own actions.

I want her to come back to me. Come back to loving me.

My heart starts to ache in my chest, realizing that maybe this was my true consequence. I'm fighting every fiber of my being begging me to cling to him, to forgive him. I beat off the temptation; it's not so easy to forgive deep seated pain.

She tries to wiggle from my grasp.

"Lean into me. I know you hate me, Teresa, but I can't afford to lose you now," I say softly into her ear.

"Alright, Viking, explain what's going on. What aren't I seeing?" she asks me, the sentence coming in shallow breaths. Too much movement for a gunshot wound. If she's looking for a distraction, I don't know if this is the right time for this.

"I don't think now is the right time," I try to say, but she cuts me off.

"Spare me the crap." *Breathe.* "Talk. If anything, distract me from the pain of a bullet lodged in my shoulder."

I can't help but smirk, "Hm, I have an idea to distract you, and you won't be able to hit me."

She pauses. "You and your damn charm," she responds. "Now, talk."

"I liked you better last time you were hurt, passed out on my couch, looking like a fallen angel. At least I wouldn't hear you running your mouth," I grumble.

She doesn't like my joke as she leans further back to squish against the door. It's adorable she thinks that it would hurt. Her eyes cut to me, glaring at me, sharp and stern.

I give in. Sometimes she makes it so damn easy to fall at her feet.

"Fine." I begin. "We've known for a while that the Falcons have been up to something. We just didn't know what. Normally, it's just the normal territorial disputes, over shipments and businesses. It wasn't until the birthday party that we had any inkling of what they're up to. There were whispers from our partners of them trafficking women and using men as sellers in other cities or handlers. We needed an inside person, someone that would benefit us, it seemed odd that the people seemed random. That was until Joaquin found a pattern, they were homeless, beaten and battered. When you were at the party, Seth and Matthew told me about you, and when Rawlings found out, well you know the ending." She eases into me, her body sinking with the truth. Something she deserved a while back.

I continue as the story unfolds, I start to count the minutes until we reach the compound, until she can get the help.

"Joaquin did some digging and with the hints from Jeremiah, we made the connection. When we found the shipping port, Rawlings figured you needed to see more of the inside, so that's why you were there tonight."

"Okay."

One word, that's all she says to that. It can't be that easy for her to give in, to not ask questions.

I want to see all the gears turn in her beautiful mind. The truth is intertwining the questions that were already going on in her mind. There's part of me wondering if this is a relief for her.

To know that we weren't lying, though we're greedy in wanting our territory back in downtown, but we would never do this. No matter what people may whisper.

We suddenly hit a pothole, and she takes another sharp breath. It turns into a hiss. I get worried that she's not going to last longer.

"Greer, how much fucking longer?" desperation seeps into my voice.

"Fifteen minutes, give or take." he says.

Fucking hell.

Please hold on, darlin'.

My hands start to stroke her hair, easing her into a light trance. I try to have her relax, after another hit from a pothole, I can't see from where we're at in the back. My hope is that the bleeding stopped or is under control.

But her body goes from at ease to almost lifeless. What is supposed to be a trance seems to make her fall asleep. I just don't know if it's the kind you wake up from. I shake her good shoulder.

"Come on. Keep those pretty eyes open, little cub."

Her head lulls to the side, relinquishing a small moan. There's still some fight in her.

"Stop calling me that, Jackson," her voice is so quiet.

"Don't think so. You're already mine. You can't escape," I rumble softly, my words vibrating against her back.

She starts to say something, every inch of strength leaving her, "Jackson, you have to stop." Her body shivers, "I meant when I said. You hurt me, betrayed my trust." There's a choked back sob trembling from her, "I felt manipulated, used. But I have to let it go, and in the end let you go."

No, you won't.

"I don't want to. There's part of my heart that still calls to you. I need to forgive you." she continues to tremble out.

I try to shush her, with the possible amount of blood loss, I don't know if this is her final goodbye, "It's okay. We'll get through this. Stop talking like this is your goodbye."

It better not be.

Her head starts to shake, "I just had hoped you would have seen me as an equal instead of a pawn. I had hoped you would trust me enough in the beginning."

"I trust you, Teresa. Just hold on for me, and I'll prove to you." I mean that in every way I can, anything to keep her hanging on. Her body begins to shiver violently.

I look around, seeing Greer gripping on the steering wheel. His eyes glance back, pleading with me as well.

Time moves quickly as the compound's gate begins to come into sight. Greer lays on the horn relentlessly. I gather her in my arms, holding her tight, bracing her for any impact.

As the truck whooshes forward the gate opens wide for us. Greer continues to speed through the roads, until we can arrive at the main house.

"Jackson," she pleads.

"I said hang on and I meant it."

"I don't know if I can hang on. Not us."

Goddamn it woman.

"Teresa, you're going to pull through and I'm going to make you see that under every star and moon, it's you and I. We're going to get out of this fucking mess."

A sob comes out of her, "Let me go," a hot wet tear drops to my hand. "I don't want to dream, if it's not going to come true."

A bunch of yelling comes from the outside. As Greer slams the brakes and parks the truck.

A beat goes by as the gut wrenching thought that she still dreams of a world that has me in it. If I wasn't ready for a war to happen over her, I am now. "Teresa, I'm not giving up easily. I'll make it up to you somehow. This won't be for nothing. Keep dreaming of us, cause it'll come true."

Hot tears start to roll down her cheeks. I pull her in one last time, putting my chin on her head. "We'll burn them alive. Take back everything, build this club's empire again. We'll save your community, your home. We'll take back our home." I kiss her head, lingering there for a moment.

The Falcons are attempting to shatter everything. Their toxicity seeps through the regions. They won't stop until they have taken everything from us and overshadow us with their built empire.

She whispers, "Home, that sounds good right now. Take me home."

D.R whips open the door, urgently getting in from the other side. His eyes strain out of him. Tessa looks up, I see a faint smile.

"Hey doc, come to patch me up," she attempts at a joke, faintly.

"Jackson, you gotta give her to me." He tries to get me to let her go. I'm not ready.

"Jackie boy, come on," Rawlings pokes his head through the opening, "You gotta let go. We can't lose her." There's some sincerity in his voice. Almost like hope.

I don't want to let go, the fear overcomes me. I'm inches away from walking away from everything I've known. Losing her would drive a stake through my heart. The coward in me is kicking at the many times I wanted to tell her that she has my heart. I tighten my grip on her, begging D.R to fix her here.

My brothers surround the truck, waiting for my movements.

She turns her head slightly, "Alexander." her voice is growing weaker. It snaps my attention. Alexander, not Jackson. Maybe she heard me.

I nod my head, loosening my grip. I lean her forward, getting her into the arms of D.R. with the help of Rawlings.

"Come on, sweetheart. Let's get you fixed huh?" D.R cradles her and takes off for the medical bay.

I look down at the empty spot where she laid, there's a puddle of blood soaking the seat. My own shirt spotted with her blood. Her very essence on me. A reminder of the cruel fate those Falcon fuckers are about to have.

Memphis opens my door, his kind eyes staring into my soul. Avery and Greer await for me. "We were right weren't we?"

I nod my head, as Joaquin curses under his breath. He stands beside Memphis. I turn towards the opening of the truck door, the compound surrounded by brothers. In the corner Matthew and Seth look at me with worried eyes. No doubt seeing the crimson stains on my shirt.

A loud piercing scream comes from the medical bay. On instinct I take off, my feet striding underneath me.

Teresa, baby I'm coming.

The light from the bay shines through the cracked door as I whip it open. I feel hands on my shoulders, pulling me back. A low gruff voice tells me, "Easy, let him work."

Something feral overcomes me seeing one of the prospects, Xavier or X, holding Tessa down. Her back arching in pain, her sobs pour out from her. An I.V bag swaying back and forth from her moving. "Stop please," she begs.

"I can't, Tessa. I need to keep going, we're going to get this better," D.R tries to soothe her.

She whips her head back, her pleading eyes begging me to make it all go away. Her chest heaves, her body fighting against X. "Please."

"Let him work, she's going to be okay." the rough voice says again.

I let loose the primal instinct to fight, to protect. I take one swing after breaking from the hold. I land one solid strong swing, my fist connecting to a face. In all of the motion it takes me a second to see whose face my fist connected to.

The person staggers grasping his face.

Rawlings.

"Twice you put your hands on me," he growls. As I try to lunge, two shadows appear now restraining me.

"You did this. All. Of. It," I yell out, power coming from my gut.

"It was the way we needed it to happen. You'll get her back." He steps closer.

"Look at her! You can fucking say that," I command him.

"I see her! She could have said no. But she didn't. She wasn't dumb, she knew that you'd be there."

"She saw everything. She set those people free, and stole the drugs."

He scoffs, "Wild one."

"The Falcons will come after her even more so."

"And we'll protect her. She's one of us."

One of us.

"Jackson," Rawlings steps closer. The fury in me still rages. "The Falcons have taken much from here."

"I want their blood." It's not a request, it's a promise.

"And we'll have it. Patience. Everything will come together. Including her."

My breath heaves in my chest. My brothers let go. "Walk away," Rawlings says, "We need to find those drugs."

"And do what?"

"Fry us some birds." There's a certain crooked look.
Timing is everything.
Time needs my patience.

Chapter 28

Teresa

The ache in my shoulder increases at any given moment. I hate this sling. Three weeks.

Three weeks go by, and between the call center, the club, and the ache, it's been slower and steadier, to say the least.

Rawlings reassures me that the club is being patient, waiting in the shadows as the threat of the Falcons still fills our streets.

But it's been three weeks since I last saw Jackson. Since that night where my life was hanging in the balance. His look of despair and pleading for me to hang in there.

I shake away the thoughts of "what ifs", deciding to not go down the rabbit hole. I should be happy, it's my birthday. The girls want to go out. I don't mind, but I still have some anxiety, waiting on word for the next move in this plan. Plus, I want to visit Jeremiah.

I lean back in my office chair, recounting my luck.

Thankfully, I was one of the luckiest people on the planet, according to Doc. The bullet didn't hit an important artery by literally millimeters. My range of motion might be compromised for a bit until I regain strength, and I need to look into physical therapy, but, all in all, I'm lucky. My mind flutters to the memories of that night.

The pain.
The aches.
The fire that burns in my body.
My silent screams grow louder.

"Hold still, sweetheart, I know it hurts," D.R says as I see through hazy eyes he's hooking up an I.V. and a bag of blood.

"Please, make it stop," I beg.

My breathing becomes harder and harder. There's another person in here, I haven't met him yet. But he seems young, fresh for a fight.

D.R hovers over me, the sweat pouring from forehead drips down, he pats a rag. D.R's sweet face makes me want to smile. His full smile can light up a rainstorm. "Okay, sweetheart, I need to put you on your right side, I need to get that bullet out," he says.

I start to shake my head no, knowing the pain would make me tremble more than I already am.

"I know Tessa, but it has to happen," he says as he rolls me over. A loud moan releases from my lips. The agony burning deep inside me.

D.R's rough hands pull the shirt, keeping me covered, but enough for him to work. He mumbles something then I feel a sharp ass pain and I screech, crying out.

I must be imagining things, it sounds like a growl and a herd of pounding feet.

"Get him out of here!" Doc yells.

D.R hits a muscle because I start to buck off the table.

"Stop please," a whimper passes my lips.

"I can't, Tessa. I need to keep going, we're going to get this better," D.R tries to soothe me, as he keeps getting the bullet out, before there's a sense of relief. We're getting close. Other hands catch me as the pain makes me buck off the table.

I whip my head back, my pleading eyes begging me to make it all go away. His icy blue eyes sear into my soul, my pain is his pain. All I want to do is caress that stumbled cheek, melt away the thoughts of hurt both mentally and physically.

"Please." I whisper.

The haze in my eyes fogs everything. Doc finally curses, possibly meaning that the bullet is out and all I have to do is get patched up and figure out my life.

Doc crouches next to me, having circled around. "Hey, buddy. Talk to me."

I softly laugh, trying to lighten the mood. "Ah, Doc. I made the connection. Sorry for the unintentional nickname. I lost a fight with a gun," I laugh again.

I hear someone burst through the door, I can't make out their words. I recognize the deep grumble as coming from Rawlings. I turn my head towards the door to see the disappointed look on his face.

A few more men have arrived, but I can't particularly tell who they are. They aren't Greer or Sparky, that's for sure. Speaking of Sparky, where is he? I hope he didn't get into trouble.

Doc brings my attention back onto him. "Listen, buddy, as much as the bullet hurt, I need you to understand that you'll be in agony for the next bit. I don't have anything to knock you out. I need you to hold on."

"I hurt him." The world starts to spin. I think I've lost a bit more blood than I thought I did.

"Hurt who?" Doc questions me from the side, gathering his tools.

"I essentially told him to let me go. I'm lying to myself, Doc." I pout. Jesus, when did being in pain feel like being drunk and out of control?

I can tell Doc knows who I'm talking about now. "You know he won't. He's more hurt that you gave up so easily. Tessa, I've seen people who would do anything to have just one more moment with their loved ones. They fought for it." He crouches back down, face to face with me.

"You think I should fight?" I look deep into his dark chocolate eyes.

"Buddy, I wish I did. It's not easy to turn back the hands of time. Don't regret things like I do." He starts to clean up my shoulder. He hooks me up to some monitors while I ponder his words. "Now, let's test that strength again."

With that, Doc starts his procedure, and the world turns black and red before my eyes and pain becomes agony.

I blink out of the memories, realizing that I made it to the hospital. I sit in the parking lot as the car continues to run. My head drops to the steering wheel. I focus on my breathing. Jackson's gone radio silent again.

What else am I to say?

At one point I was arguing with him to let me go, to forget that I was his.

Am his, that is a struggling concept.

But then the next moment, I feel his pain because it's my pain. All I want to do is crawl into his lap, his arms to circle around me and truly never let go.

It's really for the best. Maybe my words finally meant something to him. I'm lying to myself that his actions that hurt me overpowers the feelings of need and love from me. Everything is jumbled, like a puzzle with no picture and all the missing pieces.

Jeremiah woke up last week. He's taking it step by step, but the guilt is too strong, and my stubbornness prevented me from visiting him until now.

I received a friendly threat from Aggie and the girls that if I didn't go soon, consequences would be served. I can't afford for more people to be pissed at me. I'd asked if anyone wanted to come with me, but they all said I should do it by myself.

The running list of things I need to worry about and complete grows mentally.

I need to speak with Rawlings soon about ending these details. I haven't gotten any more threats. Sure, the footage of someone watching me at home and the gunshots were something, but I'm pretty sure they don't need to watch over me like a hawk.

I need to put in more work on protection. I've been putting in some work in the gym lately, particularly with my knife skills.

I need to see Jeremiah, my friend.

I need Alexander.

Damn it, when did I become a woman that plays on her strengths, only to say I need someone to solve my problems?

Maybe more like solve my heart problems, the yearning of my desires.

I gather the courage to get out and move into the hospital. I walk slowly, silently hoping he'll be asleep, allowing me more time to put together my words. Passing the nurses' station, I nod to the nurse on duty.

A man I don't recognize stands guard by Jeremiah's door. He's a little shorter than Jackson, but still towers over me. He has curly dirty blonde hair, hazel eyes, and a short beard that shapes his jawline to perfection. Add the eyebrow piercing, and he looks like a predator ready to pounce at any moment. I step into his line of sight. He takes a look at me, surveying from the top of my head to the bottom of my shoes.

"Hi," I say softly. "Is he awake?"

Without warning, I get pulled into a bear hug. The sudden jolt of my shoulder from his embrace.

Confusion.

Awkwardness.

Not the reaction I was looking for. This man is crushing me. "Um... Okay, could you let go? I'd like to leave with all the air in my lungs. And plus the shooting pain neurons are shooting through my shoulders."

He lets me go, setting me down. I adjust myself. "Not what I was expecting."

He just shrugs. "I sensed you needed a hug." This man senses that I need a hug. What is he like a human therapy animal? Well, I'm here for it.

"How would you know that?" I tilt my head at him.

"Body language. Intuition. Also, it's good to see you alive. Don't know what boss man would do if things went south that night." I tilt my head to examine him, finally realizing that he was there that night. He was one of the ones in the doorway when Rawlings peaked in.

"I don't think we need that answer, um.. What's your name," I ask.

He nods his head and extends his hand out to me. "Call me Memphis." as he flashes a smile to me.

I take his hand and look closer at him. "You from Memphis?"

"Yes ma'am, I am. It's also my name." He flashes me a huge smile. There's definitely a story there. Makes me wonder if there's a sibling named Nash or Knox or something city like.

I get to the reason I'm here. "He awake?"

"Yep, waiting on you." He gestures toward the room.

I take a deep breath to steel myself and make my way inside.

Come on, you got this. Throw the anxiety out the window.

There Jeremiah sits, working on his dinner, the television on some kind of sports broadcast. I knock on the door, and he turns his attention to me.

"You know, for a while, I thought you was avoiding me like the plague," he starts to mouth off to me. I freeze where I stand and start to fidget with my keys, trying to focus on something else.

"Sugar, get yourself in here," he commands.

I hesitate, trying to tamp down the well of emotions threatening to burst. "Ms. Tessa. Come here, sugar. I think you and I need to talk." He pats the side of the bed for me to sit. My stomach is unsettled, and I don't know what to expect.

He grasps one of my hands, and I'm taken aback. "Sugar. You hiding from me?"

His question hangs heavy in the air. How do I answer him? A simple answer comes out. "Yes."

"Thank you for the honesty," he begins, but I hold up my hand to stop him.

"I owe you an apology, Jeremiah." He tilts his head in confusion. "If I'd listened and not shrugged off your concerns, you wouldn't be here. It's my fault. You constantly warned me, and I was too stubborn. Jeremiah, you are so very important to me. You've become a dear friend and every time I'm around you and your spirit, you make me believe in the good, in the work we do. I couldn't live with myself if my stupidity was the reason you were no longer with us." I blurt out what's been bubbling up in me for a long while. Everything came out like rapid fire. This is all my fault. I hang my head, unable to look him in the eye.

"Ms. Tessa. Sugar. Come here, closer to me," he requests and I comply. He reaches a hand to touch my cheek. His calloused hands brush against my wet cheek, rubbing where tears have run down my face. "You are a stubborn ass woman. We all know this. At that moment, it was my choice. I knew if I went there, I could suffer the consequences. This is not on you. Ya hear?" He lightly taps my cheek.

"You are the real hero here Jeremiah, you are going to save so many people now." I look back him.

It's true, he called me a superhero when in reality it is him and his determination.

"You are just buttering me up." I don't deserve this forgiveness, his kindness. "Now, I need you to answer a question for me. Why do I see a wolf at my door?" He glares at Memphis.

I go pale; I knew he wouldn't like that. "Because the Wolves are helping us. It's a lot to explain, and honestly, it's not worth the hassle right now." I try to divert the conversation, but I can tell Jeremiah knows I'm lying.

"I got time. Unless you got a date like your birthday and all." He settles back into his bed, folding his hands to his chest.

I swear, I don't deserve this man. "Aw, you remembered."

"Of course, I did. Don't deflect. Start talking, child," he chastises sternly.

I sigh. There's no hiding this anymore. "Fine. I got involved with the Grim Wolves by accident. It started at a friend's birthday and I made an impression. Their VP and I got involved, but that ended badly. Now, they're protecting me and you and we're formulating a plan to take down the Falcons." I figure a shorter version is probably for the best.

"You fell for him, didn't you?" His question hits me like another bullet.

I can feel the blush creeping up my neck. "I think so, but I can't. I have much at stake and I'm not ready to forgive what he did. Honestly, I don't know if I would even if I could."

"Sometimes, forgiveness is the hardest of all when it comes to those we love," Jeremiah says. *Wait a minute.*

I snort. "Why are you quoting Mr. Rogers?"

Jeremiah doesn't falter. "The man made valid points." He throws his hand up, stopping me before I could interrupt him. "Your heart won't lie to you. You were falling for a man who made you feel safe. Now, do I approve of the man? Not completely. But the man seems to have a hold on you." he says pointing his finger.

Jeremiah speaks the truth, whether I choose to listen or not.

I try my hardest to deflect and reposition. "When did this turn into a conversation about me? Listen, the Wolves are going to help us fix this."

Jeremiah lets me change the conversation. "Falcons. I'm not surprised. They've always been at war with each other, but I don't think they're working alone. I mean, who do you think is supplying the names or locations of these people?"

Shock and wonder wash over me so quickly, I practically lose consciousness.

"You believe people are being *targeted?* Hunted down for other reasoning?" This throws a wrench into things. Rawlings mentioned that Sheldon was mixed up with the Falcons, but maybe he's doing more than we thought.

"Oh, for fuck's sake. Why didn't I realize this?" The Falcons are using Sheldon as access to the community. He doesn't need to break into the system.

I immediately reach for my phone and dial the old grump ass himself. It only takes a few rings.

"Bjorn?"

I scoff at his formality. "Would it kill you to call me Tessa?"

"Did you call to waste time or is there something you want to share?" No one could ever accuse Rawlings of being a nice guy.

"I might know something that you may not," I smirk, teasing him with a dangling carrot.

"Care to share?" he asks. His voice grows with impatience. I take a moment to enjoy the leverage.

"Hmm, not yet. Let's call it a trade, hell even a team meeting. Your little field trip was useful, but it's been weeks and it seems like you're slacking on your end." I put the phone on speaker; I want Jeremiah in on this.

I can almost hear the steam coming from Rawlings' ears. "I swear, if I'd known you were trouble from the beginning, I'd save on alcohol. When did you want to speak?"

"Sunday, my only day off. I'll come to the compound and we can catch up."

"Why not tonight? From the looks of things, your nights have been a little less busy," he sneers out.

Asshole.

"You talking from experience or busybody observation?" I tease him.

Then finally, I hear a chuckle, a brief opening of mutual common ground. "I like your wit, kid."

"Plus, I have plans to drink my weight in whiskey. You only celebrate a birthday once a year. So, Sunday." Jeremiah looks at me with a curiosity.

"Sunday, 9am. If you're late, I swear, you'll regret it, Bjorn."

"Rawlings, you just know how to make a woman quiver with excitement," I tease.

I end the call, as I glance back at Jeremiah. His soft features brings a smile back to my face.

"Ms. Tessa, how you get those men to listen to you is beyond me." Jeremiah remarks.

I shrug. "I can be charming. I have my ways. Also, it's their fault for letting a woman like me walk into their bar." I plant a kiss on Jeremiah's forehead and make my way home. Tonight, the world is my oyster, and I'm going to dance and sing the night away.

Everyone seems to migrate to my house. Brittany pokes her head into the bathroom. "Are we finding you a man tonight?"

I scrunch my nose. "Who says I need a man tonight, what if we find you one?" I say, the curling iron close to my head.

"I mean, you ain't looking and you won't be getting back with dick for brains." she asks, leaning into the door frame. "Plus, no man can handle me."

Sometimes, I think Brittany just likes to cause trouble. "I don't need anyone."

But I need him.

I stare into the mirror.

"The best sex of your life and a man who adored you," Sam yells from the living room.

"A man who has given me too much whiplash," I yell back.

I take a swig from my whiskey bottle before I check off my last thing to do today before the bar.

I dial my momma's number. I haven't spoken to them in a few weeks, and I'm starting to feel like a horrible daughter. I blame it on work and late hours, and the shoulder injury that they know absolutely anything about.

The phone rings a few times, then Momma picks up.

"I was worried you forgot us."

My heart instantly turns to mush. "Forget you, mama bear? Never. Work's just been busy, with the opening and all. How are you and daddy? How's retirement life?" I deflect before anything else comes out.

I let her talk about the latest project she's got my father working on, before she goes off on a tangent about their anniversary coming up. A ping of guilt and sadness rolls in my chest. The talk of forever love and soulmates is turning out to be too much.

I stay silent for a moment. "Baby, you still there."

"Yeah momma, I'm here."

"You don't sound like yourself."

"Momma, you ever think that if you and daddy had broken up over something that you felt was wrong, would you ever forgive him knowing how much you love him?"

I had hid Alexander from them until it felt real. Why bring home something that wouldn't last?

"You know, your granddaddy used to tell us that love is more than the happy moments, it's about how you fight for each other and the roads that come with it. After so many years, I think I can say he was right." She waits for a moment before continuing, "Baby. True love always finds a way back even through the most broken of hearts. It can heal. It can learn."

"I love you, momma."

"I love you too. Happy Birthday."

I hang up, staring back at the person in the mirror. I'm a strong woman, who fell for a man that proved to be a challenge.

I miss Jackson.

No, I miss Alexander.

I miss his smile, his eyes that stare into my soul. His gentleness and how he made me laugh. How easy it was to joke with him and be joked at in return. Mostly, though, I miss how he saw the flaws I kept deeply hidden and still wanted me.

I shake out the sadness, for now, this is for me.

Tonight, I'm dressed down in my black shorts, boots, black fishnet tights, and my Johnny Cash t-shirt. One look, and I know that heads would turn.

One last swig of whiskey and we're out the door. Reva, Sam, and Britt trail along. Reva gathers up in her SUV, majority of us feeling the buzz of the liquor swirling around a cloud of trouble. Before I get in, I see the truck across the street.

Walking over, I approach the window and give it a gentle tap. As the windows roll down the bushel of ginger hair pops out.

"I hope you like karaoke."

The look of distaste is enough to make me laugh. "I don't mind it, just don't think someone else might."

That's right, come to mama.

"Well, he knows where to find me." I throw a wink his way, throwing caution to the wind.

Maybe it's the liquor, but I'm ready for a certain someone to come graveling on his knees.

Reva introduced us long ago to a place where the mindless karaoke sways and dancing never fades. Tonight is a night with the girls, celebrating another trip around the sun, and my hope for the chance for two stubborn souls to reunite and move past this.

Am I ready to forgive completely? No, but granddaddy's words are right, it's about the roads you take and the fight that come along that brings love to soothe everything.

"You gonna grace us with your voice tonight?" Sam asks from the front seat, looking back at Reva and me. Brittany offered to drive, saying she needed a night off from drinking.

"Maybe. It's been a while." I shrug it off.

"I hope you do. Perhaps you'll get lucky and ride off into the sunset," Sam blurts out loudly, giggling uncontrollably.

"Someone may have had too many pre-game shots. Still, Tessa, she's not wrong. If you ain't looking, then at least be a good wing woman for me," Britt says checking her phone.

"I need a wing woman!" Sam whines, slumping over the passenger side.

"I swear, if she causes us to wreck, I'm gonna kill her," Reva yells.

"You don't need a wing woman, you need water and food as soon as possible," Reva says.

These are my people, the ones I know will be there in the end.

Even when my life feels like a roller coaster you can't get off of, they're still there.

We pull up to a bar, the Horseshoe. The hustle and bustle tempts us with a good time. It's busy when we walk in, the space crowded with individuals ready for a night to remember or forget, depending on your outlook.

Unsurprisingly, Sparky bit the bullet and followed us. Sam leans over to me. "Who's the cute ginger?"

Although the sight of Greer warms me, I had hoped for a bigger crowd.

I rub my temples to calm myself before I tie her to a chair. She's going to have to be watched all night, for her own safety. "The answer is no. Leave Sparky alone."

"His name is Sparky?" She looks at me, dumbfounded.

"No. And you're not going near him. Down, girl." Poor Sparky. He won't know what hit him.

We find our usual table and order our drinks. The DJ nods his head at me.

You *could* say we're regulars here.

A round of shots come to the table for the four of us. Brittany raises a glass. "To the bad ass bitch. The savior in tights. To the woman who can be stubborn and a smart ass at the same time. To you, my cousin. To the many more hearts you will break one day."

"Cheers," everyone says, clinking their shot glasses together before hitting the table and pounding the shots back.

Sláinte

One or two more shots in, we start to dance. Sam's watching Sparky, hoping he'll come dance with her. I know she has her little drunken heart set on the man making a move, but he's a little occupied with surveying the room.

Plus, I've seen him look down at his phone more than a few times.

An hour in, and I'm quite buzzed. For the first time in a *very* long time, I feel free, in complete bliss.

A couple guys have asked me to dance, and I hesitated to oblige them. They seemed nice, and fairly good looking, but no one's done it for me.

That's because no one's him.

I dance with a man that turns into a very handsy partner and whose breath is quite unpleasant. I've forgotten his name by now, and I honestly don't really care. There's an instant regret.

Not the man I'm expecting. Am I playing with fire? Sure. Do I have a plan set? Sure, make the man jealous, make him realize that we've said things that all in all, we're meant for each other. Also, the man said something about a dream and home. He promised to grovel. Damn it, I'm getting that man on his knees.

And this is the part where the alcohol stops.

"You seem like a keeper, baby." the handsy man says.

Ugh, great. Anyone can call me anything, but baby is where I draw the line.

I can feel his hands traveling around my thighs, skimming across my pelvis. When he gets a little too close to the apex of my thighs for comfort, I start looking for someone to save me, extricating myself from his sweaty hands as I look. This is not how I wanted this.

Thankfully, Reva comes to my rescue. "Hey, asshole. If a woman's pulling away from you, there's a reason." She shoves him off me, and he stumbles back. Anger splashes across his face, and I step towards him.

"Back off before you regret pissing me off." She yells over the music.

That seems to do the trick because he just flips me off and turns away. I don't give him a second thought, walking back to our table, Reva in tow.

Sparky's checking his phone again, avoiding eye contact with me.

Jesus, something crawled up his ass tonight.

Another hour in, and I manage to sip on my pale ale.

Not my drink of choice, but I'd rather not be throwing up when they call my name for karaoke. I have a song in my mind that I've been saving for a while. Brittany's following a drunk Sam, who I hope has been drinking water. Reva plops back down at the table.

"Where have you been?" I question her. She's been gone for quite a bit.

"Wouldn't you like to know?" she smirks as she sips on her drink.

I roll my eyes while simultaneously poking her hand. "You were sucking face with someone, weren't you?"

Her silence is the only answer I need.

"You shady lady! Good for you." I sip on my drink, looking around.

Reva notices. "He'll show."

Reva's bluntness yanks me out of my mind. "Who?"

"The person you're still pining for."

"Jesus, who uses the word pining?" I make a face at her outdated choice of words. Still, maybe she's right. Maybe I *am* an idiot for thinking I could get over him so quickly.

Reva doesn't let up. "Stop running in the opposite direction, Tessa. He was the first person who made you smile like an imbecile and put some color on those cheeks. Run to him." Before I can say a word, we're interrupted by the karaoke emcee.

"Alright, we have a brave soul who wants to slow things down. Grab a partner and let's show some love for Tessa Bjorn!" My name echoes through the bar. I take a gulp of my drink and make my way to the stage.

As I grab hold of the mic, the emcee continues his introduction. "This one is for the ones who want a second chance. Here's *The Strangers* by Ingrid Andress."

Couples start to sway with the melody as I search the crowd, most likely in vain. Suddenly, I can barely suck in enough air to start the song. There, tucked away in the back corner, is Alexander.

He's here and he's not alone, but he's here. A swell of joyful tears threaten to spill over. I hope he hears me. The words echoing that a couple starting over in a place where it started and wishing that she didn't know him just to fall for him again.

There's something in the words that solidify my reasoning. The reason for my own heart to sing. I slammed every door and closed off everything instead of fighting.

Music soothes the hurt and wounds of my heart like an escape from reality. All I can do is find his eyes, hoping he'll fight for me one more time.

Maybe this time, I'll say yes. The notes flow through the hall with my voice guiding the way. I'd hoped he'd hear what I'm trying so hard to say. A way to start apologizing for my words. The music fades and a thunderous applause stirs me from my trance.

I give a small bow and exit the stage, only to be pulled onto the dance floor by hands I don't recognize.

"I think you still owe me a dance, baby." The man from the dance floor slings me into the crowd, pressing his hips into me, wrapping his arms around me.. For a man who's probably been drinking for hours, he definitely has a strong grip.

"Don't owe you anything, now if you'll excuse me," I snarl back.

Apparently, he didn't. "You can't tell me you don't want to dance with me. Babygirl, I can make your world look like heaven." Seriously, where's he getting his pick-up lines?

Fortunately for me, I had something, rather someone up my sleeve ready to storm.

I roll my eyes. "No, I prefer something a bit more.. Grim." I stomp on his foot and throw my elbow into his side.

I manage to escape, only to see him turn around and knock on his ass. The fury in those icy, arctic blue eyes make my body flush. All moisture in my throat evaporates. I try to find the words, but I'm truly rendered speechless. I had all the guts to come this far, granted I didn't think I would make it this far.

The handsy guy's friends are starting to congregate, their presence behind me as I glance to see the group. I look back in Jackson's direction, seeing the Wolves gain up in numbers. They're all geared up in their cuts and boots. Their statue screams power and trouble.

Keola, Joaquin, Sparky, and a couple members whose names I have forgotten. They're all here, whether I'm the cause or the effect.

Jackson pushes me aside and takes one swing at the man. The handsy man stumbles back, trying to find his footing. I turn to see him wiping off the blood from his dripping lip. Before Jackson can charge again, I step in front.

No one else is going to get hurt. If people want a fight, I won't be when I'm around. The girls stand up from the table, watching the whole thing unravel like a soap opera.

"Fuck man, I didn't want the stupid bitch anyway." the man says. I growl, in retaliation, I smack him across the face, his head whipping back.

"Call me a bitch again and it won't be them you have to worry about." I spit out. Jackson's intense presence looms behind me.

"If you want to be slut for this guy, guess he wants something cheaper," the man spits out. This sets Jackson off, but he's stopped by Keola saying, "Take her out of here. We'll clean up the mess."

I turn to see Keola with a wide smile on his face, pat Jackson on the shoulder, pushing him in my direction.

Jackson grabs me from behind, twirling me around. His eyes narrow like he's captured a trophy. In my mind I have some decisions to make. I can either run or let him do whatever it is he's intent on doing.

Without hesitation, he hoists me up and over this shoulder. I know now that option B is my decision. As he walks out the girls give a simple wave, accepting that the caveman has claimed his woman and my night with them has come to an end.

The people at the bar don't make a move, but just simply step aside letting us pass to the outside and into the parking lot.

"Jackson, I.." I stumble over my words, trying hard to minimize the chances of whiskey and rum coming back up, "Jackson, I can walk you know."

"I'm not seeing the problem. Seems like the only way to make sure you don't run, this time," he growls out.

This is the part where I *should* be afraid.

Scary thing is, I'm not.

Chapter 29

Alexander

The blood boils in me, the sight of another man touching what's mine. The chained up animal inside wants blood for this damage.

But now, she's at my mercy. I don't plan on ever having her out of my sight. I had picked her up with ease, finding the quickest way out of this hell hole. She struggles, the damn stubbornness causes her to wiggle, trying to set herself free.

Not this time. With her still in my arms, we aim towards Greer's truck, the closest thing to a safe zone. Once I put her down, the street lights shine on us. In any light, she's an angel, giving me a taste of heaven.

I back her towards the truck, I tower over her, placing my arms beside her head, forcing her to look at me with those dark brown eyes.

I place her down near Greer's truck, backing her against it.

"Jackson," she whispers out, trying to find any clue to my next movement.

I lean closer, my face inches from her, "Teresa, what did I tell you, from the beginning?"

Her mind searches for the answer I'm looking for. She gulps as she realizes what I want to hear. "If you want something, you'll stop at nothing to claim it," her voice is like a tease.

I place my forehead on hers, "Good girl. Do you think I was going to allow another man to gawk at you? Thinking they can put their hands on you? You are *mine*, Teresa." Pure possessiveness rages in my voice.

She plants her hands on my chest to brace herself. I gently brush my lips across hers in a breathtaking kiss, melting away the chaos raging in her head. We've gone through torturing ourselves day and night, fighting what we truly feel. I need this. She needs this. I need *her*.

I break our kiss and skim my knuckles across her cheek. Her eyes hazily close, embracing the caress.

"Teresa, the moment you appeared I knew I couldn't keep you in my world. You are too good for me." I say as her eyes flutter open. "Even in the darkest views of this world, I need you. Tonight I'm going to erase the hurt we did, I did."

Her breathing hitches. I have never been this soft towards anyone other than the club and family. But she brings it out of me.

"Everything you have." My hand travels down her neck, past the quickened pulse, to her chest. "Your heart." I move down across her hips and waist. "These curves." The curves that never stop,"And this."

I cup her pussy. "This is mine." The sight of her has me hard and salivating to have more of a taste of her.

"Jackson." A flare of madness rages.

I chuckle softly, "Jackson still? We both know that's not what you will call me by the end of the night."

She smirks, she's ever so playful tonight. "No, it's Leif Erickson."

I cup then grip her ass, bringing her flush against me. "Try. Again."

She challenges me, moving closer to my face, her lips ghosting over mine, "Mm, I think I'd rather scream it."

There she is, there's my woman.

My eyes grow wide. "That can be arranged."

"Promises, promises. Jackson." she tilts her head glaring at me with passion, ready to throw down a challenge.

I finally dip my head to brush soft kisses on her neck. "Tell me to take you home. Let me show you what happens when you put too much distance between us. What happens when you starve a hungry wolf."

Her fingers trail along my side, itching to touch me and what's hidden underneath.

Her face flushes with red, I can imagine the rush of pleasure flooding her. I can see the look of pleading eyes that just scream "please". I take her lips, planting a soft kiss because tonight that's the only softness she'll get out of me.

Her eyes focus back on me after hazily looking where mine once were tracing. She whispers, "Take me home." The first ounce of forgiveness, of those barriers coming back down for a second chance, I can only hope. She says, "Alexander." with an ache in her voice.

There it is, the white flag of surrender.

The smile that spreads across my face isn't nearly the expression to show what I really feel. With her answer, I waste no time placing a helmet on her head and pulling her onto my bike only to zip through traffic. She holds onto me tightly, her warmth sends pleasure through me.

I need to get her home, rip off every inch of fabric revealing every curve and stretch mark that makes her a goddess. I want to get lost in those dark eyes, her writhing underneath me, her pleasure given by me.

I want her to lose herself, I want her to fly. I want the hungry of this wild one.

It doesn't take us long before we're in her driveway. I don't think, I just do. I scoop her in my arms after parking the bike. For the moment, I don't care what happens to the bike. What I do care is for her to open the damn door before I kick it in.

When I set her down, she fumbles with her keys. I lean on the doorway before she opens it, her face leans up towards me. I watch her gulp, her breathing shallows.

"Don't run or hide from me this time, Teresa. That's all I ask of you," I ask of her. Like a good girl she nods her head.

"Open the door, little cub," I bend down and kiss her neck as she continues to fumble to open the door. Once open, the fun really begins. I follow her, stepping across the threshold. Too much time is being wasted, I lift her up again, she wraps those luscious legs around me. She throws her arms around me, releasing my bun allowing my hair to fall. I kick the door close.

Her fingers weave through my hair. Twisting, tugging, damn intoxicating. With her in hand, we travel down the hall to her bedroom. She leans in closer, nuzzling my neck. My stumble rubs against her cheeks. Time could stay still and I would count it as a blessing.

She sighs, "I want to keep us like this." she pops up and searches my face.

"You'll always have me, little cub. Until the grim reaper finds me. Until our roads end." I kiss her softly, sealing us together, fates be damned, for the road ahead.

Something in me snaps. Our kisses turn from soft and tender to feral and hungry. Like everything in me is starving for her, starving for the moments we want to create. We drown ourselves in this kiss, she melts into my touch. My fingers gripping her ass, digging their way to feel any type of touch.

We finally make it to the bedroom, she reaches for a dresser lamp, but second guesses turning it off. I decide otherwise.

"I need to see all of you. Told you don't hide from me that also means that I need to see every inch of you." I growl.

I whip us around, sitting at the edge of the bed. She falls into my lap, straddling me. She slowly grinds against me, grinding against my hard cock. It strains against the zipper of my jeans. A light rumble in my chest prowls. She takes my lips, taking control of our movements, her hips start to move faster, her breathing heavier like she's got one goal in mind. Little does she know, it won't be the only time.

Her tongue slips into my mouth, greedy, impatient. She grinds faster. My hands dig into her side giving her more pressure to chase her release, "That's it, grinding those sweet hips. Take want you want," I growl out, only becoming unbearably harder. "Someone is being greedy. You better come little cub, because soon that pussy will be weeping around my cock."

"Stop talking, and start showing," she growls out. It's cute that she thinks she's in control right now.

"Patient," I hiss, kissing her again. My hands roam under her shirt, caressing her breast, finding her tempting, hard nipple, skimming my fingers over it, toying with it. I watch her body give in to the sensation, the way she closes her eyes like she's in a trance.

With a small moan, she bucks against me, grinding harder into my lap.

"Take your shirt off,"

It's a simple command, like a good girl she doesn't hesitate to comply. My eyes bulge out with a deep hunger as I see her push up bra, a tease pushing her luscious heavy chest. "This for me? You were hoping I'd show up?"

I play with the lacy fabric, finally pulling the straps down, revealing her soft skin. She reaches around unhooking the bra.

"It worked, didn't it," she says, pushing her chest out further. I give into the temptation. The taste of an angel is worth all this trouble. Her eyes scream "come get it", I don't waste time.

I take a nipple in my mouth, teasing it, licking, sucking. With each gasp of breath, I know she's getting to the edge of her release. Her hands reach through my hair, caressing it as I continue to play with her breasts.

"You keep doing that and I won't last," she whimpers

I release her with a pop. "Don't worry, little cub. Come if you want, but in the end both of us might be seeing stars."

I whip my shirt off of me and cut, she watches me, softly touching me, trailing her fingers down my abs. Caressing every twist and turn of muscle. She leans down kissing down the way.

She's a temptress, a delusion in the best way. My breathing hitches, knowing that I won't last longer. My knuckles brush against her backside, palming her ass through her jeans. I start to tug on them, wanting them out of the way. I'm ready to rip them off, tear them into shreds if I have to.

"Off."

One simple command ends up making her scramble off my lap to unbutton her shorts. Although they don't leave much to the imagination, but one look at her fishnets. I lay back on the bed, watching her fumble with her fabrics. It all lays to the ground like a white surrender flag.

Both our surrender flag.

I prop myself on my elbows, enjoying the view. My appetite grows as my dick becomes harder and slightly painful. I lick my lips, fixated on one thing. Her.

"Good girl. Now, crawl back over here."

She sinks down on all fours, her beautiful ass swaying with every step. When she gets on the bed, she crawls faster, hovering over me. She straddles me once again, she bends down capturing my lips as we tangle into each other. A wave of heat flushes through us, every touch and ache burning with desire.

I can't help but let out a deep rumble groan, everything just feels right. Her skin peebles under my fingertips. A deep, primal rumble sends chills down my body, pebbling my skin. My hands grip her ass again as she grinds against him, craving the pressure of our bodies together.

She tries to get her hands on me, reaching between us, undoing my button on my pants. The little minx. But I have other plans for her.

I gather the strength to grip her ass and lift her, she faces the headboard and with a force her hands plant on the board. I angle her just enough to where I want her.

"Alexander," she whispers.

"Don't let go of that headboard, this pussy is weeping to be tasted, and you've made me a hungry man." She doesn't argue or retreat.

I grip her thighs, pulling her closer to my face. I want nothing more than to be smothered by this goddess. I want her to break free, let her release take over. I want her to come all over my face.

She practically yelps when I start circling my tongue around her clit, alternating between sucking, licking, and nipping, bringing her closer to the edge with each movement of my tongue.

I become relentless, making her tremble with every stroke, as her orgasm builds, right there on the edge. Her breath staggers and she tries to lift off of me. She doesn't go far as I bring her back to sit on my face. No more of this hovering shit.

Every moan is mine. Every ounce of pleasure that I bring her to is mine.

"Jackson, I'm not going to last. Please." she's begging now, I don't give in.

I pull away for a moment, her wetness smeared all over my face. A smile spreads across my devilish face, I tsk, "That's not my name."

I pull her back to me and continue to torment her with every lick and suckle. Her thighs tighten around me.

Fuck.

"Alexander, please." she roars. I tongue-fucks her into delirium, and the waves of her orgasm flutter from top to bottom. Her body trembles, she squirms as I continue slowly, she turns sensitive. She goes to reach for my pants once she recovers. I stop her.

"Patience. If you're good, I'll fuck that pretty mouth of yours." I tease her. I flip her over, and crawl away from her. Red rushes to her cheeks as her eyes narrow on me.

I finish undressing, now she's the one salivating as my cock springs free. I stand there as she watches me stroking myself. She takes me in, a big gulp goes down that beautiful throat of hers.

That's right darlin', take a good look at what's yours.

I admire her, she lays on the bed with anticipation. The flush in her cheeks, her chest moving slowly. She hasn't felt anything yet.

She's mine.

A month ago, I would have moved on if she was anyone else. But she's not. She is perfection, big hearted, compassionate, and a light in my life.

I slide back up her body, but she gasps as I roughly stick two fingers in her. Stretching her. It's been too long. Even now she's sensitive, coming down for a fresh release.

Her back arches as my fingers continue to tease her, bringing her to the edge.

"Responsive, tight, and wet. That's my girl. Now, what do you want?" I slowly pump my fingers in and out. She knows what she wants, but words fail her. Each thrust hits every nerve, every spot that makes her whimper, possibly seeing stars. The sound of wetness fills the room, and I know she won't last long again. "Better tell me, or you'll just come around my fingers. Again." I plant kisses around her collarbone, smiling as she squirm her hips to find the best angle.

"Alexander.."

"Yes, darlin'?" I nip at her chin.

"I need you inside me."

"But I am."

"Your *cock*, Alexander. I will pin your ass to this bed and take what I want if you don't fuck me *right now*." She threatens. Cute that she thinks otherwise.

"Only because you asked so nicely." Without warning, my cock replaces my fingers. I thrust inside her, nestling myself between her thighs. Sliding in and out, stretching, filling her. How did I forget how tight and responsive she is?

Something primal unleashes in me, like that time in the woods.

Remind me to take her back there.

I wrap an arm under her leg, propping it up against my shoulder and pushing deeper. The new angle makes her and I groan, and she arches her back further, begging for more.

I take advantage of her proffered neck and brand it with my lips. I reach down to tease her clit right as I bite the juncture of her neck and shoulder. She holds back a scream, pressure building between the both of us.

I swallow every one of her pleas and moans, taking full control. She contracts around me hard, making me groan in return. I want to fill her, to take what I need, what she needs.

"Fuck. Yes. More, please. Alexander." she moans, working in tandem with me. She's the verge of tears.

I steady the thrusts, slowing down at an agonizing speed. Her nails mark my arms. "Wait, no, no. *Fucker.* I wanted to come," she's spitting mad.

Without warning, I flip her over, her ass in the air. "And you will."

I seat myself inside one more time, as far as I can go, both of us about to lose it.

Impulsively, my hand grazes her ass before planting a hard smack on it. She groans. "Remind me to paint this beautiful ass red later."

I pick up speed, I get close while she's not too far behind. We'll be chasing pleasure. Our pants and moans become the music of the night. I grind into her, hitting every spot she didn't even know she has. I reach for the back of her head, grabbing her short hair, making her back arch as I drive into her.

"Who do you belong to?" I grunt out.

Breathlessly, she says, "You."

"That's right. Who belongs to you?"

She answers without hesitation, "You. You're mine, Alexander."

"That's right. We're not going to walk away from each other again. We're done hurting right?" I keep going until we are both chasing our orgasms.

"No, I'm done running." she says, a promise that makes my heart skip a beat. She's done running.

"I'll still chase you, but right now. Right now I need you to be a good girl and come around me. And then I'm going to fill this needy cunt with my cum."

She nods her head yes, as I let her go and pound in to her. She comes hard around me, waves of ecstasy coating her body. Moments later, I'm right behind her, my cock spurting into her, filling every corner of her pussy. My cock continues to twitch knowing that I'm still inside her.

We slump down, sweaty and slick with exertion. I plant sweet, soft kisses on her shoulder. I pull out of her, walking myself to the bathroom getting a warm cloth. As much as I want to see still dripping with my cum, we have more time to see that.

She spreads a smile across her face as I clean her up. A moment of bliss.

Kisses travel up her leg to meet her lips.

She whispers, "*A ghrá mo chroí*". I freeze above her.

"That's the second time you've said that." I transition to lay next to her, pulling her close to me. Our legs intertwined. We're both sweaty and a bit out of breath.

She gives me a side eye. "It means love of my heart. I didn't realize I said it out loud."

"Love of your heart. Does that mean.." She stops me before saying anything else.

"We'll talk about it in the morning." she snuggles in closer, as if that's possible. "We have a bit to talk about. I just want this for my birthday." she kisses me softly, and I moan softly.

"You sure that's all you want? I mean, we can still celebrate your birthday." I wiggle my eyebrows, a devilish smirk on my face.

"You can't be serious?" she jerks back.

"Oh, I'm not nearly done with you. You and I are due for blissfully orgasms." I kiss the bridge of her nose. "I saw an interesting artifact in the bathroom, on charge."

Her eyes widened. Did she really think I wouldn't see that little blue vibe on the counter? I back up off the bed to the bathroom, and turn on the little helper. The buzzing may be humming in her ears and screaming danger. My mind is saying round two.

"We're just getting started, little cub."

She props herself on her elbow, watching my every step as my cock still hangs high. Her jaw drops, but then sucks in her lips. Oh she's ready.

"Alexander?" she starts.

I reach for her ankles and yank them to the edge of the bed, she squeaks. With the buzzing friend in my hand, I dare tell her, "Hang on, darlin'."

Teresa

Sometimes in the middle of the night, Seamus curls up next to me as Alexander curls behind me, arms wrapped around me, pulling me into his chest. We have a long road ahead of us, but that's what love is, right?

I nudge Seamus awake as the sun starts to peek through the blinds. I slip out of Alexander's strong arms, peering back to look at the worn out Adonis himself.

I wonder what dreams play in his head. I quickly avoid the boards that creek and head into the kitchen for coffee. Every inch of my body is sore and aching in the best possible way. Every twinge of pain is a reminder of the countless orgasms of last night.

As the coffee brews, Seamus paws at my leg, and I sit on the floor for him to jump into my lap.

"Buddy, I'm making the right choice, right?" I scratch his back as he plops his nose onto my chest. I know he can't truly understand me, but something about his spirit tells me he does.

The machine spits out the last bit of coffee and I top it off with some Irish cream. A take a sip of the hot coffee, the aroma awakening my soul.

The early morning fog is still roaming across the field as the sun peeks through the clouds, casting out the shadows of night. I find my phone, which somehow made its way into the living room, and dial Seth. A few rings go by, and he picks up.

"Hell must have frozen over," he exclaims. I can hear Ella already singing in the background.

"It happened Seth."

I can hear the panic starting to rise in Seth's voice. "What happened?"

"Him."

A soft exhale sounds on the other end of the line. "About damn time. What changed?"

I shake my head, "Excuse me?"

"Thank God, really, because I don't think I can stand his moody, mopey ass one more second. But seriously, are you okay?"

He was moody? My heart sinks, the rush of guilt returns. "I think I stopped holding back. I don't know how to explain it."

"I think it's more than holding back, Tess. There was a part of you that trusted him, no matter what lies ahead." He pauses for a moment, and I wonder if the call dropped. "Tess, is he better than Aiden? Does he treat you right? Does the man make you crazy enough to still love him through his antics?"

"In every way." I sigh.

Seth makes a happy hum sound. "You're a better person since he walked into your life. You're a fighter, you gained more of a backbone. You're someone I want Ella to idolize and adore. Even better, you opened yourself up to the possibility that you can get a happy ending. Figure out the road ahead and fight it with him."

"Thanks, Seth," I say softly.

"Also, please screw his brains out some more. Fucker needs it."

I can't keep in the resounding laugh. "Yeah, don't need to worry about that. You still having family day at your house this year?"

"Yes ma'am. I better see your ass there."

I chuckle out a yes. "You got it, buddy. I'll talk to you later. Give Ella-bella a hug for me."

Relief rushes through me. I feel lighter, like a weight has been lifted. I return to my kitchen and stare out the window, listening to the morning birds. I hum as arms circle around me, engulfing me in a warm embrace. The scent of him lingers around me, and for a moment, it feels like a dream. He plants a soft kiss on my shoulders, grabbing my coffee to take a sip.

"A little early for Irish, ain't it?" he grumbles, his morning voice deeper than I remember.

Fuck, there go the panties.

"You're complaining about having something Irish already?" I smirk at him.

"Perhaps not the Irish I want," He wraps me tighter, his mouth on my neck, nipping away.

I hum. "While I appreciate the amount of love bites on my neck, you owe me a conversation."

Alexander set his chin on top of my head. Freaking giant. "Fine, darlin'. Can I at least get some coffee in me, and move this to the couch?"

I nod. I get out of his grasp, making my way to the couch.

It doesn't help to prepare to be patient and not be overwhelmed by feelings when Alexander is half naked in my kitchen, in a pair of sweatpants.

Where the fuck did he get sweatpants? Another question for another day.

I could gawk at him all day. A man like that wants me.

"Wipe the drool, darlin', or you might get other ideas." he teases.

I adjust myself, trying to focus on *anything* else. Seamus curls up next to my side, like the good boy he is, then Alexander sits down next to us. I gather my strength and push away the anxiety.

I clear my throat, signaling the start of this conversation. "I want to allow you the time to explain things. I think we both hurt each other in more ways than one, and we both deserve to be heard."

"Where would you like me to start?" He sips on the coffee.

"When did you feel like it changed?" I know timing is everything for him.

He sighs, clearly preparing himself. "Between the night under the stars after I came to you bleeding and the night you pulled that rebellious stunt at the bonfire. I was furious you didn't take things seriously, and the thought of something happening to you stirred something in me. I'd never met a woman who challenged me, who mouthed off to me so much. I honestly didn't know how to function."

His words are honest. I feel my breath catching in my throat.

"When you shot me down at the coffee shop, after I told you we might want to work together and you pushed it aside? That's when at first I thought of you as a task. I used my charm to gain your trust. I watched you slowly fall for me, our date you were more than I expected, your wonderment, your imagination, your kindness, like a fire igniting I couldn't tell you the truth. Then things changed and when I called you mine first, I knew in the end something was going to break."

I couldn't say anything. I just listen to him, continue. He's a mess like me. "I shocked myself thinking that I called you mine. I just got lost in you and didn't know how to handle you and the club business and still be the man you deserve."

I nod. "I guess that would explain the hot and cold moments." I already know the answer, but I wait for his confirmation.

"I didn't know how to handle it. Between making runs and what Rawlings asked me to do, things got worse."

I nod again, listening to him as he continues. "This is why we don't make decisions based on emotions. When emotions run high, judgment can be impaired."

I take a second to ask another question. "So, when you told me to "behave" and listen to you, that was your stake? Dominance?"

"I had a reason for that. Yes, I need control, I crave it. But it was also to protect you."

This time, I pipe in. "I can see that, but you can trust me to protect myself. I mean, I can take you down, can't I?"

He rubs his thumb over his lip. "You can try. We have a gym in the back of the compound – maybe I can teach you to shoot too." He smiles before continuing. "Alright, my turn. You said you wouldn't make the same mistake twice. I think there's more to that."

I offer him a small, warm smile before I take a deep breath. He deserves answers, and it's time to come clean. "When I was in undergrad, I met Aiden. He was my first boyfriend. The first few months, he was so sweet and encouraging, and I didn't think twice about opening up to him. Then, after a year, something switched in him. He came from a very wealthy family. He wanted me to act a certain way, talk a certain way, just *be* a certain way that wasn't me. There was a lot of verbal abuse, but I put up with it because I wanted to please him. I thought that relationships meant taking the good and the bad, even when it was *very* bad."

Alexander moves closer, pulling me into his lap. I sigh, melting into him for comfort as I continue. "I didn't know any better. I became a shell of a person. He threatened that if I left him, he'd hunt me down, that words wouldn't be the only thing that hurt. He thought that if he didn't give me visible scars, no one would believe I was being abused." Alexander strokes my hair, trying to calm me, anchor me.

"How did you leave?" he whispers when I stop talking.

I take a deep breath. "I called my dad and told him everything. Being the daughter of a police captain does have its perks. We got a restraining order, I got an apartment as I adjusted to life again, and I got into counseling. I got my tattoo and continued on through my Master's. Raleigh felt like a place to start over, a place of new beginnings. You broke down a lot of walls, Alexander. You made me feel like I was ready to knock down the rest of them. Imagine the feeling of betrayal, lies, being a puppet in someone's plan. It was like I was back with Aiden." I trace his cheek with my finger.

"Why didn't you say anything?" His voice is soft, like he's worried I'll break if he presses harder.

"It's hard to open up to others when you're used to being alone or refuse to be a weaker version of yourself."

He doesn't press me again. He caresses my face. Instead, he asks the hard questions. "Where do we go from here? What do you want?"

I came prepared with an answer. "I want to move past this, maybe even build something together. I hear you, just be patient."

He plants a kiss on my forehead. "I can be that, just know I'll chase you if you run."

"What I'm hearing is you need me as much as I need you," I say as his grins.

"Until the roads end and even in the after, little cub." He kisses me as I melt further into his arms. He breaks the kiss sooner than I want, only to present a small, wrapped box.

"Happy birthday."

I look at him with nothing but love in my eyes. The words escape me to express it. I open the gift to find a dark green gem hanging on a Celtic knot in silver, the chain longer than normal. It's too much, tears threaten to spill over.

"Alexander. This is too much." He takes the box from my hands in response, moving to clasp the chain around my neck. I am in awe of this man.

"This doesn't have a tracker does it?" I look back at him.

He snorts. "Do you really think that we're *that* capable? No, Teresa. We're not that tech savvy. We're a club, not the mafia."

He has a point. I wrap my arms around his neck as he lifts me from the couch and carries me back to the bedroom, unraveling me with nothing but the necklace.

What a perfect way to spend a Saturday.

Chapter 30

Teresa

I don't think I've ever experienced bliss like Saturday was.

Alexander made it all better, with an absurd amount of warm-heartedness, tender-loving words, and laughter.

Seeing a giant ass man playing with a twenty-pound corgi definitely didn't hurt. There's a light feeling. Like a weight has been lifted, after recognizing that both of us were responsible for our hurt. It's not a quick fix, but it's a start.

The alarm goes off for what is going to be a long day. Part of me isn't looking forward to this. I have to suck it up. I reach over to the other side of the bed, I'm alone.

The bed is empty and lonely, cold to the touch, as if he's been gone for hours.

"Alexander," I call softly, wondering if it'd all been a dream. I force myself out of bed, walking down the hallway, hearing no noises from the kitchen or living room. Seamus trails behind me, equally as confused. I peer through the open double doors of my library office.

Be still my beating heart.

Alexander's entranced in a book, sitting by the window, not noticing as I lean on the door, gawking in amazement. I adjust my eyes to see what book he's picked up, and a heat of blush trails my cheek.

He found the romance corner.

"You're lucky we have a meeting soon and need to be on time," I say, stirring him out of his trance. "Or else I'd jump your bones in a heartbeat.

He looks up with a devilish smile, peering at me over the book. "We both know I only need two minutes."

I blush at the thought; I'm still recovering from yesterday. "I mean, you could test that theory in the shower. Kill two birds with one stone?" I look down at the floor, fiddling with the siding of the door.

Alexander pulls me into him, throwing me up over his shoulders. "Mm, I'll take that as a yes."

I don't even realize we've made it to the shower until I hear it start and feel Alexander begin to peel off my clothes.

"In. Hands on the wall," he growls from between clenched teeth. Steam circles around us as I step in, letting the warm water run over my aching body.

I'm patiently waiting for him, which proves to be more exhilarating than I thought it would. The curtain slides away as I hear Alexander join me. I want to turn away, but he ordered my hands on the wall.

"If you make us late, Rawlings will have my head on a spike," I taunt, tilting my head to the side. He doesn't say anything. Suddenly, a sudsy washcloth caresses my shoulders. The scent of warm vanilla fills my nose. The washcloth trails down my back, past my dimples, and around my ass. It continues down my legs and pulls back up.

I can't think straight, the sensation of his touch clouding my thoughts. I press back to bump up against him, aching for more. The washcloth travels to my front. He steps closer, pressing our bodies together. His other hand wraps around my neck, giving it a slight squeeze. He nips above my ear as he rubs the washcloth around my breasts. All coherent thought evaporates as he continues down the path, past my hips towards my thighs.

"Alexander," I say his name as a moan and a plea.

He drops the washcloth, my hands still anchored on the wall, my muscles starting to ache terribly. One hand travels back to my breasts and pinches a nipple, the other slipping between my folds.

"Even here, you are wet for me? What was it, Teresa? The washcloth teasing you? The anticipation?" he murmurs above my ear as his fingers dip into my pussy, the hand that was on my breast moves back to around my throat.

I disobey knowingly and place my hands on his thighs, his fingers continuing to torture my pussy and clit with small, teasing strokes.

Alexander lets out a heavy tsk. "Naughty girl, disobeying me. How should I punish you?" His hard cock presses against my back, and I buck against him, silently begging him to fuck me.

"Bend over, little cub, hands behind your back. You don't get to touch anymore." I do as he says, whimpering as his fingers slip out of me. He grabs my wrists and clutches them in his hands to keep me in place. He teases my clit at the same time, rubbing his tip up and down it before forcefully thrusting inside. A gasp tears from my throat. I might not actually last long.

"This is going to be hard and fast." Alexander isn't playing around this morning.

I nod, no words coming. He does as promised, slamming into me hard and fast without mercy. I feel full, overwhelmed by the sensations, my orgasm building quickly. Alexander hits every spot inside me, my walls starting to grip down on him as the build continues. Shrieks of pleasure escape me, breathless moans, wanting more. Without warning, my body betrays me as I come hard around him.

He doesn't stop as I ride through my orgasm. He's not far behind, finishing in me soon after, staying buried deep inside as he spills every ounce. His breathing slows as he leaves me and releases my hands, kissing between my shoulder blades.

"See? All I needed was two minutes."

I turn and smack his strong chest. *Cocky.* He gathers me in his arms and bends down to kiss me tenderly. If this is a dream, it is the best one.

In a blur, time plays well on our side and it's not long before the compound is in our sight. Alexander squeezes my hand because the last time we were here, he was begging that I didn't see into the light.

Coincidentally, even with our shower, we're on time as we meet at the Devil's Whiskey. I could use a drink or two to get through this meeting. We sit in my car, and as I go to open my door, Alexander grabs my arm to pull me back.

"One piece of advice before we go in. Stand your ground, don't take any of their shit. Do what you think is best for your community, not for me or the club." He tilts my chin up and presses a final kiss on my lips, one that seems to linger afterwards.

I went to argue with him, because we were supposed to be a team, but he stops me. The club I understand has an order, a set of laws that have been followed.

"Trust me," he whispers.

I walk in with my head held high, seeing familiar faces surround me in their leather cuts with their patches. I flip my sunglasses on top of my head; I may be small, but I walk like I tower over everyone. I'm feeling like my old self again.

Finally.

The main room is surrounded by the members but past them is a huge room with a glossy wooded table in the middle.

Rawlings sits at the open table in the middle of the room. Alexander trails behind me like a guard dog, ready to pounce on anyone who comes near.

"Bjorn," Rawlings grumbles out.

"Rawlings. Is that your first name or do you just go by your last name?" I snicker out a laugh, sitting down across from him.

"Either someone has a lot of energy in the morning, or someone got thoroughly fucked this morning." Rawlings smiles like he *knows.*

I don't care if he knows, he just knows that I'm not going anywhere. "Could be both. Thank you for asking. Johnny, could I get some coffee?" I yell at the bar behind me, seeing one of my favorite people in the back.

He smiles back at me. "Splash of Baileys?"

"Man of my heart." I flirt back. Alexander squeezes my hand, which is in his, as I roll my eyes, patting his cheek in reassurance.

"Shall we then?" Rawlings interrupts. I nod in response.

We say for the rest of the board to come in. Alexander pulls a chair up next to me. Something flutters in my stomach, it's tangled in knots.

Rawlings clears his throat, grabbing everyone's attention. He glares down at the table. "Let's cut to the chase. By now we know the Falcons are behind the disappearances as a whole. Given our history, they tend to take things that don't belong to them. We're always at war with them. What we've gathered is that they found secondary people, one for giving names and the other to do what they want with the information. We shouldn't be surprised if they're taking them to Florida."

Rawlings' commanding voice continues to tell a story, everyone seems engrossed as heads start to nod in agreement.

"Bjorn, I think you'll find this useful, we also know that someone within your company, most likely Sheldon, is working with them and covering things up. So well, in fact, that you didn't notice."

I feel like I should be insulted that I didn't catch this sooner. I cock a raised eyebrow.

I butt into the conversation, "So, we're having to cut off the head of a snake, cut out the middleman, throw a wrench into the plan. We're only focusing on here though, not in Florida?"

Rawlings looks at Alexander and back at me. I know I got it right. "Something like that."

I smirk, crossing my arms across my chest. "Why do I have a feeling that you're censoring things?"

Johnny comes around with my coffee, and I flash him a smile.

Rawlings doesn't skip a beat. "Here's the unfortunate part. It's all about timing. Something big has to be in motion for us to cut them off."

"Again, why don't you focus on Sheldon, and it will become a domino effect?" I say into my coffee.

I look back up after taking a sip to the shocked faces of Rawlings, Alexander, and quite a few others.

"That seems a little dark, even for you." Alexander looks at me with concern in his eyes.

I scoff. "Would I cry over seeing Sheldon gone? No, him and Carla have been getting to me the past couple of months. Now I understand why. I just think it's the best course of action." I shrug.

"Who the fuck is Carla?" Rawlings raises an eyebrow.

"Someone I wouldn't be surprised to see in your bed," I smirk. "Fake red hair, fake boobs, high heels that could stab a man."

I hear Alexander snicker. "She's got the red hair right." A few others snicker, even Keola. Rawlings just glares at us.

"What do you suggest then? We *wait*?" Rawlings questions.

Waiting would make things worse around here. Waiting would take a lot more lives. Save who we can, and let the Wolves fight it out how they want.

No, I don't want to wait, but at this point, I'm getting desperate. An idea pops into my head. It's risky but it might work.

"Anyone up for a masquerade?"

You could hear a pin drop, and the looks on their faces tell me they have no idea where this is going. What started off as murmurs turned into a blanket of silence.

Maybe this is why people say that men sometimes need a woman's touch, because they aren't that smart sometimes.

"Every year, the Foundation hosts a masquerade and silent auction to raise money for our projects. Get people drunk enough and they'll write big checks. This year, I got roped into hosting." I say.

"So what's the dress code to something like this?" Coda, who is typically quiet, chimes in.

"Black tie usually." Memphis says before I can. I look back at him, he jolts back, "What you think this is my first rodeo?"

Rawlings takes a moment to connect the dots. I watch as his eye light up with understanding "You might be onto something. Only time we could blend in, do what we need to and move on. You, my dear, will have an alibi so you would be in the clear. Everything else we can plan on our own."

"You do realize there's a buy-in and it's black tie attire?" I cock my head at him. Maybe I'm not giving the club enough credit, but they're more of a rough and tumble group of men.

"It's adorable you think we won't be able to blend in. Just do what we need you to do, and we'll take care of the rest," Keola laughs. I glance over at Alexander, and part of me wonders what this man looks like in a tuxedo.

Chills run down my spine.

I nod. "Perfect. Now, if you'll excuse me, I want to enjoy the rest of my weekend." I wink at Alexander.

Rawlings holds up a hand. "Hold on Bjorn. Walk with me." Something drops in the pit of my stomach. I look at Alexander and he shrugs. I would be lying if I said that I wasn't nervous.

Rawlings is even more of a giant than Alexander. The scruff and the salt and pepper hair, plus the sun kissed skin. I start to wonder how old he really is.

He holds the door for me, waiting for me to step out back near the patio. I hold my head high, trying not to show any fear. Once outside, he pulls out a chair for me to sit, and I oblige him.

"Is this the part where I'm warned again that if I'm not working with you, I'm working against you?" The nervousness sounds in my voice.

He just laughs, crossing his legs and leaning back. "No, my dear. I wanted to offer you an apology."

"Is Hell even more on fire?" Where is Alexander to shut me up when I need him?

Surprisingly, Rawlings just laughs again. "I didn't put my best foot forward with you. I acted out of what I perceived to be best for the club, for Jackson. That boy has been through a lot, and maybe I should have seen the signs. At my age, you tend to ignore them." Rawlings is rambling, clearly unsure of what he is trying to apologize for.

"The club has been through war, and even if most of my men know you, we can't be too quick. I'll admit, I thought that by putting Jackson onto you, we put our objective front and center. All this to say, he was following orders, something he's used to doing. If you're going to continue to place anger on someone, it should be on me. You seem like a good kid, with a good heart. You definitely have a hold on the big man in there."

Hearing Rawlings say this both stuns me and makes me emphasize a bit with him. The club has a way of life and order, and whether I truly believe in it or not, I have to respect that.

I reach out and pat his hand. "Don't go soft on me, old man. But I appreciate it."

Rawlings apparently isn't done. "I don't think you have a real grasp on our world, Tessa. Women don't usually have a say here. We have an order to things. We're not saints, but we run the club in a way that protects all of us," Rawlings growls out, the sweet demeanor suddenly disappearing.

I'm shocked at his tone. "I'm not asking for you to give me a spot in your club. But maybe in these times y'all need to bring in your "ol ladies", your partners. You'd be surprised. Have more faith in women, we're not all devils." I don't give him time to respond as I get up and place my hand on his shoulder to leave. He holds on to it.

"You realize the power of him claiming you as his, right?" Rawlings bites out.

I pause, looking down at his dark brown eyes, noticing the scar above his eye. "I haven't given much thought to it," I admit sheepishly.

Apparently, there's more to it as Rawlings releases a sigh, "When a member claims someone, whoever it is, it's like a shield of protection. Someone threatens you, they threaten the club. What you do reflects on the club. You may not wear the patch, but it's branded into your soul and perhaps one day, your skin. We protect our own. That extends to you as well. It's sacred."

His words ring in my ears.

Alexander called me his, laying claim, giving me more protection than I realized. It was never meant to be about property or lowering myself to him, but something he can offer me without hesitation.

Rawlings gives one last notion. "I don't think you all can afford to hurt each other again. That boy is smitten with you."

I give a subtle nod and head back in, as Rawlings looks for a cigarette and eases back even more into the chair.

Once I'm back into the building, I try to find my things. Alexander stops me before I gather my things to leave. He grabs my arms to pull me into an embrace. "Do I want to know what that was about?" he questions, nestling my head into his neck.

I snort. "Um, I think I got the "if you hurt my child" talk." He jerks back, tilting his face down to meet my eyes. I lift to my toes and kiss him on the cheek. "Now, either take me home and fuck me, or stay here to play nice with your club," I whisper in his ear.

He peers down at me with a hungry look in his eyes. I keep the silence going; all I know is that I want to devour this man. I float to the door, giving him a moment to think about his choice.

A roar of laughter soars through the room as Alexander bursts through the door, a man ready to eat.

Time passes by us again. Every day Alexander is insatiable, but that's really the pot calling the kettle black.

The man promised me gym time and a shooting range. Call me a hypocrite, but this police captain's daughter doesn't know how to shoot. Another workday ends, which means freedom. I meet Alexander out at the compound just as the sun is setting, deep reds and oranges bursting over the tops of the trees.

I see Alexander leaning against the railing of the entrance. I make my way over to him, rising on my toes to kiss him, fast and sweet.

"Okay, are we going to do this? I'm ready to take your ass down." I softly jab his upper arm.

"Your funeral," he responds as we make our way towards the back of the compound.

"What's the plan tonight? Boxing ring? Guns?" I bounce around, anxious to get started.

"You'll just have to see," is all I get as we make our way through the door into what looks like a barn. He flicks the light on and it kind of resembles Romero's gym. In the center is a ring, surrounded by weights and beams, weapons lining the wall.

My eyes grow big when I see the hilts and blades of the knives. My hand starts to reach for one, but another hand stops me. Keola's tattooed hand grasps mine and prevents me from touching a weapon. Behind him is a familiar face from the hospital, Memphis steps out from the shadows.

"Don't think that's a wise idea," he mutters as he yanks my hand back.

"Afraid I might scratch something?" I coo. "Or just happen to *miss?*"

"With you, anything is possible," Keola mutters under his breath, lugging a bag of items behind him. Memphis stands next to me. I'll never get over the fact that everyone towers over me.

"Alexander, did you invite an audience? I'm not much of a fan of voyeurism, but whatever floats your boat," I snark out. I'm struggling to hold in my laughter: the men's faces pale in terror and disbelief.

"You just had to choose her, didn't you?" Keola glances over at Alexander, shaking his head and reaching down to unpack his bag. Memphis offers a big belly laugh, and a big smile plastered on his face.

I step into the ring and walk, around testing the rigging and platform. I'd brought in my bag with me, I grab my wraps.

"Darlin', I didn't have the ring in our plans tonight. We're here to get you used to firing a gun." Alexander offers his hand out for me to jump down.

I laugh. "You didn't, but I did."

He hangs his head, glancing back at Memphis and Keola, who throw their hands up in defeat. As I finish wrapping, I sit in a straddle, working on my flexibility. I hear the clanking of metal and peek through the ropes, seeing a few guns laid out. I bend over in the straddle, propped up on my elbows. Alexander sees me watching and comes closer to me. "I was kind of hoping we'd do a little sparing, go a few rounds, then do whatever you had planned."

"You can't bring a knife or fists to a gunfight."

I can certainly try.

"Touché, but if you think that guns are the only solution, you're wrong. Why do you think I started boxing, going to Romero's? Woman has to protect herself nowadays," I say, standing up and getting into a boxer stance, bouncing on my toes. Alexander continues to look at me with seriousness in his eyes. "Tell you what, big guy, best two out of three rounds. Then, I'll listen and go along with this plan for tonight."

"Still don't think it's a fair fight, darlin'," Alexander says as he steps into the ring, stripping off his shirt and throwing it to

Memphis. His rippling muscles meet my eyes, and I shake my head to get back to the present moment.

"You are so cute when you get serious. Best two out of three," I say, giving him a wink.

Alexander nods his head. "I've pinned you down before. If you really wanted to be underneath me again, all you had to do was ask." Alexander's circling around me.

We're like two animals fighting over territory, going toe to toe.

"Don't you start flirting with me now." I tease him.

Alexander crouches down, striding towards me, his arms stretched out to grab me. I counter by staying in front of him, but he turns, reaching for my neck. My short height allows him easy access. I wrap my body around his waist, like a snake coiling around her prey, wrapping my arm around his neck. Alexander uses his weight to lean back towards the ground, and we fall to the ground hard with a loud thud, vibrating the ring. I'm still wrapped around him but Alexander, being a complete superhuman freak, starts to get up and twists us low to the ground.

We land on the ground with me on the back again, my legs still tight around him, and him still struggling to get me off his back, like an itch you can't scratch. I wait for him to tap out in defeat, but somehow, he manages to lift us off the ground. I've managed to hang on so far, but I can feel it in my thighs.

Slowly my strength is escaping me. He steps back up, and I clench my thighs, trying to hang on with all my might. His absolute brutal strength stuns me.

"Don't say I didn't warn you." I hear the anger and hiss in his voice. Without warning, he jumps up and bucks backwards, landing me on my back with all his weight, knocking the breath right out of me. I have no choice but to tap this round.

Damnit.

A hand extends out to help me up, but I smack it away.

Romero taught me to never expect a fair fight: expect your opponent to be twice your size and twice as smart. Experiences are never fair, so you do what you can to protect yourself.

Fury bubbles inside me. I get up and adjust myself, readying myself for round two with the ambition that he's going down and not gracefully. Clenching my hands into fists, feeling my nails bite into my skin, I don't give him a chance. In a rage, I rush him and I aim my punches to his abdomen and sides. I'm a force of power, fierce, unstoppable. His body takes my hits and jabs, but in one movement, he grabs one of my hands and twists behind my back.

"Anger does you no good," he whispers in my ear, roughly nipping it. Throwing my head back, I knock him off balance, and he stumbles back.

Seeing my chance, I plant a front kick to his chest and side swept his leg from underneath him. His body strikes the ground like dead weight, laying him flat on his back. I spider crawl my way up his body, straddling him, locking my lower arm onto his throat. I apply pressure against his throat, limiting his air intake.

"I quite like this position. Remind me of this when you're back in our bed." I wink at him, and he taps my side, struggling for air. I release my arms and stand up, circling around him. He coughs a bit to regain his composure.

"All tied up, brother," Memphis shouts, and Keola's interest is peaked. Keola hasn't said anything since we started, but the smirk on his face gives me a bit more satisfaction of taking Alexander down. He watches carefully, analyzing every movement.

"Don't go easy now," I say to Alexander as I adjust my bra.

"Stop playing with your tits and I won't," The snarl in his voice, the possessiveness, something in that moment made me realize that I'm his, that showboating to his brothers sparked the animalistic person he is.

One more and I'm the victor.

I'm bouncing on my toes, excited to go head to head with him one last time. Adrenaline roams through my body, my chest heaving with exertion. I take charge, aiming for his legs, but Alexander wraps his arms around my waist, flipping me up close to his head, his face near my pussy. My legs are wrapped around his neck, trying not to suffocate my man.

"If you wanted dessert, all you have to do is ask," I snicker.

I'd want it as much as he does.

He yanks me off hard, throwing me to the ground, pinning me underneath him. *Big mistake.* All his strength lies in his body weight and in his hands.

"Tap. Out,'" he growls. He tightly grips my ass, soaking in my sweat and scent. He looks up at me for a response.

"Never." I clench harder around his neck. "Keola, you might want to get Doc in here soon," I sputter.

Thank God for thick thighs that save lives. I swivel around, crawling behind forcing my weight forward, making him lean forward, smacking his forehead on the mat as I slither my way away.

This is for all the nights watching WWE with pops.

While he's still on the ground, I climb onto the ropes and launch myself up in the air, elbow ready to strike his back. To my surprise, he rolls away, forcing me to tuck in my arms for impact quickly. I land ungracefully on my stomach, smacking my head to the ground. Alexander scrambles to straddle my back, both my arms pinned behind my back.

Heat rises from me again. I'm turned on by the position, the fights, the strength, the gorgeous man on top of me. The pain in my arms shoots up again, not allowing me to move or angle myself.

The brief tingling feeling in my previously-injured shoulder returns. I have full range of motion, but once in a while, it hurts. I struggle to figure a way out of this. On my back, I could do so much, but on my stomach? Not so much. In defeat, I tap my back foot on the mat.

"There's my girl." He doesn't let go, but eases up on my arms.

"What do you mean? I fucking lost," I mumble under my breath. Not moving an inch or seeing his smug face.

"Yeah, but you put up a hell of a fight. My little wild cub. Like a raging bear wanting to fight." His hand travels up my legs and circling my ass. A twinge of pain comes from him slapping my ass. "Deal's a deal. But I'll make another promise." My eyebrows raise at his suggestive tone.

I turn my head to the side. "Listening."

"If you are good, you'll get a reward. I have something I wanted to try with you."

"Which is?"

"Let's just say, two holes will be occupied, plus the faithful blindfold," he whispers in my ear. I practically choke at his words.

I become speechless, my eyes say everything.

Fuck me, I'll be his good girl.

"I can smell your arousal, darlin'. Thinking too hard about it, huh? If I reach down right now, am I going to find you wet?" Damn. Primal, dominant, and a fan of sensory play. Who the fuck is this man?

"Get off of me, you giant." He releases me, jumping up off my back. I turn to see more sweat dripping from him, glistening in the low lighting of the barn. What is it about sweat and it dripping down a man's body that turns women into puddles?

A deal is a deal and for the next hour, they take me behind the barn and explain gun safety and how to load the clip. They test different handguns to figure out which one's best for my stature. My arms are getting sore from the endless positioning and targeting progress, but now, I've at least attempted to shoot and be okay with it. Alexander and Memphis told me that I should lay off the knives, but I'm not really about to listen to them.

I must have been focusing on the targets that it takes me a minute to realize that my phone started to ring. I bring it out and focus on whose voice I'm about to listen. I put the gun down, making sure I don't shoot anything accidentally. I look at the screen, realizing it's a video call, and my stomach drops at the name.

Lucie Lynn.

My heart sinks, like a rock in a rough ocean storm.

"Alexander," I yell, his strides bringing him quickly to my side. I answer the call and anger falls across my face.

Lucie Lynn's face pops on the screen, her face bruised, dried blood running down her cheeks.

"Lucie." That's the only word that comes from my mouth. Alexander clasps his hands on my shoulders to steady my panic. My eyes become misty, tears threatening at my friend's injuries.

"Ms. Tessa, I'm sorry to bother you," she breaks in her speech. "But you said to call if anything happens. I also didn't know who to call. I left a message for Ms. Shiloh. She hasn't returned my call," she sobs.

Her sobs are shattering my heart into more pieces. Alexander stands by me, throwing his face in the picture.

I can tell she's starting to panic.

"Who did this? Was it Ramon? *Who*?" I urge her to answer. Rage and fury aren't enough to describe what I'm feeling.

Tears stream down her face again. I will *murder* the person who did this to her. I start walking to my car, Alexander and his men following my steps. "Lucie Lynn. I need you to tell me who did this." I need the name.

Vengeance is the only emotion I feel.

"Benny."

A bird is about to have his wings clipped.

Chapter 31

Teresa

I see red, the flames rising above me.

I hang up the phone with Lucie Lynn and I turn to face Alexander, letting the fury in me grow.

"I need you to convince me to not do what I'm about to do. If you can't convince me, either help me or move out of my way and I'll clean the mess later," I say. He looks at me, placing his hands on my shoulders, then looking back at his brothers.

I'm brash sometimes, I rush into things and now is the time for him to stop me. He blinks and looks genuinely worried.

And he should.

"I know where he is and we are going to have some words. You are either going to help me or move out of my way. You got that?" I search his eyes for my answer.

No one knows he's "claimed" me and I don't bear a mark. I know what I'm going to do. I'm going to send a message to the Falcons, a threat to leave my community and Lucie alone.

I don't care if Rawlings or anyone else in the club disapproves. I refuse to let them hurt anyone I love. He would do the same if it was me.

Alexander hasn't said a word, but lets out a breath, which he seems to have been holding for some time. Keola and Memphis are waiting for his reply, too.

I'll understand if he turns me down for the sake of his club, but right now, he's starting to get in my way.

He looks at me, grabbing my shoulders. "What do you need?" Shock floods through me.

"Really?" I say, dumbfounded.

Keola looks at Alexander, probably thinking this is a terrible idea, that I'm bringing trouble and evil into their club. "Don't think this is a good idea. Whatever she's cooking in that head of hers, are you sure?" Keola says.

Something is cooking alright.

"No, you're joking with me. It can't be that easy," I shake my head in disbelief.

"What did you have in mind?" He inches closer.

Keola may think I don't hear him when he says, "this is what happens when your dick makes the decisions for you."

I twist my head, "Karma is bitch, you know that right." Alexander puts a finger under my chin and brings my face back to him. "What's your plan?"

"Send one of your prospects to Lucie while Shiloh, our legal advocate, can get to her. Legally, she needs to report this. I'm going to go have a little chat with Benedict. I'll carry my knives." I don't know why this man is shocked when I tell him, but he scans over my body like he missed something.

I snapped my fingers to grab his attention, his piercing blue eyes sparkled back, "Britt will most likely have her gun, Reva and Sam might have their tasers." He goes to argue at the mention of the girls. I stop him, "I'm not letting this go, Alexander. I protect my own, just like you do." I spit out my rushed plan.

I'll figure out my conversation starters as I drive. The time is now. After a moment of deep breathing. "I am just going to talk with him, I'm not going to start a fight."

"And how do we know that? And why bring your friends?" Keola snarks from the back.

"Because no one is going to suspect us, you want me to show up with a bunch of Grim Wolves in their joint? Because that's really smart." I scoff.

"He may have a point though. You're putting yourself and others in potential danger." Memphis chimes, showing that someone may have a calmer way of speaking to me.

"What do you need from me?" Alexander growls out again.

I keep spitballing. "I'll need back up. Maybe send in one of the prospects or if we're bold, someone without their cut with me or the ladies, I don't need you to get yourself hurt or into a turf war."

He nods at my reply as I move towards my car. Alexander follows behind, opening my car door. "Maybe if all goes well, we can discuss a mark." I say.

He smirks as he whips out his phone to make a few calls. He tells me to message Sparky after Shiloh and I speak.

I text my friends to meet me at the house and arm themselves. I'll explain when I get there, knowing full well they'll join me. The thought of them being like my own club makes me laugh.

As I drive, I attempt to repeatedly call Shiloh. She and I are more acquaintances than good friends, but I know I can rely on her, especially in emergencies.

By the third call, she picks up. "Teresa, this better be an emergency." I can practically hear the sass and fire in her tone. There's someone in the background, she shushes them. Between someone in the background and muffled music, I may have caught her at a bad time.

"Lucie Lynn." I say, knowing that is all she needs to grab her attention.

"I'll be at her place in twenty." She hangs up the phone. I shoot Sparky a message, giving him a heads up that Shiloh is incoming.

In my rearview mirror, I see truck lights and motorcycle headlights, like an armada ready to charge.

Am I acting impulsively? Perhaps.

We get to my place in record time, no time for pausing and double guessing my train of thought. I rush into the bedroom with Alexander and Seamus on my tail. Without hesitation, I whip my clothes off to change and holster my knife.

"Teresa," he growls out. I hold up my finger, against his protest.

"You can growl all you want but you and me will not be doing the sideways tango." I stand in my closet trying to find my clothes. As I finally get dressed the rush of emotions rise to the surface. A trail of second guessing happens.

Alexander clears his throat, holding out my favorite red jacket with two fingers. "Figure you might want this." He searches around my dresser, finding the necklace he'd gotten me. "This, too."

I haven't really worn it since he gave it to me. I didn't think of it as an everyday wear, but I'll humor him. As I grab the items from his hands, he holds onto mine a bit longer.

He stands there looking at me, like I might break or

"If you have something to say, say it now. Because when I step out of this house, I'm not changing my mind." I can see there's something he's holding back. The strain in his neck and his hard features give it away.

Finally, he lets out a rumble. "I'm trusting that you know what you're doing."

"I sense a "but" in there, Alexander." I know him better than he thinks.

He sighs. "*But.* what consequences come from this might end in an early death for you *and* me."

My heart melts. I cup his cheek, stroking his face with my fingertips. I may act impulsively sometimes, but there's a reason.

"You'll find me in the afterlife." I plant a kiss on his lips, tenderly, one that lingers. At this moment, I may just be falling in love with him.

"You know that's not what I meant."

"I know." I sigh. The internal fight that this may lead to an opening to show our cards to the Falcons, a standoff that they can't scare me into fearing the unknown, and a warning to stay away from Lucie. The timing is not the best but you play with the hand you're dealt with, whether you win or lose. "But you know," I start off, "I'm surprised that Rawlings hasn't busted down my door."

"I think you'd be pleasantly surprised, he was in a better mood." Alexander chuckles.

I didn't see Rawlings at the compound prior to leaving. Then again, it didn't occur to me to wonder at the time.

I hear the slamming of my front door and pull my hand away, the moment over. Alexander follows behind me as Sam and Reva pop into my front door.

"Some calvary you've there." Reva remarks.

"You call, we come." Sam says. She starts to chew on her lips.

"Better to have numbers than solo." I try to laugh off as I start to explain the situation.

With no objections, I lead Sam and Reva from my living room out the door.

The roar of the bikes sounds like thunder in a summer storm. Seeing Alexander lead the pack of wolves, like a wicked prince taking charge of his kingdom, is intoxicating. The girls and I, however, situate ourselves in Britt's truck.

"Where are we going and whose kneecaps are we busting?" Britt zooms out of my makeshift driveway.

"Violence is the last resort, I told you this. I'm just going to speak some truth and leave a lasting impression." I say. I mean it's not a total lie.

No day like today to explain the plan, omitting more information than they need to know. "We're going to the Predator's Nest. I'm just going to talk to Benny and tell him what I thought of his work on Lucie and how I feel about it," I growl, counting the knives in my pocket and in my holster.

"So, we just show up? Then what?" Sam spills out. I can sense the nervousness in her voice. I feel bad, but they have just as much as gumption and heart to take on the toughest of fights.

"You're my backup. Joaquin will be with us for initial backup," I explain. "Look, I understand if you don't want to do this. I'll love and respect you for changing your mind, but don't ask me to change mine." I don't hear any complaints and we fall silent.

Reva shares the same stern and grim look as Britt. Sam, even with her nerves, gives me a shy nod, patting her shoulder bag.

Britt parks a block away for good measure, the wolves behind us by a block, far enough to not cause issues, though close enough to intervene if needed.

My phone buzzes, "Leif Erickson" pops on my screen. I answer the phone. "Alexander."

"Promise me something."

"Some things I can't promise, but I'm listening." I softly laugh, remembering all the promises he's trying to make up for breaking.

"You come back to me." I can hear the possessiveness in his voice, the slight twist of fear.

"*Mo chroí*, always." I glance down the street seeing everyone on the opposite end. My heart though can find him in any crowd.

"Stay close to Joaquin." Alexander calmly says.

I hang up the phone before I let him talk me out of it. Joaquin joins us as he walks away from the club down the way.

I feel the hand of Reva on my shoulder, as I look back and a single nod tells me that we're ready. Joaquin stays close to us, but closer to Sam. They avoid glances, but the small smirk on Sam's face tells me something hidden.

I take a deep breath.

This is for Jeremiah, for Lucie Lynn, for my community, for adding fear that should never have been there. For creating chaos in an already unbalanced world.

The Nest is like the Devil's Whiskey, only filled with Falcons.

It's smoky. The air is pungent with cigarettes and bad tequila and rum. I tuck a piece of my short hair behind my ear and make my way across the bar as the others find an empty table. The nearly balding bartender looks at me as I approach the bar. "What do you want?" he yells over the music.

"Jameson, if you got it," I answer back, sinking more into my seat.

He slides a full shot glass, I swallow it in one go, the burning easing into the pit of my stomach. I stop him before he can move onto the next customer. "Is Benedict here?"

His gravelly voice rings out, "Who's asking?"

"I'm going to take that as a yes. Just let him know I'd like a word with him."

He mumbles something under his breath and disappears for a moment, sliding down another shot of whiskey. I watch from being me as the girls and Joaquin sit in a booth behind me, giving me a gentle nod. Moments go by and sips of whiskey later.

I'm almost about to give up when I hear a sickening voice crack behind me.

"When he said a black haired woman was asking for me, you're not who I was expecting." Benedict's voice circles around me like nails on a chalkboard. I turn around in my seat, plastering a fake smile on my face for posterity.

He stands in front of me, shaved head, tattoos peeking out at every corner, tear drops around his eyes. "What can I do for you, little lady? Something you need taken care of?"

His hand skims my arm, towards the nape of my neck. The twist in his smile is gut wrenching. I resist the urge to stab his hand to the table.

"Actually, you *can* take care of something for me, buddy." I flick out one of my stationary knives from my boot, grasping it as it sets down on the bar top for him to see.

I have no plans on using it, it's merely a prop for my words.

"Oh, you are one of those kinky bitches, knife play. You have a lot of guts coming in here like this," Benedict smirks, his face twisted with black scruff and dark brown eyes.

"I'm giving you a warning, Benny." I push the knife closer, wanting to nick him, just a little bit. The temptation is real, but I promised myself that this would be the last resort. I want to draw blood, no matter how badly that could go for me.

"Choose your next words carefully," Benedict spits out. I peer behind him as a group of men creep toward us. I flick my eyes back to him, his greasy, beady eyes staring down at me.

"If you ever touch Lucie Lynn again, I will become your nightmare. You want someone to smack around, find yourself someone who will knock you on your ass and bury it," I growl out, sensing the girls wanting to move closer.

His eyes light up with recognition, something dawns on him, I continue my threat, "I will bury you and your men. You picked the wrong woman to piss off. I will protect my own."

"Ah.... Teresa Bjorn." My name rolls out of his mouth like poison. "Took you long enough to show your face." He puts a finger under my chin, and I jerk away in surprise. "Figured you were rolling around with some dogs."

I stand up, withdrawing my knife, putting it back into my boot, readying my hand against the knife in my holster. Guns are one thing, but the sharpness of tongue has no game than the sharpness of the blades.

"Awfully brave of you. Would have never figured a *bitch* like you around here." He tosses his words attempting to bring me down.

"Stay. Away. From. Her. Stay away from my community." I hiss every word. He takes a step forward, towering over me. I ready the other hand for any sudden movement.

"You're messing with the wrong club. Pretty stupid to think you could scare us. Now, I'll forgive you if you want to..." he says, insinuating that I'd want him, my stomach churns at the thought.

I inch my hand to ready myself for what I did not want to happen, and yet wondering which vein I want to nick. He continues, "You think your band of bitches and one man, and if I didn't know better is a *wolf,* will stop me?" He laughs in my face, his breath hitting me like a ton of bricks.

"I protect my own. You so much as come near the streets downtown or Lucie again, it won't be the grim reaper coming for your soul. I will gut you like yesterday's catch." I spit out every word, letting the threat ring in his ears.

I let go of my knife and start to turn away, but Benedict grabs my hair, fire and death flaming in his eyes. He yanks me back, my back thudding painfully against his chest.

"You shouldn't have come here." He jerks my head to the side, baring my neck. His other hand squeezes; I can feel his bruising hand leaving a print. My thoughts go to Alexander and the rage he would be in right now. "No place for a damsel in distress," he whispers into my neck. Out of the corner of my eye, I see Joaquin inching closer, but Sam stops him for a brief second.

"Who says we're the ones in distress?" I say as I stomp on his foot. I pull all my strength into the floor as I flip him forward off of me. He lands hard on his back, and the sound of impact spreads a tiny smile on my face. I look down at Benedict, my lungs heaving for a breath. His groans are like music to my ear.

I crotch down, scanning over the lifeless body, "You fucking come after me or anyone else under my protection, my family, I'll come after you."

"You'll pay." he groans out.

I smile at him, "I'd like to see you try."

The girls crowd around me, a glimpse of their "weapons" of choice. "Never underestimate a woman and her fury."

The music had died at some point, and I gestured for the women to leave as we saunter out the front door, no one saying a word.

I look back to the wolves, still mounted on their bikes, ready for anything. I wave my hand to signal home, and they rev their bikes.

I can feel the adrenaline escape me, but the power remains. It's *enticing*.

Britt gets us home and I'm ready for a shower and sleep, knowing full well that work calls tomorrow. I bid the girls goodnight and ask a couple men to follow them home, just in case. *I protect my own.*

Alexander doesn't leave instead, he waits for me in the driveway, leaning against his bike, the front lights of the house illuminating his rugged features.

I walk towards him, taking my time to appreciate the sight.

"I came back." I fulfilled his promise. I shrug my shoulders, knowing he had nothing to worry about. He gathers me in his arms, my head leaning against his chest.

"Stay with me tonight," I mumble into his chest. He doesn't say anything, only planting a soft kiss to the top of my head.

He scoops me into his arms, but instead of bringing me immediately to the bedroom, he takes me to the bathroom, placing me on top of the countertop.

"Mm, this is the bathroom. I'd much rather have you in the bedroom," I say, a smirk curling at the corner of my mouth.

"I rather fuck you without another man's scent on you." I can hear the anger in his voice as he grabs a washcloth and soap from the shower. He lathers up the washcloth, gently running it across my face. I hold his gaze, soaking in the anger in his eyes. I hold his wrist with the washcloth in place.

"Alexander, if you have something to say, say it." If we're going to make things work, he has to talk to me.

He sighs, setting the washcloth in the sink, resting his hands on either side of me, trapping me even more. "I'm a little angry at your impulsiveness to step into a rival's territory, even if I went along with it. It's just...you scare me sometimes."

Shock. That's my immediate reaction. "I scare you? How?"

Alexander blows out another breath. "The way you act without thinking all the way through. You get hyper fixated on things, like a dog with a bone. You get lost in your thoughts. You go out of your way for people even in the most humbling ways. Teresa, I can sense the anxiety sometimes. I see the exhaustion in your eyes."

"I'm failing to see how I scare you."

He closes his eyes, as if steeling himself for this response. "You scare me because I never know your next move."

Suddenly, the realization hits that I never told him. He's scared of the unpredictability, the uncertainty. I cup his face. "Remember when I told you I had a superpower?" He nods his head. "I've had ADHD since I was a kid. Picture a hamster wheel endlessly spinning, even when the hamster isn't there. What you see in me, the hyper-fixation or focus, the anxiety, the overwhelming emotions, the impulsivity, the people pleasing; those are all aspects of ADHD."

"Your brain never shuts off or slows down?" he asks.

I shake my head. "I've been treated for it and it hasn't changed, it becomes manageable. Something works and we keep it that way. I'm sorry I didn't tell you, not sexy when you have to tell someone that your mind is not like others."

"You are a curious one, Teresa." He picks up the washcloth and continues to clean my face. He travels across my collarbone, then freezes. I rub my neck, remembering Benny's hands squeezing it.

"I'm okay. Just kiss it and make it better," I say softly. Like the man he is, Alexander tilts my head up, planting soft, trailing kisses along my neck. A small sigh comes out of my mouth, prompting him to look up at me and lick his lips.

"Take me to bed, Alexander. Show me the error of my ways." I place my hands on his chest, tracing the outline of his pecs.

He scoops me back into his arms. "Just remember, you asked for it, little cub." In one swift movement, I land on my bed with a bounce.

Chapter 32

Teresa

Alexander hasn't left my side as another month goes by and no progress in taking down the Falcons or their operations. My patience is waning thin.

Shortly after the Nest, Alexander forced me to take a break, and we escaped to a beach house in the Outer Banks. While it was short, it was very much needed and most appreciated.

We relished in each other, rarely leaving other than for food. The man worshiped me like a damn deity, praying to my body. It was something I needed to clear my head and regain focus.

According to Rawlings, things have been quiet since the Nest incident. I feel as though that shouldn't happen. I feel like more retaliation should have happened, a world war breaking loose.

Silence is deadlier than the whispers of chaos.

Between my body healing and the number of therapy sessions I've needed to reset my mind, the quiet has been appreciated. Above all, Jeremiah made it home, still in a few casts, healing but strong.

Shiloh had taken care of Lucie with the help of Sparky. A police report had been filed and Shiloh provided proof for an extra extension of Lucie's protective order. Rawlings had offered an extra eye of protection knowing that she is a connection to the Falcons. The sentiment was there, but I didn't know how she would feel about someone always watching her. Between Shiloh and I, we created her safety plan in hopes that things would slow down for her and she would not have a threat of danger following her like a dark shadow.

I think Greer, Sparky, has other ideas, staying close, offering her a sense of friendship.

I think I'm just waiting for the other shoe to drop. Then again, that train of thought still lingers as a night of glitz and money pulls my attention.

The Masquerade.

One of the most anticipated events of the Foundation. Every year, the attendee list grows, to the point where we've had to turn people away. Foundation staff usually helps with tickets and items for the silent auction, along with trying to sweet talk donors into supporting the work we do. We do what we do for our community. If only some of these people honestly saw what it is like out there.

I take in the moments before my night completely unravels, pulling out my dress I stare at the fabric. Sometimes I feel like I'm playing dress up in a world I don't belong to. The last thing I need is for my anxiety to spike.

I await for a herd of people possibly walking through my door as Alexander plans to come over with Rawlings to reveal their plan for the night.

I'm just offering the choice of place. A sense of nervousness and a bit of excitement roams over me.

Once my mind pushes away all thoughts, I start reading a book on the couch as Seamus lays in my lap. He rests on my legs as my sleep shirt I'm wearing offers him a place him to cuddle in. I get transported into another realm, when the doorbell rings.

I glance at the clock, it's barely early afternoon.

I shouldn't be expecting anyone right now.

The doorbell rings again before a bang resonates. My heart sinks, worried that someone may have found me.

I rush to the door and pull out the handgun Alexander stashed next to the door. I'm not taking any chances. I peek through the peephole.

No fucking way.

I quickly look down and suddenly remember that I have no pants on. I search for at least sweatpants and see Alexander's pair draped over the couch in the office.

I open the door to find Alexander, Rawlings, Matthew, and another man whose name escapes me. I rest the gun against my thigh.

"Alexander Jackson," I pause. "What the hell are you doing here? And no heads up?"

They push past the door, Seamus growls until he sees Alexander.

Traitor.

The rest push through my door, plopping down on my couch. Matthew looks at me and notices the gun.

"Who the fuck gave you a gun?" He jerks back. Then looking at my ensemble with a smirk. "Nice look."

I tuck the gun safely back in its hiding spot. "You can blame the Viking oaf over there." I nod my head toward Alexander. "Make yourselves comfortable, I guess. Pardon my absence as I make myself more presentable." I curtsy sarcastically.

I stomp my way to the bedroom, but Alexander beats me to it. I close the door behind me as the gaggle of men in my living room do what they need to do.

"Need some help?" He sits on the bed, leaning back, taking in my braless and sweatpants clad form.

"From you? No thanks. Next time you want to bring a group of men into my house without warning, I'll actually use the gun. Just give me a heads up. I'll be dressed better." I wink, finding one of my bras to put on and taking off the sweatpants throwing back his way. He catches them before tossing them on the floor.

He eyes zero in on me as he licks his lips. His eyes go from soft to hungry.

I go to turn feeling the redness of heat flushing my cheeks. He yanks me from behind and settles me into his lap. "I like you better naked anyone." He plants a kiss on my shoulder, "Only for my eyes." He nips hard, marking me. I let out a small moan as I sink into him.

"At least with a heads up, I could have put on a bra or *better* pants." I strip off my shirt. He can deal with a *slight* punishment.

"I mean, could go without. I won't have a problem." He trails a finger across the top of my breasts, sending goosebumps down my arms.

"When I was at the door, I didn't have pants on. But I'm definitely more comfortable without a bra. I can keep flaunting them, if that's what you want? I bet your brothers would like a peek," My bratty comment earns me a twist to the nipple.

"Keep talking," he growls. "Don't forget one thing, Little Cub." He punctuates each word with a kiss on each of my breasts. I reach behind his head and scratch his scalp with my nails. He'll be putty in no time.

"What's that?" I get a strong whiff of him, his woods and peppermint scent. Such a strange combination, but it works for him.

"You belong to me." He peppers more kisses along my shoulders, easing himself back up. Getting up and placing my feet back on the floor. He looks at me with those damn breathtaking baby blue eyes, the curl of a smile.

"Uh huh, you may have mentioned that. As well as you remember one thing," I smile at him, batting my eyelashes. I step in between his legs, throwing my arms around his neck.

"And." he says, tilting his chin towards me.

I go to grab his leather cut and pull him to me, claiming his lips for a hard and fast kiss. "You belong to me, Alexander."

I'm dying to climb this man like a tree, if it wasn't for the other men in my home who I have no interest in being here when I do.

"There's my little wild cub." He waits for a moment, admiring the view. He takes a deep inhale that turns into a possessive growl, "Get dressed before Rawlings comes in and your walls suddenly turn red." He leaves me standing there, my thoughts racing with ideas.

I rush to put the bra on and find a sweatshirt and jean shorts, then trot my way into the living room. "Alright, I'm guessing this is about tonight's festivities." I lean against the tv stand. "Also, did you really need an entourage, Rawlings?"

Rawlings rolls his eyes. "Don't get yourself in a twist." He scuffs before continuing, "Now, you'll walk in with Matthew, someone not well known as part of the club. Matthew will enter with you. Joaquin and Alexander will enter on their own to scope out your boss. Once that happens, one of the prospects will make a scene where Sheldon is escorted out, and we'll take it from there."

He leans on his knees, reaching into his pocket for a cigarette. He slowly puts the box back into his pocket when I give him a death glare.

Not in my house.

He sighs, "Then the rest, it's best you don't know. Not that we don't trust you, but if the cops get involved you don't know enough details."

Understandable.

"So essentially, do my normal day job?" That seems easy enough.

He grins as he leans back. "Exactly."

"Can I ask what you plan on doing with Sheldon once you have him?" My curiosity peaks.

"You really want to know?" Rawlings sneers out.

"Kinda why I asked."

"We'll convince him to leave the city and cut all ties. If it doesn't work." He trails

"Then violence," I finish his thought. He taps his nose.

Rawlings runs his hands down his thighs before standing. "You're the first line of defense." Rawlings tilts my chin up, and I can hear Alexander growl.

I suppress a laugh. It's so cute that he's possessive even with Rawlings.

"Rawlings, think someone wants to plan your early death." I laugh as he quickly withdraws his hand.

I look around to see the handy work from Joaquin and the other guy. "And this required all of you to show up at my house?" I ask.

Rawlings just shrugs. "Yes and no. Joaquin's here to finally install security cameras and Matthew and Coda usually help him." Alexander gets up and wraps his arms around me from behind.

I tense up. I've never felt comfortable with home security cameras, call me old fashion. "And Rawlings is here to make sure I don't kill you in the process"

"I figured you would fight me on this." Alexander chimes in.

"I don't like the idea of cameras in my house." I whine a bit. Instant brat mode.

"For your protection and my sanity." Alexander responds. He comes and wraps his arms around me. His warmth and woodsy smell surrounds me. His little scruff rubs against my neck.

I roll my eyes. "You're lucky you're cute, Alexander Jackson."

"Or what darlin'? You'd hurt me? Punish me?" he snickers.

"You'd like that too much." I grasp his arms, even though a wave of jitters comes through. "Look, as much as I enjoy y'all invading my home, in a few hours I have to go from country bumpkin to Cinderella," I say.

"That's fine, *mami*." Coda, the man I didn't recognize before, finally speaks as he lifts from the couch and yanks Matthew with him.

"Oh..." I'm speechless. Spanish accents will do that to a girl. If only Sam or Reva were here to hear this.

"Pick up your jaw from the floor," Alexander whispers in my ear.

The men spend much of the day installing security cameras in the back and front of the house. Not that I have a problem with them, but after years of no security, the thought of needing them now sends chills through my body.

I leave them to their work while I shower and prepare for the night ahead. Alexander leaves me as he places a kiss on my cheek as I got out of the shower. Silently, I was begging for a little more than a kiss.

"I'll see you tonight, darlin'" he says as he leaves.

I'd chosen a hunter green asymmetric dress, one that highlighted my curves and caressed my ass. One look into the mirror, and I remind myself of a sea siren.

I have plucked, shaved, and striped every hair off my body and taped my boobs in. My black hair falls in tousled waves, capped with a black lace mask. Of course, my holster is strapped to my thigh, filled with a particularly pretty little dagger of mine. Out of sight.

I make my way to the Main Hotel with Matthew, who cleans up surprisingly well in a form fitting suit and trimmed up beard. Michelle would be in awe of this man, if she hasn't already.

I try to glance around seeing if anyone else is hidden among the crowd. My heart saddens when I don't see an inkling of Alexander.

The theme this year is Around the World, and the room is set up to emulate a culture festival. It's magical; lights and different colors illuminate every corner, and the décor sparkles underneath them. A slice of different countries captivated in this room.

Unfortunately, the magic is ruined by the shrill of Carla floating her way towards me. Even in a mask, she's not hard to miss in a hideous Jessica Rabbit get-up. In an effort to ignore her as much as I can tonight, I pull Matthew towards the bar.

I ask for a distraction, and in an attempt Matthew starts to reassure me that everything is under control, hinting that this is not their first rodeo.

"So let me guess. You're all hidden in the back alley, waiting for the command?" I ask as I sip my red wine.

"Mm, lurking the shadows, waiting to pounce on the nearest prey," Matthew says jokingly. "So where's Sheldon?" He continues to survey the room, angling for a glimpse of my boss.

"Not here or Carla would be attached to his hip."

People are trickling in now, and the music is getting louder. I'm doing my job: hostess. Matthew, however, is staked out in the corner, watching everything. I spot Sheldon across the room in a blue suit with a court jester mask.

Huh, how appropriate.

He's joined by a man I don't recognize, tattoos visible along his neck, the sides of his head shaved, a full black beard with a hint of gray. His skin has been touched by the sun. He's wears a full black mask. I know the majority of people here, but I could not place him. He speaks with Sheldon before making their way towards me. I avoid eye contact in hopes that they get the hint and avoid me.

"Teresa," shouts Sheldon as he waves his hand. I twist my necklace nervously, but paint on a smile nonetheless. I look at Matthew, he shakes his head downing a glass of dark liquor before staying by my side as I usher to Sheldon.

"Sheldon, looking well," I say gracefully. "Mr. Conners can't make it, I take it."

"No, fortunately, he's globe trotting, doing some overseas. He'll be back soon, he's very anxious to come back." he says.

Mr. Conners was known to be a saint overseas, helping internationally, hence part of the reason for the around the world theme. One day, I wish to do the same, a dream of mine.

He nods in thanks. "I want to introduce someone to you. This is Jonathan Tavers, the man with the biggest wallet in the building." Sheldon roars a laugh, then looks at me and stops when I don't join in. He clears his throat. "Anyway, I wanted you two to meet and perhaps get acquainted."

Tavers chimes in. "Yes, I hear you're going to be the one in charge once the new building is opened. Two more months, I hear." He tips his head to me.

I simply nod. "Yes, we're on track, and I know our families are getting excited for the possibility of more room."

"I'm impressed with your work and the accomplishments you've made with the Foundation." He looks past me suddenly. "If you'll excuse me, I see some people I must say hello to. Ms. Bjorn, perhaps you'll grace me with a dance later tonight."

I extend my hand to shake his, but he plants a soft kiss on it instead. I feel the heat of my blush rushing to my cheeks and pray Alexander isn't anywhere nearby. I look at Tavers' hands, noticing a collection of feathers on his right.

Interesting. I look back at Matthew, his face turn stone cold. He must see what I see, but can't say anything.

Sheldon leans over as Tavers leaves. "Mr. Tavers has been working with the Foundation for a few months. He's a leader in his own association. I think he would be a good continuous partner." Sheldon continues to droll on the subject, and I tune him out, peeking around him.

Mr. Tavers continues making small talk with some donors I know very well, and I was so enraptured in watching, I didn't notice Sheldon moving off into the crowd.

"Excuse, I was wondering if you've seen Cinderella, looking for a prince?" A voice surprises me out of my thoughts, and I'm welcomed by a beautiful man in a perfectly tailored suit. More like sculptured from the muses.

God must have forged him in a fire himself, because Alexander is breath-taking. Part of me wonders how a man like that ends up with a woman like me.

Because he believes that he's the lucky one.

His mask is a quartered mask, black to match his suit, it's his eyes that reassures me that it's him. The man is the presence of strength and power.

"Darlin', you're drooling," he laughs as I rush to get a grip on myself.

I'm still at a loss for words. He walks around me, taking in every inch. I peer out of the corner of my eye to see Joaquin had met up with Matthew. I'm ripped back to the present as Alexander's voice rings in my ears.

"Teresa, you are a sight. An angel that has fallen from heaven." His voice is so sensual. If he keeps talking, I might come from just his words.

"Alexander," I say.

"Yes?"

"You have another goal tonight, *mo chroi.*" I'm practically gasping for breath now.

"Is that so?"

"To ravish me, of course," I whisper. I feel like a damn hormonal teenager.

He stalks up behind me, tracing my side with his finger. "Anything for you." He kisses my cheek before abruptly walking away.

I release a breath I didn't realize I had been holding. I'm brought back to reality when Carla bounces up to me with a mic in her hand.

"Alright boss babe, you're up." She rushes me to the stage. I groan, it's something that I'm not looking forward.

Crap, speech time.

"Welcome, everyone, to Lighthouse's Masquerade and Silent Auction. It is my pleasure and honor to be your host. My name is Teresa Bjorn, the current Call Center and Shelter Project Manager. Basically, that's a fancy title to say that I work for the community. The Lighthouse Foundation is one of the few city agencies that helps those individuals experiencing homelessness and domestic violence. It is a time in their life where they feel there is no hope. That is where the Lighthouse Foundation comes to play where we can shine hope back into their lives. So, when I say I work for the community, I work for people. I like to think that they're the superheroes, and we're the sidekicks working for them." I see nods and hear light claps around the room.

"Now, why should you keep donating time and money to an organization if the problem isn't ending? Homelessness and domestic violence will ever end, unfortunately. We are just one city, in a big state, in a big country, in a big world. Still, even the smallest ray of hope can brighten the biggest room. Here at Lighthouse Foundation, we are that ray of hope, that beacon in the darkness. Your attendance, your attention, and yes, your money, will help so many have that second chance and perhaps be a light of hope for others to come. So, eat, drink, talk with our team members, dance, and even bid on some of those illustrious packages graciously donated by partners and donors within our very city. Thank you," Applause follows me down the stairs.

To my surprise, more people than usual seem to congregate at the bidding table. Maybe this year, we'll make our goal after all.

Joaquin and Matthew circle around the room, surveying it. I wonder when the plan is going to kick in; I'm definitely getting nervous. Suddenly, I'm tapped on the shoulder to find Mr. Tavers standing behind me with two champagne flutes.

Alexander disappears on me again.

"Ms. Bjorn, what a marvelous speech. Both empowering and the truth in excellent words. I tip my hat to you." He hands me a flute and we clink them together.

"Thank you. This is my home, and I was raised to take care of it. Now, I'm curious, Mr. Tavers..."

"Please, call me Jonathan. Mr. Tavers is too formal."

"Okay, Jonathan," I smile politely.

"I am glad to see, Ms. Bjorn, that you're not a wolf in sheep's clothing," he notes, practically murmuring at this point.

A sense of familiarity rushes through me. Alexander and the men are nowhere to be found. I furrow my brows. "What do you mean?"

"Your heart is pure and not ill-intentioned. You are a humble creature. One that knows when to or not to pick a fight. Smart, really." Tavers grins. There's something not right, I can't put my finger on it.

I cock my head in confusion. "I like to think there's a hidden wolf somewhere inside me, ready to fight and protect its own. This community is my own."

He nods his head in agreement.

"How do you know Sheldon?" I take a sip of the drink as I attempt to change the conversation.

"Oh, Sheldon. What a dear friend. I finally was able to convince him to help me get your boss, Mr. Connors, to work on a project with me. I don't think Mr. Connors is fully convinced, but Sheldon and I have been working on it for quite some time." Something in the pit of my stomach churns, his charm is hiding something. I play along, keeping my face pleasant.

"What is it that you do?"

He looks at me curiously. "I work in transportation of goods, call it a moving company if you will." He says it like I should have already known.

Soft instrumental chords play through the room. He sets down his glass and extends out a hand. "Do me the honor of a dance?" I gasp for an answer, but before I can say no, he takes me by the hand. My heart sinks, expecting Alexander to come through the crowd.

Jonathan sways with the music, giving me time to spin. He smiles at me, but I try not to give any more attention than necessary. He looks down at me, and I smell a bit of cigar smoke. "Ms. Bjorn, how does a young woman like yourself not have someone wrapped around their finger?" He peers down at me, searching my eyes for an answer.

"Who says I don't?" I look back at him, confused as why he'd be asking.

He blushes a bit at his mistake. "My apologies. I ask because I saw a bid sheet for "a date with Teresa Bjorn " on the table. I must have made a mistake."

What. The. Hell.

I freeze. I'm at a loss for words. "Excuse me for a moment," I mumble as I back away, rushing to the back of the room with the bid sheets.. Before I make it to the table, I'm yanked by the arm, annoying me greatly, only to find a pissed off Alexander, chest heaving with anger.

"Teresa."

I practically breathe fire in his direction. "Alexander, this isn't the time."

He only pulls me closer. "I know it's your job to work the room, but that doesn't mean you can get cozy with them."

I'm not about to let this slide. "If you'd get off your high horse, you'd find out that I wasn't trying to dance with Jonathan, but he pulled on the floor before I could say no." His face rears back, like I'd smacked him.

"Jonathan?"

"Yes, friend of Sheldon's, apparently. Why do you look like something ran over your bike?"

"What's his last name?"

There's a weight in the pit of my stomach. "Tavers."

"I'll kill him. Matthew was right." Alexander pushes past me. I stop him, pulling back into the dark, unseen corner of the room. Pulling his jacket towards me, I trap him against me with my back against the wall. "Alexander, I need you to focus and calm down before we both blow this operation. Talk to me."

His eyes travel across my face, and I can see the fighter in him coming out. I wrap my arms around his waist, drawing myself into him. I search his eyes for the calm in the storm. "Do I need to remind you, *mo chroi,* that I belong to you and only you?"

His eyes widen and a smile curls on his face. "Wouldn't be a bad idea." His anger is put aside for the moment. "One problem: too many clothes in the way."

"Ah, I can solve that problem. Let me take care of where. Word of warning now." He leans closer to my face, inches away. Heat rushes down my center. "Stay away from Tavers," he growls closer to my ear.

"I know the man's strange, but am I missing something?"

Alexanders claims my mouth, tasting every inch of me with passion and desire. His tongue slips into my mouth, crashing hard against mine. His hand travels down my thigh, wrestling with the fabric of my dress. His hand grazes my skin inches from the holster. I laugh into the kiss as his hand retreats.

"Am I missing something Alexander?" I ask again.

"Perhaps."

"Nope, try again. Answer my question." I send a small growl his way. Still no answer. Plan B. "If you keep doing what you're doing, I'll forget my job and we can play a game here in the hotel." I nip his lip, not hard, but enough to send a surge of pain. He sighs, almost like a flag of surrender.

"I've corrupted you." He jerks back. He groans, trying to avoid the conversation, "Tavers. He's the president of the Falcons."

Chapter 33

Alexander

For an intelligent woman, sometimes she misses the signs. She draws a blank, even speechless.

"Run that by me one more time," she gawks.

"Tavers. Is. The. President." I say again. She pushes me away from her in frustration. Her mask doesn't try to help cover her anger.

"How.. what.. why.." she starts to ask, trying to wrap her head around. I can imagine a million thoughts going off in her head like wildfire. From looking like a mad bull to a seasick individual. She slaps my arm, "And you wait until now to tell me this?"

I look around trying not to make a scene, I say in a hushed tone, "You didn't tie the facts together. Sheldon came in with him."

Her eyes keep widening with each new revelation. "He said he was doing business with him. Was I supposed to have turned paranoid and question everything I know? I just thought when he said it was in regards to the foundation." she starts to pace back and forth, her anxiety kicks in a bit.

All I want to do is make her happy, steal her away from the glitz and lights. And yet the thought of whisking her away from all of this and having her underneath me makes my cock twitch. Talk about a spiral of thoughts, a thought of her in that dress hiding in the back wooded area behind her house sends me.

The thought of finding her, her trying to run while she lets me tear that dress into shreds, leaving her bare for me.

And only me.

She pauses, "Wait.. how does this affect things for the plan?"

I sigh. "We'll need more people. Don't worry about it. You have one job. Keep the face. Leave it to us" I kiss her forehead to calm her. "Where're you heading?"

"Over to the stupid tables. Apparently, I'm a prize." She rolls her eyes.

"I mean, I won your heart."

She snorts at the bad joke. "Well apparently you'll have to share, I'm being auctioned off for a date. Seriously, I'm going to raise holy hell if I find out this is true," she says, slipping past me, leaving me absolutely clueless and a smidge bloodthirsty. The idea of *sharing* sends a sickening feeling.

I follow her to the table where she starts to mouth off to Reva, her friend. A crowd of people surround auction items, possibly flaunting money "out of the goodness of their hearts" for a tax write off.

"Reva. Please tell me that what I'm hearing is not true." Teresa says with a shakiness in her voice.

Reva smirks and then studies Teresa's pale face. A face full of worry.

"It's for a date with me?" Teresa says, exasperated.

Reva's face goes blank, almost fully apologetically. Reva's a good friend and worker, she wouldn't do anything maliciously. "What am I missing? Wait, I thought you knew?"

She rushes over to the table, where the sign and sheet for "Win a date with Teresa Bjorn" sits, half-filled already. I see red in little cub's eyes, Reva notices Teresa's breathing hitches.

Reva and I pull her aside, helping her work through her breathing before the whole night goes off the rails. The need of desire turns into the need to hunt down the fucker that thought a side ploy would throw her into a tailspin.

Teresa's voice starts to sing the melody of her lullaby.

Caidil gu la laddie, la laddie. Sleep the stars away.

My soul aches to see her feel out of control, losing sight of everything. She knows this wasn't supposed to happen.

Something in her gathers enough strength to compose herself and spring into action. "Take the sign down and give me the sheet. I know who's behind this and I will bitch slap the fake boobs right off of her."

She? Not he?

She marches across the room, folding the sheet and securing it in her clutch that she had grabbed before coming to the tables.

The atmosphere has taken on another level of eccentricity. Carla hangs onto a donor at a table, laughing, clearly drunk. I watch as my woman takes matters into her own hands.

My phone buzzes, as I look, I see a message from Rawlings.

Rawlings

> D.R, Gavin, Brennan are on the move.
> Matthew is going to meet them in the back.
> Keep an eye on the bird.

Before she can march even further away from me, I grab her, pulling on her arm. I lean down to whisper in her ear. "We're getting ready to make a move. Within the hour."

She gives me a gentle nod, but I don't let her out of my sight. After another message to Matthew, I'll keep guard until I'm needed. This woman has been on the move, she seriously went from a confused state to gut-wrenching anxious mess to a fury in heels.

The event is only going to last another hour or two.

I limit her alcohol intake. I watch every move she makes. I know she wants to catch a certain red head by the roots and kick her ass. I don't blame her, but she's not the target. If anything she's a pawn, used to just make moves from a puppetmaster.

Out of the corner of my eye I see Joaquin enter the room. He had gotten here with me, but remained outside of the ballroom. Joaquin seems to have traveled across the way and found Sam. If it wasn't for work and my eyes not wanting to leave her side, I tell him that look in his eye better stay hidden.

As my eyes come back to view the intoxicating beauty of mine, Sheldon rushes to her side. My mind halts my hands from wringing out his neck.

"Tessa, make an announcement that in 30 minutes, we'll be closing the auction." she nods, but pauses for a moment.

"Sheldon, who put me down as a prize?"

Before we could walk away from a potential scene, Sheldon opens his mouth to dig his grave a little deeper, "Oh, Carla and I had the idea. Carla mentioned you weren't seeing anyone and she and I thought it would be a great way to raise more money." He laughs, like an annoying little fly from hell.

What gives him the right to indicate that she needed to be set up or that it is okay to "pimp" out his employee for something like this, without consent.

I take a deep breath to calm the fire raging in my gut, wanting to deck him. My woman speaks with command, "Sheldon, I didn't approve of that and it makes me extremely uncomfortable. I am, in fact, seeing someone," she says tugging on me, as I wrap my arm possessively around her body, "and I would appreciate it if you refrained from anything like this in the future. I took the sheet down before a PR and HR nightmare occurred. You will apologize for this behavior after this event. Now, if you'll excuse me."

She pushes past him to walk away and maintain her composure to continue on with the night. I walk behind her like a protective wall, not allowing any other people to get to her. She looks over her shoulder, whispering, "You have my blessing to do whatever y'all want with him. If there's an opportunity, I request a hit."

With an hour left in the night, we have not made the effort yet. Unfortunately timing is the name of the game and I'm not the only one getting antsy. I had given Teresa some room to work the room, give her a space of normalcy without the reminder of why we are actually here.

I see her tired, resting at a table, and I can't help myself to want to ease her mind and give her a happier memory. Something less likely to end in blood and bruises. I extend my hand

"I think I owe someone a dance." I say, curving a smile on my lips.

She hesitates for a moment before finally taking my hand and leading her to the dance floor. The soft instrumental music transports us away from wandering eyes, from all distractions and darkness of the world.

I sink into her a little more, loving being close to her. Her airy and lemon scent reminds me of home, of love. My grip around her waist tightens, I can feel the heat radiating from her body. For a moment, it feels like the world has disappeared, giving us this moment.

I look down seeing her eyes well up with tears. She tries to hold them back. The music continues to wrap us in a trance, and she sinks into my chest as we sway to the music. For a moment, the world has stopped and it's us.

I would and will burn down all those who come to harm her. She is the only one worth it all in the end. For this moment, I allow myself to continue to feel loved, accepted, and capable of happiness. Maybe after all this time, fairytales can exist.

"Come with me," I whisper in her ear.

She searches for a reason, which I don't have one other than the sight of her makes me addicted and crazy enough to steal her away. Like the good girl she is, she comes with me, trusting me. I lead her past a crowd of people, outside the event space through the hotel hallways.

She tries her best to keep up with my rushed pace. Her heels scuff across the floors, her dress ends up hiked up.

"Alexander, slow down, I can't keep up with your strides."

In one quick swoop, she's over my shoulders. I can feel her knife holster dig into my shoulder blade, possibly pressing against her own skin.

I look around trying to find a place to put her down. Finally, I find a place that might be a little risky, but my girl loves a good little secret.

I push through the door, rushing her in before I slam the door shut. There's an automatic light that turns on. Teresa's skin flushes with red, her chest heaving her delicious voluptuous boobs. Such a delightfully tempting little thing.

"Not the most romantic place ever, but not the worst." she offers a laugh.

All the self-control in the world doesn't have a grasp on me. I rush to her, grabbing her face, placing a possessive claim to her lips. It's not soft and sweet, it's demanding, a fight for control. She can't help but grab my wrists, bringing her own self closer. She gasps when her hips and pelvis meet a nice little surprise. Her devilish hand travels down to cup me, resulting in a groan.

The woman is claiming me in her own way.

"Been thinking about me?" she chuckles sinfully.

Something animalistic jerks me back with a deep sigh. Her dark brown eyes illuminate under this dreadfully light. I growl out, "Hands. Now."

Flirtatiously, she holds out her hands as if she were to be cuffed or under arrest.

We can revisit that thought after.

I undo my black tie, wrapping it around her small wrists. I can tell she just becomes more turned on. If I were to reach under that delectable dress, I bet she would be gushing for me. It would be nothing to simply just slip in, bringing her to the edge of pleasure.

"Do you know how much it hurts to see you flaunt around out there? To see other men eating out of the palm of your hand? Then Tavers," I straighten, trying to not take out any pent up anger out on her.

I trail my fingers across the top of her dress, making her ache. Every little movement she makes, makes my cock twitch that much harder. I taunt her with the lightest of touches. "Touching you, it's maddening, little Cub. Can make a man quite obsessive."

My hand reaches around, dragging down her zipper. I can't help but growl when it pools around her ankles.

A vision of her black heels, little pasties on her nipples, and her knife holster. Fucking talk about a wet ass dream. "Teresa, no panties?" My eyes widened.

She shakes her head. "Nope. You'd see the outline."

My hand trails down, fingers brushing over her pussy lips, noting how wet and glistening she is. "Tell me the truth. You were hoping for me to touch you."

"Mm, not fully." she gasps as I slowly fill her with two fingers, clutching my shoulder for balance.

"I beg to differ. You're already soaking for me." I say, pumping my fingers slowly, teasingly. My thumb roams over her clit, playing with it, making her shudder with pleasure. She tries to return the favor, but I yank her tied hands above her head instead, pinning her against the shelf behind her.

"You are a sight." I punctuate every word. "Remind me later to see you on your knees."

My pace is alluring, enticing, agonizing. I can feel her starting to tense around my fingers.

I chuckle. "You want to come around my fingers?"

She nods her head. That just won't do, she won't be coming around my fingers. As I go to remove them, she whimpers.

"Wait, no. Alexander." She practically whines at the loss.

"This is what happens when you know I'm watching and you flaunt yourself like the devilish woman you are." I undo my pants, springing out my cock.

She licks her lips, aching for a taste. I pick her up as if she's a feather. She instantly wraps her legs around my waist. My cock lines up at her entrance, teasing it, brushing against it.

"Either throw her arms over and around my neck or grab onto that shelf." She chooses the shelf, which only makes her press her chest out a little further, "Good girl."

Extra heat rushes to both of us. I give her a little wicked grin. "This is going to be hard and fast. And if you're good, I'll let you take charge."

She nods her head, too speechless to talk or let anyone know we are in here.

Without warning, I thrust into her, jolting her hard against the shelf, sending a buzz of pleasure through both of us. She tries to muffle her whimpers and moans.

She takes every inch of me, her pussy squeezing my cock hard. Hard and fast is what I promised her and she'll take it.

I want this so badly. Between her moans and my grunts, music fills the air. I grip her ass hard as we move in sync.

"That's my girl, taking every inch of me." I say. She agrees, nodding as her moans start to get louder and longer, she's at the brink. I can't lie, so am I.

"Alexander, please." she begs for release. I muffle her cries, claiming her lips again, not relinquishing control. I move across her jawline to her neck, nipping my way down.

"You want to come?" I growl out.

"Please." she's almost in tears at the exquisite pain.

"Only because you asked so nicely. Come around me, darlin'. Take me."

With that, her orgasm rips out like a storm. Her pussy spasming around me, in the moments later, I don't stop as I chase mine. In a brutaling pace, I spill into her, my own release twitching. She whimpers a little. I untie her hands as she throws her arms around me.

We freeze like this for what seems like forever. She clings to me as I kiss her forehead. I slowly pull out, setting her back onto the ground.

The sight of my cum dripping down the leg, I'd be a bastard if I'd leave it there. I turn to the side and see paper towels, I pull them wishing they were wipes. I crouch up to clean her up a bit, she bites her bottom lip.

"Would it be so bad to leave it?" my little sinful woman says. The mere thought of her walking around with my cum flaunting who she belongs to is tempting.

I'd pump her full just to see her belly full one day.

I shake the thought that will have to be revisited at a much later time.

"Don't tempt me, Teresa." I hesitate.

"Keep the heels on later tonight, darlin'," I wink, helping her back into her dress. I adjust my tie, trying to not look freshly fucked. I tilt her chin up. "My wild cub."

"*A ghrá mo chroi,*" she says, rising to kiss me one more time.

A moment of feeling protected and loved. The more I'm around this woman, I'm in awe of her beauty, her strength that she doesn't see, her sassiness that makes me smile, her heart that is too big for her soul.

I grab her hand. "Come, you have a job to finish, and we have a man to take care of." I pull her out of the closet.

"What do you have planned?" she asks.

"We paid one of the waiters to spill food and take him in the back of the kitchen where Joaquin and I will take over, getting him to the compound for a *talk.*"

"Then you'll come back to me, right?" she asks me.

I don't want to promise that always, but she makes it so damn hard to say no.

"Always."

We make it back to the event space to find everything still in full swing. I usher her away and towards the stage as she promised Sheldon moments ago that she would.

I find the little waiter that we paid off, giving him a signal to move along. I see Matthew in the corner with Joaquin. Joaquin's eyes dart to the kitchen, signaling that the plan is motion.

Across the room, the waiter performs his job flawlessly, spilling a tray of saucy food on him, creating a stir of events. The waiter starts to apologize, even though he doesn't care. Joaquin follows suit with the order, coming to Sheldon's side.

Sheldon just nods as he accepts the "help" that Joaquin mentions to him, as the men walk closer to the swivel kitchen doors, I grab Sheldon's neck and forcibly send him across the room.

No one is going to come save this man.

Chapter 34

Alexander

The scrawny man lets out a yip as we start to surround him. The club starts to zero in on him. I take off my jacket, rolling up my dress shirt. There's three of us in dress clothes and the others in their cuts.

"What the fuck is going on?" Sheldon yells.

"I'll tell you the fucking is going." I say as I cross to him.

Gavin, one of the older members of the club, yanks Sheldon into a chair, setting him down in the middle of the kitchen that has been cleared out for the next ten minutes.

Either the man starts talking, or this won't end well for him.

Sheldon looks at me, squinting his eyes, surveying me. He finally realizes, "You're Tessa's man. Or are you just playing around there?"

My blood begins to boil, insinuating that she's merely a toy. Gavin looks at me square in the eyes, begging me not to cross the line. "Keep it somewhat clean" as Rawlings had requested.

"Don't think I'm the only one playing here, Shellie." I say, throwing my hands into my pocket.

"What do you want? Money? I can't promise anything. But I can get you some money." he starts to quiver as he tries to get himself out of this situation.

"I have no need for money that you supposedly have, especially not from your so-called friends." I spit out.

Sheldon jolts back like he just hit him with a surprise. He's a good actor, I'll give him that. He starts frantically shaking his head, probably concocting his next move or a lie out of his mouth. I can't wait to see him try to escape from the severity of his consequences.

"I don't know what you're talking about. If you're talking about the fundraiser, I wouldn't say friends, mere patrons of the community." he says.

I look at Joaquin, giving him a nod to bring his tablet out, pulling up a file of what he found. Joaquin turns the tablet to my attention as I grab it. The screen lights up a face and I can't help but smile at the little paper trail that is before me.

Account statements of transactions, monthly withdrawals and transfers to other accounts, investment portfolio on a man that shouldn't have his salary but living in a life of luxury.

"I see," I say, stepping closer to the cowardly man, "Are these patrons ones that would pay you for your "work", Shellie boy?"

"I don't know what you mean." he says sheepishly.

"Better tell him the news," D.R says from the corner.

"Well, it would appear that someone has been working for the wrong people." I show him the tablet, swiping through the documents with his name on them. His eyes bulge out in guilt.

He starts to stutter, "I've never seen them. I don't know what those accounts are. I'm just a chief financial officer for a non-profit." He tries to deny what evidence already shows.

"A non-profit whose information is being sent to the wrong people to what? Cleanse the city?" Gavin growls out. I give Joaquin the tablet back, only to throw my hand up in a warning that I've got this.

"Look, you got the wrong guy. Please. I'll do anything." Sheldon keeps pleading. There isn't anything else we need from this man. Take out the middleman and the Falcon's ploy is done.

"I don't need anything from you." I say sternly.

"Is this about the sign up auction date with Tessa? We just thought it would be a nice thing."

"Who's we?" Now I result into growling like a feral animal.

Sheldon looks around, plotting his way out. Unlucky for him, there is no way out of this other than out of state, and possibly out of the country. We have our ways of making people disappear that won't get too much blood on the floor.

Or does, we're not too picky.

"Carla and me. We had the idea for a little harmless fun. When I asked Carla for help, she was more than happy to do it." He says.

We already knew that Teresa has issues with this woman. A woman who wants everything her way, someone who feels out of place. A woman who has no other connection to the Falcons nor to the disappearance of people. She works for the company, she works for Sheldon. He's just using her as a scapegoat, someone to take the fall when the ship goes down. There's no way in hell that he would throw her under the bus. The woman was a dunce, a plastic nuisance.

But a mastermind, I don't think so.

"Listen, we think it's high time that you make a clean exit. We'll give you one chance to just leave. The Falcons won't know, and perhaps we'll send you somewhere warm." I compromise.

But he only gets one chance.

"I don't know what you're talking about. I just work there," before he can answer with any more disgusting lies, D.R pinches a nerve in his neck, resulting in a slumped over Sheldon.

"Don't you think you're pushing a little too quickly, boss man." D.R says, quickly checking his pulse, making sure he didn't just kill a man.

I'm not pushing hard enough, to be honest. I feel like I'm being held back, like I won't go the extra step with him.

Because there'll be too much blood on your hands.

I shake my head at the thought. Easier to just toss in the trash and get him out of town. Whatever lies he continues to say out loud only distracts us from the ultimate goal at hand.

Well two ultimate goals at hand.

Gavin and Matthew look to me for the next set of orders. No one will miss him, Joaquin has enough alibi information to make it look like the man is taking a sabbatical like his CEO.

"Get him out of here. There's not much more that he can tell us. And frankly, I don't give a fuck," I yell. Joaquin tries to put a hand on my shoulder.

"We can get more out of him," he tries to say. But I cut him off.

"He's lucky that he's not in a pile of blood worrying which deity he will see," I jerk Joaquin's hand off of me.

"Chill brother." D.R tries to console me.

"Last time I checked, here my word goes, D.R. Either help get him out of my sight or fucking leave. We are ending this tonight." I command. D.R's face drops, he takes the higher road. D.R takes a step back and out the side door back to the ballroom. Best he does that, I'll apologize later.

The men grow silent, worried that if one toe steps out of place, Sheldon's blood won't be the only one on the floor. The anger in me bubbles and attempts to escape. The thought of not removing him from our presence and out of this equation sends me reeling. The thought of trying to protect my woman, my little cub from the dangers that circle her.

It's not a coincidence that Tavers shows up especially after the Nest incident. There's no doubt that Benny didn't run to him and tuck his tail between his legs.

He was here to strike fear and tell us that he knows everything. Over the years, they have gotten smarter, meaning that they're a little bit thirster to take what they want and leave everything to ruins. They'll torture us, take what we have, endanger the ones we love.

I'm not willing anymore to take things gently.

I did for her, for the fear that I would scare her, putting her in danger of my own actions.

I will not lose her. Even if that means she gets my mark sooner rather than later.

"Jackson, we gotta go now then," Matthew pleads as time starts to dwindle. Our window is about to close. I nod, reeling back any displaced anger.

Gavin, Brennan, and Matthew "walk" Sheldon through the back doors. His limp body should make it easier to get in the van at the loading dock without any other eyes. Joaquin leans on the center kitchen prep table. "You got something to say, say it and then leave it," I tell him.

"Just wondering why you held back? You'd be gutting that man, not letting him have a way out, probably grinning at his begging." Joaquin remarks. His answer comes loud when the voice of an angel rings through the door.

"Hello, everyone. I want to say thank you on the behalf of the Foundation."

"Because I'm trying to be the man she and the club deserves." I simply smile.

Chapter 35

Teresa

The nerves get to me. For some reason I feel more pressure than anything. Maybe it's the amount of people.

Or maybe it's because your CFO is being integrated by a ruthless MC.

The lights shine brightly on me, as the room grows quieter.

"Hello, everyone. I want to say thank you on the behalf of the Foundation. Every year, we do this auction in the hopes we'll raise funds to continue our mission. At the moment, we are so very close to our million dollar goal. Thank you all so much. Please enjoy the rest of the night and be on the lookout for...."

Without warning, I'm cut off, loud feedback screaming from the sound system.

The screeching ringing in my ears. The screens on either side of me roll a video, and I rush off the stage to stand next to Carla, who looks just as confused as me.

A loud voice comes through the system. Only chaos starts to loom over the room. The looks on our donors and guests send a gut-wrenching feeling.

It's a nightmare crawling from my deepest corners. A demon walking on the face of earth. My whole body shakes, terrified of what is to come.

"Ladies and gentlemen, folks of all ages! For decades, the Foundation has tried to be a light." Photos flash of the community, the Foundation, my work, flash across the screen. "The Foundation has been a beacon in society, but are they really superheroes?"

I quickly run to the DJ to tell him to cut the power, anything to get this off the screen. Joaquin jumps over, I don't know where he came from. I don't know where anyone is anymore.

The disguised voice continues. I look around to see where Alexander was, anyone else were or even Tavers.

I walk back to the stage, gawking at the screen, wanting to scream but nothing comes out.

"The Foundation has been sticking its nose where it doesn't belong, interrupting the lives of local people." Flashes of me in my office, of Reva and Sam.

"People have no idea what's happening in their own backyard." Flashes of Charlotte, our education director, with our students.

"Innocents, or devils in disguise?" Pictures of Maia, a housing case manager, Shiloh, women and children we've helped. All I can hear are the quiet threats.

"You know what happens when people do things they shouldn't? What happens when you play with fire?" The new building flashes on screen, superimposed with a video of a lighter. Carla grabs my hand and squeezes tight. "This is a warning to Teresa Bjorn."

My heart sinks as tears roll down my cheek.

"Don't play with fire you can't handle." The image of the lighter extinguishes. My photo with a bullet hole pops onto the screen. The crowd is silent and the video ends.

Bile threatens to climb up my throat. Carla rushes to the stage, but what she says is muffled, and I don't hear her. I feel the weight of the world come crashing down on me. My heart is sinking. My mind shutting down. The last thing I see is the floor and darkness and silence cradling my mind and body.

Silence.

Darkness.

Numbness.

The last thing I remember is hitting the floor. My body gives in to the horror and fear of the thought that something is coming my way and I can't find my way out. I must have fainted or passed out.

The memories of the dark figure and the video rush through my mind. Sunlight peeks through the room, illuminating it in morning glow. Cotton sheets trap me in warmth and comfort, caressing my bare skin.

Fear strikes.

Too many questions filter through my head, enough to make my head radiate in pain.

My eyes adjust to my surroundings, the sheets that cover me are soft. Actually softer than normal. I shoot up in the unknown bed.

I suddenly look down, I'm not in my dress, instead an extra large t-shirt and a pair of underwear.

I wasn't wearing any of them.

The room around me isn't mine, but a small picture on the bedside table shows a smiling Viking being kissed by me.

Alexander.

I'm not in my own home.

Why is that when I pass out, I'm never in my own home?

I get up and pad through the open space, looking around for Alexander.

What happened?

What did I miss? How much was actually accomplished? Who was that in the video? Was Tavers there to screw up the night, throw us off the plan.

Suddenly, I get a whiff of biscuits and bacon, and there he stands, like a warrior ready for anything. I lean against the corner of the kitchen, watching him cook, admiring the view.

I could get used to seeing this side of him, no guns, no opposing crew, no moments where the world seems to be on fire. Just these moments between Alexander and me.

"Maybe I hit my head too hard, because I don't think I belong in this heaven," I say to him, as he looks back at me, all the sadness in the world lives in those eyes.

He drops the pan and runs to me, taking me in his arms. His embrace is tight and secure. His heart beats hard against his chest. I start to worry.

"Hunny, I'm okay. I'm not going anywhere," I smile and giggle, maybe not understanding his fear. He doesn't let loose, his muscles just coil me into a tighter embrace.

"Okay, you have to let loose, or something might pop and it might be your favorite body part," I joke.

He lifts me higher and carries me to the kitchen, plopping me down on the counter with my feet dangling. He buries his head into my lap, putting his arms around my waist, still silent. His deep sighs as if a weight had been lifted. I rake my fingers through his hair, which is surprisingly not in a bun.

I've seen many sides of this man in the last few months, but this is new.

Helpless, concerned, and a bit submissive if I had to name it.

I sense the fear, the silent emotions he must be feeling. I gather his head in my hands and lift it up to meet my eyes. "I'm here. I'm not going anywhere." I kiss his forehead, letting myself rest for a beat. "I'm okay."

"I told you, you scare me sometimes," he says softly. Not yelling, not raising his voice, just gentleness. "We had Doc check you out before coming here. He said it must be a response to the stress, that you were fine. But you didn't wake up right away."

Maybe it's my body trying to comprehend what was happening around us.

"I scared you." I repeat his words.

He nods.

"You worried that you'd lost me?" I ask, possibly knowing the answer.

He nods. My sweet, possessive man.

"Look at me, I'm here. You can feel me. You can touch me." I place one of his hands on my chest. "It's going to take a lot more than a slander video and stress to take out this woman. I don't you'd allow me to leave without, *mo chroi,*" I softly laugh.

I'm not indestructible, but it's going to take a lot for someone to take me from this world. His body releases the tension I could feel him carrying. I still question myself and whether he is real or a fantasy.

"Explain what happened," I demand softly.

He sighs, as if it's a loaded answer. "After the kitchen, after we got Sheldon out of the building, D.R had run to get me and said there was an incident. Joaquin got there quicker than I could. I got to the room near the end of the video, when pictures of you and the Foundation were flickering across the screen. I saw the fear in your eyes. Carla had rushed to the stage to do some damage control, I guess, but you collapsed. Thankfully, Darius was downstairs. He said that between exhaustion, stress, and the events of the night, you'd passed out, but recommended that once you woke up, we get you checked out."

I didn't think he could do it, but he definitely explained it all.

I continue to play with his hair. "Alexander, look at me. I'm fine. Just another bump in the damn road." I kiss him gently, not wanting to spook him any more than I already have. I still wanted to be strong for him, to show him that I'm not fragile and there are other situations that I have been through that should have scared me in the end, "Also.... you undressed me?"

He cocks an eyebrow and a cynical smile.

I shove him. "Explains a lot. Kinky bastard."

"Exactly. It's easy to do this." He says as his hand slips between my thighs, under the simple black t-shirt I woke up in. I let out a gasp. I squeeze my thighs around his hand. "Ah, you're saying no."

His face twists to disappointment and a hint of ache. I want to erase that look, bring a smile back to his beautiful face.

"More like not right now. We have a day to get through. Did you forget?" I get off his counter and make my way around the island. He watches as I steal a fresh biscuit. "Family day. Seriously, how do you not remember?"

"You do realize we moved it to the compound, right?" He stands back. I shake my head. "In light of recent events, security's a must. Plus, you owe me something you promised yesterday." He walks away from the kitchen, leaving me speechless.

He heads toward the bedroom while my slight OCD tendencies looks at the kitchen, itching to clean it. "Leave it darlin'," I hear from the room.

Damn it. I shuffle to the bedroom.

"You realize I need to shower and wear my own clothes, right? Unless you want me to flash your men," I taunt, leaning on the bed. He throws sweats at my face and hands me my necklace, the one he gave me.

"We will. But can't hold it against me for wanting you just the way you are." He reaches for me, tugging at the shirt that hangs just above my knees.

I smirk. "Another time. Right now, I just need to be surrounded by the kiddos, renew the spirit. And eat some food."

"And fulfill your promise."

"What promise is that?"

He peeks through the bathroom he'd slid into. "You'll remember when you see. Get your things, we'll leave in a few minutes."

"And you'll clean the kitchen."

"Maybe," he echoes from the bathroom. I can't help but smile.

After heading to my place to get ready for family day, we head out to the compound. It's been a while since I have been to one and I'm looking forward to it. Perhaps it'll be the distraction and reset I need.

Plus, who wouldn't want to see a group of hard-ass, serious bikers become like marshmallows around kids?

"Alexander, do you want kids?" I ask as we get closer to the compound. We're jerked across the road. He swerves the truck in shock, someone laying on their horn.

He looks back at me. "Umm... you're not.. I mean."

I put my lips between my teeth to keep from laughing. "As much as I love to see you stumble over yourself and leave you speechless, no there is nothing to worry about" *yet,* "I'm just curious."

Alexander thinks for a moment, his eyes straight on the road. "I won't lie to you, darlin', if you asked me and I wasn't in the club nor the life I have right now, I'd say yes in a heartbeat. This club, this life, can be brutal and dangerous for families. Too much heartbreak if something were to happen," He slides his hand over my thigh. "I'm already concerned for your safety, and to put another innocent life in danger, it's not fair."

To say I'm disappointed in the answer would be a lie, and my face must show it, because he pulls the truck to the side of the road. He turns and looks at me, right as a small tear rolls down my cheek. I don't mean to be emotional, damnit.

"Darlin', if it was another life, I'd fill a house and land with kids and bikes and animals. I would choose you and kids."

"But not in this life." sorrow fills me internally, trying so hard not to show him my own heartbreak.

He looks down, saddened by my reply. "My darlin' girl. I want to fill your world with happiness and joy. I want every morning to be laughter in the kitchen, I want every quiet moment when you have your nose buried in a book. I want to show you the endless love I feel for you. I want to show the world that you and I could do good in the world, even when we have to do things we are not entirely proud of."

Wait a damn minute.

"Say that last part."

"Show the world that you and I could do good in the world?"

I shake my head. "Before that, Alexander."

"To show you the endless love I have for you."

"You sneaky bastard." I shove him. This is the moment he chooses to say he loves me? "You can't just slip in that you love me and think I wouldn't notice."

"Teresa Saoirse, I love you, in this life and the next." He reaches over and grabs the back of my neck to pull me to his lips.

"Motherfucker," I murmur against his lips.

He nips my bottom lip. "And yet you've fallen for me, little cub."

"Completely and maddening sometimes." I smile slyly. He pulls back to the road until we reach the gate. We couldn't ask for a better day. But to think that the one thing in life that I might have to compromise for, might be something that will float in the back of my mind for years to come. The one thing I don't want to regret, at least to try.

Rolling up to the compound, I'm shocked at the 180 change from a worn down, multi-faceted compound to a kid and family filled area. Bubbles, games, balloons, cookout food are all lined up on a long table, music filling the air. Alexander leads me towards the party, only to be practically trampled by two little ones. With arms wide open, I scoop them up and embrace them.

"Sasa, you here!" Allie screams in my ear, not letting me go.

"I told you she would be. Especially cause Mr. Jackson promised." Ella looks at Allie.

"Sasa, he your prince?" Allie whispers, as if the secret was so powerful that no one could hear it.

I glance back at Alexander, the smile on his face spread from ear to ear. I knew he could hear her. "I think so, Allie-cat." I kiss the top of her head and set them both down. Allie runs off to play with a couple of the other kids. Ella, she grabs my hand and pulls me across the gravel to our group of friends. Seth stands up and hugs me tight.

Michelle stands up next. "Jesus, woman," she sighs and goes in for another hug. She hugs me tighter, as if to make sure I don't slip from her grasp.

"I'm guessing your husband told you everything." I cough out from her grip.

"Made my heart stop," she teases, embracing me again.

"If you're all quite finished with the hugging and embracing, Teresa has something to fulfill before we continue our family day. It might be a couple of hours," Alexander sneaks up behind me and grabs my shoulders.

"Alexander Jackson, I swear to all things God..." He silences me with a deep kiss, making my knees weak.

When he breaks it, he whispers against my lips, "You can scream for him later, Teresa. Much rather my name though,"

Fucking hell.

I see Rawlings sitting in a lawn chair, chatting with Johnny, I tip my head to him as he raises his beer. Alexander leads me into the main building, stopping in one of the empty rooms. At least, it was supposed to be empty.

Instead, there sits Memphis, sitting in a chair with what looks like a tattoo gun and equipment. His long waves cascading around him. He seems a bit too excited for this. My mouth drops open, but nothing comes out.

"Explain." I step towards Alexander. He takes my hands in his and looks deep into my eyes.

"There's a tradition in our world, especially in our club, that when someone's in a committed relationship and has found their 'old lady', their girlfriend or partner is tattooed with our emblem and typically 'property of' whoever the person is. When we find our person, the emblem shows that you're one of us."

He places his hands on my cheeks. "I'm asking you to be mine, to show the world that you're a part of my world, part of this family."

I look at him, his rugged features, the scar above his lip, the light stubble on his jaw, his slight dimples. Am I willing to make the sacrifice? There won't be children, no big bustling family, possible danger. Just him and me. Together. I think I am. I want him, only him.

"I mean I thought I was already yours?" I say, grinning at him.

"Yeah?" he asks again, with a slight shock in his voice.

"Yes, *mo chroi.*" I smile. He hugs me tightly. "This is what you meant by two hours." Alexander smirks at that.

Memphis chimes in for a moment. "What did you... oh.." It clicks with him.

"You crazy horny kids," Memphis inserts himself in the conversation. He pats on the table and I hop up. "Where would you like it?"

I point at my right shoulder. Close to the art on my skin already. Two worlds colliding. We have some time to kill and I need a distraction.

I turn my head to Memphis, "Memphis, can I ask you something?" One of the only men so far that I truly have no information or story on.

"Sure, I guess," The tattoo buzzes off for a moment.

"What is your story? The first time I met you, you gave me a huge hug and said 'You seem like you need it'. How did you know?" I ask, Alexander inching closer towards us, leaning to hear this.

The tattoo gun continues, prickling on my skin. "Well, like you I was once in the helping field, counseling young adults. But the city of Memphis is not what it used it to be when I was growing up. Unfortunately, I lost quite a few young people." He takes a pause.

"I guess you could say that I didn't handle all the loss completely well. One day I showed up to one of the local bars and sat, get this, Johnny. You could say right place, right time."

"I take it that Johnny talked to you." I say to hear the rest of it.

"He did. Told me a bit about the Wolves and being a family. I needed a distraction for a while. What turned from a distraction with an expiration date turned into a family that gave me a bigger purpose."

"What purpose was that?" I inquire.

"That I will tell you another day. But for now, I need to finish." He says. I have a feeling my friend has not truly found a purpose, maybe we need to reignite that fire of helping people.

For the next two hours, I grip Alexander's hand as Memphis rips into my shoulder. This is what love looks like, like a reminder of forever. Forever and always until the road ends and even after. And also suffering through getting tattooed to show your dedication and loyalty.

"We have one last thing to do," Alexander says, helping me with my shirt. He's almost giddy, like a kid on Christmas morning. He leads me out back to the open air, lightly grabbing my left shoulder.

What do you have planned, buddy?

He clears his throat and everyone looks our way. This much attention is overwhelming.

"I wanted to formally announce that Teresa is mine and agreed to be a part of this family. You all know what that means."

"Hands off, fuckers," most of the men respond with cheers and claps.

I smile big. I have another family. One that is dysfunctional, but would drop anything to protect their own.

Even better, I have Alexander.

Alexander takes me to talk with everyone I haven't met. Out of the corner of my eye, I see a bubbly, blue-haired woman sitting on Johnny's lap.

"Johnny, my man." Alexander claps him on the shoulder in greeting. "Teresa, you remember Topaz, right?" Alexander nudges me, playfully.

I flash a large smile. "Nice to see you again. What brings you around here? Thought it was for families."

She giggles. "Oh, I am family."

I jerk back, confused.

"Topaz is Johnny's daughter," Alexander snickers out. Everyone's laughing but me. I'm so stunned that I'm at a loss for words.

"Um..." Guilt, complete and utter guilt. I had already played nice during our first meet, but did not realize she was more to the club. "I'm so sorry... I didn't give the best impression and I got territorial and then you became fast friends. I'm ashamed of myself."

She gets up from Johnny's lap and hugs me, careful of my shoulder. "Oh. No, I admire that. Shit, if he screws up with you again, can I shoot my shot?"

Wait a damn minute. "You're.."

"Got eyes for only women? Yep." she winks at me.

I can't help but laugh. I've been an idiot, thinking someone was going to slide in and occupy Alexander's time. I think this may be the start of a beautiful friendship.

We spend the afternoon meeting more people, and I commit myself to learning everyone's names. The mark I agreed to is permanent, a reminder of the decision that will alter my future.

That future is Alexander, even if a family may not be in the cards. I look at this man who has captured my heart and I can't help but smile. For the first time in a long time, I don't feel lonely or lost. I feel accepted, secure.

The moment of bliss ends abruptly when my phone buzzes in my back pocket. The world stops in place. Aggie's calling me, and I feel the ground beneath me dissipate. My hands shake, my body trembling, and I look at Alexander from across the way.

When he sees the fear in my eyes, he's bolting to my side. I have no choice but to answer. "Aggie."

"Child, you need to come to Memorial."

"Jeremiah?" I'm panicking now.

A pause. "You need to come down to the morgue. Something's happened."

No, God no please.

Chapter 36

Teresa

I can't breathe.

I can't find the air in my lungs to bring me back to life.

My world stops.

Everything freezes, no movement, no voices to pull me back from the edge. The well of emotions bursts. I beg and plead to God that those words aren't true.

Alexander gathers me in his arms and says something, but all I hear are mumbles. He'd picked up my phone and must have been talking with Jeremiah. I feel dead inside, numb, no feelings. I can't move my body.

My mind spirals as the thought of Aggie being harmed. Was Jeremiah just a warning and now Aggie paid a price?

A body for a body? A soul for a soul?

How long can a person remain a strong force until the scales of life turn the other direction? My answer, not very long. Everything can be taken from you in a heartbeat.

Alexander rushes me to the car, straps me in, and we take off with no regard for the speed limit. My mind is racing a million thoughts, and everything feels like fire, spreading and destroying everything in its path.

I haven't cried yet but it's only a matter of time. I hear mumbles, a voice trying to pull me out of this daze and numbness.

"Teresa, say something," Alexander says, reaching over to rub my cheek, stroking my hair. I look at him, trying to create a coherent sentence. "Come on, darlin'. I know you're scared. We're going to figure out what's going on."

His words echo. *I know you're scared.*

I *am* scared. I'm scared the truth is what I am imagining, the worst thoughts reality. I'm scared to find my world come to a complete stop and never get back into motion. The fear that evil has won this war before I can even get into battle.

Alexander parks the car and gets out.

I don't move. I don't speak.

Cape Breton doesn't sing. He appears by the door and taps on the window. I look at him.

Please don't make me go back in there. First it was Jeremiah, and now, I'm frightened who is taken from me.

Someone took the chance for happiness and more memories. Someone stole someone from my life.

He opens my door, the creaking grabbing my attention. He pulls me into his chest, wrapping me in his arms. I feel my walls breaking down, collapsing under the weight. He takes my hand and guides me out of the truck, towards the entrance. The steps feel heavy, as if gravity has doubled down.

The sliding doors of the hospital open, a gust of air welcoming familiar senses. The information center is in front of me. One step at a time, the saying goes. What if I don't want to walk? Will reality slip away?

"I'm.. I'm looking for the.." I stumble, emotions riding high. "the morgue." I hear the clicking of keys, the person behind the desk staring at me.

"Name?"

"Tessa Bjorn." My voices as my name comes out as barely a whisper.

More clicking. "Ma'am, just follow the directions," she said, pointing to the map on the desk, noting the first floor layout, down a flight of stairs to the lower level.

I nod my head, looking at Alexander. We head towards the stairs, each step echoing the words "it's her." I want to run. I want to erase time.

When I turn into the hallway, and when I find Jeremiah, I feel like I see a ghost when I find Aggie, bare face, wet streaks down her face. Jeremiah's twisting his hat in his hands behind her. She moves for me to walk past her, a man at the entrance waiting. I look at Aggie, and she can't look me in the eyes. Guilt rams through me like a train.

So, if it's not Aggie, and it's Jeremiah, it's then another fear runs through my body.

"Ms. Bjorn. Thank you for coming." The man's eyes narrow, still waiting for me to take responsibility. "Please come with me." I look at Alexander. I can't do this by myself. I reach back for him, wanting his gentle touch.

He takes my hand, his body language soft, comforting in an unknown time.

I don't know how much longer I can pretend I have everything intact.

I walk past the man as we move down the hallway. The doors swing open to the next and hopefully last room.

"You're the emergency contact for Ms. Rivera." We stop at a closed window. "I'm going to go in and open the window; we just need you to verify her identity. The police have already taken photos. If you need anything else, please do not hesitate to ask."

The sound of her name makes my stomach drop, nausea threatening to weaken me. There's pounding in my head that comes from my heart in my chest.

Lucie Lynn.

Numbness doesn't cover what I'm feeling right now. A flicker of hope extinguishes.

A pure soul taken from us too early.

I have no one but myself to blame. I made a move to the Falcons, I made the choice to stick my nose into a world I have no business being in.

And yet the mark on my skin tells me otherwise.

I feel the shame and the guilt rises in my throat choking on every emotion. A spiral of thoughts, my own impulsive thoughts and actions is to blame.

All I can do is nod. I just nod. My body vibrates with nerves. Alexander lets go of my hand as I move towards the window. I wait for a reveal that might break me.

The clanking of the curtain opening hits my ears, opening into a cold, metal room. He moves towards a table with a figure under the sheet. He slowly grabs the sheet and pulls it back.

The curls. The curls are the first thing I see. Her curls sprawled out across the top of the table. The sheet uncovers her face, her button nose and full lips. I don't see her eyes. Her eyes are closed.

The harsh, cruel truth of it hits. My mind tried to pretend it would be a stranger, someone to just scare me off. Scare off the club. But it's not a stranger.

This is truly my Lucie Lynn, cold and gone. All sunshine and warmth is gone from her smile. Innocence taken away too soon. My knees buckle and Alexander catches me.

Should have been me.

I ignore all the rules and burst through the doors. She's just laying on the table. No one to hold her hand, keep being her cheerleader.

Lifeless. I comb my fingers through her hair. My sweet friend. My fighter. My beautiful girl. Tears sting my eyes. Tears, warm and wet.

Reality soon sets in. My body trembles, shaking with the truth that I'll have to say goodbye. I have to let her go. My chest is heavy with emotions that I can't release here. I search for her hand, grasping it in mine.

Her body is cold, soulless.

"Teresa," Alexander whispers.

When he says my name, I lose it. I break a wall, the full emotions wail out like a banshee. Moments move as the tears spill out and ravage my body.

Alexander looms over me like a silent guardian angel. Giving me the right amount of space, but staying close enough for when I crash.

I gather enough strength to speak, only to convey the only thought I have left within this shock, this emptiness.

"I don't want to let her go." My voice is shaky.

"I know, darlin'." He places his hands on my shoulders, trying to bring me to him. He slowly moves to gather me into his arms. Soothe whatever is left. I can hear his heart beating steadily. I guess sometimes life can be easier when someone is there beside you, holding you up.

"We have to go. I know you don't want to leave her, but we will fix this." I look at him, mascara running down my face. He wipes away one of the fallen tears with his thumb. "I'll take you home."

"How can this be fixed? You think you can bring her back to life?" I start to raise my voice, with the slightest of anger.

"I know. I promise that her name will not be forgotten," he says, grasping my shoulders.

I make my way back to the hallway, Jeremiah consoling Aggie. Aggie's dark eyes flick to me, reaching out to embrace me. I hug her tightly, like I never want to let go.

"How did Aggie..." I say silently, as if the words refuse to come out, couldn't say the rest of it.

"What do we know?" Alexander asks for me, keeping me beside him.

"She said she'd been calling you, saying someone had been following her. She tried to shake them when she called me, but I heard her scream." She pauses and shudders. "I told Jeremiah to call 9-1-1. They traced her phone, but when they got there, it was too late." She takes my hand.

Someone set out to kill her. She wasn't a warning.

She was a punishment. To the club.

To me.

I nod, looking at Alexander for strength. There isn't anything else to be said. I don't know when the pain will stop and the healing begins. We leave the hospital, I feel hopeless as there's nothing left I can do, but lead myself into a spiral of self-loathing.

My jaw drops as we reach the parking lot. A roar of engines, a congregation of brute force, a group that stands for family and power.

A pack of wolves on their chrome steeds. I look at Alexander with a puzzled look.

"We protect our own," he whispers in my ear.

Their *own*. They came because of what happened. They'd come because of me. Johnny with Topaz on the back, Seth and the kids in his truck, Matthew and Michelle gazing into the crowd, Rawlings leaning against his bike. Everyone else here. Joaquin, Memphis, Coda, Keola, and a few prospects standing tall.

I wrap my arms around me as Rawlings approaches, his eyes boring into mine. "We express our condolences, Tessa. We know she meant so much to you and the foundation," He rubs my arm, expressing his sincere apologies.

I look past him and find Doc, his saddened eyes and body slumped over his bike. I see Greer, sniffling as he looks at the pavement. The sorrow in his stance, his eyes full of grief. It doesn't take much to know that he'd established a friendship with Lucie.

I move past everyone to stand in front of him. I offer him a weak smile, still numb inside.

"I'm sorry Tessa. I wish.." He starts then stops mid-sentence, at a loss for words.

"I know, Sparky. If we could change time." I rub his arms. "You'll help me plan something, yes?"

He nods. He won't shed tears, but I know they're there.

We need closure. We need to have a moment to say goodbye. I pull him into a hug, his leather cut biting into the embrace. He pauses, waiting for a sense of permission before wrapping his toned arms around me. His breathing shutters. He doesn't have to tell me what he's feeling but I can only sense that there's blame. I can feel his heart break.

There's nothing that he could have done. Alexander grabs my shoulder and as I look he does the same to Sparky.

Alexander takes me home, not saying a word. The roads become a blur.

It doesn't take long before we make it back to my house. As soon as I get inside, I go to the kitchen, find the nearest liquor bottle, and twist off the cap. I know it's not the healthy way to grieve, but fuck it to hell.

The front door swings open, the screen door creaking shut. Seamus's little paws hit the hardwood floor. I crouch down on the kitchen floor, letting my body sink down. Alexander's heavy boots collide with the wood, inching closer, crouching down close to me. He attempts to whisk the bottle away, but I growl at him like a feral dog, Seamus perking his ears up.

"Teresa, this won't take the pain away," he tries to say.

"If you care about me, you'll take your hands off my bottle and shut up." I yank the bottle back and take a swig.

"I know you're hurting but.." he starts, and my eyes go cold. Wrong words to say.

I laugh. "Hurting isn't the word to describe it. I failed." All the pent up emotions I've been pushing down for the past few hours are now surfacing. My anger, my fury, comes alive.

"I failed one of the most innocent people I know. So yeah, it fucking hurts. And you know what?" I stand up, towering over him, slamming the bottle down. "I started the fire. I started her death sentence. That night, I went to the Nest and sent a message to the Falcons. I know this is them!" I start walking, before his booming voice yells after me.

"Don't walk away. You have a habit of doing that."

I turn around and shove him. "I'm not walking away from you. I'm walking away from the stupidity that might come out of my mouth." I jerk my head up to stare into his eyes. "I failed her. I put her in harm's way. That should have been me on that table," I yell out. It should have been me. That last one I don't say for fear of what would come.

Alexander takes a step closer to me, but I jerk back, keeping my distance. I shake my head, fearful that anything else I might say would be out of anger.

"You didn't fail her. This isn't your fault," Alexander says softly.

"It's not her fault either," I cry out. He steps closer. I move away.

"I know. Unfortunately, she was in the crossfire of a war the Falcons started. You can't blame yourself. You can only do so much." He slowly takes a step forward. "I know you want to help everyone. One of the things I love about you is that you want to care and protect everyone. So much compassion can be exhausting."

I shake my head, my body shuddering as I take a breath. "I should have known better than to think everyone was safe. Her death is on my hands, on all our hands so don't stand there and tell me it isn't." I'm yelling now, screaming with frustration. "Her blood soaks my hands and I can't do anything about it." I step towards him and hit his chest.

He takes a step back.

"That's it. Hit me, cut me, use me! Take what you need." he says. I huff out a breath. "Maybe I should have stopped you that night. Maybe we could have done something more." With each of his words, I smack his chest, punch his sides, screaming my frustration out.

"That's it. Harder, Teresa," he growls out. I raise my fists again and again. "Tell me who's to blame."

"Me." Again and again.

"No! Who's to blame?" he asks again.

Hit after hit, my knuckles and hands ache with pain. I slow down, my body ready to slump to the ground.

"The Falcons." I let my hands fall to my sides. The white hot anger has dissipated.

"There she is. There's my wild cub." He takes my head in his hands, kissing it softly. "We're going to end them." A moment goes by, wiping the tears, and trying to compose myself. At that moment, we sink to the ground, pausing for a moment. We stay wrapped up in each other.

"I want their heads. I want their blood to drip from my fingers."

"My ravenous cub." He lets me sink into his body. He scoops me into his arms and takes us to the bedroom. Sleep came hard like a train.

Chapter 37

Teresa

There's not enough time in the world for healing to be complete.

Two weeks definitely isn't enough.

The first week was the hardest, keeping up appearances, avoiding interviews after someone leaked that Lucie had gone through our program and "died in a vicious attack". We held her service and burial the Saturday after that.

Not only did the Foundation employees come to the service, but the club came to pay their respects as well.

The weather allowed us to celebrate a lost soul. The sun shone bright cascading around her grave sight. The roar of the bikes as they helped parade her in, laying her to rest. I could feel Alexander staying by me the entire time.

I could see the heartbreak in Sparky's eyes. It's a heartbreak that he closed off, as his eyes looked lost and distant. We all felt it, especially some more than others.

This gives me more reason to burn the world, to seek out revenge. Now, though, I want revenge. It's part of the grieving process to feel anger and acknowledge it, but this goes beyond anger.

I want to see the Falcons fall. I want to see their empire fall and burn. To see them squirm under my boots.

Rawlings calls for a meeting tonight and honestly, it's about damn time.

I just have to get through the work day. I'm looking forward to walking Aggie through the new building today. I'm not saying

I'm back to normal, but doing something good helps me feel a little bit closer to it.

A knock at my door pulls me from my thoughts. Carla stands in my doorway, carrying a mountain of files. I haven't seen her since the chaos of the masquerade. She clears her throat, like I hadn't already noticed her presence.

"Yes ma'am, what can I do for you?" I say absentmindedly, checking emails and glancing at the door.

"Well, since Sheldon isn't here, we have to pick up the slack," she announces, plopping herself down on my couch. *We?* When did *we* include *me?*

"You're asking me to do what?" I raise an eyebrow.

She looks at me like it's an obvious answer. "Run the committee meetings, meet with the board. And now you're looking at me like I have two heads."

I sigh, massaging my temple. "Carla, on top of overseeing the new building, running the hotline, and directing the section committees for services, I don't have much time to spare." I lean back in my chair.

"Maybe you can just do the monthly financial reports and I'll attend the meetings instead."

This isn't worth the fight and I know it. Who knows, maybe this will light a fire under Mr. Connors' ass to find a competent CFO this time. But I know that Sheldon isn't coming back if he values his life.

"Sure, Carla. By the way, I meant to express my gratitude for handling the situation at the masquerade." She better not make this difficult on me or I swear, it'll be the last time I ever thank her for anything.

This is already hard enough to give her my appreciation while I have the suspicion that she's attached to my current situation in more ways than I could think of.

Her response is to stare at me in shock.

She shakes her head, like shaking thoughts away. "That wasn't a pretty picture, I'll be honest. You froze. You never freeze. You fainted." She leans closer, arms on her knees. I nod my head.

"Are you going to take my thanks or what?"

She scoffs. I don't think she believes me. "Whatever. We just have to keep up the illusion that nothing's wrong, even if someone's pulling more weight than others. If people keep missing, this foundation will go down in shambles." She keeps fidgeting with the folders in her hands, ignoring me completely.

Her words echo in my head about people missing. It's too eerie.

"What did you say?" I jerk my attention.

"People like Sheldon or Mr. Connors." She clarifies.

I shake my head from the paranoia.

I'm tempted to groan, but I sigh instead. "I'll help out as much as I can. Where'd Sheldon disappear to?"

Her head pops back up, "I have no idea and frankly, I'm disappointed and so is Mr. Connors. I spoke with him today."

"Still enjoying his sabbatical?"

She nods. "Lucky him, yes he is. Another couple of months and he'll be back."

It's been a while since I've seen Mr. Connors. At this point, he feels more like a name than an actual person. Part me wonders if Carla actually murdered him or something. She places the folders on my desk and leaves without a word. I roll my eyes. Piles of paperwork on my desk on top of the mountain of paperwork I already have is just what I needed.

Sam walks into my office, her face scrunched. "Mt. Carla came through here?"

I scoff and nod. "More like a hurricane."

Sam just shrugs and changes the subject. "I wanted to show you something, boss." She inches closer and hands me the June reports, which she follows up with the February ones.

I take the reports but realize there's probably more to her visit when she avoids eye contact.

"Sammie..."

"We're down by two hundred," she says sheepishly.

"Two hundred over time?"

She shakes her head no. "Two hundred between May and June. Two hundred people who haven't checked in since April. We're talking category one people, literal homelessness. Things are escalating, boss. More and more people are disappearing." She looks at me like she's frightened she'll be next.

"I know, Sam. I'm meeting with Rawlings later tonight. We're going to come up with a plan. No matter what, I'm ending this, somehow, some way," I reassure her, a hand on her shoulder.

But first I need to see Aggie. The more I go down this rabbit hole, I'll get lost. This all just needs to end, somehow some way.

Aggie's at the construction trailer waiting for me as I park my car at the new building. I see a truck and a motorcycle behind me in the rearview mirror. Alexander has double the people watching over everyone now, and I can't help but wish he'd declare himself my permanent detail instead. I recognize the truck as Sparky's, but I'm only familiar with the motorcycle in passing.

"Ms. Aggie." I reach out for a hug with a smile on my face.

"Child, you don't have to fake a smile for me," she answers back, returning the hug. I fix my face, flashing a happier smile.

"That's better. Now, show me around." She links her arm into mine as we start our tour. This building has come such a long way, and I can't help but smile at the new possibilities this will bring for the shelter.

"Ah, there's that smile." Aggie wags her finger at me. "I'm worried about you."

I try to brush it off, but I know Aggie isn't going to let it go. "What do you mean you're worried about me?"

"You've got yourself tangled in a web of lies, betrayal, and danger. I mean, hell, you have a bodyguard watching your every move."

I shake my head, trying to downplay her concerns. "It's just a precaution. Once this is all over, everything will be fine."

She looks at me like I'm crazy. "You say that like it's a one and done deal. Wake up, child. Just because we take off one head of the snake doesn't mean it ends."

"So, we keep fighting." I raise my voice' I'm going to spiral if this keeps up.

"When is it going to be enough? When you end up on the table?" Her words hit me like bricks, suffocating me. I jerk back at her words.

Aggie seems to realize what she just said. "No, Tessa. I didn't mean that." She tries to reach out to me, but I flinch away. Sparky's lurking in the back, ready to bounce at the first sight of something off. I wave him away, knowing I'm not in danger with Aggie.

"Aggie, I've, for some reason, been oblivious to what's going on. Someone has to fight. I'm not naive. It's a lot to figure out. Have a little faith. Do you really think I'd risk everything, including my *life*, getting tangled up in a motorcycle club? No offense, Sparky." I look back at him over my shoulder.

"None taken," he mutters back.

With a deep sigh and a small grin, Aggie backs down. I know her heart is in the right place, but this is my mess and I have to clean it up.

We continue to tour the building, looking into every new area and talking shop. "What do you think, Aggie?

She peers around, nodding. She continues to roam through the corridors, staring into each room. She looks back at me. "We could plan something together. Only if this threat to the community stops. The foundation will continue, I know it will."

"Agreed," I reach out to her, putting my arm around her shoulders.

I walk her back to her car and wave her off, Sparky still a shadow behind me. I glance at him as the sun begins to lower in the sky. He's hiding in the shade, waiting on me.

"Shall we, Sparky?" I ask him, glancing through my glasses.

"I have a name."

I chuckle. "Yeah, and it's Sparky."

He mutters something under his breath.

"I'm sorry, what was that?"

"You're lucky you're the boss man's woman," he answers back.

"Oh Sparky, that shouldn't scare you anyway," I say as I get back into my car. I start my car. The playful spat plants a genuine smile on my face.

As we head towards the compound, the hopes for a plan and what's to come is high. Time passes too quickly for nothing else to happen. The twitch of my mind to take matters into my own hands.

Tonight's the night we finally figure out when to make a move. For once, Rawlings lets me get involved, with the understanding that normally, women don't get involved with club business.

We weave our way to the compound as the sun sets, bringing in the darkness of the night. I park my car nearby, and a chill runs down my spine when I sense a large looming shadow waiting for me.

The door opens for me, more like being ripped off its hinges. I exchange my sunglasses for my actual glasses, since I left my contacts at home.

"Darlin', if you don't get out of the car now, consequences will follow," the shadow growls out.

"You act like I should be scared." I try to get out of my car.

"Mm, maybe a round of hide and seek will change that." The devilish, tempting smile I adore peeks out.

"Maybe later." I get out and tap his cheek.

"Mm. Yes ma'am." He leads us into the main building, into the bigger meeting room. The smell of smoke and grease fills the air. A long oval table sits in the middle of the room, with swivel chairs surrounding it.

On the table are maps of the cities, photos, and a mock-up of the shipping yard in Wilmington. Rawlings, Keola, Doc, Memphis, Joaquin, and Coda are already there. There are still a few older members that I don't recognize very well, but their appearance and body language of me being here, sends chills down my spine.

"Bjorn, have a seat," Rawlings commands, his face twitching with frustration. I take a seat closest to Alexander: not at the table, but not out of sight.

Rawlings doesn't wait to dive in. "As we're all aware, the Falcons have overstepped and somehow claimed our city as their own. We knew they were back but we now have a clearer picture. Thanks to the intel gathered by Bjorn, we understand that they're murdering the homeless population in an attempt to 'clean' the streets, and the ones they're not murdering, they're using for trafficking, transporting drugs, and other exploits." Everyone nods in agreement. The looks in their eyes are thirsty for what's to come.

"Unfortunately, it's getting closer to the club by extension of the threats to Bjorn's Foundation and the death of young Lucie. We thought by taking care of Sheldon took care of the problem. Obviously, that's not true." I look at Rawlings, confused.

"What do you mean that's not true?" I snarl out, staring at Alexander.

Why didn't you tell me about this?

"Joaquin." Rawlings sits down, allowing Joaquin to speak as he rounds the table towards me.

"There seems to be another person. The night you were at the Nest, I was able to tap into their network and look into their server. We found emails, some coded messages, hinting at someone called the *Siren*. Could it be that there's another person linked to this? Possibly. I've run every data point there is," I look at the email copies he has and thumb through them, glancing at the language they're using.

"Any ideas of who?" Coda asks from across the table.

Only one person is enough of a snake to play the innocent act and call herself the Siren. My gut feeling has led me here.

"Carla Martinez."

All eyes turn to look at me. "Who?" Rawlings asks for confirmation.

"Carla, as in bottle red head in your office?" Alexander says in disbelief. "Darlin', that's a stretch"

"The fuck it's not. The woman is a puppet master. She walks around thinking that with one bat of her eyelashes that men would fall at her feet." I huff.

"Tessa, that is a very big assumption," Memphis pipes up in the back.

"When you've worked with this bitch for years, you'll feel the same. There's no doubt she's involved. Think about it. Alexander, Joaquin you were there that night at the masquerade. How calm was she? Enough for her to put people at ease," I point out. Joaquin, a man of few words, nods but shrugs.

"I don't know. Other than your comparison of emails, it's a coincidence. What if someone set her up?" Alexander considers the other side.

"Go ahead, run her name, do it here!" I scream out, a wall of anger comes tumbling down.

Rawlings gets a look from everyone, he just nods his head and waves his head. The man has no desire to listen, even if I'm right. None of them will.

"I don't see why she would get involved?" Doc raises a question.

Honestly, I didn't either. But the blank stares at me hoping that I would know something or be more productive is getting too intense.

"Who knows. Maybe money, maybe to get back at me, or maybe she's just a bitch that will do anything?" I rattle off a list of my reasons but not ones that would stick.

I blow a breath waiting for results to come. And it does as a ding goes off, Joaquin and Coda return to the tablet. They shake their heads.

Nothing.

I hold out my hand to grab the tablet to see for myself. There's no way that she wouldn't pop up with something.

But the screen is blank. No jail time, no tickets, nothing that would incriminate her as this so-called *Siren*. I shake my head as the pit of my stomach drops. This isn't right. It must be a flaw in the system.

"Run it again." I say, sliding the tablet across the table.

"That's enough, Bjorn." Rawlings growls out in a warning.

I look at him dead in the eyes. Telling that it's enough, like I'm to be silenced.

"There's nothing else here. You're out of assumptions. There's nothing to show for it." Keola scowls at me, crossing his arms in front of him.

I look around the table, my face drops to the many eyes that look at me like I'm wrong or something is wrong.

But deep down, I'm not wrong. I might detest Carla with a passion, but what leverage *does* she have? I look to Alexander with pleading eyes, asking for him to say something. He's been holding back. The thought that he will choose the club over me looms like a dark shadow. The spiral of thoughts lead to me thinking maybe he's right, that the thought of kids would make it harder for him to choose the club, let alone me.

Something sparks his support, as he takes my hand in his under the table. Alexander looks back at Rawlings. Rawlings groans, wiping his face with his hand.

"We can put a tail on her if you have a hunch," Rawlings suggests, dismissing the rest of the notion. "But no promises,

Bjorn. We're putting our resources into a dead end when we can cut off the meeting point, the shipping yard."

I raise my hand, like an idiot. I'm already looking like I'm the crazy person, the one who doesn't belong here. There's a few snickers before Rawlings coughs.

"Bjorn, did you just fucking raising your hand?" He cocks an eyebrow at me.

I put it down and speak up. "If the meeting place is so important, why wasn't this done before?"

"Because we don't know who's all involved and taking over a territory doesn't happen overnight. Know your enemy," Rawlings sneers.

I feel heated, like I'm going to explode. If the man would just *listen* to me.

But the pieces of this puzzle keep fitting. They aren't here mainly for me, the people are second thoughts. Or that's how it's perceived. This is all about money and territory. I can't scratch the itch in my brain. How is this fair?

"So for weeks, barely months you've been sitting on plan B for what? To keep your business going when it benefits you or to play along and use what you have a ploy. At this point, what is the point? Why keep me involved when clearly it's a territory game, and my community is in the wrong place at the wrong time. Just claim the shipping yard as your own already? What's the point of using the foundation? Risking the lives of your club members for what? Look, I know who this other key player is and instead of trusting me.."

"Watch what you say next, Bjorn," Rawlings warns. He stands, getting closer to me. "You may be the old lady of the VP and I said you could be a part of this, but I will not entertain your outbursts. We care just as much about the community as you, but it is about territory at the same time." He points a finger at me and I smack it out of my face.

Oh, he's going to get it. "I told you to trust me and you have. Have I steered you wrong at all? I don't care what the data says, it's the gut feeling. I never liked the idea. But she said something earlier!"

Rawlings has an answer ready. "This is business, dear. We take back what's ours and keep your streets clear of trouble. Therefore we're voting for plan B, taking back the shipping yard."

"I don't get a say? You say be a part of this meeting, sounds like I didn't need to." I say, yanking my hand away from Alexander. The man can't stand up for me or side with me.

"Tessa, that's not what he means. You're just as important, this might ensure more safety on the streets." Memphis tries to say.

"Just trust us, as we have trusted you," Doc begs me with a hidden silence.

"I don't have fucking time for a bigger wolf to take over something because they feel threatened," I growl out in frustration standing up. I feel Alexander pulling my arm to get me to sit back down.

"This big bad wolf is taking back what's ours in revenue, businesses, property, and yes, our streets. So sit down and shut up before you piss me off." Rawlings backs me into my seat. *Fucker.* "That emblem on your skin means you're loyal to the club. What we say goes. You'd do well to remember that." He sits back down and waves at Doc. "DR, continue explaining the plan."

Alexander shoots me a look to mind my mouth. Instead of having my back, he sits there quietly, reviewing the plan. There is a twinge of pain with it.

"Their meetup is next week, loading up and shipping out. From what Jackson and Greer have explained, we have the access points and weak spots covered. We'll have our vans at the entry point to rescue the individuals they wrangle up. We'll have them outnumbered, send a message to the Falcons, and reclaim the shipping yard." Doc points to the mockup of the shipping yard and docks.

While the Falcons are going to be ten steps ahead of you. I get a few eyes over to me. I snap my eyes back. I'm keeping my mouth shut.

"If we kill a few birds in the process, then no harm, no foul," Keola pipes in. He's been silent all night.

Memphis punches his arm. "Ha, another bird joke." He starts to laugh from his belly.

Rawlings straightens up, "All those in favor."

Hands across the room shoot up.

"Those opposed?" Crickets of silence. The urge to throw my hand up takes over. But my voice stays silent.

Rawlings takes back control of the conversation. "Alright, next week. We'll split into teams led by Joaquin, DR, and Jackson. Bring along Johnny and Matthew as well. Oh, and grab the prospects, get them to handle cleaning and stocking weapons."

"Thursday, we ride at 8 pm," Alexander adds to the orders.

Rawlings collapses his hands on Alexander's shoulders, giddy as a maniacal man seeking the rage and weakness of his enemy.

"I'm merely a decoration," I mutter under my breath.

Apparently, Rawlings heard me because he laughs. "No, my dear, you keep your head and ears down on the ground. Keep your man happy." He peeks over his shoulder, not paying any mind to me.

I roll my eyes and stomp out of the room, slamming the door behind me. I don't look back. Am I just a *toy* to them? Again! Did I just throw a tantrum, yes. And I'm not apologizing for it.

So much for this 'family'. So much for Alexander wanting me by his side. He wants someone who will sit down and shut up and take orders like a submissive woman.

I'm raging mad. I fumble with my keys. Cursing every word in the book, I go to open my door and a hand plants over me, pressing the door closed. My chest heaves out in heavy breaths.

"Don't leave here mad." I hear Alexander behind me.

I don't look at him. I don't do anything. Apparently, I've served my purpose and should be a quiet, meek mouse of a woman. A shell of someone of importance.

"Say something, please," he whispers.

"Oh, now I'm allowed to say something?" I shove him with my back.

"I told you Rawlings is a traditional man. He doesn't completely trust and believe that women are allowed to do business or make decisions. Club first, pussy second." I shove him completely back with my hands.

"Pussy huh?" I throw his words back.

"Little cub, that's not what I meant."

"Rawlings isn't the only one on my shit list," I yell at him, trying to hold back the frustration and emotions I'm holding.

He hangs his head. "You're mad at me."

"Damn skippy I am."

He's putting it together. "Because I didn't fight back."

"Give the man a reward for being a good little soldier biker." I say.

He growls in warning. I continue, "You didn't support me. I get why you said what you said in the truck that day. Because in the end, you'll always think of the club first. It's the way it's always been."

He jerks back, but then steps closer to me, holding my face in his hands, forcing me to look up at him. "You are always first."

"That's the thing, Alexander, not in this case when it comes to money and claim. That's what this meeting was about, reminding me that the club takes what they want even if they share a common interest. I have no doubt that you all care, but it wasn't shown."

He lets go and rubs the back of his neck, preparing his next words. Carefully. "I can see how that was bad."

"You think? Oh, and imagine Keola or Doc not siding with you, making you look like you're spiteful or better yet, incompetent, that you're throwing every assumption book." I say back to him.

He goes to say something but withdraws. "Imagine how it feels now that, according to Rawlings, I'm only good for one thing and everything I have done for this club now is done and means nothing."

"Like you were a puppet again," he adds. Correct. "I fucked up a bit."

"Yeah, you did."

"You, Teresa Saoirse, are a damn gift."

Then wrap in a bow and tell me I'm pretty.

His eyes hold my attention, the way he looks at me melts me into the gravel road I'm standing on.

"What can I do, then?" He comes closer back towards me, wrapping his arms around my waist.

"You can tell Rawlings that I'm more than a toy or a puppet. I can do more than just sit back," I press him.

"But you're my toy." He inches closer, placing his forehead on mine, trying to be a damn flirt.

"Only in bed." I peck a kiss on his lips. "I mean it, Alexander. You know by now that I won't back down from a challenge." I flick my eyes to him.

"I know, little cub. I will see what I can do." He goes to kiss me, but I duck my head and slip into the car. The look on his face is priceless, the look of rejection. "Little cub."

I turn the car on. "Fix it and you can come play with your toy." leaving the tall viking of a man in the rearview mirror.

Chapter 38

Alexander

"I don't know how she doesn't make you want to pluck your eyes out," I hear a voice coming from the back. I turn from where Teresa just left a moment ago. Keola leans against the bannister, hinting that he's been watching the whole thing.

"I don't know what you mean," I shrug off his comment, straightening my cut.

He gives me a hesitating look before speaking, "Meaning the mouth and demands, seems like you got your hands full."

Most of the time I do.

But I won't tell him that.

Could I blame her entirely? No. She isn't wrong about me staying silent. In our world, in our lifestyle, disobedience from an ol' lady isn't common. Though accusing another person rather than our target makes it look like we didn't do our due diligence.

"Don't bust my balls."

"Nah, she does that for you," he snickers.

I fucked up in her eyes, and to see the pain again surely doesn't sit well with me. Then she had to bring up the damn kid talk again, which hits even harder. She thinks that I don't see, but I see the small defeat in her eyes, the saddened disappointment.

"You'd talk like that if you had someone that challenged you and everything you've known. She may have had a point." I walk towards the main clubhouse, stopping to sit in one of the chairs that sits on the porch.

"There's no evidence, so what we go chasing a dead end?" Keola offers. "We can't chase ghosts or innocent people."

"Trust me, that Carla woman is no innocent woman. You talk about Teresa busting my balls, Carla acts like she owns the place."

Teresa makes her feelings known about the woman and then some. The utter distaste she has for Carla can make Teresa talk in circles about the day to day interactions she has with her. Partially I don't blame her for the strong dislike of her, but also we know it's not a good enough reason to accuse her of being a mastermind.

"It's not enough," Keola says. "Look, back in the day if I had taken those claims to chief, my ass would be traffic detail for a month. It's the same feeling here."

One thing I have respected from Keola is that he takes his force days into perspective, answering the "what-ifs" questions when regularly breaking a law or two during the week. He makes for the prime devil's advocate, also helps that understanding the law helps with the accounting books.

I shake my head from the thought. The thought that we're missing something, jumping from one plan to another. Moving towards ending it all, but ending a war. Or the thought that when I say Teresa's first, she feels as though she's not.

She's not wrong. The club, it always comes first. In life, in business, and in morals.

"You haven't felt like we're missing something?"

"Are you saying that because she said otherwise?"

I shake my head, "No one is that damn clean. Not even a simple speeding ticket. For fuck sakes, I could understand indecent exposure for this broad."

Fuck!

I hate her questioning everything, trying to prove something. I hate that I'm in love with a stubborn but clever woman who seeps into my every thought. Making me wish that I could give her everything she wants, the house, the life, the family, hell even a ring on her finger.

"What are you gonna do? March back in there and move forward with her demands?" Keola questions me.

Pretty much.

But not in the way that is going to show that I can't keep her at bay and not at our throats.

I get up without answering him because he knows the answer already. The cocky motherfucker just grins as I pass by him.

As I push through the double doors, the clubhouse still rattles with noise and hustle. The smell of smoke and grown ass men surrounds everyone. I roll my neck, knowing I need to find Joaquin or Coda, someone who is better at searching through the damn dark web.

Walking through the main gathering, I see Greer at the bar top, head hanging low. The poor fucker still feels the after effects. Blaming himself for the murder of Lucie Lynn. A lightness in his eyes has disappeared over the days. I don't know whether he was close to her as a friend or something more.

It's times like this where the brotherhood and family come to surround him. But he won't ask for it. Though it won't have a choice because he'll dig himself into a self-pity grave and create a harder shell of a man we all know.

Ambrose, an older member and overall decent guy to talk with, walks by me. I grab his arm, he turns his attention to me. "What's up?"

I look at Greer before coming back to Ambrose, "Keep an eye on prospect over there. I'm not confident that the boy is okay in the head."

"Afraid his ass will be stupid?" Ambrose cocks an eyebrow.

"Something like that," I admit.

He nods his head, slapping an embrace on my shoulder, "You got it. I'll make sure he's alright."

We can be ruthless, but we at least look out for each other. Maybe not in emotions but man to man rather.

I scan the room to find my next target to speak with and it doesn't take long. There at one of the wide farm tables is Joaquin, raking his hands through his short, dark hair. His face scrunches up in frustration.

What the fuck has him so riled up?

I walk over towards him, slightly hesitating as not wanting to piss him off any more than he appears to be.

"You good?" I ask, as he faces me. His expression didn't change. "Woman troubles?" I randomly ask.

"You could say that," he openly admits.

What woman does he have now?

"Then I might not want to add to that problem," I mutter.

"What do you want?" he growls out. I pin a look to him, narrowing my eyes at him, reminding him who he's talking to. I hate pulling the rank card. He backs out, softening his face and hopefully his tone.

"I need you to run Carla's check again." I command. A couple of eyes, including D.R., look at me.

"We already are going to have a tail on her, what more you wanna know?" D.R. questions me.

"Call it a gut feeling?" I shrug.

"More like a ol lady feeling," Joaquin says.

My blood begins to boil, wanting to knock him on his ass.

But the fucker is right.

"How did you pull her up?" I ask. Joaquin jerks back as if I insulted him. Maybe I did, but call me curious about running with a thought.

"Typical name search, DMV records, court records, the woman is clean. She may be a viper in the office, but," he says as I cut him off.

"Watch what you say next, Teresa may be my ol lady but she is ultimately a friend of yours." I warn him as his mouth closes.

"But, whatever Tessa says about her co-worker, wasn't enough for Rawlings or any of us to say otherwise." D.R says for Joaquin, being mindful of his words.

I sigh. Am I pussy whipped? Or do I actually trust Teresa enough to go against everything that has been hardwired in my upbringings The test of loyalties.

"Then just fucking humor me so I can ease her down then. Do facial recognition then. Don't use her name." I ask him. Joaquin looks back at D.R. who hasn't gotten up from his lounger. He looks for permission or at least a second opinion. He twists his face as if to say to give in and do it.

Joaquin groans and twists back to his computer. "Fine, but if we still don't find anything, you know what you have to do."

Like I need fucking reminding.

Chapter 39

Teresa

What is it with men and thinking they know what's best when it comes to relationships and what to do? This is why women tend to live longer than men.

I'm still waiting on Alexander. It's been days. Okay, a couple. He's supposed to fix this mess, while I sit back and do nothing. I'm more useful when I get my hands in the mix. Alas, Rawlings still doesn't trust me.

If I wanted to take down the club, I would have by now. I won't lie, the thought comes across my mind once or twice, but Alexander reassures me that this is the only option. If anything just to piss him off, and maybe Rawlings.

Is it? Or, are you putting all your faith into a man you're still getting to know?

My mind bounces back and forth between the club and my relationship. I sit back feeling like I'm twiddling my thumbs.

"Tessa, do you have a moment?" I hear Sam and one of the specialists calling my name. Boxes are everywhere, organized chaos as we organize our upcoming move to the new building.

I trample over the boxes in the hallway. I see Sam hunched over one of our specialists, staring into one of the computers. It makes me nervous, we don't normally have issues with our technology. Sure the call system or reporting system, but rarely our computers.

I round the cubicle, joining Sam and the specialist. "What's going on?"

Sam looks at me with a strained grimace. "I don't know. Bethany said the phone call she just logged isn't showing up. We tried closing out of the tab and then restarting it. Half the calls she took today are gone."

I pull out my phone to call one of our providers. "Hey, this is Tessa Bjorn from the Foundation. I think we're having issues with the homeless reporting system. The call system's working fine, but I have a specialist whose call records for today have disappeared."

I give the provider some information and the line goes silent for a few moments, only to be revived with, "Huh, that's interesting. I'm not seeing any specialist with that number."

You have got to be kidding me.

I look between Sam and Reva, who's joined us in the chaos now.

"Boss, what's going on?" Reva chimes in.

"I have no fucking idea, but something isn't right. Do me a favor and get Joaquin on the phone."

Sam blushes for a moment. I try to surpass a laugh, but it comes out like a snort.

I bypass Alexander, as I'm fucking pissed at him. Though if Reva calls Joaquin then maybe Alexander won't have my ass.

Maybe that's what you need.

Damn my intrusive thoughts. When I hang up the phone with the representative, more chaos erupts.

"What the hell!" I hear a voice from the other side of the cubicles.

What the fuck now?

Any minute I'm going to wake up in my warm bed with Seamus tucked behind my legs because this is a nightmare. In the back of my mind, I think that this is too much of a coincidence.

"What happened?" I ask. I'm starting to get annoyed, everything seems to be shit now.

Another specialist looks up at me, with worry in her eyes. "Sorry, Tessa, I'm just frustrated. That was my fifth bounce call.

I've never had issues before, you know this." My poor specialist voice cracks feeling a sense of guilt. I rub her shoulders trying to calm her down.

"Today? It's probably just the phone. I'll get you another one," I say before I'm stopped by her response.

"Not of the day. In the last five minutes." she says sheepishly.

In the last five minutes.

Coincidence, I think so.

Sam and I stare at each other. Something's going on. No, not something, someone has to be doing this. A scare tactic. Before we can troubleshoot, Reva comes back from her cubicle.

"Okay Joaquin is twenty minutes out." At this rate, twenty minutes might as well take us to the grave.

"Umm.. Boss lady!" Another specialist pipes in. "My screen just went blank."

"What do you mean it just went blank?" Sam asks, reading my mind. My eyes close as an attempt to not overreact to yet another problem.

"I was typing in notes from this call and it went blank." they say. I rush over to them.

Could this be a hacking attempt? An attempt to grab more information about out community? Creating new targets?

I think of all the families, all the women and children, men, everyone!

I examine everything. I push my specialist out of the way, crawling under the desk to see the outlets.

All charging ports and cables are good. Nothing is bent or fried. Nothing is out of the ordinary or misplaced with the outlets and cables.

I can't figure it out. Call records being erased, specialists not being in the system, bounced calls within minutes of each other, screens going blank. Perhaps there's one thing left to do, and consequences be damned.

"No, no, no, no." I'm practically screaming now, sprinting back to my office. "Everyone turn off your computers. Now!"

I struggle to get mine shut down before the building goes dark. Complete power shut off.

I walk back, all my specialists confused, looking at me for guidance. I rush downstairs to check out the other offices and our lobby. People are just as confused as me.

There's no storm, no clouds in the sky. I see Joaquin and Alexander standing at the lobby door, and with no power to our building, my receptionist can't buzz them in. I go to open the door and Joaquin zooms past me without a word.

"What's going on, Teresa?" Alexander glides his way to me.

"I wish I knew. Maybe just a power surge or something. Or someone truly fucking with us?" I walk away from him, heading to the stairs. He grabs my arm before I can get far.

"Still upset with me?" he pouts.

I yank my arm free. "Not the time nor place for this conversation. Some things are not all about you, Alexander," We make our way back upstairs, the power still out.

Joaquin is circling like a bloodhound looking for a scent. I pray that he can make sense of everything or get us back up and running. At least give me good news that it's not in my head. That someone is not out here wanting to ruin everything and take the community away from us. I choke back my tears that threaten to swell up. I can't control anything.

It's like a damn itch.

Reva and Sam stand beside him, looking around for answers. Suddenly, a woosh of sound sends the lights flashing back on. Our screens flash, resetting from the sudden power down, but there's a haze of sounds and pictures with it.

It's like someone is scratching their nails down a chalkboard. I wince, scrambling to find the power button to our big call monitor. Before I can get to it, a hooded figure walks across the screen.

The same one that threatened to burn down the new building, telling me to stop and stay out of the business. The fear rushes through me.

I was right, it's an attack, striking even more fear to me, to us. What. The. Fuck.

I don't take a minute to gather my thoughts. "Joaquin, get this bastard off my screen, now!" I flag him down around the corner.

This fucker will not do this here, *again*. Joaquin scrambles to get out a laptop and plug into the interface, I'm assuming. I try to push the power button. Nothing. I try to grab the power cord from the outlet, but it's stuck. My heart plummets.

"How many more warnings do I have to give?" The hooded voice booms through the room, ringing painfully in my ears. A voice that is well-hidden and changes with every pause.

"Apparently you didn't get my message, Teresa Bjorn." The hooded figure leans into the camera. The voice is unrecognizable, taunting.

I see the horror in Sam and Reva's eyes and the guilt in Alexander's. This message is for me and me alone. My responsibility. I hear the clicking of heels and turn to find Carla behind me, fear in her eyes. She's a great actress, I'll give her credit. A puppet watching her work?

"Ms. Bjorn, you have until Saturday. Leave everything behind, be a good sheep. Leave behind this facade of heroism, you're no hero." The snarl in their voice ripples down my spine. "I would hate to see Mr. Jackson end up six feet under." Their laughter haunts my ears.

If something happened to him because of me, I wouldn't be able to live with myself. The ticking of a clock echoes through the room; then, the screen goes dark.

Silence, a well-known friend, greets us. Shock, horror, and fear slides across my face, and I hang my head in defeat. We've wasted time and planning getting this far, only to be taunted and laughed at by the opposing team. If the club won't do anything, I will.

"Joaquin, tell me that you have something. A name? A location?" I whisper, knowing that if there *was* something, we'd know by now. He gives no response, as I'd expected .

Carla breaks the silence, her heels clicking on the floor as she clasps her hands together. "I think it might be best if the call center closes down for the week. Everyone, take the next few days off. Your fearless leaders and I will come up with a plan."

Who the fuck left her in charge?

Everyone looks at me for confirmation, and I give them a nod. They slowly make their way out, leaving Joaquin, Alexander, Sam, Reva, and myself standing with Carla. She plastered a fake smile on earlier, but as soon as everyone leaves, she sits down and gestures for us to join her. I choose to stand.

She pinches the bridge of her nose and lets out a deep breath. "Someone better start talking."

"Depends on what you want to know," I mutter.

"Don't play coy with me. What did you get yourself involved in? And why are there two bikers here?" Her face twists with disgust.

I can feel my temper rise. "First off, we welcome all people into the Foundation. Second, there's a problem, but I'm sure you know more about it. Honestly."

She jerks back in astonishment. "Excuse me?"

"I don't think I stuttered. People are missing, people have something to do with the Foundation," I challenge her.

"Why the fuck would I do this? Last time I checked, they're the reason we have jobs." She retorts back.

She flat out denies it. Any involvement. But her eyes, her body language, there's no genuinity.

"Look, whatever insanity is going on here, leave me out of it. Tessa, you dug yourself this hole. Get yourself out of it and fast, for the sake of the Foundation." She stands up, wiping invisible dust off her skirt. "I'm just surprised that Mr. Connors hasn't fired you already. Good day." She turns to leave, and I turn to pummel her into the ground, but I'm held back by Joaquin and Alexander.

"Retract the claws. Don't let her get to you," Alexander says, but I yank back in response.

The idea of smothering the light out of her. She's hiding something, I know she is. I don't buy the fact that she would easily walk away, away from the chance to get rid of me. The chance to take charge to show Mr. Connors that she can be the boss.

"We need to make move *now*! I don't care about the damn hierarchy. No one is allowed to threaten me, the Foundation, my loved ones, or you." I step up to him, looking him dead in the eyes.

The people around us quiet down, watching, waiting for someone to explode or even to tell me I'm wrong. Alexander stands there, grasping my shoulders, not taking his attention off of me. The heat coming off of him is alarming.

Don't tell me I'm crazy.

"It doesn't work like that." Alexander stares right back.

"Make it happen." I lower my eyes. I don't back down. "Find a way. I'm not waiting on Rawlings anymore. If they want a fight, they'll get one."

Alexander pulls me into this chest, attempting to calm me down. I don't want his comfort right now.

I want his fury, his anger, his desire to take out the enemy. I want him to be pissed off like me, that people are fearful of his wrath.

He doesn't let go, an attempt to silence me.

I push back on him. "Excuse me, but I have some paperwork that I need to grab before I head home. Reva, Sam, enjoy the next few days. I'll call you later." I head into my little hallway to my office. I can hear mumbling and feet shuffling, but I don't look behind me.

I feel defeated. I feel like a damn failure. A spiral of thoughts surround me, choking on every light, darkening my mind. Burning the ounces of hope that is left over. My hands shake, my body shivers.

Make it stop!

While the feeling of being useless in my community, I guess there's nothing more I can other than try to keep somewhat of my job. Rolling my chair along my desk, I search for my computer, notes, and other items to bring home. One aspect of my job may be out of commission temporarily, but other responsibilities beg for my attention.

I hear the door open quietly, shutting with a click behind him. I know it's *him.* No other person would want to come near me in this state. Silently I had hoped that he would come back to me.

"You have five minutes," he announces.

"Excuse me?" I look back at him, throwing my glasses onto the desk.

"You have five minutes to get everything out that you aren't saying. Darlin', if you're going to put a mask on, at least make it pretty." He leans on the door.

Fucking excuse me? The nerve of this man. I wasn't hiding anything. I made my voice known, I was just turned down when for once I'm ready to fight even more.

"You've got some nerve, Alexander Jackson. Be careful with your next words. Wouldn't want you six feet under." I throw my hands up.

"You have four and a half." He folds his arms.

"How? How can you stand there when someone's threatened your life? What do you want me to do? Sit back and wait and look pretty? New flash Alexander, I won't."

He growls at me. "You think this is the first time that's happened? This is an empty threat. It's showboating, scare tactics. Something to scare you. They won't win. We won't let them."

I walk back around the desk and stand closer to him. "Just because you have no regard for your life doesn't mean that I'll ignore it. I'm tired of Rawlings and the club telling me I don't need to be involved or not to worry about or that I'm just a woman and I can't do anything. That I don't have a say. I get it, Rawlings is a bit of an old-world control freak. But frankly, I don't fucking care." I shove his chest, banging him back against the door.

That feels good. Something primal awakens in me.

"That's it, darlin', let it out." Alexander strengthens his stanc e."Use me, take it out on me."

"Choose me, listen to me! You didn't stand up for me, you said nothing other than no!Nothing!" I punch him lightly on the side. "You sat there and gave me a look like shut up and take it! I've proved my loyalty time and time again, I've chosen you! I've chosen the club. I have your brand on my shoulder, for fuck's sake!" Another couple of punches land on his side. "Then, when I asked you to involve me, to fix it, I got nothing. You did nothing! You don't need me anymore!"

The haze of words flow and the anger continues boil. I hate being angry, I hate feeling like this, uncontrollable.

When my final words blare through, this time, I smack him across the face. My hand stings from the impact, and his cheek is stained slightly red.

I stop, looking at his cheek, stunned. Tears threaten to spill over my eyelids. I pushed the limit. The immense rush of guilt floods.

"I'm sorry. I'm so sorry." I rapidly repeat my apologies. He doesn't move, the slight redness on his cheek shows me my reminder of what is done. His eyes soften as I keep going, "I didn't mean to, I'm sorry, I'm sorry," I shake my head in disbelief that I went that far.

I may push him or shove or even take him down in the ring, but never a smack. I intentionally hit him. My mind pushed to actually harm him.

I try to reach out but end up step back away from him, overwhelmed by what happened, the emotions, my actions.

"Oh, little cub. I will always need you." He takes a small step closer. It's like he didn't even feel the slap. "Without you, it's hard to breathe. I need your love in my pitch black days."

He reaches for me, arms outstretched. He tucks a hair behind my ear, tilting my chin up to him. "It's going to take more than pushing and a loud attitude to change Rawlings' mind. But I need you by my side. You are my life, if I have to keep reminding you that I'm here that I'm not leaving, I'll do that." He bends down to kiss my forehead, attempting to erase all thoughts of being a screw up and lost.

"One day, things will change, I promise you. I know it didn't seem like I was there, but I am. We'll figure this out. No threat will take me away from you." The glimmer in his eye, the sincerity, the beautiful words behind a bit of doubt. It all makes me want to crumble into his arms.

"I got out of control."

"Just a little bit," he winks, softly pressing a kiss to my lips. His peppermint and woodsy scent is intoxicating. I deepen the kiss, rising to my toes, throwing my arms around his neck.

"Darlin'," he moans into my mouth.

For a moment, he quieted my mind that was spinning out of control. He promises me that I'm more than what I appear. Promising that nothing will happen to him. All I want is to believe that with my whole heart.

But easier said than done.

"Mm, that's not my name." I throw his old words back at him, breaking down all walls of anxiety for a brief moment.

He smiles against my kiss. "Oh, little cub, little cub."

"Take me home, you big, bad wolf."

With a sweep into his arms, he tries to make good on his promises.

Save the community, take back our community, and fry a bird or two.

Chapter 40

Teresa

Alexander can't get out of here fast enough. The look in his eyes when I told him to take me home, like a feral animal ready to pounce at any moment, thrilled me.

A distraction from an endless world view of worry and destruction. As we leave the Foundation, I see him on the phone, I don't need to guess who. My only hope is that he's truly finding something to do, to move the timeline.

He glances back to me, as the rumble of his bike echoes the empty lot. He shakes his head as he talks and I worry even more. Rawlings may not do anything. Perhaps too much of a risk. Perhaps something else is stopping him.

This day, let alone this month, has been shit and not what I expected nor wanted. One thing is for certain, though, when Alexander has sex and desire on his mind, he fulfills every wish and grants you more.

I honk the horn at him, knowing that the more he paces around the bike the more Rawlings isn't going to do anything. The disappointment that Rawlings is allowing more time to give the Falcons more power. What happened to a rough and tough club taking charge?

When he turns back around, I decide to leave him, giving him an ultimatum.

We get to my house, Brittany's on the porch with a mug in her hand. Alexander eyebrows scrunch inward for a moment. He gets out and yells at Britt to go home. In response, Britt throws an attitude at him, as expected.

"Last time I checked you don't own the mortgage," she retorts. I swear, they would end up killing each other if left alone too long. He looks back at me, practically begging me to do something.

I bite back a laugh. A simple distraction. That's all I need.

"Britt, kindly go home so Alexander can toss me around like a sack of potatoes." The shock in his eyes, in disbelief that I'd say that. Her reaction is like pure heaven.

"Natural selection, my ass," she mutters, giving a small salute to me and a middle finger to Alexander.

"I don't know how she's related to you," he mutters under his breath. He looks at me, clearly confused about what just happened. I just shrug.

"Get your pretty little ass in the house," he commands.

"Awe you think I'm pretty?"

Oops, the brat might be coming out.

"We'll see how far that mouth will get you." His eyes darts to me as I walk towards the house.

"I seem to remember it getting me pretty far." I smirk at him, knowing that's going to earn a few swats on the ass. "But first you have to catch me."

I bolt from the front of the house towards the back, into the nearby wooded area. I don't look behind me, knowing that Alexander is cursing under his breath, but secretly enjoying the chase. I swear there's a growl that echoes when I round the corner. My mind flits back to our first date, how unusual and sensual it was. I shiver in anticipation.

With the sun setting, low light shines through the trees. The woods snap at every footstep that strikes the ground. Every twig, every leaf under my feet crunch loudly.

I only hear my steps, and it's terrifying, and exhilarating at the same time. I don't bother turning around to see if he's following me. I know he is.

I slow my strides before coming to a complete stop, questioning whether he did, in fact, follow. I don't hide, I try to but something in my gut tells me that he didn't follow me. I give up too easily. I back track towards the open back yard, looking around and not seeing anyone. The yard is empty.

All I see is Seamus in the window, wiggling his bottom. The birds and crickets surround me with sound.

But no Alexander.

My eyes drop down, my mind saddened at the disappearance of Alexander. When I look down at the ground, noticing my shadow, another joins, forming a larger one. Hands clamp down on my upper arms. All the blood rushes to my face.

"You're mine," he says. His voice tickles my ear, a primal lust filling his tone.

"Oh no, whatever shall I do?" I say sarcastically. I narrow my eyes, giving a small smirk.

"House. Now" He growls, like his beast is ready to claim its prey.

"Yes sir."

I march inside, Seamus looking comfortable on his back side from the window bed, not paying any mind to me or Alexander.

Alexander is on me before I can get back to the kitchen. He guides me into the bedroom and shuts the door, locking it behind him, as if he's expecting guests. He shrugs off his cut and starts to unbutton his shirt. "Do I need to remind you what happens when you run and hide from me?"

"Guess I forgot," I shrug.

I don't hesitate this time, planting my hands on his shoulders to hoist myself up and wrap my legs around his middle. I press a hard kiss on his lips, telling myself that he's fine and I'm fine, that perhaps nothing will happen to either of us. His hands tangle in my hair gripping my scalp, gaining control of the kiss.

It doesn't take many steps before he lowers us onto the bed. His hungry hands skim my shirt and reach under to palm my breasts, a small whimper escaping me.

"You are wearing too many damn clothes."

"Someone should fix that," I whisper.

The savage beast rips my shirt open, I hear the buttons clamor to the floor. "Hope you didn't like the shirt."

I'm exposed now, clad only in my pants and bra. He kisses me again, deep this time, sending heat exploding to my pussy. I will never tire of this man. The passion in him chokes out any sense of loneliness.

I fumble with the rest of his buttons and slide his shirt off, grasping at his defined muscles, the hairs that strike a path to something I desperately need right now. He snaps the hooks of my bra open with one hand, yanking the material off as my breasts fall free, my nipples instantly pebbling from the cool air.

He hovers down over one of my nipples, sucking it into his mouth, using his other hand to rub taunting patterns into my skin. I buck against him for more friction.

"Greedy, aren't we?" he says, reaching to the night stand and pulling out the tie from the masquerade, tying my hands above my head. I pout in response. "Good thing I left this here when I was grabbing some things from last time."

He smirks, testing the tie, ensuring I have no slack. He continues to suck and flick my nipples with his tongue, the coil inside me tightening.

He pulls my pants and panties in one, smooth motion off, leaving me completely bare. He presses against me, straining against his jeans. I want to tease him, taunt him, feel him in my hands, twitching with every touch. Without warning, he slithers down my body. He hoists my legs over his shoulders and peppers kisses along my inner thigh.

"Please," I whimper, twisting and turning in need. The fire in me builds, begging to be released.

"Please what, Teresa?" he presses his lips inch by inch of my legs. He's an animal playing with his prey, his dinner.

"I need your mouth." A little swat on my pussy makes me jerk. His breath lingers around me, creating an unbearable sensation.

"Let's see if you can come before I fuck you senselessly." He lowers himself down.

He takes slow, delicate licks at my wet center, throbbing and hot with need. He leaves me a sweating mess. I want to reach down and grab his hair; maybe if I lower my hands, I can reach. As soon I lower my hands, he yanks them back up, clucking his tongue as he goes.

With every click, his tongue lashes at my clit, making me jump. Without warning, he thrusts two fingers inside me, and I almost come undone. He starts to suck my clit at the same time, and I'm hurtling towards the edge.

"I don't want to come around your fingers. Please." I say completely ignore his own command. He doesn't listen to me. He continues at a determining pace and I'm ready to explode. Fireworks flutter in my body as my orgasm pulses around his fingers.

I want to thank him, thank him for silencing my mind.

He doesn't let time pass before his fingers leave me as he tugs off his pants and shoes, leaving him naked, his cock springing free. My eyes grow wide with need.

Yes, yes, yes.

Mine.

"Is this what you want? You want my cock, to come again around it," I nod my head.

He crawls up my body, kissing me hard and fast. His knees push my legs further apart, his tip teasing my entrance, his hands grabbing the tie and holding it steady as he glides into me, stretching me so much, I'm sure I'll rip in half. He lets a groan escape as I moan at the feeling.

Nothing is between us. Just him and I in a blissful moment, feeling ravenous, like one.

Pleasure builds as he takes his time, slowly setting the pace. It's an agonizing pace, so far from the hard and deep thrusts I need. I want more, I need more. I give into his control, even with my hips bucking for more. With his slow thrusts, I feel full and stretched, compensating his size anew with each push into me.

Eventually, I wiggle my hips for him to move faster. He doesn't let up, instead Alexander flips me onto my knees, hitching my ass up so my chest hits the floor.

"I know what you need," he says, landing a few smacks on my ass. My ass flares red from his hands. The thought pools more heat and pleasure to my center.

"Don't stop please."

"I wasn't planning on it."

He grabs a hold of my hair, forcing my back to arch as he sets a harsh, brutal pace, thrusting harder, deeper. I can feel my orgasm licking at the edges of my body.

He leans over and nips at my shoulder, placing open-mouthed kisses on his emblem, his initials, the paw print. His thrusts come quicker now, more urgent.

His hand sneaks around, and with one well-timed flick of my clit, I'm screaming his name, feeling the rush of my release pooling where we're connected. He's not far behind, his thrusts losing their rhythm as he spills inside of me.

His primal grunts as he empties himself is reward enough, knowing that I can do that to him, allowing him to get lost in us. It's feral, it's dirty, it's us.

He drips out of me, running down my leg as he pulls out. He gathers me in his arms as he lays on the bed, both of us spent. I notice that my wrists are still bound, and I take the loose end with my teeth and pull it loose.

"Oops." Alexander watches as the fabric falls.

I look at the door, still closed. I tilt my head towards it. "Worried someone's going to come in?"

Alexander's eyes stay closed, his heart rate resting easy. "Habit from the compound."

"Good habit to have in the future," I reply. He bends his head to meet my eyes.

"Future?"

Crap.

I was insinuating children. "Never mind." I try to put the conversation to rest.

He isn't going to let it go, I know. "No, no. What did you mean?"

"You know, when little feet grace the hardwood floors," I mumble.

A deep sigh comes from him. "A dream, I know darlin'." He rises on his elbows, and I circle the outline of his pecs with my finger. "The idea of bringing a little one into the world right now, it's not the right time."

"So you're saying there will be a time?" I inquire. His silence is the answer I was waiting for.

I don't know why I get on this subject. I mean is it so wrong to want more. We all do "scary" things every day but how you overcome it determines on you. Between all the chaos, maybe I'm hoping that it would be reality.

Then again, I don't want to lose him.

"There might not be a right time," I say with a straight face. I hide the disappointing look when he doesn't try to correct me, even just saying that there might be a future little one. Maybe this is the wake up call to put that dream to rest.

"I'm going to get something to drink." I get off of him and grab one of my shirts to head to the kitchen. I feel a slight guilt for leaving before any other discussion.

I should have known that Alexander wouldn't want children right now, or anytime. I know I accepted that he would be in my life, but seeing him around Allie and Ella, I thought he would have changed his mind.

The thought of a stubborn little blonde haired, blue eyed child walking around, keeping us on our toes, made me smile. I imagined playing in the backyard, an older Seamus chasing them. Our kid in Romero's gym, picking up boxing gloves, chasing them away from the knife dart board. I can't say he hadn't warned me, but I'd hoped.

In the kitchen, I start up the coffee pot, lost in thought. Seamus paws at my leg, and I pick him up to cradle him in my arms. "Decisions, decisions buddy. You may have to fill the hole in my heart." I kiss his head, his nose in the crook of my neck.

I can't help but let a single tear come down my face. I start to hum Cape Breton, immediately thinking of granddaddy. He'd know what to say to calm me and ease my thoughts.

I hear the creaking of the floorboards, turning to find Alexander standing at the opening to the kitchen.

"I'm fine, Alexander. Just give me time." I turn my back to him. I don't want his sweet words right now. I look out the window, watching the storm clouds gather for a summer storm. How appropriate for the mood of the day.

"I hate to see you like this," he says. The hint of worry in his voice.

"It's okay, this one is on me," I hang my head, holding back the tears I know what to fall.

"It hurts me to see you upset and hurt." I can sense him moving forward.

"No, *mo chroi*. I hurt myself this time. I wanted a family. The notion that there will never be a good time, I got it. I made the choice when I got your mark, some dreams may not be safe, it's just taking me a while. I chose you and this life now. Just give me time." I brush past him and head to the bathroom, grabbing my phone from the bedroom and shutting the door behind me. I put my hand over my mouth to muffle the cries escaping me.

Why is this so hard to accept? I don't want to make him feel guilty. Maybe I'm just looking for a way to pick a fight or fight something else.

Because I am picking between the future in front of me over the future I planned in my head. I'm picking him.

I went from being hopelessly in love and wanting to protect everyone at all costs to a mess on a bathroom floor, hoping no one sees this struggle or weakness. My phone dings in my hand. I open it to see a message.

Unknown

> **Ready to end everything?**

My heart sinks, knowing that this isn't spam.

> **Who is this?**

Unknown

> **Someone who can end everything, end the pain, the worry, the sleepless nights.**

This could be a trick. A trap. But part of me is desperate.

> **Friend or foe?**

I wait for a response. My heart races with the anticipation, knowing that this isn't a game.

Unknown

> **I'll let you decide, Ms. Bjorn. Wouldn't want anything to happen to your love.**

I can't wait anymore. This is my opportunity, end the fight. I'm ending this once and for all. For the community, for the foundation, to protect Alexander from harm.

> **When and where?**

Unknown

> The new building, 9 o'clock tonight.

> I'm under watchful eyes. Not exactly the easiest to slip away from.

I tap my thigh in impatience, still waiting for their reply. I become restless with the fact that someone may have my fate in their hands.

Unknown

> Leave that to me. Just be ready. Tell no one. You get one chance, Ms. Bjorn.

I lock my phone.

One chance.

One chance to end everything in one foul swoop.

One terror leaving the streets.

One less threat. A chance for Alexander and the club to breathe. I await the signal for my chance to leave. I look at the clock, I have an hour and a half and Alexander isn't leaving anytime soon.

I hear a knock at the door startles me, "Teresa, I have to go."

Damn, that was quick. "Where are you going?" I inquire.

"Meeting at the compound. Something's come up. Rawlings didn't request you, but I'll fix that, little cub. You gonna at least open the door for me?" I can hear the weight of his body hit the door, possibly leaning against it.

I oblige. I open the door to find him towering over me, completely dressed.

"There she is." He cups my face with his hands and bends down to softly kiss my lips, a slight note of love and tenderness. I melt. His intentions are genuine, mine feel like a small lie.

You should tell him.

No, I won't. This was my battle to begin with. If it means that my loved ones and people will sleep better, I'll do whatever it takes.

"I love you. We're not done with the previous conversation. You hear me?" he says, pulling my body into his, "I'm coming back you know."

"I know, *mo chroi,*" I whisper, as he places a small kiss on my forehead and leaves through the front door.

Once I see him leave, it's time to put on my armor. Things are going to change tonight.

Chapter 41

Teresa

My heart beats and hums louder as I rush through my room.

Alexander's only been gone for fifteen minutes, but it doesn't take long for me to get dressed. I have an hour to get out of here and to the new building.

For once, I won't be late, not by a second. A million thoughts happen inside me, I've never had to do this. My life has turned into one protective factor, a shield of watching what I do and say.

I could be walking into a fire that has no extinguisher. I could have said I love you to Alexander one last time before I walk into whatever hell awaits for me. There are a lot of things that I could have done.

I grab the hand gun in the first drawer by the door.

Better safe than sorry.

I return to my room to take one final look. I tuck my necklaces inside my shirt, feeling the cold metal against my skin. The rain picks up, a slight wind whipping around the walls.

As the night shadows my thoughts during the drive, all the second guesses come quickly. My heart races as the streetlights pass me by.

Am I making the right choice?

Should I have told someone?

It doesn't matter now as I have to follow through with my decision.

Lost in thoughts of second doubts, I arrive at the new building. There's an eerie feeling as I hear the rain pattering against my car.

The on again off again rain doesn't help my thoughts of danger and the impulsive decision to do this on my own. It's the suspense of what's to come, trap or not. I lock my door and give one last glance at my phone. No missed calls or messages.

I leave my phone in my car and lock the door, adjusting my jacket and readying myself for what's to come.

I make my way through the front entrance; I have no specific instructions, but this is my turf, my building. I walk through each corridor, staring at the partially finished rooms. Offices explode with color, areas open and warm to invite people in.

We'd planned in the next few weeks to start moving in and planning the opening ceremony. The echo of my footsteps creak.

I scour for any signs of anyone else being here, other than workers who may come and go. The empty education rooms are haunting as the rain sneaks through and distant thunder roars in the background. I make my way up the stairs to the second floor of the shelter.

Checking every room, I see nothing but wrapped up furniture awaiting residents. I look at my watch seeing that it's nine and I feel like a dumbass waiting for this mysterious person.

I've given up hope. This was a cat and mouse game. Suddenly, the screeching of a mouse skids across my foot, making me jump.

I need to remember to call pest control in the morning. I make my way through the services area, the open cubicles and meeting rooms. It all makes me smile; I can't wait to get back to work after this is all over.

There's no sign of life, other than me and that rat. I think I put too much faith into this; time to turn around.

One last look, and I head to the call center area, where my new office has begun to feel like home. I'll miss my little hallway, but this will be closer, more open and inviting. I take a deep breath as I spot something moving in the shadows. I turn on a work light, shining it around the room, but no one's there.

Perhaps my paranoia is getting to my head. I pat my jacket down, checking to make sure I still have everything with me. Gun tucked in my side holster, check; knives still weighing heavy in my boots, check.

Teresa Saoirse, time to go. Enough of this scooby shit.

I turn back towards the grand hallway, only to feel something come down hard across the back of my head. All I see is pitch black and the ache radiates.

A long, wide field stretches in front of me, nestled in a deep stretch of mountains. A slightly warm breeze whispers against my cheek, ruffling my hair. A small figure stands just ahead of me. I feel drawn toward it, to its pine and wet grass scent. Its light brown hair rattles a memory free. I place a hand on its bare shoulder and turn them around to see the warm brown eyes of a friend.

"Lucie," I whisper, wanting to pull her into a hug, but my eyes drift downwards.

She's covered in bullet holes. This is no memory or ghost of the past, but a haunting nightmare. No, I need to wake up. I don't want to relive this guilt. No, no, no, please!

Her ghost stares at me, with blood stain tears and a hand reaching out. All I want to do is tell her I'm sorry for everything. For her getting tangled up in a mess that I'm partially to blame. For making the impulsive, stupid threat for the Falcons to stay back.

She continues to step in front of me. The fear shivers down on me as I walk back shaking my head.

No, Lucie, no. I scream.

"No!!" I scream out. I scan the room, slowing my breathing down.

I'm still in the new building, the rain still tapping on the ground. It's a full storm now, thunder roaring and lightning lighting up the sky.

I know something is off when the sensation of tightness surrounds my wrists. I try to move my hands, but find myself in a chair, my hands bound behind me with what feels like a zip tie.

"What the hell?" I mutter.

Fuck, of course I'm the dumb that falls for this. This was a trap. Ignorance is truly both bliss and a curse. "Son of a bitch."

"Oh good, sleeping beauty is awake." A cringy voice I know all too well joins me. Without her stepping into the light, I want so bad for the tie to be broken, so I can wrap my hands around her throat.

"I was fucking right." Take that Rawlings, you motherfucker. "Honey, you might as well come out of the shadows, though I suppose that *is* your natural lighting." I couldn't help myself.

"Seriously, I should have shot higher last time." She steps into the light, the construction bulb beaming like a burning flare.

Last time? This woman had a gun pointed at me at some point?

"What do you mean 'last time'?" I think back to the times I'd been shot. My mind flashes. She wasn't at the shipping yard. No, the first time, the time that Alexander threw himself on me, tackling me to the ground.. In the screeching cars that zoomed past the entrance.

"That was you!"

Carla snorts. "Wow, she *is* smart."

My temper flares. I can either play it cool or let my temper get the best of me. I'm going to go with cool. And choose revenge when the time is right. My temper continues to rage in me, like a burning fire waiting to breathe.

Her high heeled boots clack against the hardwood floor. She traded her skimpy tight skirts for black leather pants, plus a bustier, pushing her fake boobs higher. Any higher and they might touch her ears.

"Can I please shoot her?" She reaches behind her and pulls out a gun, waving it in the air.

I'd like to see you try!

I don't know exactly who she's speaking to, but I have a running list. Sheldon, the weasel. I wouldn't put it past him to come back, regardless of the price on his head. Jonathan, that cockroach. They'd make a wonderful villain couple. A tall, shadowy figure flicks a lighter on, lighting a cigarette, puffing out a cloud of smoke, and gravelly voice.

Idiot, you should have told someone where you were. And your phone is in the car. Stupid mistake!

Lightning cracks suddenly, illuminating the area. The air in my lungs leaves me, my body failing.

"No," I stagger out. I shake my head, trying to disprove what I think I saw. Someone who we may have missed, just not in plain sight.

"She's not very smart, is she boss?" Carla says, continuing to wave the gun around like a toy. My heart sinks further in my chest, my palms sweaty as hell, and my head rushes with silent prayers that someone will find me.

He comes closer and closer, diminishing the space between us. A cloud of nicotine circles my face, making me cough.

"Good evening, Ms. Bjorn," a dark, deep voice grounds out.

A lump in my throat forms. "Mr. Connors."

The man who took a chance on me. The man who grew the very foundation and building we're now in. He'd been on sabbatical for less than a year, but never did I expect this. He'd been the kindest man, the gentlest man, who cared about the work we did. This is not that man. In his place, I see a twisted man, greedy, hungry for power and wealth. I don't recognize him, and I don't want to know him.

"Awe, I think she's heartbroken." Carla mocks me, then snickers, leaning against an empty desk.

"You, my dear, are a stubborn woman. I really thought you'd back down after the first threat to your life. Jonathan was right." He takes another puff, then pinches my jaw and twists it in his hands. A twinge of pain. I yank it out of his hands.

"So, I've been told, on more than one occasion, " I sneer at him.

"The harder you pushed the more we took." He pushes my face. A sense of disgust spreads across my face.

"Care to share?" I bite back.

He laughs and slinks back. "I suppose I can. I anticipate ending our little road block anyways." And by road block he means me. "The fear in your eyes. It's a beautiful sight."

A tear runs down my cheek. *Alexander, please, for once, find me.*

"Why? Why take out the very people you started a whole foundation on to serve?" The question has been circling around me and I'm desperate to know the answer.

"Haven't you figured it out yet, Teresa?" I shake my head.

"I want to say it, boss." Carla raises her hand, starting to circle behind me. She lowers her head down to me. "It's a good one."

I'm starting to wonder if something's still in my boot. I carefully try to move my foot around to see if it's still there.

Yes! They didn't get my knives. Now who's the dumbass.

"Mind getting your skank self away from me? If I wanted to smell like a tramp, I'd ask for it," I snarl at Carla.

She yanks my hair, pulling my head back. "You're lucky that I'm not the one doing the honors. I'd make your death slow and painful. Perhaps send a video to dear old Jackson." She throws my head forward.

"Carla, be nice. It's not ladylike to play with your food," Connors coos.

Carla scowls, like a child whose toys were taken away. "Fine but hurry up. I have plans to screw the brains of a little birdie." I gag a little bit. The Falcons can have her and her spite.

"My dear Teresa. You got yourself tangled with some ruffians. I had higher hopes for you," Connors tsks.

"Really? Like what? Joining you?"

"So dramatic. I was hoping you'd join me in furthering the cause, ridding the streets of its infestation, of its pile of worthless life choosing to defile our cities." He looks like a dictator on a pulpit.

He's making it seem like the whole foundation is a lie. Instead of a beacon of hope, it's a beacon of deception.

I'm nauseated at his speech. "Excuse me? No one chooses homelessness."

"I very much believe they do, Ms. Bjorn. It's our duty to make sure they're taken care of." He takes another drag of his cigarette before giving me a Cheshire cat smile.

"People don't just decide to be homeless! We all know there are factors and life situations that happen. You know that! At least you did. What happened to you?" I bite out. I'm disgusted, but his diatribe is stretching the clock, giving Alexander more time.

"Such pretty words, Ms. Bjorn." Connors just smiles again.

I'm going to be sick. "So what, the Falcons found you and made you a deal you couldn't refuse?"

Carla laughs in my ear. "You could say that."

Connors smirks. "Carla had a hand in that. I mean, she *is* the goddaughter of Tavers."

Bile rises in my throat. Of course there was another connection. Carla was enough of a snake. "Ah, that explains the siren nickname floating around. I would have called her Medusa."

She smacks the back of my head, hard enough to where I'm seeing stars.

"Enough, Carla." Connors growls.

"Told you we should have duct taped her mouth. What Jackson saw in her, I will never know." Connors steps forward, snuffing out his cigarette on my leg. I can feel the burn through my jeans as it hits my skin.

He drags a finger across my cheek, the roughness of his fingers nauseating, nothing like Alexander. His touch sears my skin. "You're a pretty little thing. Ignore her. Too passionate for her own good." He brushes my hair behind my shoulder. "Lovely.

Too bad you've been in my way. We would have had such fun together."

He inches closer to my face. I have to think fast. I swing my head back and thrash it against him, knocking him back a few steps. He growls out, covering his nose. I hope I broke it. He smacks me across the face, knocking me to the side before yanking me back up. "Feisty. Too bad you aren't begging, little one."

"You think I'm afraid of you, Connors? Think again." Blood is dripping from somewhere. Is it from me or Connors? I hope it's from him. If I'm going to die, I'm going down swinging.

"You never told me why you're doing this," I ask, clearly stalling but still playing to their egos.

"Duh, money. Jesus. Seriously, George, you left her in charge?" Carla spits annoyingly. Mr. Conners, George twists back in her direction.

Connors smiles wide. "Money, Ms. Bjorn. Money and ridding the city of the vermin infesting it."

"Like your little Lucie Lynn," Carla laughs, high pitched and deranged. My eyes grow wider.. "Oh, who do you think gave her whereabouts to the Falcons?" I thought it was Benedict.

Carla told them.

Carla has her killed.

I want to throw up. I want to break down and cry. I want to watch the world burn at the same time. My eyes fill with defeat.

"Oh look, there's the heartbroken face I wanted. Lucie was naive and too easy to get rid of. You should've done a better job at protecting her." Carla's nasty voice taunts me.

A flash of lightning shoots across the sky. A roar of thunder follows, but there's a new noise along with it, a screech of tires.

Alexander.

The slamming of a car door echoes through the rain and the wind.

No, no.

Connors and Carla turn towards the noise.

Please be smart and have someone with you.

Footsteps hitting hard on the ground. I do the only thing I could do, to prevent terrible things to happen.

"Alexander, RUN!" I scream, hoping the echoes will carry my voice. They turn back towards me with scrunched faces. The slight worry in their faces tells me that they didn't consider Alexander or anyone else coming after me.

"Watch her! Looks like I have to put down a dog." Connors takes the gun from Carla's hands and leaves, going to kill the love of my life.

What did I do?

Chapter 42

Alexander: couple hours earlier

I get on my bike as I see the storm clouds are gathering. It hurt my heart to see my girl locking herself in the bathroom after hearing that what she wants may not come true.

I'd give anything for her to smile, to not see her cheeks wet from the tears that are shed.

I hate having to have the conversation that would make her almost regret the choices she's made. Ultimately feeling like she'll regret me. I can't bring another innocent life in this mixed up world. A child should deserve all the love and safety we have to give and I can't promise that.

At least, not right now.

My head rattles through the last words she said to me, to give her time, that she's hurt herself.

The rumble from my bike attempts to bring me back to the present. Rawlings called earlier at the house telling me that a couple brothers and a prospect were knocked out at the shipping yard. That supposedly there was a tip that one of the front businesses that the Falcons have was a meeting point.

I have some hope that this is true. Though, it feels like we've been down this road before. Underestimating the Falcons at this point and time is an early death sentence, one that I don't intend on Teresa planning.

There's a pain in my chest to think about Teresa shedding more tears if I wasn't here. The pain that would cause her would turn her into a broken person, a ghost of the beautiful woman she is now.

I shake my head of the troubling thoughts, trying to erase any negativity that lingers. I just want this to be fucking done so I can go back to her and wrap her up away from this nightmare.

Time passes me as I meet with some of my brothers. Some are on their bikes and some within their trucks.

The street is empty, only the street lamps start to illuminate the road. Darkness is starting to spread across the sky. The roar of my own bike echoes through the emptiness.

"We got Brennan, Owen, and Nolan being transported to the side clinic, but we need to get our asses over down on Second street. We got a tip."

Moments ago it sounded like Rawlings was ready to go, but as I arrive the men look to me with confusion.

I don't blame them, we have been led down the path into uncertainty and misleading information. We truly become like dogs chasing their tails expecting a different outcome.

Keola waves me down as I slowly pull up to the gathering. I shut off the bike, but hesitate to get off. No one looks ready, no one seems to be willing to make a move.

What the fuck are they waiting for?

"Someone having second thoughts?" I question my brothers.

A nervous wave hits them, Keola looks to Joaquin, Joaquin looks to D.R and Memphis. Coda clears his throat as he inserts a cartridge of bullets, then takes off his safety. A heat of anger rises, feeling guilty for leaving Teresa if this is what I'm walking into, a group of brothers that aren't ready or not willing to go through with it.

"I swear, I will put a bullet through someone if someone doesn't answer me." I growl out, about to reach my own piece.

Finally, someone speaks up, it's Johnny, as he pops his buzzed gray hair through the crowd of people. "I think we've been set up."

I blink, and start to sarcastically laugh, "I'm sorry, you want to run that by me again?"

I whip my head back to my board of brothers who stand there, waiting for me to explode. I get off of my bike, adjusting my cut, finally reaching my piece. The clinking of the metal punishes the silence, the coolness of the metal lays in my hand. "Someone better explain, because the pass couple of days I've had, I'm not in the fucking mood." I yell.

Fuck being quiet.

"We already surveyed the building, it's completely empty." Keola finally speaks up. He folds his arms across his chest. "When I say empty, I mean not even squatters have been in that junk place."

He keeps rattling on and I walk down the street turning the corner to see this bullshit myself. As I turn the corner, the storefront has a sheet of window across giving me a peek into the empty. It used to be a video rental store that shut down at the age of streaming services. I see the barren shelves, the mess of trash left behind, and the beads from the "adult" section swaying to whatever is blowing on them.

At the corner of my eye a couple of my brothers come around the corner. My breathing becomes heavier, with each rise and fall of my chest becomes another moment to not put my hands on someone.

How do we believe every little piece of information, we're thirsty for revenge and power that we jump at everything.

A hand rests on shoulder, "We're chasing a ghost right now."

"We're always chasing ghost," I shake my head, turning to see Memphis and his soft, empathetic eyes, "We're grasping at straws just to take back power and prove that no one fucks with the club, and yet here we are at an empty building to do what? Chase the tail and then tuck back in?"

Memphis tries to say something, but quickly changes his mind.

A flash of light shines at the corner of my eye. I whip back my head chasing the light, curious to know where it came from. A thought that maybe it was a gun or someone recording this for their own pure enjoyment.

"We stick with our plan, check on Nolan and the others," Memphis starts sputtering, but I shush him. I see the light again, coming from the same direction. I take another step, finding that there's something in the video store.

There's no other evidence to prove otherwise.

"Go get Joaquin or Coda, someone get me in this building. Make sure we don't set off an alarm." I command. Memphis blinks confused at first but then quickly scatters back around the corner. Last thing we need is the cops, no matter who's in our pocket, to come here and see us breaking into an abandoned video store.

A rush of shuffling feet come my direction, Coda whips out his lock picking tools as Joaquin rapidly presses his fingers to his tablet. Within a minute, Coda has me inside.

The dust in the air swirls around me like unwelcome visitors. There's a small dusty fog that clouds us. A crew of men stand behind me as I look about the empty room. We take our time walking through the aisles.

Nothing shines through, nothing pops out as a threat.

Then a faint sound like a moan or groan sends a chill down our spine. If it wasn't for the quietness, we would have missed it.

I freeze in my place, waiting for the sound to do it again. I hold my hands up, signaling everyone to stop, then tap on my ear.

Where is that sound?

My head turns in every direction waiting for the sound to do it once more, I have to close my eyes to focus on it. I steady my racing heart and the raging fear, silencing everything else around me.

A whisper in the wind, the sound happens again. But it's not a whisper, it becomes louder. My eyes snap open only because that's not a normal moan or groan. I know that sound.

As I begin to step closer, the rain begins to pour, almost drowning out the sound of the moan. The sound happens quickly, as I get closer.

Coda jumps in, "It's coming from the back."

It's never a good sign when an eerie sound comes from nowhere. It's the gut feeling of needing to turn back and get out of the damn building that becomes stronger.

With the gun in my hand, I rush to the back, the old adult section, pushing past the door hanging beads.

A light comes on, as I pass the threshold. At first there's nothing, not until the sound echoes again. Our heads turn in every direction.

My mind races to soothe me, convincing me that it's not Teresa, Teresa's not here, that she's back at her home, waiting for me.

The sound goes off one more time, this time the low lighting catches in the direction of the sound. An old bar stool stands in the middle of the room with an older CD boombox. The sound becomes more frequent, reaching to a piercing scream that I swear speaks my name.

Almost as if the person is begging for their life. A knot in my heart grips me and no longer are my thoughts soothing me. The sounds keep getting into my head along with the rain pouring down on the roof above us.

My skin itches for relief from the chaotic noise, from the chance that this is all a nightmare and I just need to wake up. My hands tremble for a moment before the barrel of my gun rises to meet the damn machinery, pulling the trigger to bring back the once pleasant silence.

The kick from my gun rattles me, as my breathing becomes heavier. I feel a hand easing my arm down from the stance I'm in. There's some smoke that flows through the air, circling from the electronics. I don't move from my spot, but Memphis walks past me and checks out the exploded pieces.

There on the floors lays a silver CD that glistens in low light, beckoning to be uncovered. Memphis picks it up, then his eyes grow wider, hesitating before looking back at me.

The damn anticipation is enough to send me to the hospital in a straight jacket, I yell, "What is it?"

His face straightens, his expression stern. "This is a message to us this time."

He walks towards me, handing the disk. In black permanent marker the disk reads, "Should have kept her close."

There is no second guessing of who they mean but her.

I throw the disk down, bolting back out to the street. I yank out my phone, pressing her number. The phone keeps ringing and ringing. Then straight to voicemail.

I call again, then the call goes to voicemail. I call once more, only to hear no rings.

Her damn phone is dead.

I never wanted to do this, but now I have no choice.

I press on the little app, watching her dot move around at the... the new building. What the fuck is she doing there?

This wasn't the trap, she walked herself into it.

I don't care at this moment what's around me, my bike just needs to fly faster than anything, for I fear the worst is about to come.

Chapter 43

Teresa

He can't be here, he wouldn't be that stupid to come alone. He wouldn't leave himself unprotected. I can't hear anything between my own breathing and the sounds of the rain pouring down.

I don't know where Alexander is, but Connors hasn't returned nor will be unless there's blood on his hands. A man I thought I knew, corrupted by the power of greed and hatred.

Carla watches me with careful eyes, never once breaking eye contact. She turns for a moment, stomping her high heeled boots across the floor. She's possibly afraid that I'd ruin her plastic looking face. I know one thing, I'm not going to sit here looking like a damsel in distress.

Time to fire up the fake redhead.

"Skank." I let go, the first thing that comes to mind. But something about releasing that word frees something inside of me.

Carla rears back, shocked I spoke, cocking a stupid look on her face like she can't believe I just said that, "Excuse me?" she scoffs.

My own grinning face taunts her, "Cunt." I let out another word, because damn it feels good at this moment to say it.

If my mother heard me talk, she'd have my ass.

"Name calling, really?" She rolls her eyes at me.

Her annoyance just fuels me to keep going. "We get it, you have a big head, but the world doesn't revolve around you."

"You're annoying." She rolls her eyes again, so hard I bet she saw her own brain. I just keep going, rapid fire. I don't have a plan, but I'm sure one will come along. If I get in the right position.

I snort. "Yeah, keep rolling your eyes, sweetheart. Maybe you'll find a brain back there. Though you won't know how to use it."

"What did you say?" That got her marching back towards, only to stop like I'm feeling threatened by her movements. If only she'd just come a little closer.

"Don't worry, scarecrow, you'll get a brain. I'm sure some birdies would love to come screw you again like the whore you are," I say in a taunting baby voice.

Oh, that gets her. She's sneering now, definitely irritated. Her brows furrow, anger rises in her face, or what I can see in this dim lighting. "You little bitch."

"Not the worst insult I've ever gotten. You got anything better?" I snicker.

She finally stomps my way again, and though my legs are bound, I have an idea. Balancing on my toes, I hunch with the chair and swing like a baseball bat to hit her, knocking her against the door frame. She collapses, not moving. I hear a gunshot in the distance.

Not this close in the distance. The sound echoes through the empty halls. I don't hear any yelling or rants. But the eerie feeling in my chest is not banking on what I think I know.

Fuck.

I doubt this'll work like in the movies, but it's worth a shot. I gain enough of a bounce on my toes and launch myself into the air, trying to land on my back, to break the wooden chair. Luck is on my side one of the wooden legs breaks, releasing one of my bound legs. I kick my leg back to my hands, hoping I can slide my knife from my boot.

In one swift motion, the cold metal cools my hand.

The knife in my hands, I flick it open and get to work cutting myself free. I work tirelessly, one goal in mind.

I keep sawing until finally, the knife slashes through the last bit of material. I hear a moan from Carla, and I rush to free my ankles. The last thing to freedom, to finding Alexander, and getting out of this hell hole.

Finally, I'm free, the material escaping my skin, but it comes too late as Carla charges after me. I don't think, I simply do, waiting for my instincts to kick in or meet my adrenaline.

It isn't until she crashes into me that we both go down hard against the floor. Her limp body slumps over me, flopping to the ground. I scramble to get out from under her.

As I roll her over, I see my knife sticking out of her chest. Thick red liquid pools around us, spreading like a sickness, coating me in her blood.

There's no noise, nothing left between us. A small thrill of what I see enlightens the heavy burden on my chest. One soul is avenged, knowing that this person would never have control to harm anyone else.

I thought that killing a person would be more traumatic, more sorrowful. Maybe it's the adrenaline, maybe it's the thought that an evil has been ridden of the world. I should feel guilty for taking a life, even if that life seems like a waste.

Carla meant nothing to me, but a nightmare in heels. As much as I truly believed that she was a part of this, part of me hated to be right. But the other part wanted to rub it in Rawlings' face to prove that a woman's instinct can lead you in the right direction.

I yank the knife out of her and stand to my feet, staring down at her lifeless body. "That's for Lucie. Burn in hell, bitch. You won't be missed," I flick the knife closed and look around.

They found my gun while I was knocked out, that I know, but I didn't see it on them. I have no other way to protect myself. I may not be the smartest sometimes, but I know that it won't do me any good to come to a fire fight with a knife and the will to charge.

I search around me hoping they stashed it out of sight, if they were smart.

Flipping through drawers and desks, moving furniture as quickly as possible, I scramble to find my weapon. As success pours into me, I see it, tucked into an empty desk in the corner. I check the ammo and put the safety on. One goal down, last one to go.

Alexander.

I pray that he's somewhere safe, away from a crazed lunatic. There's enough blame and guilt to go around, all I pray for, to any one that is listening, is to get out of here alive.

I hunker down around the corner, peering to see if Connors is nearby. My legs and body start to ache from injuries.

My body can tell its own stories at this point.

I can't see anything distinctive. No signs of another person, no marks that I can see. My thoughts conclude that either Alexander is hiding or Connors took off.

Whichever way it may be, Alexander's still somewhere in this building. I just don't know if he's either dead or alive. My heart and soul ache more than my physical body at the mere thought that Alexander is dead, laying on the floor, with the thought that we didn't have forever.

I throw my hand over my mouth to silence the incoming wail that threatens to expose me. A knot in my throat makes my breathing harder.

He's not dead. He's not dead.

I try to swallow the pain and the intrusive thoughts, I force myself to push past this feeling and march my way to answers, even if I'm not ready for them.

There's no clear signs of Connors, or even Alexander. I don't know whether to count it as a blessing or a sign itself. The hallway is bare, enough for me to quietly make my way to a conference room, taking a shortcut between hallways and intersections.

The grand area looks clear, so I move into the service department. The empty desks that one day hold the promises of the future. At least, I had hoped they would be. My mind shifts to replay the words that Connors spoke. Everything seems like a lie, a front, a show that I don't know if it will go on.

How can it? One look into this and the media is going to explode with hatred and views for the worst.

The rain seems to be letting up after hours of pouring. The light sound of rain still hits the roof, but I start to realize that my sound coverage is going to paint me a target if I'm careful.

Sweat drips down my spine, my pieces of falling hair stick to my neck. My breathing attempts to steady as I try to think of my next steps, silently hoping that Alexander will come behind me and wrap his arms around me, filling every prayer that I have been saving.

The silent wish isn't coming true right now.

I peek into the service department, looking around and moving from corner to corner, hiding behind every desk, underneath every table, until I feel confident he isn't here. Only the late night lights and moon illuminate the room, as the rain has turned into a misty fall.

You never think a moment like this is going to happen. But in the end, life throws you curves you never expected either.

Jumping from desk to desk, covering myself in case he finds me, I make my way to the corner desk.

I hear the creaking of the stairwell door that connects the shelter from the services team. I cover my mouth with my hand and say a quick prayer. The door flings open as the heavy metal door slams against the back wall with a force.

The floor feels like a bomb has gone off with the amount of force behind the thrust. The slamming of the door makes me jump. I close my eyes, easing the jolt of fear from the danger ahead of me. When I feel there's enough distance between me and his footsteps, I peek over the desk.

Connors walks towards the call center area, and I can see blood on his neck. Or is it Alexander's?

God, please. Please don't let this be Alexander's!

His shoes click as he moves through the opening. The sound pans through the hall, as he steps outside of view. Every click echoes in my chest as my heart can't take the agony of the sound.

As he exits the service area, I crawl low, making sure he can't see me as he passes. A feeling of relief washes through me, one less thing to worry about. I wait a few extra moments to move past the opening of the area.

I make my movements light as if my own feet hover over the concrete. I head into the shelter area, quietly opening the doors, but head toward the third floor of shelter rooms. I don't see any sign of Alexander or anyone else, for that matter.

Alexander, you call me impulsive. No back up?

Making my way to the shelter rooms, some of the emergency lights shine through, only enough for me to see where I'm going. My eyes have already adjusted to the dark moonlight shining. I scan each room, seeing if there is any sign of trouble or life.

My searching comes to a halt as a roar of anger echoes through the emptiness making my skin jump from where I'm at. My heart pounds in my ears.

He must have found Carla, laying in her own blood like the worthless bitch she was. But this doesn't get me enough time, he'll be prowling through the hallways like a vengeful demon until he's found his prey.

I scurry faster, yanking a door open. I have to find Alexander, quickly, before Connors finds me. I hear heavier footsteps coming across the service floor, echoing in the stairway. The man is relentless, craving some blood, more like my blood.

I find an empty room and hide in a big closet in the main family room. It's enough to cover me and peek through to make sure he walks away. I have no idea where he's at, but I'm not about to survey to find my own answers.

I can hear my heartbeat in my ears, my breath staggered from nerves. I shake with the anticipation of getting out of here with my life intact.

My own breathing isn't the only one. I didn't notice another body behind me in the blind rush. I feel a large, rough hand roam over my stomach.

A hot breath in my ear. I know this touch all too well. Tears start to pool in my eyes. I lean back into the other body. I just sink into the only happiness I can feel right now.

"Little cub." he says with the tiniest whisper.

Mo chroi.

I press into him, as if to mold us into one.

I was stupid to think that I could solve all our problems and instead of him causing the trouble, it's me.

I allowed this madman to get to me, play into my head with the need to be the hero of it all. Giving me a sense that I could protect everyone that I love.

Yet we're here with the risk of both our lives and possible more around me. My sobs threaten to spill as the pure happiness of Alexander being in my reach but the sadness that life is in the balance.

Alexander shushes me, calming me down. He tightens his grip on me, making me stand so I don't crumble.

"I got you," he whispers. He repeats this, over and over, pressing his lips to the back of my head.

"I'm sorry." I clasp his hand in mine. More like I cling on to him as my life depends on it.

Don't let me go.

His head leans into mine. The gentle embrace searing into my skin.

The stomping of feet jars me out of my revelry. We can hear him, like a raging bull, aiming for his prey. He's peering into every room, tearing down every plastic sheet and box there is. Opening every door, making me jump further out of my skin.

Alexander's grip tightens more, almost cutting the circulation off of me.

Connors isn't going to stop. But he didn't expect me to escape, to fight.

"You vicious little girl. Can't blame you, though. Carla was a nuisance. She played her part. Almost too well. Had too much of the ear of her godfather," His voice echoes in the hall.

"But, if you think you can outsmart me, my dear Ms. Bjorn, you are so very wrong. I will find you and rip away every last thing you love. I will finish off your lover and dance on his grave."

Alexander pulls me tighter, kissing my hair again, telling me that he's still here.

"Then that pack of dirty moguls. You could end this all and still save everyone." he bellows out. I don't move, another ploy to get what he wants.

He wants me to sacrifice me, even if it was his original plan. I don't trust him. Just like I wouldn't trust a demon at the crossroads.

"Tereesssaaa," he sings out my name hauntingly. He moves past our room, but I can tell by his footsteps that he's close. I let out a breath I didn't realize I was holding when I hear his footsteps die away. The sounds of rolling thunder clap in the distance.

We have to leave if only to just move out of the stop. Time wasn't our friend.

"Where's your gun?" I whisper.

"At the main entrance."

Well, fuck. "I have mine. I'll cover. We need to leave."

"The club is only a few minutes out."

Time hasn't been a thing this whole time. For me, time has been slow, testing me at every corner with every second.

"Then let's go now!" I say sharply.

As we open the closet door, he pulls back my hand, the one stained with the dry blood. "Who's blood?" His voice rumbles heavier than the thunder outside.

I smirk. "Mine and a dead redhead bimbo's."

"He touch you?" his possessiveness teases out.

"Not important. Let's go!" I rush him to the front north staircase, being careful that Connors may be close, still searching for us.

We get to the staircase, careful of every step we make. We make it to the second floor, back where the service department is, and quickly try to cross the open floor.

We're going to be home free, at least that's what I think until my foot catches a plastic bucket in a hidden corner. I start to trip and tumble over it. I start scrambling to regain my balance, but it's too late.

As Alexander tries to stead me, we hear Connors rushing in with long strides. Alexander pulls me up by the arm, practically dragging me to the front staircase.

"Come on, darlin'. Almost there." Alexander goes first down the stairs as I trail behind him. I can see his gun by the reception-ist's desk. He's right we're almost there.

The sands of the hourglass run out before my eyes. We stomp down the stairs but halfway down, a shot rings out and Alexander goes down, falling down the second half of the stairs. Blood trails down the steps.

My feet guide me to Alexander, screaming for him. Connors shot him in the back of the leg. I scream with hot tears of fury as I whip out my gun, unlocking the safety and pointing it at Connors.

He laughs cynically, approaching from out of the shadows. He comes out with his hands up dramatically, toying with me. A cruel smile spreads across his face. I glance quickly back at Alexander who's at the bottom of the stairs.

The rain picks up a bit, the sound covering the groans of Alexander.

I aim my gun at Connors as he walks with his in his hand. I just need to hold him off a couple more minutes until the cavalry shows.

I can do that. I can distract him.

"So close and yet, nothing accomplished. You're not going to shoot me, dear." Connors taunts me, waving his gun in the air.

I don't know why I'm hesitating.

"And why is that?" my voice shakes, choking back any ounce of weakness.

"Weakness. You're weak. You won't risk his life to kill me." His voice sends nerves down my spine. Alexander groans in the background.

"Aiming at you says otherwise, I'm not weak."

"Oh, but you are. He's lying there, on the ground. Your heart is aching to just walk away, pretend this was a nightmare," he sears his response.

"I protect the ones I love," I say shakily, taking one step slowly, as he creeps closer and closer.

"And what a fine job you've done. Jeremiah, Lucie, and now that pathetic little pup, Jackson." His words echo louder than the thunder booming around us. "It's time to rid the streets of pathetic, ungrateful, insignificant vermin."

I shake my head. His words of disgust make me cringe. To think I may have idolized this man for "the goodness of his heart".

Evil words.

Disgusting words.

I'll find a way to erase his name and build something greater. He starts to step down slowly towards me, "Take another step and I will end you, Connors!" I yell, inching closer to the bottom of the step.

I go to shoot the gun, but nothing happens. My anxiety and nerves get the best of me, and the gun locks for some reason. I panic.

No, no, please.

"Little girls shouldn't play with guns," he laughs.

Alexander starts to get up, but the fall took something out of him. I look back at Connors. Another roar in the distance swirls through the air. A call to me, like a beacon of hope.

It's not thunder, but the engines of bikes.

They're here. Light at the end of the tunnel.

"You lose," I snarl. A weak grin spreads across my face. I feel a brief moment of relief that is soon washing away as I see Connors shake his head.

He points his gun, not at me, but Alexander. "No, you lose."

I quickly realize what he's doing. He won't take my life, that would be too easy. I'm not the weak one he's realizing. I shake my head, "No, please. This is the part where you lose everything, ending your poisonous ways!" I scream.

"We'll see about that," he chuckles as he goes to fire. Everything is slow now, but somehow, I'm faster, or just stupid. I jump to shield Alexander, just like he did for me.

The bullet hit me in my lower side, and the impact jerks me back. Pain radiates through my body. I see the blue eyes of Alexander staring into mine. I landed on top of him.

I'm sorry mo chroi.

His body vibrates in shock. He yells but all sound is muffled. Time and sound have slowly disappeared on me. Movements turn into a slow moving picture, my body lays on the ground, as Alexander hovers over me.

I jerk my head up, see Doc and Memphis coming in first, guns up and firing. I collapse back down.

I watch Connors' body shake from the impact of bullets impaling him, his life ending in one fiery swoop. His body collapses to the ground before me. A roar of muffle yells surrounds me. I force a smile, a final feeling of relief.

An enemy is out of the game. No more harm can be done.

People will be safe. We did it. If I have to go, at least I know everyone is safe.

I see the scared look of my Alexander's face, searching for a way to stop the bleeding. His hands roam over me. It feels numb. Almost ghost like.

I thought in the end, fate would be good to us. But we all have a destiny that we never asked for. And the people that come along for the journey, make us the true blessed.

My sweet, protective man. It was my turn to save him, as he had saved me from a life of feeling unloved and unwanted.

Alexander cradles me in his arms. "No darlin', Teresa, what have you done?" his voice trembles. His wet, blond strands stick to his face, his breathtaking baby blues hold my attention.

My breathing becomes heavy. I caress his cheek. "Oh, I don't like the sound of that. I'm in trouble when you say that." I laugh a little. My chest contracts from the laughter.

"You.." he tries to say, trying to be stern and angry at me.

Let him.

"Stubborn woman." I finish his sentence.

We both smile, even if I know his is fake.

My body is aching, I don't know how much time I have or what's left, but I'm happy I'm here in his arms. The man who brought me back to life when I needed it the most.

"Stay with me, darlin.' You can't leave me." He kisses my forehead. "We'll get you to a hospital. Fix you right up."

Don't cry, my love. It takes a lot to get this woman down.

"Never, you know I won't. We did it, my love." I start to say, my eyes growing heavy and tired.

"Yeah, we did. You did. You beautiful woman." he stumbles to say.

Doc comes over to rest his hand on Alexander, but Alexander just shakes his head. "I'm not leaving her. Not again."

I shush him, his hand caresses my cheek, my hand tries to hold on to his, "Until the roads end and in the after, *a ghrá mo chroi.*"

There's a bright light, so warm and comforting. I close my eyes and fall into it, with Alexander holding me tight.

Chapter 44

Teresa

There's something about life flashing before your eyes that is supposed to happen when you see the light or walk towards the light. For me, the image of Alexander's sorrowful face is the last thing I remember. I have to believe that my life was full of love and life and my purpose has been fulfilled.

Perhaps I'm made for more than one purpose?

I find myself back on Granddaddy's porch. Sitting with a lemonade in my hand and a white summer sundress to style. I can hear the chirping in the back. A warm breeze greets my face. Then one of the most majestic sights I see.

"Granddaddy."

"My brave little bear." The hint of his Irish accent melts my heart. "So brave."

"I did it. Are you proud of me?"

He cupped my cheek. His gentle smile, his kind blue looking into mine. Burning away darkness that dares lingers.

"I have always been proud of you."

I can't help but wonder. My mind plays tricks on me. My mind tells me one of my safe places is with Granddaddy.

"Am I in heaven?"

He shakes his head.

I'm alive? How? I thought the gun shot would have ended my life. With the extensive injuries. "Then what is this?"

"Think of this as your mind telling you to rest and fight"

"My mind... "

"Your mind giving you a friendly face of strength."

I stagger my breath out. "So I'm alive? And..."

"And you have been through a lot. Been shot, three times."

I'm not deep in my faith, but I wouldn't have been upset if this was truly heaven.

My mind is giving me a comfortable place away from nightmares. Even though this isn't heaven, the thought of a life with Alexander, a second chance, a chance to be with him. But on the other hand if I don't fight, I have the chance to be reunited with the ones I love. I hear a faint beeping in the background. I turn towards it.

"He's never left your side."

"Alexander?"

Granddaddy nods his head. His handsome features, I loved him so much. And yet I miss him, it aches sometimes.

"Listen.." He says. He gestures to the open, sunshine sky.

I turn to where the beeping was coming from.

"Teresa, come back to me, please." The softness in his voice, but the emotional sadness that follows. "Come back to me. I need you."

"Mo chroi"

"Ah, you gave yourself to love." I look back at him. I nod my head, tears, or what feels like tears pool down my face. I did Granddaddy, I opened my heart like you always told me to.

His smile becomes bigger. "Keep listening." He turns my head back around again.

"I'll build you a house. Enough rooms, even a big library, to fill with your little fantasies. Come back to me, so we can make mini you's. Ones with little feet that will remind me of the most incredible woman that has entered my life and how lucky I am. My light in my darkest time." He shutters. I broke his heart. "Please." He says in a soft prayer.

I turn back to Granddaddy looking like a giddy school boy about to have a treat. "He's a looker, that one. The viking essence.

Can you imagine wee boys with his features and demeanor or your stubborn and feek looks."

I whimper out, "Yeah. I can."

I want that. I know he didn't mean for it to be a bargain. Something tells me we will over more, once a choice has been made.

I look back at Granddaddy caressing his cheek in my hand. I grab him for a hug, reaching for him, embracing him. The strength of an Celtic warrior and the gentlest of men. The smell of the fresh Irish mountain morning. "A stóirín. I love you, my treasure. Keep doing good in the world and know I will always be here."

"Goodbye granddaddy."

"May the sun shine warm upon your face, The rains fall soft upon your fields, And, until we meet again, May God hold you in the palm of His hand. My brave little bear." He kisses my forehead and a bright light covers my eyes once more.

I know this is my unconsciousness conjuring up something, but everything seemed so real, perhaps this is a long awaited goodbye, somehow saying what I wanted to say.

The weight of the bed has sunken from Alexander slumping over.

Monitors beeping, machines pumping, IV bags hooked into my tubes coming from my hands. As my eyes start to adjust from the hospital lights. It's bright, between the hospital lights and the late sunlight beaming in the room. My body is still aching from what happened.

That's what happens when you let stupidity make your decisions.

Alexander slightly snores in the midst, the television turned on to the news with low volume. A local headline reads "Corrupt Founder brings terror".

Something tells me that our problem got a little bit more publicized than we would have liked. That is for later. Cards and drawings from the girls. Flowers surrounding the room.

His hair cascading around his head. I want to see his face, those breathtaking eyes. But I go to adjust and feel every bone and muscle sting in pain, aching with instant regret. My hand may have to wake up this sleeping giant.

I brush his hair out of his face, tucking it behind his ear. Tangling my finger in his soft white blonde hair. He starts to stir, taking a second to shake his head before he realizes that I'm awake.

His eyes, dark circles under them, even darker than before. His mouth agape, with zero sounds coming out. Possibly surprised, overcome with shock.

"I fucked up." I say, my voice crackles, my throat dry. Returning the favor words, every word scratching against my dry throat.

He lightly chuckles at my words, rubbing his hand along his jawline. "Yeah, you fucked up."

He stands up, pressing the nurse call. Putting his forehead on mine. It seemed like there was no one else around until a nurse walks in.

"Finally, after a few days, we were starting to worry about you. How you feelin'" She comes in checking my vital signs and checking my fluids. Charting away, waiting for me to answer.

"Is it too soon to say 'like I got shot'?" I ask lightheartedly, my voice still trying to find it's true nature.

"I'd say no, but your guard dog here may say otherwise." She gestures to Alexander who is stroking my hair.

If he keeps doing this I'm going to fall in love with him all over again. Or fall back asleep, which wouldn't be a bad idea.

"Too soon, darlin'" He presses a kiss to my forehead. Something vibrates in his pocket, as he reaches in and answers it. He steps outside for a moment.

"You got a good one there." the nurses says.

"Yeah, I guess I will keep him." I shrug. Even though I can see him, I miss him. It feels like an eternity has passed.

The news was still flashing the story on television. I listened in, following along. Apparently, the police had found the linkage between him and missing people within the area. They had said that Connors and Carla had been in "conspiracy" to work for a mysterious underground drug trade and using the homeless population to do so.

There's no mention of myself, or the Grim Wolves, or the Falcons for that matter. I wonder why the turn of events, now that the police may be involved. There were a lot of unanswered questions but I know the way to get my answers.

As Alexander comes back into the room as the nurse leaves, I can't help but notice he's walking with a small limp.

Wait, I almost forgot. "Your leg! You got shot too." I almost got out of bed.

Alexander stops me. "I'm fine. ER patched me up and I'll be fine." I know he was hiding something but it could wait until I break out of this hospital.

"You up for a visitor or two?" He asks.

I nod my head.

And hell must have frozen over because I see a salt and pepper man himself walking in with Seamus in his arms. Never in a million years did I imagine this man handling my dog. Nor him choosing to come see me.

"Dear one."

"Rawlings." I nod my head as he lets Seamus down on the bed. "Oh my baby boy! I'm so sorry. Mama missed you."

He sniffs my feet before he gently walks towards me. I reach my arm out to scratch my hand. He licks in response. "That's my buddy boy." He seems to sense that laying on me would hurt me, so he pancakes in between my legs.

"Tessa. I want to apologize." Rawlings beings to say.

I snap my head up. My heart rate monitor is spazzing out because I'm in shock.

"Easy, darlin'" Alexander puts his hand on my shoulder.

"Run by that me again, big man."

"I want to apologize." he reiterates.

"How do those words taste like?"

"Unusual." he smacks his mouth with his tongue.

"Proceed." I grin, knowing that it took a bit of his strength to speak those words.

"I want to apologize. First, for my behavior. When I said that this club was a family and it extended out to you, I didn't treat you like family. It has been hard for me to think that we need to give our ol ladies, our partners, more of a voice. Second." He pauses and steps closer to me. "Second, you were right about a few things and instead of listening." He looks at Alexander and back at me, "I may have put you into your dumbass..." Alexander clears his throat, "Your plan of action when Connors reached out to you. It seemed like they were a couple steps ahead of us." Rawlings comes closer to the bed, acting like he is going to break me if he gets closer.

I gesture to him to come closer to me and lean in. When he does, I plant a small kiss on his cheek. Why hold grudges? Family is family. They came for me not because of Alexander, but because of me.

"That was kind of you to admit."

"Well, you took a bullet for our man here," he places his hand on his shoulder. "It's the least I could do."

"While you're here can you answer a couple burning questions." I look at both of them. The president and vice president.

They both look confused. "I guess?" Rawlings did not know what to say.

"First, explain why the news has no other connection to Connors and Carla." I wiggle in my bed.

Alexander steps in first. "Just thank Joaquin, kid got us out of more news articles and evidence to tie any of us with it. Including yourself."

"So what you're saying is." Waiting for the other end of the shoe to drop.

"The less you know, the better it is for you in the future if any cops ask you."

"Try again. It's my agency, my life."

Rawlings hangs his head. "Fine. Joaquin was able to hack in and erase any notion of us, the Falcons, and you. The only mention is that you were a casualty due to you checking into the shelter project and defending yourself."

"But there wasn't any justice, there is so much more."

"This is our fight. No one else needs to get involved." Alexander chimes in.

"What do you expect people to do? People have seen you all associated with us." I point out. Knowing that people within the agency will not forget random bikers around the foundation.

"We will figure out that piece. No one has come forward." Rawlings states.

"*Yet.* Keyword there." I say.

"We're doing everything to take the heat from you and us. You are one of us. We protect our own." Rawlings caresses my cheek. His words ring with sincerity.

The dots start to connect. Protection in this is better. The knowledge of what is happening is a sign of trust and a long road ahead of us. More like a fight is waiting for us.

"One last question. How did you find me?" This one I know had to be an explanation because I remember I turned off my phone beforehand.

Rawlings grins wickedly. "Yeah big man, how did you find her?" His soft deep chuckles rumble. He crosses his arms, cocking his head at a not-so-innocent looking Alexander Jackson.

Alexander goes to move, "Alexander" I say to him as he moves to get a baggy with my possession and starts to fish out something.

"I, um…"

"Oh, this is going to be good." Rawlings leans against the wall.

He pulls out the green gemmed necklace with the celtic symbol that he gifted me.

What the hell.

He hands it over to me, dangling in my hands. The cool metal in my hands. The weight of it weighing heavily in my hands, I have missed it hanging around my neck. I unclasp it and put it on me. Noticing that all rings and earrings are missing. I guess I didn't notice when I woke up.

"Remember when you asked if there was a tracker in it and I said no." He sheepishly grins.

I knew it!

"You lied." giving him a stern look. I should have known better.

"I lied."

Replaying the words in my head, making the note that he said that they don't do that or have the equipment for it. "Anything else I need to know?"

Rawlings kicks off the wall. "We have just defeated one threat to us, but there are many more out there. I'm asking for your trust in return, and know that I do trust you. You're a part of this family now and I know that you can do good things for us."

Something in me pops an idea.

An idea to insist on why the club had been hanging around the foundation, but also put them to work for the greater good of this community.

"Ever thought about community service?" I raise an eyebrow.

"Community service?" Alexander chimes in.

"Could always use volunteers at the Foundation, if the foundation is still standing." I suggest. If the club wants to keep their name out of the police or the community in regards to their image, helping the foundation in many ways could help.

"May not be a bad idea, boss, actually." Alexander agrees.

"Bust out of here first, and we'll talk." Rawlings winks.

He heads out, embracing Alexander one last time, they give each other a nod, as Rawlings strides down the hospital wing.

Alexander grabs the bag of possessions and brings a chair around back towards me.

"I'm sorry, sweets." I say, noticing that Alexander still hasn't expressed his happiness or joy. Not completely.

"You can't die on me anymore. My heart and my hair can't take it." his light grim expression, showing his fear.

"Well, I wouldn't have to die, if people would stop shooting at me." I say, pointing out the true fact.

"Teresa," he growls in warning, "Your sass, your attitude, you can't leave me." He shakes his head. "You're too important to me."

I don't want to leave him, it's like a missing piece that would be forever missing, lost to the unknown world.

"Yes sir. Help me put my rings back on would you? I feel naked without them."

He raises an eyebrow. "Gives me an idea or two. We definitely have some time to make up for."

"No, no. I don't need you to break me anymore than I am. All this has been punishment."

He snickers. "Not even close, little cub."

Oh promises, promises.

He slides some of my rings into the correct spots, tells me that he has been paying attention, a little too well.

Except one. My claddagh ring. I have been placing it on my right hand with the heart pointing it in, which is a traditional Irish way of saying that you're in a relationship.

But something in Alexander doesn't follow suit with that placement. He slides it on my left hand with the heart pointing outward. I shake my head, "My love, wrong hand. Wrong way."

He pats my head, "No, it's not. It's meant to be there. And in some time, the heart will turn one last time." My eyes grow wider.

The only reason for the ring to be there was for a moment, pointing outward meant intention, one step before a white dress. I didn't think would come, let alone with this man.

"Alexander Jackson Jones. You are not saying what I think you are saying." I say in disbelief. I try to get up, but the rush of getting up makes me dizzy. The room spins in a blur.

Alexander steps to help me, his hands tightens around my forearms.

"And what if I am?" He cocks his head.

"You are asking me," I start to question his true int

"To be mine forever." he says, leaning in closer to my face.

He did his research, following the traditional placement when one is engaged.

"To build a home?"

"As long as there may be a few mini you's roaming around." he says brushing a few strands of my hair back.

"It wasn't a dream." I say.

No this is better than a dream, this is my reality, my own slice of heaven. A man obsessed with me just as much as I'm obsessed with him. A man willing to burn the world for me, take away any pain as much as it pains him to see me in pain.

My heart is so full. This man does want it. Maybe not now with what we have going on. But in the future. Little blonde babies riding their tricycles. Little ones curled up beside us with a book.

"I knew you could hear me." He says, I grab his face and pull him in for a long awaited kiss. This kiss is so full of passion and love. A kiss waking up the princess from a long deep sleep into the arms of someone who will love her for the rest of her life. Alexander tries to hold back, but I press hard, sinking further into it. We have years to make things how we want it. I'll choose him, again and again.

"Alexander, come help me please." I yell from the bedroom.

In an instance, he comes to my side already fumbling with the hem of my shirt, "Help with what? Devouring you? Of course I can." His lips trail along the curve of my shoulder, sending tingles down my spine.

Not what I had in mind, but I can't say no to this god of a man. But I can't be late.

I shrug him off of me, "You big oaf, not like that, help me with my shoes."

"What do you say," he mumbles over my skin, going back over the same spot that makes me even weaker in knees.

"I said please," I say, sternly.

He rests his forehead on my shoulder, sulking because he knows I can't afford to be late, at least not this time.

A month has gone by and countless physical therapy appointments and exercise have been beneficial. I am not saying I'm back to fighting style, but soon I will be. Unfortunately we had to push back the opening of the center due certain "circumstances".

I was able to work remotely as well to continue the projects, though Alexander proved to decline my recovery by him being a walking temptation. He said he knew the right medicine, that he knew how to "take care of me".

After popping a few stitches and a couple calls to Doc, Alexander knew he had to be completely hands off. As much as it has ached the coming months were going to be worth it.

The cleaning and construction crew I know worked tirelessly to complete the new building project, pushing the opening to today with the grand ceremony. Little by little we are moving in and my heart is overjoyed with the outcome.

The board, unfortunately, had to take over since two of three general leaders were, well indisposed or out of the picture.

More like no longer a part of this Earth.

And the other one, me, is partially out of commission. I detest the work from home option especially with two guard dogs at my feet. One with endless cuddles at my feet and the other one attentive and gives amazing, toe curling kisses.

From the news and the slight media, the minor truth of my whereabouts on that night had gotten to the board. After being spoken with about the dangers of taking responsibilities a bit too far, the board "apologized" on behalf of Connors and Carla.

But today is the day that we open the doors to new better futures.

Honestly, I didn't know how I was going to move on as my soul and purpose with the foundation was shattered that night. A foundation that I was starting to believe was nothing but lies. We are supposed to be helping those who need help, striving towards their own hopes and dreams.

It took some time to decompress and with a little help from Joaquin and Coda, they helped me see that the foundation was safer. Although, after Jaoquin had done more digging and reverse image check, he proved with evidence that I was right about Carla, unfortunately a little too late.

Today is the day that I have longed for. A brand new start, with a brand new hope. The moment to open the doors to the foundation and hopefully start anew with traditions, engagement, and further help out our community. Giving back to the community and to the cities. Maybe once and for all, we can put an end to this.

Today we are surrounded by the community. The warmth of the sun beams on my face on this bright September morning.

Aggie and Jeremiah sit together appearing to be holding hands, a small curve of a smile appears on my face.

My ladies who have stuck by my side, Reva and Sam, alongside Britt, already tear up at the sight before them. A wave of support collectively shows the rest of the agencies, dignitaries, donors, and many of the previous people we have helped in the past.

The one that makes my smile wider than before is the line of chrome bikes standing guard like a protective force from anything that dares challenge the goodness here today. The men, Topaz, and a few of the ol ladies stand together trading in a rough up look for something more clean and casual.

As much as this is a new start for the community, it's a new start for the club.

A new start for me.

Anderson, one of the older board members, steps up to the podium, tapping the microphone to begin the ceremony. "Welcome ladies and gentlemen and people of all ages. Thank you for coming to this joyous occasion. I never intended to put this part in my opening. But many have heard about the recent events of our former founder and we the board were in disgust and horror to find this out. But the Lighthouse Foundation has been a beacon, and pardon the name, within our city of Raleigh and the surrounding areas. It was the workers, the ones working tirelessly to help the community, the true heroes of this community, to convince us to let the foundation continue on this path. One in particular." He gleams over to me. I simply give him a nod, waiting for him to announce this new person who would be the leader of this new start.

Anderson's blissful, aged smile grows bigger. A certain glint in his hazel eyes focuses on me.

"And I think it is a great honor and most deserving to announce the new Director and CEO of the Lighthouse Foundation. Ms. Teresa Bjorn."

Wait, excuse me. Huh?

No, they have the wrong person. Do we not know what happened the last time I was in charge.

A shout of cheers and applause and whistles welcome me. The shout becomes a roar of thunderous applause. The overwhelming fear and shock numb me, keeping me in the chair I'm sitting in.

I hesitate to stand up but the other board members usher me to the podium. I didn't have a speech prepared nor what words to actually say.

Let alone, I don't deserve this. There are way more qualified leaders and workers out there that can do a better job than me.

I look around at the faces of the people standing as I still haven't moved. The smiles, the cheers, the people's faith in me.

Maybe I can do this. I start to stand slowly, making my way to the podium. My hands start to sweat with the nerves still rattling my own body.

When words in my mind begin to fail me, I look to see Alexander have the biggest smile on his face. His face glows with pride. My eyes roam over to my friends and the rest of the club. They believe I can. The crowd starts to take their seats, and I let out a nervous breath.

"Um.. Okay well. You'll have to excuse me ladies and gents, I did not expect this. I was pretty much planning to just smile and wave." I laugh, and the crowd joins in. "If you had told me a few months back that this would be happening, I would have laughed, calling you crazy. If you told me a few years ago, I probably believe that you were joking. I still feel like I'm in an endless dream." I take a deep breath.

Looking back to Alexander in the crowd, he nods his head to tell me to keep going. I wet my lips, waiting for more truth to transpire.

"But here's the thing, I didn't do the work to get here. I let my heart, my mind take the lead. I did what I thought was right and made an effort to change it, not because someone told me to, but it's the human thing to do." a whisper of murmurs silently agrees with me.

"I always have the goal in mind that if I could change one person's life for the better, that was all the success to me. The Foundation isn't perfect, far from it, but who is? Unfortunately, the person started it all, perhaps let power, wealth, and a tainted viewpoint get in the way of the true vision of this foundation." a lot of people's eyes grow with the harsh reality of events.

"This foundation, though, is going to be stronger. We won't back down for the people who want to tear it down. I think I can speak for myself and my colleagues, my partners in this community that we won't let anyone else take away our light from our Lighthouse." Heads nods and whispers begin to take place.

"I love this place. My only hope and goal is to continue on our mission. To be a beacon of hope to all who need it. This is only the beginning of a new chapter and I, for one, am ready to welcome it."

I say the last part with strength as a promise to myself and to others that we continue the fight. Though the fight isn't going to be the one most think.

With the thunder of applause returning, I gently bow my head, then turn to shake a few hands, welcoming the congratulations that come with it. I ended my speech with the message of hope, and a bit of a warning to all who think they can tear it down.

We won't back down anymore, we're not going to lose a fight. But we'll definitely call on a wolf to go into battle with us. In the end, there won't be anything that will tear our two forces together.

Epilogue- Three Years later

Teresa

Three years! It has been three years since Alexander Jackson Jones walked into my life, and a few months in our marriage. He wanted to wait until things were calm within our city and no threats to us.

We have one final thing to finish, more like to end the terror, but everything else has been blissful.

Every day is an adventure with him. I love him, I love him so much it hurts to bear the thought of one day not having him. When I opened myself up to him and let him love me for me, inside and out, that's where the fairytale continued.

Alexander wants to take a ride to our first date spot, to celebrate our sixth month anniversary. I don't feel like it counts, but Alexander is relentless.

He sits on the couch in my office, waiting for me to get done with work. "I'm celebrating every moment with you, darlin'"

I roll my eyes. "When do you not celebrate?" I raise an eyebrow at him. Looking at my email one last time before we rode off to whatever destination he had in mind.

I walk over to him, and straddle him. "Always with you Mrs. Jones." He says

"Excuse me?" I smack his chest. Then wrapping my arms around his neck.

"Sorry, Mrs. Bjorn-Jones." he presses a supple kiss to my lips, grinding against me, and I return the favor by pressing into him tight. "Finish what you start Teresa."

"Yes sir. Let me go and I'll show you how I finish." A smile curves on my face.

The bike between my legs, my arms wrapped around him. For the brief moments, this was where I wanted time to freeze. The warmth from his body, the humming and vibration of the bike, and the open roads in the early morning.

At this moment, nothing could harm us, it is just Alexander and myself. I tuck his gift in my jacket, safeguarding it. Normally, it's Alexander that spoils me with gifts, both physically and affectionately.

We make our way to the park, parking the bike in what feels like the same exact spot as the first time. Before I can get off the bike, Alexander reaches behind me with all his strength and whips me around to the front of the bike.

Instead of straddling the bike, I'm straddling his hips. I reach for his helmet to take it off, to reveal his beautiful face. His once long blonde hair now shortened with a high fade. I miss grabbing it in more ways than one, but it will grow back. But his bright blue eyes and his full lips, his prominent cheeks, the devilish grin on his face.

"When I took you here you were so nervous."

"Duh, you are an oaf and I was just an innocent short woman. You overpowered me. But I thought you brought me there to kill me." I tapped his nose.

"Innocent would be the world I would describe you." Alexander laughs.

"You corrupted me," I say in response.

"Then soon, it was you who overpowered me."

"I have my ways." I plant a kiss on his lips, grabbing his head with both my hands.

The park has not changed, still the trees lining up in various directions. Every inch brings back the memories of a once scared woman who was afraid to take a chance on love, take a chance, relinquish the fear and take control of the wild side.

Alexander takes my hand, guiding me through the woods. The one place that good memories live in a world of fear.

This was my idea. Because for once, I have something up my sleeve that he will never see coming.

In our tracks lies the bridge that we had stopped at, where Alexander unleashed a primal idea that unleashed something within me. It makes sense that my own idea plays off here. I stop Alexander jerking back my hand.

"Teresa," he says.

"Remember when you brought me here. I thought you were out of your mind, talking about how you are not a good person but you are not a bad person either." I start off. Alexander nodding his head.

"Originally there was another purpose behind it."

"Right, but you said to take a chance. To say yes to adventure."

"I remember, darlin'" He says, taking a step closer.

I brought out his anniversary card out of my pocket. "How about we start our new adventure?" handing the card over.

He looks at me puzzled, tearing open the card, reading the front of it, then slowly opening it to the inside. Inside is the secret that I have been hiding.

His eyes are growing larger but softer. "You really are?"

Inside I had a special patch made for him giving him a new title of "Papa wolf". Something that matches the other patch reading "Mama bear" in my pocket with a pregnancy test alongside it.

"What do you say papa wolf, you ready for a little cub in the house?" I ask, as he gathers me up in his arms twirling me around, slamming his lips into mine. This was all the answer I needed.

He puts me back down. "You know how hard it was to make Memphis keep a secret?". I know full well that if we have a girl there is only one name I want to name her. *Lucie.*

"Probably torture." he says. "Honestly, I thought you really wanted to walk down memory lane."

"I mean, no one says we can't." I give him a coy smile. Part of me is excited for this.

Then a bit of his eyes turn dark, the hunter has arrived. There is a small growl coming from Alexander. He starts to back me up off the bridge near the opening of the trees. "I don't see you running, mama bear." he growls, as I relive the memory that somewhat started it all.

Legs don't fail me now.

Acknowledgments

Oh my lord almighty y'all. I did it!! My ADHD did not fail me this time. Let me tell you, this has been a dream of mine to just write. What started off as a fever dream (really melatonin and cold/flu medicine sometimes has not mixed well with me). One of the main reasons I wanted to write was to write about someone in my profession as a social worker since I have not seen or read many ones that were. Another reason is to bring light into a community that is close to my heart. This is such an achievement and I made it to the end. To those that are reading my work for the first time, I just to cry and hug you and say thank you. I wanted to at least put myself out there and take a chance. I never thought I would do this, just a hobby I had when I was bored in class or had down time.

Side note. My world in social work is fast moving. There would be days where both myself and or my supervisor would be out of the office and in the field or constantly on the phone with community partners or clients or even both. The fast pace world that Tessa is in, is my own depiction of what it seems like in my field. To my social workers, counselors, educators, advocates, and my other helping field professions. This one's for you as well. We are social workers that help change happen, we speak for those who have lost their voices.

To my parents, who I know is reading this even though I warned them, for always telling me that I needed to get into writing and when I did encouraged me every step of the way. Even if I don't become a bestseller, I did it and you are part to thank you all this. Love you.

To my two grandfathers who unfortunately, I never go to know. I hope you are looking down at me and smiling and proud of me. I have a feeling your spirits were involved with this.

To my ladies of the round table. Thank you for putting up with my antics and the late messages. I truly and deeply love you all and thank you for allowing me to give these characters part of your sparks.

April, my dearest April. You my dear, I don't have enough words to thank you deeply. First, for always being there when I need you or anyone, being my rock through my process, boosting my ego when I needed reminders, and being my second eyes. Don't worry, I plan on spoiling you tremendously (and yes... I did misspell that and spell check caught it). Love you my dear friend.

To my alpha pack (yeah I'm still working on the name, don't come at me). Boy y'all took a chance on this social worker turned author. I can't thank you all enough for reading WC and giving your thoughts and most importantly your love and dedication to it. Also, putting up with my rambles and giving all the support.

To my betas. I did not know how I would do with critique, but I wanted honesty and I got it and look where WC is at now! It's been a journey. Also you all caught things that I overlooked!

To Sam, Caelyn, Cala Riley, Mariah, the ones that checked in with me and gave me the support to continue on whenever I started to doubt myself

To anyone who says that they are not able to do this, just start doing it and let your mind roam free.

Afterword

There's so much we can do for our community, helping those thrive. You can volunteer your time, donate, or simply educate others around us. If you or anything else is experiencing homelessness, domestic violence, suicide ideations, or anything else please utilize the numbers below.

Homelessness:

- Check out your local shelters or google for a HUD (Housing and Urban Development) phone number.

- Volunteer, donate, advocate

Domestic Violence:
Call or text: 800-799-7233
Visit their website: https://www.thehotline.org/

For Rape, Sexual Assault, Abuse, and Incest National Network
Call: 800-656-4673
Visit their website: https://www.rainn.org/

Suicide Hotline:
Call: 988
For more information: https://www.samhsa.gov/find-help/988

To those who feel unheard, unseen. I see you, I hear you, you are safe with me.

More Books and What's To Come

Grim Wolves MC
Wild Cub
Savage Angel
Shiloh and Rawlings (Coming Soon)

The Treasured Outcasts
Buried in Sins
Outcasts 2 (Coming Soon)

Saint's Outlaws MC: Memphis Chapter
Hound Dog's Howl
Shooter's Saving Grace (Releasing April 2026)

About the Author

Jamie Fritz is a full time social worker with her masters in Social Work, that works in various populations such as family services, veterans, homelessness domestic violence, and pediatric health care. She lives in Eastern Virginia, where the weather never is correct.

She is known to write stories with wild, unhinged, burning romance with happily ever afters. She hopes that her writing will shed light into the vulnerable communities that have a special place in her heart. Author of the Grim Wolves MC series, Saint's Outlaws MC: Memphis Chapter series, and the Treasured Outcasts series.

She's still waiting for prince charming but he might have gotten lost or the dragon burned him to a crisp. When she is not immersed in the community and writing, she is attempting to go through her TBR list with her dogs, and surrounded by family. She enjoys a good whiskey and coke, while doing whatever her ADHD tells her to do.